The *Professional Widow*

The *Professional Widow*

CORSETRY with LOVE

To ~~Bernie~~ Alan wil very good wishes and Thanks for incredible wisdom x

MILTON GAZE

&

SVETLANA BABENKO

To order additional copies of this book, contact:
Xlibris LLC
0-800-056-3182
www.xlibrispublishing.co.uk
Orders@xlibrispublishing.co.uk
307095

Preface

*W*hilst this is a novel, much of the narrative is based upon fact but interwoven with fiction. There is a psychic element and I recall many of the events described as if they were yesterday. The two psychics were remarkably accurate in their predictions; one cannot of course guarantee accuracy from any 'see-er'. As in real life, some see more clearly than others.

I have not tried to write an erotic novel. In the late 40s and 50s, women in the Western world wore corsets as a matter of routine. Until the First World War women of any standing wore rigid corsets every day. The war brought changes and women could no longer dress as they used to display themselves. After the war, the silly season took over and women bound their natural curves and dressed to look boyish. They flapped around.

In the late thirties, and again after the Second World War, society women demanded a change to firmer ways and they yearned to re-take their shape by means of stiff foundation garments that controlled excess and dramatically improved their natural curvature.

This story is told through the eyes of Mary who was introduced to corsetry by her actress friend and colleague, Colette. Intentionally, it discusses corsets in a detail few story-books have ever attempted. The narrative takes the reader through some harsh times and some joyful occasions but often coupled with the enjoyment of wearing restrictive clothing and the effect such garments had upon loved ones.

There is a general perception that being dressed in corsetry is bound to be uncomfortable. This is positively not the case provided that made-to-measure is the rule rather than the call of an insistent shop display. Did women really wear foundations all day and for some nights, too? Oh yes; very definitely. This story of Mary and others is based entirely upon fact and what and when they wore their very controlling corsets. They wore them with total pride and the dramatic differences so achieved led to startling changes and dramatic improvements in their life. When will the fashion again turn full circle?

Be dressed for success!

# Acknowledgements

I owe a debt of gratitude to my wife, Svetlana, for her fortitude in up-putting with the hours I have spent holed up in my study. For her part, she spends a great deal of time chattering in Russian to her close friend who is an expert fashion designer.

Laure Lincker has helped to transform my schoolboy French into language as it should be described or spoken and to her I owe many thanks as she has had to understand my English so as to follow my lines of thought. She has had access to a number of documents relating to France in the period around which this novel has been written. Historical accuracy is important and even in the relatively recent late 1940s, changes have occurred such as The Eiffel Tower which was regarded then as a shabby object around which nobody who was anybody wished to live. In 2013 the area is populated by the diplomatic corps and visitors swarm over the structure and indeed France uses the image to promote Paris.

Our good friend Deborah Cooke who may shortly leave England to stay in Paris used to work in television production and her expertise has been invaluable in assisting me with text, particularly where titles, summations and biographical detail has been used on the book covers. Her method is to use brain storming to great effect. I thank her for her kind wish to become involved.

The staff at The East Sussex Library in Lewes have been unstintingly helpful in locating reference books, such as Kelly's Directory, information about steam trains running in Sussex in the 1930s and even finding old timetables. They seem to be refreshed and so helpful when one mentions that a novel is under construction.

One of the world's finest websites must be *www.corsetiere.net* which is written and operated by Ivy Leaf, a former corsetiere and the wealth of detail given on all matters foundation garments has to be seen by any aficionado. It is superbly illustrated, with plenty of true-life tales and hardly a question goes unanswered. I have drawn upon information gleaned from this site for this novel, typically for garments worn by Mary and permission was given to me for this purpose. So, thank you Ivy Leaf.

A similar website is operated by Thomas B. Lierse from Virginia USA and his website *www.staylace.com* has a substantial quantity of information relating to rigid corsetry such as garments worn by Coleen within this novel.

There are other websites but, in the past, I have learned a great deal about corsetry in general from these excellent Internet websites and I have also written a book How to Get into Shape. Those who wish to find out more need look no further but if greater detail is sought or recommended English makers, do contact *mmg1@hotmail.co.uk*

I cannot forget to mention the often derided Google. I have had to research so many little pieces of information relating to the period around which this novel has been constructed; I was too young to notice when I was born, so Google has avoided many howlers such as my describing a story from Kathleen Hale's *Orlando Buys a Farm*—which was not written until 1942—well after the story's 1935 trip to Drusilla's farm and children's zoo.

 *Chapter One*

1 May 1944

'Be very prepared; your husband will not come back. I am so sorry.'

Eleanor Rich was a near neighbour but not a particular friend. She had vivid dyed red hair, dressed in flowing outfits and was known to be a spooky psychic who tended to keep herself to herself unless she had something of import to say. She was accompanied by her unruly red-setter, Domino, which tended to leap and bounce about instead of guarding his mistress. People avoided her because she was known to have strange ideas and came out with news that often disturbed. What made matters worse was the fact that Eleanor was also known to be right more often than not. So, people tended to avoid her and took evading action if they could see her on a collision course in the street.

In 1944 many servicemen failed to return home, so Mary did not take Eleanor's bald statement too readily; but in August she received the dreaded telegram from the War Office. A year later, Mary and Eleanor, still with Domino, met again whilst climbing steep steps in Withdean. Mary said,

'You were right . . .'

Interrupting Mary, Eleanor said,

> 'There's more bad news, I'm afraid, but you will be glad when
> it's over and there's a new existence. It's your Mater this time.'

Mary grasped every fibre of her self control and thanked her and turned around to return from whence she had come. Eleanor still had her all-too-vivid red hair, was aged about fifty and was probably reckoned to be an attractive lady who dressed quaintly and always appeared in flowing long skirts and loose patterned blouses which did not match. She stood out like a beacon; but not a beacon of light, sadly. More often than not, she accompanied bad news.

Mary was desperately unhappy. Reaching her mother-in-law's home where she was staying, she lost control and burst into tears. Tears were not for Martha but Martha's son James who, alone, called his mother "Mater".

James had been hit by a mortar bomb in August; and October was all too soon to have more grim portents even though the news may well be good. Martha hated Mary but was in need of every bit of help she could attract from her daughter-in-law as she was terminally ill. Mary was reaching the end of her abilities—nursing, cooking and cleaning were taking a toll upon a strong and active woman who just wanted to return to her world, the London ballet scene and fashion. She needed to pick up the pieces of her much valued work and to try to forget the awful year when she had lost the love of her life whom she had seen so little since James had joined up in 1938 and been whisked into the Artists Rifles where he served, unable to say too much—or anything at all—so little or no news, stories or information reached his beloved Mary. The time was much of Careless Talk Costs Lives and this was of strategic importance in lesser known and secretive sections of the services. All that Mary knew was that James was involved with training—hardly a cause for so much inscrutability. But one did not ask questions as leave was often short or grasped for little more than hurried moments when duties allowed and there were much more important things to share between loving couples and their baby son, Peter.

2 Classical Upbringing 1918-1930

Martha's only son, James, was sent to school in Devon at thirteen following his Bournemouth preparatory school. The transition from being a top-of-the-class prep-pupil to fagging, the lowest-of-the-low new boy at public school had to be taken on the chin. James was a lonely child, probably a nuisance to his parents who were not living together. He was forced to accommodate acute change and to learn to survive in a vicious and disciplined environment where, for the slightest infraction, punishment was inevitably the cane. Both masters and prefects handed down punishments, dependent upon the seriousness of the rule breach. Fagging was a requirement to act as a personal servant to an older boy, cleaning shoes, army kit, sweeping and dusting seniors' studies. Poor workmanship always resulted in a dose of the slipper or the cane applied in the dormitory where beatings were carried out without a sound being heard from the miscreant. Dorms varied in size and were separated by age and each holding some dozen boys in barely heated wooden floored rooms with iron bedsteads and a single small cupboard by each bed. The matron held all clothes and issued these when required. Obviously, newcomers were prone to a harsh start but, given time and experience, all pupils learned the ropes and experience led to a quieter life and only occasional wheals on their backsides which were regarded as badges of honour by some hardy souls.

James thrived and in the third year started to specialise in classics and European languages. He was also good at several sports but excelled in athletics. The army corps, Combined Cadet Force, was also a great interest, but one of his main hobbies was woodwork and sculpture where he found he had artistic talent. School for James was really a child-minding institution. His mother and father lived separately, both abroad. As a result, shorter school holidays were often spent with masters and their families who were happy to entertain a bright boy who'd help with household chores and looking after their younger offspring. It was only during the summer vacs that James went abroad, normally to Paris to be with his father. Consequently, he became a fluent French speaker as his father had lived in Paris for many years.

He was also a German speaker but by no means assured; halting would be more accurate. However, with Hitler and the Nazis and war a possibility, he was advised that a good knowledge of European languages was a passport to working in intelligence or even in special ops of some kind.

He was handsome, with dark hair, well built and muscular as he was a schoolboy athlete. He had dark brown eyes which saw everything and helped him to miss little. In the holidays, he dressed well, had an allowance that enabled him, often accompanied by a master's wife, to purchase quality suits and separates and shoes, some of which would last him well into his twenties.

Games were a major part of school life, taking almost as much time as academic work and masters were selected at interview for their sporting ability rather than their scholarly prowess. The school was expected to win above average at rugby and away matches were watched with great intent and expectations and particularly enjoyed by those involved. Charabancs queued up on Saturdays to take boys as far as could be driven in the limited time as all games had to finish before darkness began to fall. Cricket was an exception as the days were longer and competition for the few team places was stiff.

Being a good sport helped James to advance and he became popular as he was a fair person and did not choose to take it out on his subordinates or new-boys. He regarded strong discipline to be in the form of a good discussion with a boy who had broken the rules whilst whacking a cane on a book and watching the petrified rascal awaiting his turn instead of the book. Books suffered; boys survived. His results proved better than those of his colleagues who also learned that talking was preferable to violence and junior boys worked harder to achieve standards that were acceptable. In his penultimate year, he was advanced to a prefect and in his last year was voted to be Head Boy. His closeness with many masters, because he often stayed in their homes during the holidays, led him to bring many changes to the harsh discipline that he had had to suffer as a new fag and into the first two years of public school life. Beatings used to be a daily affair also meted out in the prefects' common room; now, they were a rarity. Personal discussion worked better: the canes took a holiday.

Apart from masters' daughters, girls were rarely observed and only junior matrons were to be seen in the houses or grounds. Sometimes prefects had friend-girls and such alliances were not encouraged during term-time. Such girlfriends that were known started during holidays and correspondence continued when possible. Dating a young matron was an offence and if found, the prefect or senior was immediately demoted with further onerous sanctions and almost certainly a visit to the dreaded prefects' common room.

James looked forward to his summer holidays because his father was liberally-minded and actively encouraged alliances with friends' daughters but these were strictly controlled by the parents concerned. Nevertheless, this did enable a good background as to what girls were like, what they liked to do and, importantly, how to behave. The difference in dress was also of great interest and some intimate garments became a source of amazement for him. This led him to appreciate corsetry which all Parisian girls of that era wore as a matter of course and, in truth, as an honour for being grown-up and able to suffer the rigours of firmness that dated from the previous century. Parents used such means to ensure that daughters did not stray from the accepted line when meeting or mingling with boys. A cuddle was not really practical when wearing firm boned controlling undergarments. But James did notice the fantastic figures that some late-teenage girls possessed.

One girl, called Sylvia was always heavily contained by a rigid form of steel busk-fronted corset that seemed to be excessive. They had something in common because Sylvia was British but living in Paris with her parents but supervised day-to-day by her governess and at a finishing school in Switzerland during long periods of the year, so she was not often with her girl-friends sharing a moment for a coffee and croissant.

James liked Sylvia because she appeared to be fairly plain and yet spoke with a wisdom quite unlike her Parisian friends. Maybe that was a result of her special training in Zurich. On one of the few occasions he saw her he asked,

'What do you do when finishing, Sylvia?'

'It's an amazing place, run by a woman who has our interests at heart but along lines that were last to be seen in the mid eighteenth century. Then, girls were expected to be elegant and to converse as if it were second nature. So we learn to talk on almost any subject; we read a great deal of relevance but we also develop practical skills such as household management and staff direction.'

'But you are so tightly corseted; why?'

'Part of the regime, there; and it is reinforced by my governess who never permits me to appear "*sans*" as she infers casual dress. In the 1750s, stays were worn by all ladies of standing and even boys were breeched and wore corsets from the age of about ten. The current Principal has changed the dress for us and we now have to be attired as for the late nineteenth century and hence the stays I have to wear appearing so controlling. I like them; they are demanding but they do give me control and a close feeling which I adore.

'We are not permitted to wear make-up or to resort to hair-styles that will enhance our looks and in fact, she insists that we appear drab and positively unattractive but conversely, have perfect manners and deportment. Strangely, we are expected to have tiny waists and to accentuate our rears with some horsehair padding and to push our bosom up and eliminate any natural curvature there.'

'Sounds terrifying; do you like this regime?'

'Oh yes, I do. I'd like to return to teach there. It has given me so much that I simply did not have when I first went. My parents are in the diplomatic and they now expect me to converse with leaders from all over the world when they are staying here, in Paris. I'd have been too shy and speechless before Zurich. Now, I am at ease with myself and the dress and lack of any adornment and styling mean that I can be me without seeming to be someone I am not.

Just look around you; all the girls I know are dressed to excess, in reality to attract men. I do not have that requirement so nobody I meet formally has any interest in my looks. So, I hide behind my plainness and spend ages making myself especially plain. James, you should see me when I am myself.'

'I probably should not say this, but I am attracted to you and your fabulous form of tight dress.'

'Well, thank you. It is tough to wear but it gives me the requisite shape and I am now used to the regime, and use it as a means to hide my true self. Governess, as I have to call her, dresses severely and sees to every aspect of my apparel and also insists I am never out of some form of foundation which means I am used to being stiff, rigid, re-shaped and appearing to be plain ugly.'

'I must go; but Sylvia I have to disagree with you—you are far from "plain ugly". I consider the transformation is incredible and it makes you so attractive by its understatement.'

'You have just spoken as the Principal does. "Understatement!" Good day to you.'

He knew what his girl would have to look like; what she would have to wear and how she would impress him and everyone around her. Sylvia was certainly stunning when out of her formal dress and she spoke with considerable poise and wisdom. He was positively attracted to her and had in fact, been so for some time but she was unattainable and was never about without a chaperone or her governess.

3 Work starts 1932 - 1936

James left school with his Matriculation which gave him a connection with an Oxford college but he did not feel ready for another round of scholarship. Truth was, he did not have any idea for a career. His choice of learning tended towards the classics and languages which interested him greatly but was not exactly leading to any single vocation. Perhaps the classics were useful devices for medical secrecy, and the law used Latin terms unjustly to confuse clients. Government service appeared to be mundane.

He was an effective man outside the classroom and enjoyed making things and the Woodwork and Carving Club had been a good deviation from the rigours of athletic training and the modicum of academic work required. Canborne had been an excellent hands-on and artistic tutor; he normally taught physics, but James was not a scientific pupil, so never attended Canborne's classes apart from the WCC meetings. Rugby and athletics were high on his non-academic interests but these did not lead to gainful employment. Money worries did not surface as a Trust funded his school fees and provided a stipend. It was enough to keep things afloat provided there was not too much splashing out.

He whetted his appetite for a Morgan car so he had to keep the Trustees a little less agitated as they felt this was extravagant and a wasting asset. They also urgently pressed him to find a suitable profession but agreed his lack of physics and chemistry would eliminate medicine and his dislike of the law did not bode well for top careers. Architecture, perhaps, was the latest trustees' topic for their promotion. James thought the Services would be a suitable career as he was well used to discipline and he considered the navy or the army to be an easy option as he was entirely content with the regime. Many of his colleagues had entered either the army or navy and a few had become high flyers, literally. The Air Force did not attract him because the aircraft were ungainly and inadequate for purpose in the thirties.

A group left school together; some were up for Oxbridge but a few were also uncertain and James was amongst them and he did not like the idea of a five year architectural trawl through the inner workings of ghastly buildings that looked so out of place in much of modern England. Why not recreate classical structures, he mused, and thus he closed the door on smoky offices with wheezy old men at drawing boards designing mock-Tudor edifices.

Sydney Allard was a couple of years older and he'd met him at a schools rugby convention during one of the hols. He was heavily into motor cars which really did interest him. He raced, owned a Morgan car—hence James copying his *alter ego*—which was racing green and had three wheels which was customary for this marque. Stability was not a strong point, and there were just two seats and a tiny rear locker.

He contacted Sydney to suggest a meeting but before he could bring up the possibility of a job, Sydney told him that he was setting up a workshop specifically to convert Morgan three-wheelers to have two full axles and much greater stability as a consequence. Pay was to be minimal, probably little more than travel costs and a few coffees but both felt that there was a good future upon which to build experience as well as racing, hill-climbs and trials which were quite a new sport in the early thirties. This was the real dawn of motor cars and long gone were the conversions from horse carriages made by continental firms such as Daimler and Mercedes.

Morgan-conversions were just a few a month but, as word spread and after winning a number of races at Brooklands, the new banked circuit just outside Weybridge, the Allard car name widened. James could see a good future working there and he and Sydney worked happily together. Sydney had visions of a motor vehicle plant whereas James was more race-minded and less inclined to see the tills turning and a staff wage bill mounting by the week. He did have the small private income from the family Trust, so money worries were not high in his life. He lodged just outside Cheltenham with a young couple who had twins of nearly three. His apartment was at the top of the house, well away from the incessant yelling which had all the potential for putting him off children for life.

James had some near squeaks whilst racing but his worst accident had nothing to do with speed, more to do with a narrow road and an embankment. Late one evening, lights approached, he slowed but the oncoming car was going far too fast and so he took to the upper slope to try to protect his beloved Morgan. It rolled, of course, and relatively minor damage was occasioned to the bodywork, easily repaired at the Allard works. Sadly, his front teeth were not repairable and a false plate had to be worn if he was ever to smile again. He booked his Morgan in for a two axle conversion as well as some other mechanical improvements plus some creature comforts. Cars were primitive in those days but most of the work he did on his car was managed during his breaks and after hours when the crew had gone out for a customary sup at the Rag and Bone, their name for the local Stone Stag pub.

He mused, often, as to where his future really lay. Unlike his mother, he did not own a home, he was young, single, just 23 had no unofficial children and was professionally unqualified. He was upwardly mobile and went to Paris frequently to see his father and also to spread the Allard and Morgan names amongst specialist dealers who were springing up in the French capital as well as in Chartres and also Pontoise, to the North of Paris. It was his lack of formal qualifications that concerned him most and he would take a cigarette break to ease this tension. His answer was Services; reconsider the Services.

Otherwise he was happy, without an especial female diversion—although there were plenty on the sidelines in all forms of motor sport. He did wonder, once, whether he had a quirkiness like Oscar Wilde as girls did seem to leave him cold and uninterested apart from what they wore to keep trim or maybe to help attain a curvaceous shape. That fashion fascinated him as did many shop windows showing elaborate fitted foundation garments—abominations he called them, just like Mater wore. No, a trial run in a Parisian establishment had assured him he was far from being in the least odd.

4 Mary's Early Days 1932/33

Nothing if not ambitious, nascent actress Coleen and her father found a vacant shop premises and whilst it needed some fitting and redecoration, this was well within the family capabilities—so started her women's wear shop which they called Dress Address. As she had to be readily available for stage parts, Coleen needed to have a helper: someone she could trust and depend upon as shop hours had to be maintained as a priority. Idly, she wondered if her somewhat distant friend, Mary, might be interested. The two girls hit it off so well when they met awaiting an interview and had remained in loose contact ever since. Having decided to start this small business, Coleen needed a helper and Mary was an obvious choice.

Mary was living in Maida Vale and Coleen remained with her parents in Bethnal Green. Mary was more successful in finding work, menial and boring, but it paid the rent. Coleen helped her father as best she could and started to prepare for opening Dress Address. There was a great deal to do as she had no real contacts and had never worked in a shop, let alone a specialist outlet. But, her RADA training was broad and instructive in ways that fell into place in her small stage. She had to set up and dress her shop, its windows, its lighting, its furnishing and fittings and she felt that this was ideal to gain experience for any stage management job—a route into acting in rep from whence almost all successful actors became well-known by the public.

Writing to Mary, Coleen explained she was completely naive but well trained and needed a senior assistant who would be able to man the ship and captain the vessel whenever the need arose due to her acting commitments. Could they discuss this proposition?

Mary leapt at the chance; she was anxious to work in fashion, dress or fabrics and had a natural flair as if it was genetically built into her make-up. Notice given, Mary left dreary Woollies where she was a trainee and was on Dress Address' door-step by 7.30 Monday morning; luckily, there was a cafe across the street so she could watch out for Coleen who must have had her Irish hat on. Are they late by nature she conjectured?

Dress Address still needed a great deal of work before it could open to the public gaze. Between them, they decided upon who was best suited to what work to frame the store. Contacts and suppliers were non-existent and it was proving difficult to find the first few. There was not even a telephone book and references and suppliers had to be researched in the local library where Kelly's and other trade publications were invaluable. With so much to do in the days, Mary agreed to visit the reference library in the evening and the City Library was ideally suited as it was situated in the East End, a major area of London where all forms of dress, fabrics, accessories and lingerie were manufactured often by the large Jewish community.

It was the Jewish readers who proved to be so helpful to Mary. Oddly enough, her unusual nose seemed to attract them and they thought she was one of them; not disabusing them, she was certain to be found out one day as she did not frequent any synagogue and knew none of the phraseology and chants. She was taken under their wing, and managed to make long-lasting friends who would be of invaluable service to her in future years. In her late teens, she could not see the future.

In her thirties she would have a commanding job and great responsibility in the higher echelons of the London stage and theatre. If Coleen could just see Mary's potential—far beyond being a shop assistant.

Daily, parcels started to arrive and with amazingly little argument the shop came alive and displays were arranged. Both girls had a natural aptitude and Mary took over the window dressing—something Coleen thought she would do but Mary seemed to have the innate gift whereas Coleen had the training but lacked enviable artistic talent.

The shop was small and rectangular and rails were arranged on one wall holding new dresses, mainly evening-wear suited for the forties age range upwards. There were some island display stands holding special dresses. Behind the sales counter which had a measuring 'yard' built into the top as well as a glass surface; underneath were drawers containing accessories, gloves and some haberdashery. Behind the counter and the till was a wall fitting with drawers holding items such as scarves, tops, jumpers, display items for the windows, stockings and some underwear. The colour arrangement was pale green and blush red—just to be different, Mary thought. The ceilings and non-shop areas were white. The back of the shop, a private area, held the cleaning equipment, a small table for snacks and space for coats and hats, new stock and boxes. There were washing facilities, too.

The opening date was set for April 18, 1932 a Monday—no specific reason, just that most of the list of To-Do's had been completed and all that was wanted, now, was custom, people, reps, sales and fewer bills. Mary would be 19 in a couple of months. Coleen was 21.

The window displays had had time and money spent and they did look the part. The impression was of movement and Mary had toured the West End to see what the major stores were doing—but they had so much more space, so she looked for the marginal ideas and for the concepts that appealed to her imagination. Anyway, well before the shop opened, people had started to glance in and then stop and stare at what was happening in the windows. Mary felt like being on stage when she entered to add something or change the look with people staring in. It bode well, she thought.

She thought she recognised one of the potential customers looking in; an actress called Josephine Baker, an American African girl who must have been in her mid-twenties. Why were we not open, she reflected?

5 Train Meeting 1933

James spotted an interesting girl on a train journey and determined to find out more about her. It was impolite to talk to strangers, so he watched and noted her dress, the absence of rings, little but effective jewellery, a gold watch and a set of real pearls arranged as a double row beautifully accentuating her neck. She had bright blue eyes and a large thin nose which made her face really interesting but far from flattering: but, James loved it. The unusual attracted him and he was not in the least interested in chocolate-box glamour pusses. He did notice she had a medium figure, with good rounded breasts and trim waist and hips.

Hiding behind *Euripides Iphigenia* which he had been awarded as a school prize, he did notice an interested glance from his fascination. Maybe just a glimpse, but quite enough to tell him that he had scored a point. Dressed in a continental fashion, wearing a good tweed suit, plus-fours and elegant shoes with patterned socks, finished with a tailored shirt with an elegant silk cravat he did have a confident bearing and clearly appeared to be well out of the ordinary when travelling Third Class for the short journey from Three Bridges ticketed to Preston Park late in the afternoon on the newly electrified line from London which was still undergoing live active passenger tests.

James resolved to find out more about his compartment-companion and was ready to get off the train if she alighted short of Preston Park or at any other stop well outside his relevant journey. In his mind, he willed his target, "Anne" in his thoughts, to alight at Preston Park a suburban stop just a mile or so from central Brighton where the train terminated. He was a mind-person. He really did feel that thoughts were transferrable and could influence others. This was a subject he'd love to research.

Anne evidently had a travelling bag in the overhead rack directly above her seat. People did not place their valuables, cases and purchases anywhere but directly above their seat if at all possible. Maybe they seemed safer. Her case was a smart, patterned, but a light valise with a handle at one end and made, possibly by Louis Vuitton as the monogram looked Parisian. There were no clues such as labels stuck over the case so *Anne* must be a visitor rather than a regular traveller: regulars had small bags or briefcases. *Anne* also had a handbag which she held close to her on the seat shared in the compartment by four other travellers on the opposite side; all facing the engine, an expression reminiscent of the steam age.

She sat one away from the window but did not appear to explore the view; maybe she knew it from past experience. He did notice that the window had mirror-like qualities but he could not see what she was looking at. He hoped she could see him. Trig told him that the angles were right and she did move whilst appearing to look vacantly out of the carriage window—or at the image sustained therein. James recalled Alice through the Looking Glass and had thoughts of what creatures were visible in the passing countryside or which ghouls lurked in the tunnels as the carriages clattered through.

There was no movement from *Anne* as the train approached Preston Park and the next and only stop was Brighton Station, a terminus with a modern glass roof suspended over a number of platforms, barriers a dominating clock, rest rooms and small shops and restaurants for passengers awaiting a connection or an arrival. The station smelled of smoke and steam as most local routes were not electrified. The noise was always interesting; announcements, guards' pea-whistles, louder train whistles and the occasional weird deep-noted horn from the modern electrified stock.

James saw he had a chance. *Anne* looked strong, probably five feet eight inches at most but would have to struggle with a valise. Gallantly, he offered to help—reaching up for the handle before *Anne* could refuse, just as the train was slowing towards the buffers and the wheels were squealing along the rails due to the platform curve. The lighting flickered and the under floor compressor started to run sounding 'dud-dud-dud' like a garage machine. *Anne* smiled and her eyes seemed to glow with happiness with someone daring to help an angel in distress. However, *Anne* was far from any distress; she was clearly a seasoned traveller but was cautious and like most women, needed help when it was offered in an acceptable manner. Her helper was well dressed, smart and articulate and she felt at ease and gave a rare winning smile to say thank you.

> 'Where are you going? Maybe we could share a taxi as I am going to Withdean.'

> 'I'm going to somewhere called Dyke Road Avenue, which I'm told is on the way towards the Devils Dyke' said *Anne*.

> 'Yes, it is close to where I am going, so a taxi would be ideal for both of us.'

The Streamline cabs were all black and cream and known to be safe and reliable. Now James had to act really fast without seeming too forward; the taxi journey would last ten minutes at most.

> 'May I introduce myself? I am James Compton and my mother lives in Withdean. I'm spending the next few days with her as I'm at a loose end until Tuesday.'

> 'I'm Mary Porter. Silly name when I'm on a station as I want to turn whenever anyone calls out wanting . . .

> 'I christened you on the train; I had pondered who you were because you were smartly dressed and patently not a local traveller. Have a guess what I called you'

Anne giggled and suggested Edith or Thelma.

> 'No, I had you as an "Anne"; with an 'e', Mary.'

> 'Now, that is strange as I was christened Anne-Marie but I'm known as Mary as my real name sounds elaborate and calls for too many explanations.'

> 'So, what should I call you?'

James was astonished and taken off-guard by the incredible coincidence; really strange. The thought flashed that he was a little psychic. But to admit that would not be the thing to do.

'You will know me as Anne-Marie, please. I'd love that.'

'Here is my card; it's my Mother's address and number. May I be presumptuous and know where you are from, please?'

'I really did not expect you to ask; silly me. Of course; I am living and working in London but was brought up in East Anglia-Norwich, as my father works for a large insurance company based there.'

The taxi-driver said,

'We are approaching Timbers—it is Timbers you want isn't it?'

'Yes, please'

'Best to call me on CUNningham 7846 but I'm working most days. Good luck and keep trying. Thank you so much for the taxi and for help with my case. Have a good stay.'

All too soon the taxi drove on, towards a right turn called Tongdean Lane. A quaint name for an area losing its countryside feel in exchange for encroaching urban sprawl with an army of marching 1930s mock-Tudors and lesser semis. James recollected and stored his memories.

"Mary or Anne-Marie Porter from Norwich living at CUN 7846."

He was quietly thrilled; Anne-Marie was so at ease and happy and he longed to be able to know far, far more about her. His stay was short, unlikely to get more leave for several weeks as his motor industry work was preparing for racing at the new Brooklands Circuit. Arriving at Mater's home, he had a really rash idea. He'd look up the local Kelly's directory giving the names of people living in homes and flats in the Brighton area.

6 Finding Out 1933

Kelly's listed the family living at Timbers, Dyke Road Avenue, as one person: Alfred Palmer. This must be the head of the household and not whom Anne-Marie was going to visit. What should he say if he telephoned Timbers? It would be inappropriate to call in person but the telephone was new-fangled and less restricted in modern usage. James decided to sleep on it and see if a flash of light would give him courage and an idea to forward his means for introduction. It was no good asking Mater what to do: he thought she'd have no idea at all. But he had reflected without his customary pre-assessment.

Martha was worldly wise; he knew she had lived in Burma for many years; knew she had separated from her husband and it was likely she had formed a relationship with an expatriate. But how had they met? Where did they live in Burma? Many unknowns and whilst James was her son, she did not confide much, if anything, of her relationships. He did know that she had been content in Burma but with a proviso. James was instructed, strictly, never to mention to anyone where his mother had gone to live, let alone with whom. Just say I took a long holiday, she instructed.

James awoke quite early on this morning, a Saturday, and he did have a flash of wisdom. There was no time to tell you what I was doing today, and it might interest you and your friend, he mused. Unusually for James, he felt acutely nervous; it was as if he were on the side of a precipice, not certain which way to climb down. He knew that, if he made an error, it would be unlikely that he would see Anne-Marie again. The competent Sylvia came to mind; her training and manner was just made for him to overcome his fears. Treat the Palmer household as she would have so done. Be a gentleman; stand tall; appear groomed and speak without any hesitation which is a huge give-away if not practised.

But, he did have the London CUN number, of course. On the other hand, the ancient idiom "strike while the iron is hot" is as true today as in the sixteenth century. Undoubtedly Anne-Marie would have something planned—maybe the whole family were going somewhere, to a wedding or perhaps to a christening. The unknowns were obvious and endless. Chance had to take a hold. If it is meant to be, so be it! O Henry had used a line in a book title *Cherchez La Femme* and loosely translated could mean "there is somewhere the woman." James was amazed that he could be so excited by someone he really did not know. A few glances in a railway carriage were hardly enough upon which to instigate a relationship. And who says Anne-Marie wanted that, anyway? But she did exchange her number; she did not dismiss James, she clearly was glad to receive caring assistance and a taxi. What did he have to lose? Everything and nothing. He checked the local telephone directory.

Quarter past nine: a suitable time for a telephone call, neither too early nor too late into the morning's events. By now James was unbelievably nervous, almost shaking. He had never, ever, felt quite like this even before an important school away rugby match but somewhere there is a woman in Dyke Road Avenue. He thought mentally of Sylvia: what would she do? He picked the black telephone receiver and heard the gentle purr of the dialling sound and this was comforting. 4,8,1,4 he dialled, and almost immediately there was a giggle at the other end, a young voice saying between her happy chuckle

'Who can this be so early in the morning?'

'James'

'James who?'

Anne-Marie butted in,

'James, the man I told you about; we met on the London train'

'Oh, yes, Mary did say you'd helped her with her case. How may I help you? Did you lose something? Shall I pass you over to Mary?'

'Anne-Marie here. This is a surprise. How did you know my number as I'm staying with a friend, Jane.'

James' anxiety had reached fever pitch. Was this questioning a line of reproach or just natural curiosity? O Henry's title came to mind again *Cherchez la Femme* as he and his mentor, Sylvia took courage.

'Anne-Marie, I was down here to go to a dreadfully boring meeting of the BHMC—cars and things—but when I awoke this morning I remembered there was a new zoo or something at Drusilla's, near Eastbourne. I considered whether you two would be interested. There's an interesting village, nearby where we could arrange tea'

Muttered conversation was inaudible as the receiver was held covered.

'Jane says wonderful idea as she has noticed the hoarding and it's quite new. Do let's go, James.'

'May I come at about 10.30 to pick you both up because we'll have to take a train or something?

'My car is at home, I'm afraid, and anyway, it's too small for three; it's a Morgan.'

'Good. We have just enough time for a quick bite and to get dressed. What should we wear, do you think?'

'Oh, Jane suggests 11.30 would be better. Find out about trains and things, please.'

'Dress smart-casual; we are in the country but wear walking shoes as stations are near, but a walk away. I do not know the location, never been there. I heard about it from Mater. See you both at 11.30 sharp.'

'What a magic idea. Jane is beaming, don't quite know why. See you soon.'

"What a magic idea". This resounded in James' mind. And "Jane is beaming". He wondered what they had planned to do, anyway. Maybe go to the Pavilion or Hannington's or even go for a paddle at Black Rock. Who knows; I'll ask. He called the railway and enquired about trains to Drusilla's and gathered there was a station close-by at Berwick on the Eastbourne line via Lewes. He was warned not to take the express as it did not stop. Locals run at 42 past the hour and only hourly. Mater told him that Alfriston was a charming village which had tea houses and a few interesting shops—and a church and a cricket ground that she had been to at some time. James called the taxi firm and booked for 11.25 at Withdean.

He thanked Sylvia for her training which had clearly given him the courage to be strong, relaxed and utterly in control. That is what the diplomatic did for people. A career move? No; they required graduates with first-class honours and another three years of study. I'll think, he thought.

7 Drusilla's and Alfriston 1933

As the taxi entered the driveway, two laughing girls came out. No sign of the parents who must have felt that their daughter would be safe as a trio. James was out and asked who was going to sit in the front for the short journey to the station. Jane jumped in and said she'd tell the driver where to go. Anne-Marie beamed at James as if they had known each other so well and she took his hand and squeezed it hard but did not release him until the taxi arrived at the station. James leaped out to pay the fare but was beaten to the task by Jane who proffered two ten shilling notes and accepted some of the change.

'Why did you do that?'

asked James.

'Because, when Mary arrived yesterday, all she could talk about was you, James. I've known Mary for many months, now, but I've never seen her as content; she's been reclusive and did not appear at all interested in men. Just what did you say to her? She has been transformed before my jolly eyes.'

Anne-Marie looked either really embarrassed or maybe just sheepish to hear this outpouring from her close friend.

'We'll talk about this a little later, please; maybe when we've found a good peaceful compartment. I shall be the one who is getting a really red face and I do not much care for beetroot, Jane.'

James moved towards the clattering departures board but there was nothing, so far, indicating the slow train to Eastbourne.

'Speak of the devil.'

Said Anne-Marie as a shunting-engine drew a carriage-train puffing smoke and wheezing steam as it slowly came to a halt at the buffers beside a platform. James was now holding both girls' hands and smiles and glances were flashing about whilst the two girls were avoiding the steam and smoky atmosphere. They led James away from the activity but he was interested in matters-trains and was awkward about being moved slowly away from interesting goings-on. There were four carriages, all of which had seen smarter days but the journey was quite short. The guard shouted to the few waiting passengers:

'Do not board this Eastbourne train.'

And he blew his whistle as a caution. With the arrival of another engine, tender first and also moving slowly, the carriages were buffered together with a clunk and squeaking as the new engine closed the gap between the rear carriage and the tender. Men in blue overalls and oily working caps jumped down onto the track to ready the train. James was now anxious to see what was happening further down the platform and he tried to urge Jane and Anne-Marie but they seemed to have installed brakes in their shoes and listened to what the officious guard had to say. This train did not have a corridor, just compartments; and every brass-handled door was emblazoned with Third in gold letters on green background, the SR livery.

Steam trains still operated as the SR system had been part-electrified but neither on this branch line nor the route towards Eastbourne and Hastings. This was a good alternative to the newer stock; the smell and noise of a working steam engine, its deep puffs and chugs as it pulled its load interested James who appreciated all things mechanical but such mundane activities left the girls unimpressed and looking to avoid inevitable smuts thrown up by the smoke stacks. The carriage nearest the engine was chosen where there was an empty compartment; it smelled of stale cigarette smoke and maybe some unwashed passengers.

'This is Third Class for you, make the best of it.'

Said Jane with her aquiline nose held a few inches higher than customary.

Jane was dressed in a grey skirt with a blue blouse covered with a coarse-weaved round-necked grey-blue pullover which clinged to her interesting, rounded figure giving an overall picture of a girl at ease with herself. Her hair was natural dark blonde, so James thought, and arranged with the side lengths tightly curled up above her ears in a modern fashion. James would have preferred her to have had free-flowing hair but she had, of course, been to the hair salon before Anne-Marie's arrival. Neither girl wore much, if any, make-up apart from lipstick which was quite bright and appeared to flash when either spoke.

There was a mixture of scent but James could not differentiate who wore what but he did think Chanel No 5 was there but he was no expert in such intimacies.

Anne-Marie was dressed rather more smartly, wearing a suit jacket and skirt made from gentle tweed together with a cream blouse and a blue and green neck-tie-choker which was rather fetching and unusual. She still wore pearls, now only just visible. The suit rather hid her figure but her face shone and she looked happy and at ease. Her light-brown hair was framed in a bob-style and came down each side of her face to curl, a little, at chin level. No earrings were visible but maybe, if there was a gust of wind during the walk, James would be able to see a few more secrets. He thought she was ideally dressed for a countryside trip and a walk of a mile or so from the station to Drusilla's and maybe, onto Alfriston, another two miles. Neither of the girls was wearing anything but sensible dark flat shoes and beige stockings. It was a real joy to be out with such an attractive pair who were clearly at ease with each other and not at all abashed by James' presence.

Who was the worldlier and more experienced of the two, James mused, idly. Jane as she tended to take the lead and the initiative with all that was going on. There was not a great deal of chatter whilst everyone took in the rather sad ambience of SR's best when Anne-Marie asked with a completely straight face,

'Shall we order some tea and biscuits?'

to an ice-breaking gasp of laughter. Once the train had started to move, conversation was permitted and Jane wanted to see the line running through the Brighton suburbs towards Lewes. There was no real view apart from when the train took to the viaduct as it trundled north-easterly clanking and squealing over the points or curves in the track.

James turned to Anne-Marie, saying,

'I know so little about you and I am desperate to know what you do, where you work, where you went to school or

university, what games you are good at and what your home or
flat is like, how it is decorated, and what you wear, normally'

'Oh so much to take in and I cannot wait to tell you'

This was the first real conversation they had enjoyed since taking
the taxi from Timbers. Being a threesome and a stranger to the other
two, James felt a little uneasy about opening a normal discussion.
Once again he recalled the training that Sylvia had in Zurich and asked
himself what would she have said or done had she been introduced
to some leading dignitary. There had to be a recognised disease called
tied-tongue as so many men and women suffered at times. Maybe
he should set down a number of questions to ask when in a tight
spot. Mnemonics and acronyms came into his mind as a solution to
the problem. After all, "Richard of York . . ." enabled the colours of
the rainbow to come to the mind's forefront when the sun caught
raindrops. James had asked Anne-Marie about her background and
schooling but had not received an answer before he jumped in, again,
asking,

'How do you know Jane so well?'

At this, Jane who had been listening intently instead of busying
herself with the awful back views of terraced houses beside the railway
line said,

'Keep counsel, please; James is still a stranger.'

Ignoring this imperative, Anne-Marie carried on saying that they
had met at a musical evening in London and had gone onto a Fuller's
Restaurant for a light meal afterwards where they talked incessantly and
seemed to be like old friends from that moment onwards.

'We have only known each other for about eighteen months
but have similar likes and enjoy fun things to do. We are
both interested in clothes and fashion changes, of course, as

these seem to move so fast particularly with the American and French influences. I've been invited down a few times now, and it seems like home-from-home. Mr and Mrs Palmer have treated me like another daughter, which is lovely as I do not see much of my parents.'

James was thrilled to be talking openly with Anne-Marie when Jane, who had been looking at the view of the Sussex Downs and the Cuckmere levels, said the next stop was Berwick and it was time for walkies as if we were a litter of yapping puppies. Luckily, the weather was bright but chilly. All were glad to leave the rather stuffy compartment for the fresh air. They asked the station porter which way to follow for Drusilla's and Alfriston.

'Easy; just cross the line here, keep on past the Inn on your left and walk down Station Road 'til you reach a crossroad, go straight across and on, same direction, for about a mile and Drusilla's is on the left after the road junction just after a farm. It's quite new. Alfriston, if you want to see that, is on the same road but about another mile walk. Good pub, there. Have a good outing and enjoy.'

The Berwick Inn was modern and uninspiring and walking hand-in-hand they walked briskly past towards the south. The road was interesting with straights and bends with a few scattered houses and businesses then mainly fields seemingly with crops growing and a few sheep and cattle sheltering in the lea of thick hedgerows. Trees stood along the field boundaries and the scene was singularly placid and the walk would be classed as "easy". The South Downs were clearly visible in the middle distance and they appeared really inviting.

Conversation was still venturing upon enquiry rather than discussion of interests and Jane took most initiatives which did not really appeal to James who was bowled over by Anne-Marie. There was so much he wanted to find out about her and Jane rather stopped this line of questioning. Anne-Marie was happy to let Jane lead.

Did Jane fancy James? Anne-Marie thought so but retained her composure and she knew from slight eye-contact how James was feeling. Apart from some musical interests, neither of the girls was struck madly by modern Jazz, The Charleston, Fred Astaire but preferred classical orchestras. James retained his comments as he did like the modern age and the American influence of the Deep South but did not wish to enter into a musical discussion: simply not his scene.

Drusilla's leaped into view but there was not a great deal to see apart from a sign recommending a tour of the animals and a tea shop. No bets were taken as to what everybody preferred, first. The thatched building was quaint and the inside was set out with a mixture of household chairs, mis-matched tables that were un-commercial but the counter was laden with delicious-looking cakes and fresh bakery. Two girls were in charge but looking somewhat bewildered as if the head waiter was on leave. Schoolgirls came to mind but the older of the two came over and spoke with a cut-glass accent and enquired of everyone what they'd like to eat or to drink. She spun off a list of homemade cakes and the selection was quickly made. She had teas and coffees but recommended their house speciality brew which was a mixture of Indian and Chinese leaves which did prove to be unusual and refreshing. The menu card called the place a Tea Garden but this signified a garden set out with rustic tables and atrocious chairs. The interior had twisted old beams, white painted walls which were far from upright, exposed timbers in the walls and doors that were not straight out of a brand-new box. Yes, definitely really rather a good site for a tea room, but a pity to call it a garden.

'Shall we all go and look at what animals they have to offer?'

Suggested Jane, in charge as usual.

'The cake was really good, didn't you think so James?'

Anne-Marie moved closer to James and took his upper arm from behind and squeezed it firmly.

> 'Let's go explore; there must be some form of attraction to retain those girls in a Tea Garden; I'd get fat with all those delicious cakes mercilessly tempting me all day long.'

James and Anne-Marie went out, still linked together and both feeling really content and happy. Jane was also exploring, looking at the printed cards and a map of what animals or birds were available and what was planned to be opened. Drusilla's was going to become something—someday soon, she felt. The grounds were naturally of a farm that was no longer an agricultural enterprise. It was clean and over-tidy. Old sheds and barns and many large trees helped to give Drusilla's the air of an attraction-to-be. It was not quite there, as yet but money had been spent on cleaning the enterprise and installing walkways which looked inviting as well as being workable.

> 'Let's go over there.'

James suggested, and walked twenty-five yards to another barn that was clearly old, constructed of Sussex flint walls with a locally tiled roof and high windows. Inside, there was a farm smell—of animals, but not the usual kind of large farm animals but neither exotic nor zoo creatures such as zebras or tigers. This building was set out as a children's attraction and all the animals could be petted and some of the enclosures were made especially for children to enter and to stroke the inhabitants as if they were dogs or cats.

Neither Anne-Marie nor James were animal-wise. Breeds and names of farm animals had been learned from children's books. There were informative labels and these told children what they were looking at and what they ate and where they were from. There were goats, rabbits, small pigs, and a few adorable calves. All quietly domesticated but children were enjoying themselves and were screaming for their mother or father to come and see how tame were their new friends. Anne-Marie found she was enjoying being near these lovely gentle animals which gave the impression of content. Jane, appeared to be completely at home with animals and with the layout of Drusilla's.

'Where is Jane?'

Anne-Marie asked. Outside, Jane was nowhere to be seen but they knew she would not just disappear so they agreed to look in an interesting building which was quite newly built to see if Jane had meandered there. Otherwise, she'd be in the tea garden, and was leaving Mary and James to be together for a while.

> 'Jane works for a veterinary practice, near Devil's Dyke so knows a great deal about animals and farms. We do not need to worry about where she has walked.'

> 'So, what does she do at this practice? Is she a vet, herself?'

> 'No, she works as an assistant to the trained vets who, on the face of it, cannot manage all the procedures on their own. The animals are all large and often must be held firmly whilst they are examined or injected. She hugely enjoys her work and finds it fascinating and the male company jolly good. But, no, she is not interested in any of her colleagues, most of whom are married or attached.'

> 'Have you seen her at work, yet?'

> 'No, never. I could ask but would prefer her to invite me, first. She does not discuss the Poynings Practice much.'

The next building was set out as a museum of ancient machinery, discontinued farm implements; most had shafts for horses to pull and polished metal blades used to till the soil. All a bit strange for one not brought up on a farm. There were clearly printed signs which were instructive. At the other end, where one day there'd be more exhibits, the management had installed a children's play area with ropes, swings and some frames to climb and to slide down again. These were in some demand. James and Anne-Marie lingered awhile to watch the children. Both thought they had missed out on an agricultural upbringing. There was so much more to see and to do on a farm than in a town house with office-working parents.

'I'd like to have a farm to bring up our children.'

Said Anne-Marie.

James looked at her in astonishment and Anne-Marie realised what she had said. She looked foolish and said,

'I have been so happy with you today; the kids bit just fell out naturally. I do hope you do not mind or think me presumptuous. I so want to see much more of you.

'I'm really rather reserved and unused to men's company and you are the first I have ever felt like being close, safe and wanting to love. I have never, ever, been in love with anyone and have rejected all advances—and there have been a few, I can tell you.'

'My astonishment has nothing to do with being upset. I have been taken by surprise because I feel exactly the same about you and have been wondering just how to talk to you and to try to explain my feelings. I am almost a complete novice with girls but my father has been trying to impose various friends' daughters upon me with indifference on my part except for one called Sylvia.

'She's British but living in Paris with her diplomatic service parents and a governess who is likely to be a tyrant and insists she wears figure changing corsets all day and probably night, as well. I have the impression that they are supposed to be good for the soul but they do give her a wondrous figure, too.

'She has a trained mind developed at her finishing school in Zurich where she wants to go back and to teach when she graduates. I have been thinking a great deal about her—not because of her looks which are positively plain but for her innate wisdom and ability to converse. Other Parisian girls were vacant-minded individuals who lacked a vital spark that you have in abundance.'

'Oh, my darling James—here I go again—I feel happy beyond measure. I hardly slept last night and my thoughts were with you for hours and I did not know what to do to make contact. It is just not appropriate for me to telephone you and Jane warned me off doing so as etiquette and formality are valued beyond measure. And then you telephoned this morning. Both Jane and I were thrilled and we'd have come out at six o'clock with the cockerels had you suggested something daft like that.

'We must go and find Jane, now. She is hiding somewhere to leave us alone. I'll tell you more about our first meeting when we're on the train back to Brighton.'

Jane was not in the tea rooms but she had left a message with the waitresses to say that she had walked towards Alfriston and was just going to explore but would not leave the direct road. If you don't find her, they said, she'll be waiting in the parish church at five-thirty.

'There she is.'

Said Anne-Marie. She had spotted her looking over a farm gate. Some cattle were waiting to be let into one of the steadings, nearby.

'Jane I'm so glad to find you so soon; are you alright?'

'Of course. I left you two so as not to be a cuckoo in the nest: you looked so happy together. Anyway, I wanted to move on and to see what Alfriston looked like as I'd heard it was an attractive village. So, let's walk on and find another tea room and then, maybe, we could hail a taxi to take us via Seaford which has a railway station. I am not quite sure which line it's on but it cannot be impossible to get to Brighton'

'Great idea, Jane; you are a good organiser and full of ideas.'

James said.

'Are you happy to do this, Mary?'

Jane asked.

'Of course; we'd love to see the much-mentioned pretty village; so, let's walk onwards and a shade upwards so that we'll be ready for second tea and maybe scones and cream.'

After a half-hour walk, Alfriston came into view, stone walls, flint featured buildings alongside brick and hanging-tile-clad homes vying for position with ancient timbers supporting roof structures. With so many varied methods of showing off its homes, working properties, shops and inns, Alfriston had much to offer the casual visitor. Market Cross was where a few cars, vans and charabancs all vied for space with horses and traps used to give visitors an interesting tour of the area. There were several restaurants and tea houses. Badgers Tea House looked inviting and, inside, it had a wall map showing exceptional points of interest with historical details. James decided to have a closer look at the village and suggested he left the girls to have a gossip and giggle.

Even so, they wanted to look at what was on offer and to explore the small shops. Needless to say, there was a smart dress shop and all went in and James was surprised to notice the well set-out range of corsetry destined for the village women-folk as this was a well-to-do village and its inhabitants would need to be well dressed, and booted and suited to match.

Both girls noticed James' interest and Jane asked,

'What do you think about girls being enclosed in such foundation-wear?'

Embarrassed, James said,

'I like it. My Mater wears things like this all the time and she has given me an interest; so, yes, I do like women to have the need to wear good support and I like to feel it when I give them a hug or dance with them.'

'You're not giving me a hug.'

Said Jane with forced vigour.

James had already established that her clothes were too free flowing and clearly she was not clad in anything tight—almost to his disappointment. Anne-Marie admitted that she did not have any need for support-wear apart from a bra and a suspender belt but that she'd been thinking of having a look as there were so many shops offering incredible garments with stocking clips and things that appeared to have brassieres built into the things which would enclose the whole of a woman's torso.

'Jane, do you think that one of those long things would be easy to wear in your work?'

'No. It would be hot and impractical in my work but I do have something like that which I wear when going out to smart dinners or to dances. Mother insists, much to my annoyance, but I know she is right as I feel so much more contained and collected—and safe—when I have something enclosing me tightly which she bought for me in Hanningtons.

'So, on balance, I do like having one and I'll tell her about this interesting shop. She is never without a foundation garment and she changes hers at least twice daily. Being a good mother, she does not impose her preferences upon me but it does get mentioned quite often as she hates to see me scruffily dressed—but that's part and parcel of my job. My job is often dirty work and I do have to strip to my bra when required to glove-up and venture into an animal's backside to feel its ovaries or to see if it has a growing calf—or two.'

# Chapter Two

1 Coleen's Story

*C*oleen was mildly jealous of Mary's probable success in finding a handsome soul-mate. It was a matter of luck and although she spent days meeting fellow workers in theatres, the magic component seemed to be elusive and she did not like men who just happened to be around. Yes, she was acutely fussy about who she assessed to be a close attachment with her. She'd rather see nobody than anybody and was determined to settle down with just one partner for life. No hurry, she was young and able.

Just now, her priority was to get into her profession and to succeed with a really good part where she'd be noticed by a producer. "Your time will come" she had been advised by her tutor at RADA. At least she was not idle whilst resting. The shop was proving to be a success and takings were definitely increasing, slowly, but certainly. Word was spreading, too. Coleen was mad keen to tell everyone she met about her enterprise and a few did look her up.

Recently, she had been to see Jen, a corsetière she had met at a theatrical function, to have a consultation and had decided to order. The meeting went well and Coleen explained that she so enjoyed the feel of an Edwardian busk-fronted corset that she had to wear for a part in a stage play where she was working as an understudy for the retained actress who was in hospital and then recuperating for a few weeks. Six days a week she was required and on four days there were both matinees and evening performances. It was unwise to dress and undress during a full performance day so she found she was encased for entire days at a time in the corset that was provided for her.

The magnificent corset had been specially made by Angels, a leading theatrical costumier. It was designed to give Coleen an 'S' shape and initially this took some days to get used to the feel and complete re-shape this particularly rigid garment enforced. At first, she really hated the feel; it cut into her flesh, it stopped her moving as she would normally and it so re-shaped her figure that she felt she was unrecognisable if she went out in the street for a coffee in a corner house. She had to hold herself utterly erect and sustain the incredible curves enforced by the close-fitting garment. Was this a curse of being an actress?

As days passed, she began to look forward to being helped into the blue and white creation once again and she did not protest when the laces were customarily tightened expertly, by one of the dressers. They did not close the two corset halves all at once and insisted that Coleen rested after the first closure for a good half-hour before they attempted fully to wrap the corset around her and attain a waistline of just twenty inches as well as a change in spinal curvature required for the Gibson-Girl appearance with an accentuated bust and posterior together with a hairstyle which added inches to her height.

The result looked and felt quite superb. After another rest, so as to regain her breath and to start to respire correctly, she was released from dressing room control in the first required costume, complete with an ungainly bustle and an immense wig to await her call by stage staff for her entrances. She really hoped that she'd be noticed; the part was not that complex and the director was happy to have her as an understudy. It was normal for new understudies to have a hard time from directors as they had to come specially to re-train an actor and, of course, they did alter the directions where a slight change would improve the performances as a whole. Coleen relished the new directions and worked remarkably well with the cast and stage managers. That she put up with her shape so well and did not complain impressed the director. That the crew and company asked her to accompany them in the green room and to some after-performance get-togethers indicated that she was surviving well.

As the time came for her part to cease as the original actress was to return full-time, Coleen really regretted the thought of being unable to have her new shape for much longer. The two girls worked together for some weeks with a two-days-on and three-days-off basis but slowly Coleen was eased out entirely.

She determined to buy a new corset and discussed what would be appropriate for modern-day living with Jen Johnson whom she had met at a function arranged by The Stage newspaper. Coleen decided to be fitted and Jen had been instructed to arrange the tailoring of the garment. She could not afford more than one and that was almost a step too far, financially—but needs must, she thought. If it influenced any directors, then the outlay would pay-off hugely.

Her corset was due any day now. Jen telephoned and arranged to meet at her home, as was customary. Coleen was so excited; she longed to be in harness again and so hoped that what Mme Vermeuil, had constructed would suit her, fit her and support her. When Jen came to the door, Coleen was just a little taken aback; she looked worried and this was not Jen's way with customers.

'Hello, Coleen; I have been looking forward to showing you this creation but it is really so unusual. That is why I appear concerned. I always examine new garments before I bring them to a customer and this is the most unusual I have ever had to deliver and so wonder if the maker, Mme Vermeuil, has managed this to perfection. I know I measured you correctly and what I wrote down was exactly what the tapes said but she may have taken you a little too literally.'

'Come on, Jen, let's try it on for size—and see what it does to, or is it 'for' my shape?'

The new corset was a fabulous creation but not at all of modern appearance; it was made along the lines of a real Victorian, rigid busk-fronted well boned garment that was designed to cover Coleen from over her bust to just above her hips. The steel busk was gently curved rather than being straight. This would follow, more accurately, the female abdominal line. Would this corset feel like being encased in a straightjacket? Jen had seen such corsets in the past, but nobody ordered such items these days, preferring to be able to move freely but in modern controlling creations; this one was not at all modern.

> 'Please put on this chemise, first. It will be close fitting but will protect your skin from the rigours of the corset's construction which will need literally to be broken-in. Initially, you will need to dress in it with some care. Is the chemise on?
>
> 'Please stand straight whilst I place this corset on you and try to attain its correct position. I will need some help from you, too.'

Taking the corset, Jen put it around Coleen's body and closed the lowest of the six busk studs. She asked Coleen to support her breasts with her hands and then closed the top stud of the six. Then, using the top stud as a form of lever, she closed number one, then the other five, one by one. She said she could now release her breasts. The garment was not in the least tight, yet, as the lacing had not been applied.

> 'How do you feel in this corset, Coleen? Are you ready for some lacing-in?'
>
> 'It's superb; but it's not tight, yet, is it?'
>
> 'I am about to apply some intense pressure on your trunk when I start to lace you in with considerable force.
>
> 'I know you are well used to being laced in but I will take my time.'

Turning Coleen round, so that her back and lacing could be adjusted, Jen eased the laces towards the centre of the corset, at waist level. Jen moved down and up as all the lacing had to be evenly moved through the grommets, thus starting to close the two halves of the corset. When the halves were two inches apart, Jen asked Coleen to sit down and take a rest and to start to breathe normally.

'Let's have a cup of tea; I'll make it.'

Jen implied as an order rather than a request.

'You just take it sedately and get used to the feel. It does look really good on you. The experience you have had on stage has prepared you for this creation. Had you not been used to being corseted, you'd never have got this far so quickly.'

Coleen was trying to work out how this new rigidity suited her frame. It was incredibly tight and restrictive but she liked the sensation. Her bust-line was raised and her breasts looked amazingly good. Defying orders, she stood and moved to the long mirror on the wall. The laces at the back were dangling but ignoring them her figure looked so elegant and much slimmer than she had dared to hope. She found she could move, almost normally. She decided she'd be able to do any work demanded in the shop and she tested her ability to bend from the knees.

'You do look exquisite, Coleen; quite lovely. Have you rested enough?

'I'd like to move towards the final closure of the rear panels so that the lacing is completely tight. Normally, you'd have to wait a couple of days for me to do this but you are well used to the power of ceintures like this one. Please lie down on your bed, facing the mattress and do not worry; breathe normally, please.'

Jen knew it is much easier to close a corset with the wearer lying prone and so it was the case with Coleen; it closed entirely in a couple of minutes and Jen tied off the lacing into a neat half-hitch and bow and tucked excess lacing under the bottom of the corset so that it would never be seen. She clipped this into place so it could not fall out—a Mme Vermeuil design idea.

'How does that feel, Coleen?'

'Incredible; no tighter than when it was left before. I am really amazed and longing to see the measurement of my waistline and how it looks in the mirror; how do I get up, though?'

'With ease; you just slip your legs to the side of your bed. Now, bending at the knee, lower your legs to the floor and help yourself upright using an arm for support. And stand upright. At first you'll feel a little strange. If you do feel breathless or faint, sit down. Your body will need to become accustomed to its new exo-skeleton.'

'It's like a form of bondage, Jen. I'm tied into this suit of armour but Oh! I like it; I really do like it. It feels so comforting, controlling, firm and as if I was born wearing it. You are a wonder, Jen. I cannot tell you how pleased I am to be dressed so well. I know that I'll have to force myself to wear it, all day and every day, but I have done so before and will attain normal composure in a matter of days. Please mark my words.'

Coleen was beaming with delight. This corset was all she had ever hoped to receive. It fitted her beautifully and nowhere did the stiff whale-boning attack her flesh. The stiffening avoided her major hip, rib and pelvic bones and any of her protuberances. But the waistline was clearly defined and flesh had literally moved within her abdomen—as it had in the theatre corset. Her breasts were so defined now, and looked as one with her body. They were firm and there was no possibility for any unsightly bounce. Her waistline was a full ten inches less than her bust and hips thus resembling an hourglass.

'May we dress and go outside for a short walk, please Jen?'

'Of course; but this is quite unusual for someone newly in a rigid costume. A wise move is to get used to this first and to have some real air into your lungs. How is your breathing, now?'

'Breathing is straightforward; remember, I am used to being controlled and have mastered diaphragm control having been looking like a Gibson Girl for weeks on end. At least I do not have an S shape, a bustle or a huge wig. This Victorian design is looking and feeling fabulous. My waist feels strange but I expect I'll get used to the constriction. Let's go.'

Walking downstairs was easy but Coleen thought how it would be on the ascent. She was young and fit but her rib-cage did not move in and out as it did *sans-corset*. She reflected upon how she would put this garment onto herself without any help. She recalled that Jen had discussed this problem when it was being ordered. Two things would help: a strong hook or a doorknob; and maybe Mary at the shop.

The fresh air was balmy and cooled her down. She managed to talk quite normally and took in the street scene and watched what was happening. Nobody could see what she was wearing nor could they see what a wondrous figure she had suddenly achieved. Jen looked proud and unconcerned. They moved towards a small park situated within a square of properties and found a bench where they could rest a while. Jen talked to Coleen and asked her to describe what was expected from her in the part she had played. Both felt that they needed a good strong coffee but there was nothing nearby. Standing, they turned and walked towards the flat and found a small cafe. This will be a test, Coleen thought.

'I'll buy.'

Coleen said.

'May I have two coffees, please, milk in both but sugar in one, please.'

'You look well, today, Madam. Doing something interesting?'

'I feel on top of the world.'

If you did but know.

'Thanks for the refreshments, anyway.'

'Now Coleen, I want you to take this calmly and not to rush up the flights of stairs. Grip the handrail and stop if you are out of breath or if you start to feel faint. Do you hear me, Coleen?'

Taking a step at a time, only a little slower than usual, Coleen took the first flight easily and stopped for breath on the half-landing. Her face was just a little flushed and she was smiling radiantly. Moving on, she started up the next flight; only one more after this. She managed to control her breathing a little better and used her diaphragm more effectively as she had been instructed by one of the theatre dressers; there, she had to project her voice to reach the upper circle seats. Coleen took the last two flights at a steady pace and entered her flat. This proved she was fit.

'Jen, I'll manage, now. Have had experience taking myself out of corsetry and it's straightforward once you know how to loosen the reins and unclip the studs one by one. I want to stay in this for the rest of the afternoon and will try to go the evening as well. I may see if Mary is still at the shop. What is it, COV 6684.'

'Good bye Jen and so many, many thanks.'

Mary was delighted to come round to Coleen's flat and was really amazed at what she saw. She wished she had had the same type of garment made; it looked quite exquisite, feminine and flattering. Mary determined she'd have one when enough of her allowance had been saved up. They decided to go out for a snack and a small drink to see how it felt and looked when on show. Coleen felt her tummy was tight and had little or no room left for much food—at least she may get slimmer.

The girls had a delightful evening and Coleen did not show a minute of discomfort. On the contrary, she stood and sat so much better; really erect but satisfied rather than imprisoned. She looked at ease and clearly, the theatre training had been an absolute boon. Just one area was a slight discomfort—her thigh tops where the corset ended when sitting—the stitching was cutting in a little and she wanted to see what sort of mark was left on her thighs. Her stockings felt cool and the suspenders were holding the corset and her hosiery delightfully in place.

Mary decided, there and then, that she would have another word with Jen, the corsetière. She had liked what she had seen in the Alfriston shop and knew that James was more interested than he should have been but she appreciated the feel of modern corsetry.

2 Paris Learning Curves 1933

James and his father had a regular coffee and croissant in the Neuilly district in outer Paris and the girl who was working there was called Claudette. One day father said James should make contact "to see what you can get." As father walked out, Claudette walked over and sat with him bringing her *tasse de thé* plus a generous smile. James spoke fluent French but was naive with girls and definitely with ones who were slightly *risqué*. Elfin faced, with pert breasts to die for, she was also singularly forward and suggested James come and meet her towards the night, say 9.30? Madame, she said, would not mind my having a friend round for a short rest. I'll see, said James, and accepted her address-card as if it was from the local builder. School had taught him all he thought he needed to know about night-girls, the need for rubber-wear and for avoiding being caught up in any form of agreement-to-repeat for a valuable reduction.

Other cafe customers entered and Claudette was behind the counter in a flash, without even giving a smile. She was red-haired, certainly out of a bottle, but she had an interesting face with delicate features, a small nose curved at the tip and big round eyes. Something was incorrect and as he studied her, it was clearly the hair that needed professional attention. Dark or black would be far more suitable and the fringe needed a decent—more expensive—cut so that her hair fell around her face.

Her breasts were filling her *soutien-gorge* without space to spare and they gave a firm impression and were tightly supported. James longed to feel them and see if they were really like his mates' descriptions of being soft, supple, round and bouncy when released from their harness but warm and suffocating when nuzzled.

He decided to take the offer and walked out with a glance that said "I'll see you later". He did not want to fear his father's mock outrage if he did not do as he suggested. Father had been leading him on for long enough, considering he was over 21 and still not yet a man of the world with necessary experience and bed-time wisdom and manners: so important in Paris, he said. He stopped and bought a copy of *Paris Soir* to help while away a couple of hours and then walked a short distance to find the card address and to see just how awful it might be. It was not; a great surprise. The concierge muttered something which was not quite polite but waved James towards the stairs and said '*troisième*' without the *étage*. There was only one entrance door and he knocked and a woman of about fifty beamed a wide smile standing in her over-corseted figure clothed in a shapely dress but worn with a bow-tie which gave some sort of message—rather lost on James.

'You must be James for Claudette; may I ask you for just ten, please.'

She meant francs but at least the formalities and the transaction was completed without any *embarras*.

Claudette had heard and swept out of her small room within the apartment giving a smile that would win freedom from the Bastille and holding out a hand she grasped her trainee warmly but her breasts were also on display, looking astonishingly lovely and definitely naughty. James had never seen her dressed for *le travail de chambre*.

'How shall we begin?'

She queried, undoing a further button from her tight blouse so as to expose her white SG which was working wonders supporting the volume. Her breasts were filling her *soutien-gorge* without space to spare but they were firm and were clearly very tightly contained.

James felt absurd. He had never had any experience of this sort of advanced behaviour and desperately wanted guidance from Claudette. Looking crestfallen, she took the stage and was used to in-experience and took it with great charm as, to upset one so new would create a lifetime of angst. She leaned over and took James' hands and moved towards him so that she was close but not touching his body. Her smile was now comforting and wildly attractive and she was softly talking in her native French little words of encouragement. She took James' coat off and undid his shirt and cravat and placed them on a nearby *chaise* being careful to fold things as if she was a maid. A lovely touch, he thought. She removed her blouse and placed it with his shirt too. It looked spotless and quite well made. Apart from her SG, she was now naked from the waist up.

Her breasts were supported by a new clean SG of some construction with wide straps and a wider back band and side wiring but with the contents literally inclined to pour out, she took James by his waist and hugged him and pressed her upper body lustily towards his. He could not contain his feelings and inched away which Claudette recognised instantly and she started to undo his trousers and take them off together with his shoes leaving him standing in pants and socks. She was still in her underwear and long lovely stockings and suspenders. Carefully, she removed James' pants but neglected the socks and she removed her knickers leaving the suspender belt and SG. James was uncertain, again and looked longingly at her voluptuous parapet. She fumbled, meaningfully, with her rear strap and asked James to help her with the hooks and eyes 'c'est difficiles' she said, pretending. Dropping her garment onto the chaise, she took James' head and placed it right in the midst of her most ample feature. James noticed that without her SG, there were deep red marks around her chest where it had been tightly encasing her breasts. He found these indentations decidedly erotic.

He wondered what real corsets Claudette had in her room; he would like to see and to feel her tightly sheathed in a vigorous corset that made her waist really tiny. He placed his face into her much reduced cleavage and rapidly found that it was far more attractive when supported; he could breathe and the flesh would not suffocate him as his pals had wrongly suggested. James moved to take a nipple and to work his tongue around an areola which tasted mildly salty.

By now, fully erect, opening a small packet, Claudette eased the smooth rubber onto his member with great care and attention to his needs. She was clearly experienced but almost clinical in her practicality. She moved onto the centre of the bed and teased James to her side. Her breasts were now spread out on her chest and were by no means as attractive as they were when she stood up. This amazed him. Anxious not to have a failure on her hands, Claudette took James into her right hand and placed him close to her upper thighs and willed him to enter her, soothingly suggesting that he moved and caressed her stocking-clad legs. The actual movement taking Claudette was relaxed; he had expected tightness and felt that great pressure was required to enter. She was wet and expectant and pressure was not an issue. She moved with a swaying motion, as best as she could, and hugged his face close to hers but nowhere near his lips. She suggested, simply, '*prends plaisir.*'

Surprisingly, for one inexperienced, it took James about half a minute to reach a climax and he did so with a deep groan of release which felt as nothing before—certainly far, far more ecstatic than mere masturbation. The nerves within his member had come alive and were throbbing. Claudette put on an expression of satisfaction and then said that was sensuous for me, too. You have manhood with which to be really proud. Use it well and you will be a content man with a wife who'll never get enough attention without demanding more. You have done well, really well. Let me help you to dress as she grasped her *SG* and hooked the back strap with practiced hands. She took his protective from him and passed him his pants as it was necessary to cease all embarrassment from this venture. James admired her for her professionalism and clearly she took a real pride in teaching youngsters just how to feel and to behave in the boudoir.

'Do you have *le corset?*'

Claudette was a little surprised but knew that James had a special interest and she took his hand and walked towards the *armoire à glace.* Opening it, it was filled with lovely fripperies and interesting costumes used to create an atmosphere: some uniforms, some work-wear, some bathing costumes and most interesting, some real corsets made of coloured satin and rigidly boned and with laces to tighten.

'James, you will need to return to see me in one of these.'

She said, holding a superb example of the corsetière's craft with two hands and rotating it as if to demonstrate its construction and abilities.

Seeing James was aroused, again, she took pity and undid the busk rivets and placed the garment around her body, attaching just one of the rivets. She undid her SG and dropped it to the floor and attended to the remaining four rivets and adjusted her breasts to fit into the corset, leaning forward to assist the correct fitting. Standing, she asked James to help her with the laces but looked at him as if to say "I bet you cannot help."

Needless to say, James had no clue but just looked flustered and fumbled with the complexities of the back closure of the corset which was not at all tight nor particularly supportive.

'Let me help you.'

She said, taking the laces and placing them around a pair of hooks set firmly into the wall. Moving away from the wall-hooks, the laces closed the back of the corset, forcing her breasts upwards and making her waist considerably smaller. James placed his hands around Claudette's waist but his fingers would not touch; the laces needed much more tightening—and experienced hands were necessary.

> 'You will have to learn to help me to tighten wholly *le corset* if you are to be able to span my waist with your fingers. I love this one as it is extremely firm and tight when on me. For now, this is a demonstration and when you come again, I will be wearing it, as now, but we'll close it together, and then . . . James, I have so much enjoyed helping you and look forward, greatly, to your next *visite*.'

With a chaste kiss on his cheek she parted company and Madame asked how he felt without needing to hear any answer. Maybe, Madame kept her for this purpose, alone. This was why Claudette was not in attendance until later in the evening.

Father was delighted to see James when he walked in as if nothing had happened but a look that said the cat had found the cream said it all. He told James that he often sent young friends of friends to

Claudette but had never been there himself; he had a mistress who lived elsewhere. From the reports he had received, this girl was a delightful teacher and never failed in her mission to complete the task and to relieve the poor young man of his virginity. James slept really well that night. He lusted to see Claudette encased tightly and firmly in one of her favourite corsets. He felt pleased that he had had the courage to ask especially, and to see her range of interesting clothes. A real worry was lifted from his tiny mind.

3 Jen Advising Mary

Anne-Marie had returned to her flat in London's Maida Vale after the most fantastic weekend and especially meeting James almost out of nowhere. She recalled she had studied him from her seat on the train by viewing him in the window that had quite miraculously become like a mirror. Nobody could have realised what she was doing—least of all the hugely attractive man sitting opposite—and she pondered just what he was like and how she could strike up a conversation. Impossible; the carriage was filled and it was not done for anyone to open a discussion in so public a place. So, she dreamed and hoped for a miracle. When she arrived at Jane's home she regaled her with the events of the journey and her wild hopes. Jane did suggest that a telephone call to his mother's home might be a possibility but this was thought unwise as James Compton might be offended by their presumption. After a night spent wondering and somehow hoping, the telephone rang during breakfast and she had had a magical day with Jane and James.

Now, in London, she was expected at work in the small dress shop she helped her actress friend Coleen run in-between parts and auditions that she had to negotiate in the hope that a producer might require her evident looks, dancing ability and training for this most difficult of professions.

The shop was located between the British Museum and Covent Garden and there was a constant flow of passing public and a few women did venture inside as the window display was always glamorous and inviting and often had a theatrical theme. Anne-Marie worked miracles with the shop front simply out of interest and her art school training.

Fabric was her selected *point fort* and she got to know many of the wholesalers because of her looks and not really because there was a raft of sales as the shop specialised in finished evening wear rather than cloth by the yard. Mary, as Coleen called her, had considered materials-by-the-yard but discarded the notion as the range of shades, fabrics and types was just too vast for a relatively small boutique venture.

Meeting so many fabric sources was of great interest to Mary and maybe, one day, it would prove useful. Life itself was unpredictable and she found that things often fell into place, rather than having to be researched. Coleen had to audition for parts and they did not materialise by chance. Did Mary have a streak of luck in her being or upbringing? Or was it, perhaps, help from "them above"?

Mary had a fitting arranged with the corsetière, Jen, who had been introduced by Coleen after a short run in a period-costumed play that ran a trial in the Home Counties before being taken up in the West End. Coleen said she adored the feel of Edwardian fashions and she had urged Mary to try some modern corsetry styles to see how she looked and felt and they both agreed that if Mary's looks were enhanced by a fashionable curvy figure, then turnover might increase as women did like to copy what they saw. She already knew that James loved to see and to feel a well corseted figure so the meeting with Mrs Johnson would go well. Mary felt in the mood to be advised what best to wear to satisfy both James' desires and Coleen's hopes. Oh: and hers, too.

Mrs Jennifer Johnson arrived, promptly at 11.30 and was smartly dressed in a light suit and carried a large bag and wore gloves to great effect. Initially, she was businesslike and clearly interested only in a sale rather than in offering advice. Mary needed the latter before she could stretch to a sale. Tea and biscuits calmed Jennifer down and they discussed what they had done in the past and how much Mary liked working with women in Coleen's shop. Jen, as she preferred to be called, explained how Mme Vermeuil worked and how Mary would be fitted with a sample test-corset which would take the vital measurements, similar to the Spencer method of taking dimensions.

Mary asked what Jen could do for her figure which was average, but one that did not need heavy corsets like her grandmother wore as a matter of course. Jen suggested that, where Mary was on display in a clothes shop, she would benefit from using every means at her disposal to re-shape, improve her curves and to dress in a manner that would grasp people's attention after the awful Flapper Age of the twenties. Jen said:

> 'I'd like to see you dressed in the modern manner but one that accentuates the Victorian image with a small waist-line and firm bodice we used to love and now miss so much.

> 'Your bust would be held high, uplifted from below rather than with modern brassieres that are not wildly supportive with breasts bouncing and dragging down from your shoulders.'

> 'I entirely agree.'

said Mary with feeling.

> 'I dislike the sloppy feel that bras have and the absence of competent support.

> 'I wear my bras tight but then they cut into my flesh and become increasingly uncomfortable during the day.'

> 'Mary, you are telling me what so many of my customers say. Modern breast supports do not fit the need, they are ill-made and lack the structure and firmness required to hold up weighty breasts that most women have to carry.

> 'I'll be able to show you how to change your foundations and to be able to wear a single garment that will utterly transform

the way you dress, the way you feel, the way you stand and even the way you walk.'

'What is "foundations", please?'

'I'll tell you.

'Waistlines are reduced by about three to four inches so that you'd be able to wear really curvaceous suits or dresses that cling to your improved figure.

'Your breasts would be supported without any strain imposed upon your shoulders; they would be uplifted from below.

'The abdominal area would also feel supported and less inclined to fluctuate every month or change with eating habits—or even the occasional excess.

'The method will be to use a foundation garment, also known as a corset, which you will wear as a matter of routine every day—just as I do. I am never seen without my foundations.'

'Jen, why don't more women subscribe to this concept you are promoting for me?'

'More and more women are realising the benefits but I have too few hours in the day to see more flagging, sagging bodies! It is also a matter of expense.'

'I would be interested to see and to feel what you can do for me, Jen. My colleague, Coleen wants me to dress with panache to help sales and James has taken a fancy to corseted Parisians.'

Mary, it is not an undemanding solution. Nobody can jump into a new garment and hope that it will perform miracles. Your existing clothes may well have to be altered to suit your revised figure when you have new foundation wear . . .

Jen came across as a little concerned as she realised Mary had little idea about corsetry—what its benefits were and what changes would be necessary both to existing wear and to daily lifestyle. A sale was important as income depended upon getting a sale rather than advising benefits. Her valise contained garments much more suited to a mature figure but she did have one which demonstrated what Mary might particularly appreciate. Jen showed Mary what she had in mind:

'This single garment looks complicated but it is made to dress a woman from her breasts down to her lower hips with only minor shoulder support; most will come from below, from the waist upwards and your stockings will keep the lower corset firmly in place even though, ideally, it will be firmly in place around your hips giving you a superb trim, flat tummy as well.'

'I have recently come from a small shop in Alfriston where they had garments like this on display. I was with Jane and a friend, James and we did discuss the need to wear such apparatus but it so depended upon one's work. Jane, for instance, is a vet and would find such control out of the question. As you know, I work in a dress shop and Coleen thinks that I should appear formally dressed and to be well controlled.'

Jen's hopes leapt and she could see a sale was now obvious—and maybe there would be an opportunity for her to be able to meet some of the customers who came to Coleen's shop.

'Older and firm foundation garments will change the shape of a wearer and will smooth out life's lumps and bumps that occur following childbirth or those who have had too many dinner parties. These are definitely not suitable for you, Mary.'

'Oh no.'

Mary said with some vigour. She was going to ask why a simple foundation was so complicated. But she did know it was expensive and that it was vital to be expertly fitted. Coleen had explained what she had to go through, so Jen had been reinforcing Mary's limited knowledge.

> 'If I may, I'll show you what I am wearing under my suit. I am never, ever, out without my excellent foundations and I do not think that you noticed that I was well corseted—and at ease, too. I wear some for day-wear and always change for the evening into stronger more waist-enhancing garments that maybe less agreeable but give me an enviable figure and sometimes I even wear them all night. I really love the sense of control and the firm hug that I wish my husband could offer more often.'

> 'Please, do show me what you wear. And, yes, I did notice that you stood upright and had a figure much appreciated by all discerning women.'

Jen went into a corner of the sitting room and carefully removed her outer suiting and blouse leaving her standing in her corset, stockings and drawers. Her breasts were well supported and her waist was surprisingly small and she did not appear to have any excess weight or curves where they should not be seen. Her stockings were held by clips hanging from the corset and these were definitely better than garters that tended to slip allowing stockings to concertina at the ankles.

Mary was amazed and considered how she would look if her own breasts were racked up a little, and if her waistline was re-formed by the three inches or so, as suggested by Jen. Her hips were already trim and needed no assistance at all as there was no excess weight being carried and her rear was interestingly curvy, a feature she'd like to keep.

She was sure that James would like a really good figure; he had said as much as an aside whilst they were at Alfriston. Mary did like the figures that were seen on some advertisements, the Underground posters and in the cinema.

'Well, this is me in all my glory. What do you think, Mary?'

'I'm astonished. You wear these corsets so well and comfortably and nobody would know unless you undressed.'

'Please tell me what this is that you are wearing, now.'

'I'm in something called a corselette and it is made as one garment which, as you can see, stretches from my breasts, supporting them, down to my pelvis where the suspenders take over and support my stockings so well.

"Suspenders"? I called them clips. Are they instead of tight garters?'

'Yes, an American invention I believe, sensible and functional.'

'But what happens if you sit on one of the clips—sorry suspenders?'

'Interesting point, but if you look carefully, you'll see that the rear suspenders are set a little to one side as well as up so that, when sitting, they do not press into your flesh at all. That's not quite true; just occasionally, a suspender manages to press into my flesh and it is irritating rather than painful. Moving does correct the annoyance. They hold up my stockings satisfactorily and when, occasionally, I wear a patterned pair, the design has to follow the leg precisely—and stay so placed.' I also need my stockings to hold the lower corset firmly in place so that it does not move upwards—ride up—as we call it.'

'My corselette is, in fact, made in two parts, an upper and a lower section. The lower part is heavily strengthened with bones or stays and is laced up as tight as I wish with the centre set of overlapping cords or laces, as we call them. This part runs from just below my ribs and controls the waistline wonderfully. Above this is the shaped section that supports my breasts from below and also stops any tissue bulging above my corset. It is firm, and you can see more lacing at the sides of the garment. It is important to have these adjustments so that my chest can be eased off when I need lighter pressure.'

'Isn't this a bit too much to bear, all day long?'

Jen again sensed the danger of a lost sale.

'I do wish I could show you my body, *sans* corsets, as you'd be able to see that there are almost no marks on my skin. Here, I'll loosen my bra section and you'll be able to see and to feel for yourself—no indentations, wheals or discomfort whatsoever.

'It is surprising how this garment fits me. It is of the latest designs. Mme Vermeuil trained with a leading international corset-maker and she has new ideas and regularly copies patterns from the Americans and some English makers. She has an incredible eye for detail and her customers come specially from all over London and from further afield to see her. I work away from her shop and deal with all home visits but you can always go to her salon for a shop fitting too.'

'What if fashions change, again, and the Flappers get back into vogue?'

'Doubtful; ladies like being well corseted as the foundations give the wearer a much better shape upon which to dress competently. Clothes slide over their garments and do not wrinkle as much.

'Tell me Mary, do you wear tight well-fitting shoes?'

'Of course; they have to be well fitting so they do not slide off and are often tightly laced in place, too.'

'It's exactly same with a well fitted corset. After a short time, you do not realise you are wearing a pair of shoes. Same with a pair of corsets—and you'd be really lost without them. Nowadays, we do not refer to a "pair"—just to a corset.

'Remember what I told you; you would need a garment to be fitted exactly to your existing figure and it would be constructed to show off your waistline to perfection. I am not wearing a heavily waist-tight corset because I have to keep bending to take measurements. But in the evening, I have a 21 inch waist measurement and I do look quite dramatic and this brings me new business because dinner guests want to copy a figure like mine. You would do the same in your shop because you and Coleen look dramatic and that is what customers want to see—and to copy.

'I'll get dressed again.'

Mary had a few moments for introspection. What will James think? Will Coleen approve? Will Jane think I am quite mad? Most importantly, will I be able to wear a garment like Jen's each and every day? Of course; it is exactly what I want. I am going to move from being ordinary to extra-ordinary.

Coleen would approve and would be the first to say she needed a version too, if the new foundations made a dramatic difference. It might just help her to win a great part and so leave me to run the shop and make more money for myself.

And so Mary agreed to be measured by the strange contraption that Jen had briefly shown her. It felt incredibly tight and was not at all gentle against her flesh but Jen stressed that it was a tool of the trade and not for daily wear. Finished garments always had lacing adjustments built-in so that firmness could be changed to suit the day, mood, hormones and the weather, for that matter.

The finished fabric and construction was discussed and finalised. Both garments were to be nearly identical in similar white satins, with some elastic material as well as firm sections with grommet-holes for laces. The bodice section was to be made with some firm stretchy materials so that breathing was not hindered in any way.

'Now look at me more critically as you know what is underneath—my foundations.

'Knowing what gives me my appearance, my confidence, the way my outerwear hangs, please take mental notes of what you should look for in other women. There are clues: just be aware.'

'Agreed, lets place an order for two of your corsets and I'll consider what to do, if anything, for evening-wear. I'd prefer both to be white but slightly different, please. I need to be more used to being really tightly corseted as part of my job before considering how to reduce my evening waistline.'

Jen thought this approach to be entirely correct. Mary thought that whilst the garments were expensive—the cost was quite considerable and much more than had been expected, the extra business that was likely and the attraction generated might just make this venture worthwhile. She had the money as she had an income plus an allowance from her father which was invaluable.

And so Jen left the flat in a really happy frame of mind. She and Mary had got on well and it was likely that a friendship may well develop. Maybe Mary could come to one of her dinner evenings.

Mary realised that, to show off her clothes, she'd need to make alterations to many of her dresses; she may have to ask a tailor how to re-seam some of her suits.

§§§

A month later, Jen brought her valise, again and was superbly dressed with a clearly smaller waist, higher bust line and she wore the inevitable white gloves. She was utterly calm and was smiling broadly.

> 'Since I saw you, I've had a really good month and have managed to amaze Mme Vermeuil with my work and fittings. She has had a job to keep up with new orders and she has had me photographed for the shop window and for a publication. I'm thrilled.'

> 'Do let's see what you have made for me, Jen. I cannot wait. I've spoken to Coleen and she's really keen to view the result. I just hope she and James will like your made-to-measure contraptions.'

> 'Foundations,'

Jen corrected.

> 'You look so elegant, today, Jen. What have you done to achieve a transformation? It looks to me as if you are wearing an evening garment to show off to me. Am I right?'

> 'Of course you are. I chose a suitable ensemble that might impress you today and here I am in all my glory and feeling decidedly agreeable as I like being held tightly and able to wear my nicer clothes so effectively. The only disadvantage is that my body will have some interesting red marks and my shoulders are feeling the straps because my breasts are held higher and are more controlled than usual.'

> 'So Jen, please encase me'

4 Dressing Tightly

Jen looked so glamorous in her evening foundation. She held herself upright and her waist and bust were in symphony with each other that was quite amazing for a person in her mid to late forties—maybe more. Her outer clothes hang as if possessed by some inner spook but flowed in and out and around her figure as if stitched into place.

> 'Let's show you what I have brought from Mme Vermeuil. Here is the first corset; both are the same—we would never change an order, even if we thought there'd be an improvement, so both are identical apart from the fabrics she used. Oddly enough, because the fabrics differ, they may feel unfamiliar—tighter in places but that may just be imagination.
>
> 'You must wear a chemise, first, and I've brought one for you to try. It protects you from the harder corset and the corset from your softer skin and natural exudations—sweat.'

Mary looked at the complex design and thought how it would be fitted onto her frame. She started to find the garment quite sexy; but was it wearable . . . each and every day from now onwards?

> 'Stop looking quite so alarmed, Mary. These are quite fantastic and *Mme* has worked wonders for you as your figure is quite juvenile—smaller than she is used to dressing. Let me explain.
>
> 'Your corselette is made with several sections which can be taken apart from one another. Normally, they appear to be in just two parts—and upper and a lower section and both are adjustable using the lacing sections after the hooks and eyes have been closed. Normally, you'd put the lower section on first, and then concentrate upon the upper, bodice piece. You

don't tighten anything until the entire corset is in place but not closed up.'

Jen handed Mary, dressed in drawers and brassiere, the chemise and one of the two new garments. Chemise on, she stepped into the lower section guided, carefully, by Jen who held onto an arm as Mary stepped gingerly, teetering on one leg at a time. Both eased the foundation into place; it was loose, so readily slid over the chemise. Jen made an adjustment, tightening the waist a little.

'Now we need your stockings on, please.

'I have a new pair, especially for you.'

'You'll need to put them on, without my help. Take care with your nails—do not ladder them. I put stockings on first, before stepping into any corset I am wearing; you will find that to be easier. Never put stockings on after you have closed the corset in any way; you're certain to risk snagging one or both and they are expensive. Please remove your drawers, now as they need to be outside all foundations.'

Mary began to enjoy the sensation. Nothing was tight yet, but the feel of the new garments was well, strangely voluptuous, definitely unusual and provided an entirely new feeling. What was her body going to sense as it suffered the compression about to be applied by Jen?

'Mary, please will you do up the hooks and eyes that connect the main corset; they are to the left side, here. All must be closed, and do not miss any out or you'll spoil the garment because of excess strain. Good; now we must close the lower corset using the laces. As this is your first wearing, we cannot close it entirely. You and the corset must get used to each other and this will take about a week at most. Now, be prepared for a changing sensation. It is bound to feel strange at first.'

'Bound? Am I going to be bound like a parcel?'

'Yes you are, and it will feel quite strange but I do know that you'll feel sensational when you get used to the wicked new control. I love mornings when I step into mine and cannot wait for that surge of pressure that my body now expects from my firm foundations. I adore the sensation; I cannot describe it except that it takes over from my un-corseted body which seems to anticipate a tight covering. It's amazing; quite wonderful.'

Mary allowed Jen to close the laces and she did so with little or no tugging and pulling. She applied her fingers carefully and they did seem to know, by feel alone, what they were doing. Mary felt the steady closure. It was a comforting feeling. Her waist became smaller almost instantly, her hips were firmer and encased but the design had made little or no difference to her mildly rounded seat of which she was really proud. Then Jen started again with the laces and closed them up until the lower corset was within a couple of inches of full closure.

'How does that feel, so far, Mary?'

'Jen, it feels exquisite. I simply cannot believe why I have not copied my Gran or my Mother in all these years. Let's do the top, now. My breasts are just itching to be supported adequately and you can put my bra in the bin. I'll take it off, now, so don't look!'

Jen adjusted the upper section of the corset, making the whole garment into a corselette.

'Please lean forward to that your breasts engage with the prepared spaces, we call them cups, and then we will ensure that the support comes from below and just watch your shape change as pressure and uplift is applied from below and not from bra shoulder straps. The lacing will ensure that support is total. The new awareness will be so exotic compared with what you've been used to since you were a teenager.'

Jen made adjustments and considerably tightened the support offered by the brassiere section of the corset. Mary could see her breasts changing shape by the second. They became rounder, almost squeezing out of their new confines. She thought they were a little over-exposed, at first, but Jen said they'd settle into place quite soon. She was right. Within a minute, her breasts were well supported and there was no room remaining in the upper part of the corset; flesh had replaced space. Comfort was quite amazing. In fact, there was no discomfort whatsoever. Finally, Jen adjusted the shoulder straps into place; these were not at all tight and were used to give a secondary fixture in case of any accident or loss of support elsewhere.

'So, that's it, Mary. Now move around the room a little and try bending, stretching and some usual movements that you'll make in the course of your day and work. Try stepping, onto a bus platform, for example.'

'How are you progressing, Mary?'

'This is utterly fantastic. I cannot get over the new me and the feel that's being applied to my unfortunate body. It is beyond doubt quite lovely—but I have to admit, this is early in the day and I might have a great deal more to say after an hour or more of its confinement.'

'I'll leave you, now, and will telephone you mid-afternoon to see if there are any problems or comments. I am here to help you and to support you—mentally.

'Bye, Mary. You have been a terrific customer.'

Mary was utterly thrilled to be dressed so exquisitely. Why, oh why, did she reject the approaches of her elders and betters who would have given her every chance to be dressed, firmly dressed, from an early age; age when she thought she knew better. Jane came to mind.

Jane's mother, Mavis wore corsets at all times and yet Jane rejected her advice and only occasionally did she subscribe to her mother's suggestions. Maybe Mavis was too forgiving with her beautiful daughter.

4 Work and Play

Anne-Marie missed James so much. Two months had passed since they last met. The shop was doing well and many customers were intrigued by Mary who looked to have grown taller or, maybe, she was just standing better—more erect. Her waist was undoubtedly smaller and her bust higher but it was impossible to see the effect of the new foundations because most of her clothes required alteration to take advantage of her changed physique.

Both Mary and Coleen modelled shop stock to advantage and enjoyed choosing dresses that were suitable and which would show off stock to promote sales as well as bringing their amazing figures into public view.

Mary had to spend many evenings altering costumes for both of them as stock sizes never fitted them perfectly. It was impossible to make temporary changes with pins as both had to work whilst demonstrating the items that the shop sold. It was fortunate that Mary had a natural aptitude for dressmaking which she first learned whilst at school and her mother honed her natural ability whilst a teenager. This was one of the few tasks that she and her mother enjoyed together.

Anne-Marie was really lonely and longed to see James. She decided to take an initiative. She wrote:

> James, it seems an age since I last saw you and had a wonderful
> couple of days. Much has happened here in London. You have

not telephoned me but, of course, you may have missed me when you tried. I did warn you that I was often out or at work but I do have another telephone number for you to use; it is at the shop that Coleen and I run and it's COVent Garden 6684, so please do ring me sometime as I am longing to hear your voice again. You did promise to keep in touch.

You mentioned that you were interested in fashion and I have some news. I have a new shape and Coleen has changed hers, too. More when I am with you and you can inspect the result. I am standing taller and you'll be amazed, I think. At least I do hope so!

The shop is not struggling as much and sales are now made every day and it may well be because we are appearing better dressed and modelling stock. Poor Coleen has been out of work, resting as they call it in the profession, for ages. She auditions, regularly, but has not been chosen for any really good parts that may run for a few weeks and hopefully, longer. She has had some school work but that lasts just a day or so and does not bring much cash for her. She is a little despondent but working as an actress is difficult and she despises the producers who want a physical bodily exchange for a fair part. Like me, she is very fussy indeed and I intend to stay that way for you.

As Coleen is here most of the time, I could arrange some holiday. Can we meet and spend some time, maybe near where you are working?

My dearest James, I love you so, so much . . .
Anne-Marie

A week later, James wrote:

What a fab letter; thank you so much, Anne-Marie. I had been hoping to hear from you and every day I longed to get home to see if there was a note or a longer missive.

I have been incredibly busy and races take up so much time as everything has to be absolutely as near perfect as we can make the machinery tick. Also, we have been spending more time away at race tracks far from here and it's almost impossible for me to spend time writing. Tomorrow, I will telephone you on COV and if I cannot get you there, try CUN again. Yes, I have tried CUN 7846 but there has been no answer.

What on earth have you done to your shape? I did not know you could alter it at will apart from if you chose to wear reshaping corsets like they wore in the late 1800s and maybe what we saw briefly in Alfriston. I'd be impressed if you have managed to do that as I'm a great fan of the old styles that faded soon after I was born. I've not met Coleen, yet, but if she is statuesque, she may well win parts because she is different. Please tell me more about her—I promise I am not interested in actresses, so don't worry!

I told you I was working with Sydney Allard but he was concerned for his future and wanted to get into manufacture of his marque of cars. As you may have gathered, I am more interested in speed on the track, touring and some hill climbing, so have joined forces with a well-backed chap, Kaye Don. Have you heard of Sunbeam cars? Well, he is endorsed by the makers and has had some remarkable successes. He is brilliant, Irish, and also demanding of his colleagues who have to keep up with him, literally!

My darling, I do think of you every day and I certainly do miss you so much. Right now, I am going to find a telephone box and I have some coins . . .

My love to you and to your tight corsets, Anne-Marie.
James.

The new shop telephone was remarkably silent. Well, it was a new device and not many callers had its number, yet. It sat, glumly, on a small table at the rear of the shop where one could see what was going on if it spoke or rang. Suddenly, the familiar trill was heard and Mary was alone in the shop. She dashed to it in hope: and it really was James who just said:

'Are you expecting me?'

Once the connection had been made correctly, the distant operator said,

'You're through, now.'

'My dearest lovely one, how have you been since we parted in Brighton, oh, weeks ago?'

'When can we meet, James? I am really anxious to see you, again and I have so much to tell you and to show you. I have never stayed away with any man, so you are my first encounter, but is there an Inn or somewhere we can share a roof—but each in a separate room?'

'I know just the place. I'm here, now. Don, as he prefers to be known, and I eat here some late evenings and they are friendly. It is not far from London in a village called Marshalswick near St Albans. It's an ancient settlement dating back to the thirteenth century, so has some really interesting buildings—a bit like Alfriston, maybe, but they do not have flint construction here. The inn is called Blackbury Jack'

'James, please make a booking for me. Can you make a few days from next Sunday, perhaps?'

'I'm fairly sure that that will be viable with Don but if I need to be away, I am sure to be back in the evening and maybe we can all meet. I'll check and will book rooms for us and let you know. Glad I can get you readily with your new number.'

'James, I have to go; shop to run and someone is hovering.

Love you, love you, love you.'

The rest of the week dragged. Coleen was happy for Mary to have a break and to meet her new beloved. She wished she had a man with whom she could share her life and its seemingly unsuccessful future.

James had made a quick call saying, come to St Albans station at about noon and meet in the main station hall. He suggested I find a cafe at the station if he was delayed.

Just after Anne-Marie left her flat, she thought she heard a ring like a telephone. Maybe not mine . . .

5 Appearances

Coleen was Irish but brought up in London's East End where her father worked in heavy construction. A carpenter by trade, he had made his way up and was now a general foreman. There were three daughters in the family and Coleen was the middle child and from a young age she had yearned to act, starting at kindergarten where she was a stage angel, then onto primary school where her parts and abilities strengthened and by the time she left she had a lead in a play written by the music teacher which gave her great confidence and eventually helped her to get into the Royal Academy of Dramatic Art where she thrived on the intensive course-work, learning a new part twice a term, gaining knowledge of stagecraft, dress making and design, stage lighting, how to make stage flats and to prepare and paint scenery. As she had a strong Irish accent, elocution lessons remodelled her voice so that she could speak normal southern English as well as imitate other nationalities and regional British accents. She found the course mind-blowing and so demanding. She felt privileged as RADA was known to be one of the best drama schools in the world.

As soon as she graduated, she did win starter-parts but nothing memorable; her time would come. She discussed the resting with her former tutor and he was adamant that she had passed admirably and was capable and well-trained; what was to stop her progress? Time and patience would be needed. She was advised to have a business to tide her over, or to work in a menial employment such as reception where she could come and go as parts surfaced and then, if necessary, get another temporary post. Many other budding actors and actresses faced the same task and 'temping' was a way of life. Keep looking, keep asking, and keep eyes on repertory theatre companies who always wanted new faces as their core crews were plucked off for taller orders.

Learning lines frightened Coleen and she mused how she'd manage at RADA. But every other student there, apart from a small minority who had photographic memories, was in the same slave ship: hard work that became easier as the slave's brain adjusted to the need to recall and to remember lines. Initially, repetition was necessary, say, one hundred times. Quite perceptibly, this manic work fell to fifty, then twenty and lastly to about ten or a dozen repeats before the part was embedded. Truthfully, every old hand at RADA used to tell newbie's that they must not worry but they must work instead.

Coleen found that this aspect of RADA's craft helped her to manage her business using her brain rather than endless notes. She did not forget meeting dates and times; she remembered what had been ordered; she learned to recognise faces and put names to them and she found that recognising a former customer almost invariably led to new orders as a person recognised felt they were a client rather than a mere customer.

Mary was not as good as Coleen with her memory but watching her employer manage customers so eloquently made Mary think that effort was worthwhile and she started to pick up a few tricks from Coleen such as giving a customer a second name—Ellen Smith became Ellen Hat Smith or Agnes Jones became Agnes Aber Jones because she was from Aberystwyth. As soon as Coleen asked when "Aber" was due, Mary would recall that Agnes Jones was arriving. Tricks like this work: well done RADA.

Both Mary and Coleen found that being well dressed and looking as if the store was theirs, appearing better than presentable—neat hair, groomed fingers and nails, matching shoes, sufficient but not excessive make-up—encouraged customers to become clients. Many clients asked who prepared their foundation garments—particularly of Coleen whose incredible silhouette was visually stunning—maybe a little too much for the age but it did bring business because clients were fascinated and invariably asked a question or two.

Mary, on the other hand, was firmly dressed rather than rigidly encased. When Coleen used to explain the difference to those who wanted to know, the pair would often provide an ad-hoc demonstration using the shop as a catwalk and showing what could or could not be done whilst wearing superb made-to-measure foundations.

Nothing defeated Coleen. To pick up a dropped pin was no problem; she bent from the knees like lightning. This was far, far more elegant than stooping from the waist, of course. Both knew what sizes and makes of dresses could be worn and demonstrated and if two or three clients came together, they'd quietly prepare a small changing stock in the back room so that the show was effortless and smooth to the eye. The business this brought was hard to quantify but sales rose every month. Some clients did ask when the next show was to be held.

'No date, just bring a few friends when you wish and we'll wear the fashions that have just arrived. We so enjoy doing this for you.'

Husbands and men-friends were often aghast and fascinated by the elegance shown by Coleen and it took the older ones by storm: they had been used to the curvature and elegance displayed by pre-1914-women and they did not expect to see a demonstration outside the theatre in the 1930s. How many wives were coerced into being similarly dressed is not recorded but some clients did return rather better dressed supported by sound foundations than when they began as new customers.

6 Blackbury Duck Inn 1934

Noon at St Albans came and went and no sign of James. Anne-Marie wished she had raced to her telephone but, by the time she had dashed up and fumbled for her flat key, it would have stopped. She was peckish so she did as she was told and found a cafe serving the station. The newsagent had magazines and she bought a copy of the American publication, Vogue which always had interesting fashion news and articles. She ordered some soup and a pot of tea. After three o'clock, Mary was getting genuinely restless and anxious.

Her new foundation was making its presence felt, so she took a walk around the station and it became easier to wear and she was happy with it once again. She was really keen to let James see—and feel—her new shape. She knew James would not let her down and he must have been delayed by Don with some matter that tested his stamina to destruction.

She could take a taxi to the Blackbury Duck but could not leave a message for James—or could she? There was a booking office which suggested that it had information and so she told the clerk she had a problem:

'I was due to meet my friend, James Compton, at noon and he has not arrived. Would you kindly say I have gone ahead to the Blackberry Tuck to wait there?'

'Of course; if I see him or if he asks. He may look worried so I'll spot men without any hair. By the way, it's Blackbury Duck; I know it well. Have a good stay there.

'How do you know I'm staying?'

'Obvious, my dear Watson: you have a case.'

'Thank you; you have been really kind in my hour of need. Good-bye.'

Anne-Marie was beginning to think that she had made a huge mistake when there was a knock on her door. It was James and he looked utterly frantic. It was nearly seven o'clock in the evening.

'Oh my darling; what has happened?'

'There was no means that I could contact you and tell you that Don had had to go to Wolverhampton with me to sort out a problem with the Sunbeam.'

'You must be utterly shattered. Darling I love you so. I am so relieved. I was worried sick'

'I was so worried, too, and this is the last thing I needed when I had made all the arrangements we agreed upon. There'd have been no way that we could call each other. I did try your phone at Maida Vale but there was no answer. After that . . .'

'Come on, lie down here, James, and tell me about yourself and your day. I'll go down and see what is available to eat. I'm sure you must be famished—I am.'

Anne-Marie came back to find James had vanished—gone to his room but she did not know where that was in the Duck. She could not ask as she assumed they'd throw them both out for behaviour unbecoming or something. She decided to have a walk around the upper floors and see if she could hear anything or at least find James. She wished she could sing, but James had never heard her rather poor singing voice, so that was a non-starter. Then her mind clicked into gear.

'Would you kindly take a message to my friend in his room?'

'James Compton?'

'Yes, he booked the two rooms for us and was supposed to be here shortly after noon today but only arrived sometime after six. Now we've passed each other between our rooms'

'Of course, what shall I tell him?'

'Just that I'm waiting in reception please'

Newly washed, shaved and fully dressed, James came down after twenty minutes. He looked really handsome. Whereas when he arrived he was a real mess in a suit which was rather stained and now needed the cleaners, with untidy hair, smelling of old cars, shoes covered in some sort of dye, or could it be oil, maybe? The leather was stained badly. Anyway, now he was really fresh and Anne-Marie was desperate to give him a huge hug but that would be improper, right here and now.

'Let's pop outside and have a short stroll and some fresh air, suggested Anne-Marie.

'I think you'll find it's raining, but I'll try to borrow an umbrella.'

The evening was drizzling but quite warm, and it was not dark. The Inn's umbrella did keep the rain off and they wandered into the garden and found a small pond with a nearby shelter.

'Ideal.'

James exclaimed.

'James, I have been waiting literally hours, to get my hands around you and to give you a crushing hug. Here I am and I'm starting to weep; I'm just full of emotion. Sorry, I cannot control myself. If I go on like this I'll need a bath, too.'

'Am I allowed to take you in my arms, my darling?'

'You do not have to ask. I need to be closer than close to you. You are the man in my life and I want to show you how I feel. Now hold me; hold me, grasp me tightly—please!'

James took her closely in his arms and, for the first time, he kissed Anne-Marie gently on the cheek, then the other cheek, then on the back of her neck. He felt her body and noticed it was firm, structured but not soft like the Parisian girl, Claudette who trained him in the art of seduction.

James was keen to explore Anne-Marie's body as he was really interested in the type of firm garments that his mother wore and he was thrilled to feel similar constructions, now. He kissed her again, this time on her neck and then on her forehead. He carefully touched her nose, with the tip of his nose.

'Icelanders do this'

Anne-Marie was so excited and had seen couples kissing in cinema films she and Coleen had seen. She decided that enough pottering around had been done to satisfy any watching elf, so she grabbed James' face in her hands and moved to kiss him on the mouth, just as it was done in Hollywood.

James jerked away and said:

'Darling, I'd so much like a good kiss but I have a problem. My front teeth are sort of, false; I have a dreadful plate and you'll need to be gentle with me'

'James! What else is false?'

'I was going to tell you but we have not had a chance to discuss anything, well anything, sort of private.'

'Whether you want a kiss or not, I do'

With that, Anne-Marie grasped James' head, holding him by his cheeks and gave him a gentle kiss on his lips and then took one lip and kissed that softly and then the other lip slightly more firmly as James did not stiffen quite as much. They had not reached the stage of tongues meeting, yet, and the films did not really demonstrate how this was done. All she knew was that she literally wanted to eat him.

James began to get really excited and so enjoyed the kisses which he started to reciprocate, being careful not to dislodge his dental plate. Should he take it out and put it in his pocket but he feared Anne-Marie might have a fit seeing his face without its top front teeth.

Hugging Anne-Marie, it was starting to become obvious that there was something firm in his trousers.

> 'James, there is something else false about you. Why have you
> got a stick or splint in your leg? Have you broken your thigh,
> perhaps?

They went back to the Inn and asked after some food and found that dinner was served until 8.30 and that they'd be welcome. Sitting next to each other at a table they'd found situated away from the other guests and their chatter, they held hands and talked about their love for each other. James said he had a tummy-ache which had come on whilst they were fondling each other in the garden. He had never experienced this pain ever before and wondered if anything was wrong and decided to ask the doctor when he next saw one. This really did put him off his meal but he struggled with his so as not to upset Anne-Marie and angled the conversation towards what she had to say, saying less about himself.

For her part, Anne-Marie was still encased in her newish and firm corset. Upon arrival, when she got to her room she had loosened it, having taken off her outer clothes and washed as best as she could, sort of bit by bit rather than having a preferred bath, as she thought she should have, but did not know where James was—so put that delight off. She then lay down and had a short rest and maybe a sleep; still in her corset. This was a first but she did sleep, quite well, but woke with a start suddenly worried about James. Was he here, yet?

She got up and adjusted the laces so that her waist was really controlled and measured some four inches less than her natural measurement. Jen said her waist would be nearer five inches smaller, allowing for the corset's thickness.

On this garment, there were three lacing sections, front and both sides, and she managed to close up the lacing. She had not eaten so there was no real discomfort but she really did like the incredible pressure that she felt. She also liked the support offered to her breasts as the underwear pressed them upwards, so that they were just starting to be visible if she wore a low cut top. What had she brought with her, she asked herself. She was really anxious to please James and to show him her superb new figure—even if it was assisted a little.

He had said, on a couple of occasions that he did like firm supports. She knew what her grandmother and to some extent her mother wore but had never taken a great deal of interest—she was young. It was only in the films that she had seen younger ladies firmly dressed in Victorian corsets which looked so good, tightly laced with small waists but they always moaned when their maid pulled them in tightly. She now realised that the moaning was for show. Her new corset, she had only tried one of them, was not at all uncomfortable and she remembered what Jen had said. that people would not have worn things like this if they disliked the feel; for a few days your new corset will feel tight but it has been made to fit and precisely follows your figure. So, she had experimented and tightened the three laces as much as she could. In the mirror, her figure looked really incredible. Why had she not done this years ago? Why had she not asked her grandmother for advice?

She was not particularly close to her mother but her grandmother was a kind person and was close to Anne-Marie and they did talk about lots of things but rarely what undergarments they wore. Granny was interested in getting the correct brassiere and told her about teddies and camiknickers which were underwear that loosely covered a woman's body from stockings to breasts.

Evidently, it was fashionable in the late 1920s and teddies were often worn, alone, without outer dress when at home for the evening. Anne-Marie did not have one, though, and Granny had not pressed her to buy one but she did insist she wore various brassieres as she felt, strongly, that women needed the support or they'd all look like native women in the jungle. So, Anne-Marie had bought a number of designs and even tried wearing two at once to get the effect as she wished. There were some shops that specialised in getting the correct fit and they often did sell conventional corsets but it did not occur to them to suggest a young girl aged 18'ish should try one.

> 'James, Darling, I am starting to tire and would like to see my bed, soon. I do want you to see my new foundations, though. I know you are interested. Do you recall the dress shop in Alfriston—you were quite fascinated, as I recall. If we go up together, the Innkeeper may not notice us. Do you want to see if we can?'
>
> 'Can, of course we can. At worse we'll be thrown out and have to spend the night in the pond shed'
>
> 'You lead, James.'

Anne-Marie pushed her door open—and then closed it and slid the lock across. After some surprise, James came and took her in his arms and kissed her passionately, just as before, but he asked,

> 'May I please remove my awful plate? You must promise not to look.'

His kiss was really firm, this time, and they enjoyed each other's company as if they had never kissed ever before.

'James, I want you to have a look at my new foundation-wear as Jen, the corsetière, calls it. You must wonder why I feel so firm. I am not used to showing anyone, so please be gentle and kind and I'll throw you out if you dare to laugh.'

Moving to where there was a small screen near the wash-handbasin, Anne-Marie took off her skirt and blouse but retained her stockings, knickers and shoes. She peered around the screen to see what James was doing. Good; he was sitting on her bed, looking perplexed, maybe. She noticed he had his entire set of teeth in place, again. She said she was ready and with that he got up and started to look in her direction. She slowly walked away from the screened area and moved across to James whose face lit up and he smiled from ear to ear. He was utterly amazed and thrilled with what he saw. The whole ensemble looked really spine-tingling, erotic and attractive. He had seen corsets in the films but never ever expected to have been able to touch and to feel someone so dressed. Well, not quite true: he had seen and had felt Claudette for just a minute or so. But she was, well, Claudette: a good teacher.

'May I hug you, again, Anne-Marie?'

He was faintly formal with his request, fearing that she'd push him away and not let him touch her corsets.

'Of course you can. I've been waiting since noon today for you to hold me tight, tighter than my corset, and to give me the hug I have been aching for, all day.'

'Darling, Anne-Marie, you are stunningly attractive and this material makes you far, far better than I had dared to hope. Only you and I are able to see this, so closely, so it is private.'

'Well, not that private, James. Jen and Coleen have both seen me in it, and if I ever have to go and see the medical doctor, he might have to view what you can see.'

'Can you bend as if you were unsupported?

'With care I can, but not from the waist. I have to bend at the knees and that keeps my back straight. Have you noticed that I appear to be a bit taller? Did you notice my behind and its roundness—and firmness?'

'Now you come to think about it, yes, I had noticed, but did not comment. Your shoulders are much further back than when I recall you in Alfriston. And your breasts appear better and rounded—up-held better. They are an improvement upon someone I saw in Paris when I was last there. She was a showgirl, of sorts.'

'Who was that, James?'

'Someone my father knew; she ran a small cafe where we used to go for a croissant and coffee and she had a sumptuous figure and one day she had to undress because she had spilt something and I saw her top without clothes—I shouldn't but she did not mind being seen and I remember she gave me a wide grin. My father did not see as he was facing the other way. Do not worry, she was not my type of girl and anyway, she dyed her hair with something red.'

'Yes yours are much firmer and I love the way they are supported from underneath rather than hanging from those awful brassieres which they call SGs in France. May I have another hug and feel what your corset is like, please?'

James took Anne-Marie and held her closely and ran his hand over her covered body feeling the materials, the stiffening, the laces, the smooth satin strong parts, the suspenders that supported her stockings, and the various lacy materials that ran up towards her breasts. He noticed that her posterior was also covered but differently; it was rounded yet firmly encased in a material that he had never felt before. The suspenders kept this in place and Anne-Marie looked well and competently dressed.

James had, again, managed to have an artificial leg and it was showing through his trousers. He gave a knowing look towards Anne-Marie who exclaimed:

> 'James, what have you got there? I have never seen anything quite like that. May I touch it? Is it really all you? Does it grow like that normally? Does it hurt you? You were not well over dinner, this evening. James, I have so many, many questions. We both have so much to know and to find out about each other. I really do want you to stay but that would be improper.'

> 'When a man gets physically excited by a wild film, maybe, a girl who excites . . .'

> 'Like the Paris cafe-waitress?'

> 'Yes, possibly her, too, but with you, I get a firmness in my penis that I cannot control; it just happens and I suppose it wants to be ready to inject itself . . .

> 'James, there is so much I want to know about you. I do not have anything like that. I love your touch but nothing seems to happen to me except that I feel like I've peed in my pants a little—and I want even more of you to feel and to touch. I suppose this is all quite normal, normal for both of us. You will have to instruct me what to do, one day.'

> 'Now, James, it is past our bed-time and you must disappear—much as I do not want you to go but I am sticking to my good-girl image. What time shall we meet?

> 'There's so much to see and to do. 8 o'clock? Downstairs?'

'Goodnight, my darling. Hope your tummy ache gets better. 8 o'clock it is'

Anne-Marie was quietly amazed that James was so well mannered; he had never touched her in any way that might have been seen—or felt—to be improper. She realised, he had never felt her breasts, at all; had looked at them but that was all. She wanted him to feel what they were like but that will do for another day . . . evening. She was more than convinced that James was HER man and that she'd never meet anyone who was so kind, caring, gentle and really loving. And he appreciated her and allowed her to look, feel, touch and to enjoy his body. She had not moved in closely and had not touched his intimate parts—but he had not touched her, either, so they were equal, so far. She had noticed his rough cheeks and chin when he had just arrived from Wolverhampton, and she felt this was quite strange and not really soft near her skin when they had briefly touched cheeks. She'd sleep well and would dream about someone . . .

7 Dressing Alone

Anne-Marie was awake early at the Blackbury Duck. To be ready for eight, she had to bath and she hoped nobody would be in there first. Wrapping herself in a cloak, she opened her door and looked about; no sound; nobody about. Returning to her room she took her personal washing things and padded quietly to the shared bathroom for the landing. The hot water took an age to reach the bath and she did not dare to take too much, so was not able to wallow as she'd have liked but at least she could be clean, fresh and ready for the day ahead. The two towels were solidly made, off-white but were able to dry well and hoping nobody would try the door, Anne-Marie sat on the side of the bath and waited for nature to help dry her assisted by the towels. She had decided not to wash her hair as it took too long to dry and then set in rollers—doddermans she called them. Instead, she brushed out her locks and eased her comb through her curls and patted them into place. At least they look as if they've been cared-for. Nobody about, she crept back to her room and locked the door. Footfalls went by outside. She thought it was James but they belonged to a female voice. Thank heavens, she thought; she had not held anybody up queuing for the lavatory.

Now dry, the first task was to put on her stockings. These were expensive, made of artificial silk and not readily available and the slightest nick from a broken nail would render half a pair useless. She was always careful and tried to buy the same make and style so that un-laddered items could be matched to other lost souls. Sitting down, Anne-Marie took a stocking and eased her hand inside towards the toe and carefully folded the silky fabric into a ring moving downwards until she reached the ankle area. Passing the folded stocking over her foot, she eased it past her ankle and slowly allowed the gentle texture to slide over her calf, past her knee and upwards towards her thigh. She always liked the sensation of coolness and slight firmness and smoothness on her legs. She repeated the operation with the other stocking, trying hard not to snag it. She loved the feel of the material on her flesh. It was not at all tight or firm, just a feel she liked because it did give an element of warmth and enclosure as well as the sensation of smoothness when touched. The material reached her lower thighs but now needed the pull from the three suspenders on each leg. With care, the stocking would stay in place until she had put on her corset. Danger for stockings lurked all over a room: splinters in the floorboards, a coarse part of the bed rails, a shoe-lace aglet, or a chair leg and particularly from corset boning or a metal part or hook—oh, great care was vital.

Standing and moving carefully, Anne-Marie reached for her corset. It felt quite heavy, and it was cold but it would soon warm up and then it would hug her wonderfully. She had rapidly found that she loved wearing a corset—as so many women had in the past. It gave her a sense of well-being, a means of control over her flesh and body. It made her stand straighter and hold her shoulders back but, best of all; it reduced her slender waistline to give proportionality to her bust, waist and hips. She knew that both men and women much admired a slender waist whereas men usually ogled a large bosom. Some men even spoke to a big breast which made girls want to cringe.

Anne-Marie stepped into the corset, having relaxed its laces and unhooked the bodice section so that it would slip over her hips. Taking care not to snag a stocking, she moved the garment slowly upwards until the suspenders were close to the top of the stockings, now at about knee height; time to fit the suspenders to the stocking tops. Jen had shown her how to do this and it avoided a great deal of twisting to reach the rear pair of suspenders. Easing the corset upwards, ensuring the upper section was always in place, she helped her stockings into place, pulled the laced part of the corset well over her hips so that it felt snug and the tops of the stockings were within a couple of inches of her upper thighs.

Now time to adjust the bodice which was in place but not closed and the shoulder straps were not in place, yet. Taking one arm after the other, she slid her arms into the crossed bands so that they were placed correctly into the depressions just by the curve of her collar bones. Now, the corset needed to be laced up, tightening its control over her waistline. This she greatly enjoyed. The laces slid with ease through the grommets and she tied the closed lower section with a half-hitch and a tidy bow.

Now her breasts needed to be held and confined in place so that they could not move. Another laced section closed the two halves of the bodice and squeezed her breasts upwards so that they were supported completely from below. She used her hands to ease each breast into its place so that they emerged rounded, supported and snug. The shoulder bands were only used to keep the garment in place, not to give support. They were removable and maybe, when completely satisfied that the new corset would not let her down, she'd remove the crossed straps and free her shoulders. Finally, time for the teddy, a form of slip which helps outer clothes to slide over the foundations. The teddy is an attractive, fine, light garment that pops over her head and hangs from shoulder ribbons and makes the corset less obvious but gives a luxurious feel and matches her knickers that had lightly elasticised waist and legs for comfort so they will not move out of place. These were part of a set with the teddy.

Anne-Marie felt she needed a cup of strong tea. It had taken her about forty-five minutes to wash and dress so far. It was almost seven o'clock. Time to finish her dress for the day; not certain what she and James were going to do or to see, so she opted for simple outerwear that could be changed after breakfast—and so that James could see her foundation-work from earlier this morning. She so wanted to dress with him there, with him there so that he could help with the awkward parts of the corset so that she did not have to wrench it into place. This brought to mind the feel of the corset; it had warmed up and was doing a wicked job of controlling her body. The corset contained her and she felt so much better when competently enclosed. She wished James could embrace her so well, too.

Placing a wrap over her shoulders she applied some powder to her cheeks and nose, which were shiny from exertion. Her lips were always glossed with Elizabeth Arden lipstick; a shade she had worn for about four years and she was disinclined to change as she felt at ease with the stability of its texture and hue. It was a rite of passage, too; a symbol of adulthood. Standing, she looked at herself in the cheval mirror which was a lovely touch in the room. Her hair needed a small adjustment and her waistline needed definition, so she searched for a suitable belt which she placed around her waist but without tightening it; it hung close but loosely so that its presence accentuated her corseted curves. Lastly, she slid on her small-heeled shoes to give her a couple of inches of additional height. She now stood about five foot nine inches tall and felt confident to go downstairs and see if James was already up and waiting for her.

Need Anne-Marie have worried. Of course James was there, awaiting her and had been at their table in the area set aside for breakfast for about half an hour. The room was set out in a homely fashion and was apart from the drinking areas and used for evening meals, too. The walls were panelled in dark wood and had various pictures of horses and racing as well as some harness brasses. Two vases of flowers made the space attractive and welcoming. Newspapers had not been provided, but James found an edition of Sporting Life to keep him occupied.

'Good morning, my darling. How are you? Did you sleep well?'

'Incredible night, thank you; I did wake quite early but it takes some time to bath, dress and prepare for the day, so I could not have come down sooner—unless I was undressed.'

'Anne-Marie, I have a few ideas for today; we could go into St Albans and look at its cathedral or we can seek the local shops and see if there is a good museum and the Alban Arena which also has exhibitions. Failing that, we could go for a walk along the Ver River and lakes and maybe look at the watermills and consider having a drink at Ye Old Fighting Cocks public house, which I'm told is the oldest pub in England.'

'I would like a walk, please, and the river, mills and ancient pub sound lovely; we ought to give the cathedral a visit to show willing, if nothing else. I'm not that religious and you told me that chapel was thrust down your throat at school—enough to put anyone off until sense prevails.'

'Let's have some tea and toast and whatever else the Inn can dream up; I'll call the young man.'

'James, have you had a chance to explore this area before we came to this village?'

'Of course, Don and I regularly come here for a sup and a meal sometimes, so I am well known. I don't get much time to explore, though, so our adventures will be new. I have my car, so we are free to go where we wish. You have not seen my Morgan, have you?'

'What is a Morgan? I am not much used to motor-cars; my father has one but uses it only for his business. I take the London Underground and a double-decker bus when necessary. The main-line trains are also satisfactory for me.'

'A Morgan is an unusual three-wheeled car—or it was until I modified it—which is made in a county called Worcestershire in a small factory where each one is hand-made. These are beautifully made but can be temperamental at times. As a three wheeler, they are not really stable enough and that is why I have missing front teeth—it rolled on me. But I still dearly love my vehicle. Maybe I am a fool?'

'Will I be safe in this dental-cart?'

'I have given it an extra wheel now and it is much safer but less exhilarating. Being an open-topped car, it will be draughty and your hair will blow everywhere but am certain you'll enjoy the ride and the view. Have you a warm coat to wear, and some gloves, too?'

'Of course I have a coat but I think I may need more. After brekky we'll go up to my room to see what I have. As I only brought a small case, I am not prepared for the anti-arctic and gale force winds. Maybe you'll have something I can borrow to make my ensemble quite idiotic, my lovely one.'

'Strangely enough, the small windshield, just in front of the two seats, will deflect most of any headwind away from passengers and up and over the car; even light rain is deflected but that should not give us a problem today; it looks bright and sunny so far.'

'How was the shop, what do you call it—Dress Address—yesterday? Had any good sales, interesting people? Anyone I'd know, perhaps?'

'Nobody yesterday but an actress friend of Coleen came in to try some evening wear last week, and she came with Linda Darnell. Yes, it was Ann Sheridan who was over from America, looking at London theatres for opportunities. She bought a fantastic gown and we had to take dollars which caused some confusion, I can tell you.'

'I have not heard of her, have I?'

'We do seem to attract stage persons, thanks to Coleen. The stage clans tend to stick together and Coleen attracts them like a magnet and she's not a shrinking violet so tells them about her shop: probably bores most of them stiff but its business.'

'Let's go. But first we must see what you will wear to keep warm.'

James followed Anne-Marie upstairs and, first things first, wanted a kiss and a hug. Taking off her cloak, she thrust her head back and was taken into the wondrous world of a lovely gentle kiss and enjoyed the smell and taste of a real man. James started to feel her body and the firmness of her corset, even through the fine teddy she was wearing.

'Come on, I must not attract tummy-ache, again or your lovely body and tight corset will be the death of me. I do so enjoy looking at and feeling you; you are utterly gorgeous and I'm so happy to be with you; why did I not meet you years ago?'

'You need to take more trains; maybe you'd have caught me earlier, and have a few more teeth.'

'Let's go and meet Morgan. Grab your coat and you'll need that scarf, too as well as your black gloves. You'll look the part, so don't worry.'

So the day started and they did not return until well into evening when they were hungry and thirsty—but much more in need another firm cuddle.

8 Jane's Work

Jane was mad to know how Mary was faring with James. She had said she was nervous because this escapade was entirely new to her and although she trusted James completely, anything could go amiss: she might say something out of turn, he might be difficult over her privacy; he might see Mary in a conflicting light or maybe he has met someone else recently. All manner of worries came flooding in when they last spoke on the telephone a few days before the Blackbury Duck adventure was mooted.

Urging Mary to take life as it came; Jane tried to give her some wise advice as her wisdom was based upon experience. She had not been quite so rash and rushed away with someone relatively new. She had slowly nurtured a close friend for a couple of years. He was now away and working as an engineer in a distant oil field for Shell-Mex and she missed him dreadfully. She was just a little jealous of Mary. Both girls had their distinct outlook on life. Of course, everyone is dissimilar; with different genetic make-up but at heart, both girls were from a similar background with similar ambitions, hopes, feelings and desires. She wished Mary great luck, happiness and a life to be lived.

But, was she living her life to the full, she considered to herself?

Every working morning, Jane took a Southdown bus to the village of Poynings where she worked as a veterinary assistant. The practice specialised in larger farm animals rather than domestic pets unless occasionally a farmer had a sick dog or cat when exceptions were made—specialising was all well and good but if needs were not met, then the back door may be left open for another practice to move into the agricultural environment. Compared to domestic pet ownership, there were far fewer farms and the working radius was limited and many farms were arable and had few, if any, livestock; just a few animals casually reared for a season, maybe. It was the dairy farms that provided most of the practice turnover but every spring sheep and lambing kept all the staff awake for impossibly long hours. Occasionally, Jane had an orphan lamb to rear with a bottle and it went everywhere with her, even on the bus if it was still young and not boisterous. Passengers used to find a lamb so appealing and bright-eyed.

Some wanted one as a pet, little realising that they grew, needed to be sheared, and needed their backsides to be cleaned so that they did not get fly-blown. Sheep lived in groups—flocks—and had to be controlled by shepherds and their collie-dogs but a hand-reared lamb stood apart from the flock; it was always un-fearful of humans and would come close to a walker in a field whereas naturally reared stock maintained a cautious, watching distance. Jane loved it when a grown ewe recognised her, especially when it was lambing and there was closeness between a birthing animal and its helper who was kind and caring and, above all, trusted like a mother. She would regularly receive a lick from mother to say "thank you for your help."

One day, Jane hoped to take exams and maybe become a surgeon but years of study lay ahead if that life was to be adopted. For the time being, she did much of the work that the vets' did and farmers took to her and her striking feminine manner and attitude with their animals. Many farms knew their dairy cows by name and, of course, Jane had to get to know hundreds by name and always spoke to them by moniker and this really did have a calming effect because the presence of these green-coated people often meant pain or being tied up whilst some intrusive procedure was necessary. Wariness became instinctive but Jane had such a close bond with animals that less stress was caused; the farmers really did notice and learned from her.

Travelling was now by car and the age of the pony and trap had gone but in really cold winters when roads were snowbound or icy, the trap came into its own again but it was oh, so cold. Jane was always accompanied by a veterinarian and could never work unsupervised but her exceptional skills were invaluable and she was regarded as an equal and often asked to give an opinion, usually when confronted by a stuck calf or an unborn lamb. She would frequently have to feel an animal and even had to don long gloves up to her armpits to make an internal inspection so that an informed opinion could follow. Such inspections had to be carried out partially undressed with just a bra and trousers with a covering smock-cum-apron. Everybody knew the score and how to behave together and it was rare for a testy word to have to be said before laughing off a discrete touch.

Jane often thought about Archie, who was with Shell-Mex. Letters were few and far between, both because of the distant location and the fact that he was always busy looking after, or for, oil. Apparently, he had something to do with mud but she did not really understand. Was there mud in a desert? She did not think so.

There had never been any intimacy between herself and Archie but they had been to a few dances and she knew that he was attracted to her. Did she find him attractive? Probably, but was he the Mr Right she dreamed of marrying, one day? She could neither say Yes or No. Simply, she did not know Archie well enough. Also, she could not face being apart from her husband for months at a time. This answer inferred that she really did want the closeness that a husband and lover would bring. But Archie was neither, yet.

Jane was a well built and comely girl with a good figure, strong arms and working hands used to the necessary farmyard mess. So, clothing was not fashionable but was suited to the workplace. Tops had to be taken off regularly or replaced when soiled. There were times when a wash was necessary in a farm water trough, sometimes having to wash head and shoulders when an animal had made a mistake. Her mother did not mind laundering for her daughter—so long as she changed out of her work-wear on the back doorstep and looked—and smelled—fresh as a daisy in the home.

Mary would not have been happy in the dirt and mess that wreaked farm-life. They rarely talked about her work and she thought that Mary would imagine that milk was made in bottles at a factory somewhere. Farms were to be enjoyed whilst on a country walk but what went on in the buildings was an alien world to Mary. If cows wore clothes, that might have given her an entirely novel outlook.

Chapter Three

1 Engagement and Marriage 1935

*A*nne-Marie was ecstatic. She and James had been together for about twelve months and both had met their prospective in-laws. Neither approved of their new daughter or son-in-law but that was to be expected, sadly. James was not close to Martha and Anne-Marie rarely saw her parents in Norwich.

'Darling, will you marry me, please, dear Anne-Marie?'

'Definitely, but when and how soon, dearest; I have wanted you to ask me for months, now. What took you so long to ask?'

'I was not certain that you wanted to spend your life with a dirty, grubby motor-car mechanic.'

'No, I am not coupling up with a mechanic; a racing driver, maybe. I believe you are a born racing driver with all your vital wits and pieces in order—save for a few teeth.'

They decided to try to get a special licence and called at the local births and deaths office—they would know the form.

'You need to apply to the Archbishop of Canterbury . . .'

And with that, both burst into gales of laughter, probably to the horror of the assistant registrar of all human dysfunction.

> 'Well, that is out; we do not want a church ceremony, just to be able to get married as soon as practicable. How do we do that?'

The registrar went through the processes necessary, the swearing and the affirmations required and what documents they'd both need to prove eligibility to marry, such as passports. So, assuming all paperwork would be in order, they arranged to get married in a civil ceremony in six weeks time.

The momentous date would be Saturday April 13th 1935, at 11 o'clock. Enough time to be able to request the company of a few close friends and for courtesy, her parents and particularly, James' father who would not come if Martha was there. So Martha was not asked. Anne-Marie wanted to take her out for a meal where they would explain that she'd never have liked the noise and the crowd.

The ceremony was to take place in Crawley near where they had set up home in a rented cottage—Yew Cottage at Ifield, which was close by. Crawley was an attractive small town and there was a good railway connection at Three Bridges which was on the main London to Brighton line from Victoria but London Bridge was also an option.

They needed to have a small group for a drink and a light meal; nothing formal or elaborate and nobody to dress for the part: just to come in normal day wear. They chose a small public house, The Plough Inn at Ifield which had a meeting room and would be able to provide some light refreshments.

Hilarity, un-rehearsed speeches and tales went on and on and the afternoon came and disappeared and before long it was time for dinner. Lunch had been sandwiches and other snacks together with a gruesome mixture of champagne and local ale.

Both James and Anne-Marie were fast tiring and they were looking forward to their first night spent together in one bed. Both had seen each other almost naked but had reserved themselves for a unique first night. Their senses were at bursting point and wishing everyone would just go home quietly; but no, it seemed they were in for the duration. OK James thought, folk don't get to a wedding every day, or even every month; so let them enjoy their fun. Standing, he raised his voice, then, to pretend he had cymbals, beat two plates together, smashing one.

> 'We are off, if you'll be glad enough to release us; it's been a hard day . . .'

> 'And it'll be a harder night, too, James'

Archie, the resident comic called out. Anne-Marie—or Mary to many of the guests—raised herself, and feeling quite tender within her bondage-like corset, she took James' hand and led him towards the door threshold. They both waved and wished everyone well and said a belated thank-you and were gone.

Outside, they felt they had had just a little too much to drink so walked the half mile, glad of the fresh air, free of smoke and the smell of spilled beer. Their clothes were in need of an overdue change and Anne-Marie was quietly suffering inside her corsetry; she had laced it in to the limits. She could sense more places it was biting her flesh than was clear of the controlling fabrics, the strong boning and elastic. A small problem was the itching and she longed to take it off—and have a good scratch. The joy would come when she began to take it off, loosening the laces and enjoying that awesome feeling of release that she relished so much. She adored being held tightly and with release, oddly enough, looked forward to the next morning's encasement. James rudely suggested:

> 'You are a natural for being held in bondage, as, with all the laces, you're literally tied up and trussed like a boiling fowl ready for the oven.'

I'm ready for your oven but not for cooking. Buns will have to wait. Have you brought some whatsits? I'm ready for a scratch, if you'd kindly oblige.'

'Just where do you expect me to start de-lousing you from your ticks?

'Well, my back. I cannot reach the long bony thing running down the middle; have you seen one before now?

Reaching the porch, James picked Anne-Marie up and with ease carried her inside and, with a couple of bounds almost to the top of the narrow stairs. Between them, they managed to scramble and muddle onto the awaiting bed where James fell upon his new bride and tried to suffocate her with his kisses.

'Forgotten the promised scratch?'

'You are still en-corseted. I cannot find anywhere.'

Anne-Marie wriggled, pushed and shoved and pretended she was not at all pleased but gave up the effort as James was so much the stronger of the two. Relaxing, she inferred that it was time to undress and James felt the message and started to undo some of her buttons and to take out the flowers wilting in her hair.

Whilst James had a quick wash, Anne-Marie undressed herself and tidied away their roughly discarded clothes, and joined her husband at the small basin and, head-to-head, brushed their teeth.

James looked at a vision he had never seen before: a lovely pair of breasts dangling in front of his face. With each brush-stroke, they appeared to dance with happiness and this made his lust all the stronger.

He suddenly recalled what Claudette had told him: always, always stroke and tease your partner and encourage her before attempting *passer a la vitesse superieure* as she put it rather sweetly.

Recalling more of the Paris lesson, James turned Anne-Marie to face away from him and placed her face down on the bed, but near to one side. On bended knee, he stroked her back and using his knuckles, gnawed her spinal vertebrae which made Anne-Marie twist and turn with utter joy, pleasure and excitement. Soon, she started to moan, loudly and he changed the movement to an examination of her shoulder blades before turning her over onto her back. James noticed that Anne-Marie's back was quite marked by the indentations left by her corset. It was these marks that itched, so he ran his fingers over the redness and tried to soothe them. This action excited Anne-Marie considerably and she moaned with pleasure.

'More . . .'

James turned his wife over and found more red marks to play with. Under Anne-Marie's breasts were red badges of honour left by the supporting structures and the lacing and these needed his unique attention.

'Pass the sandpaper, please.'

He was starting to enjoy the feel of her exposed breasts and waiting nipples which, by now were standing on ceremony, or so he thought.

Anne-Marie was so, so wanting to feel what happens next. She had heard penetration was painful but was oblivious to that, just wanting to feel James' huge new limb inside her. She felt as if she had leaked and worried about that for a moment but soon started to encourage James by stroking his hips and lower back with an intensity that surprised her.

She had no experience whatsoever. Apart from a few risqué cinema shots that disappeared with the censor's pen as soon as any interesting part . . . was left to the imagination. Even grand-mama had never broached the subject of sex—"breeding" as she coyly put it one day.

Anne-Marie wondered how James knew so much on this, his first married night. She determined to find out as a matter of priority.

The enquiry would await morning, sometime now in the far distant future . . .

2 Return to Work

After a few days' snatched holiday and enjoyment of each other and no regrets, both knew that they had to return. Don had arranged some races over Easter and James was a lead driver and there was no question of delaying. Coleen had not telegraphed after she had returned from the Plough Inn, so no new parts were in the offing.

Coleen had looked stunning at the wedding breakfast as the inn-keeper insisted upon calling the beer-fest. The few single men were entranced by her fabulous figure and she felt safe because all clearly wanted to see more of her and were like animals struggling with each other for her attention—so safety in numbers. She did fancy Don, but he showed no interest and James told her he was happily married and that his other half had had to stay at home with their youngest who was ailing. No actors were at the wedding and she did prefer to mix, socially, with fellow professionals. The stage is a difficult act for couples who were not similarly occupied as the hours are impossible and home-time would create unbearable tensions between the irregular calls for "stage left".

After Easter, Mary found the shop had been changed a little and was glad that Coleen had put in some time and thought; change that was her time, her thought, her wisdom and artistry. The window dressings were a total surprise and had been made to represent a special wedding event. This had, seemingly, brought in custom. Later, Coleen told Mary that she had sought some guidance from a friend working at the Gaiety Theatre who was an ace at set design.

Coleen looked dramatic in her new corset but had not been able to lace it up as tightly as she wanted and Mary had to assist in the back room whilst she bent over the table permitting the laces to be eased into place. Jen's ideas for doing the final closure were excellent and nothing like the occasional film scenes where the girl was impelled to hold onto a bar whilst a maid struggled and the lady moaned—theatrically.

Today, Coleen was dressed simply and elegantly with a wide leather belt just placed loosely at her waist so that it had the effect of enhancing her incredible 20" waist. Her breasts were also standing proud and it was clear that women shoppers did notice and some were inclined to ask, quietly, how she had achieved such a delightful figure. Was it uncomfortable? Was it like a form of bondage, one customer asked? Coleen said it was a form of restraint but was not at all spartan once used to the lambency. It was far more supportive than the modern sloppy brassieres. Did it hurt at all? This she answered not at all, but it probably has to be made to measure, as hers was. Where did she go? And another asked what it cost and really wanted to look inside her clothes. Coleen drew the line at that and said she had to reserve that pleasure for the stage but she'd introduce the corsetière with pleasure . . .

Fewer noticed that Mary was also heavily corseted but whilst it gave her an excellent stature, it was far less obvious unless, of course, Mary bent over when the shape of her back would become apparent to anyone in the know. Her clothes were worn much more glamorously and they hung from all the correct places and had been altered to accommodate the new foundations. Mary really loved the feel and vowed never to be without her new shape and wonderfully refreshed clothes. Idly, she pondered whether she should take after Coleen and her vastly altered shape. She'd talk to James when the moment was right. He had not noticed too much about Coleen at Ifield as he had been otherwise occupied.

Mary and Coleen thought about devoting part of the shop to selling some corsetry but realised they did not have enough experience and would need a 'Jennifer' to guide them. They decided to talk to Jen and maybe have a mannequin suitably dressed to encourage questions and to see if leads would generate income. The dress shop in Alfriston had been of great interest to James and Jane when they were there many months previously.

New seasonal stock had started to arrive and space was limited so the girls marked some older stock down in price and called it Special Deal Week. It brought in custom, mostly from new clients who appreciated the lower pricing. By the end of the week, several garments had flown from the rails and some were to go to the alteration ladies for minor restructuring. They considered whether to have more Special Deals but realised that profit was made from full-priced goods and that they could not survive on half-income. Mary was learning a great deal from helping to run this shop. Experience was always useful and she had a feeling it would be handy, one day, maybe in her own store. If Coleen gained a few dramatic parts, she'd want to release the lease, rent and taxes to Mary, on her own.

Thoughts for the future.

3 Married Life and War Looms 1938

Anne-Marie and James were blissfully happy together but this spirit was severely overshadowed by news from Europe and the Nazi politics which were utterly abhorrent. Mary especially felt this because of the new Jewish friends she had made who often called upon her at Dress Address. They were in despair because relatives and friends left behind in Germany and Austria were suffering horrendously. For them, there was little or no escape route. The secret police were impossible and brutal. James was certain that the new SS political police would spread and could imperil England with their demanding practice of extreme violence towards suspects under coercion for little or no reason whatsoever.

At least pregnancy had not loomed and both had carried on with their work but James could see that racing was not going to be a profession; it was a young man's game and he felt he was starting to age, even at twenty-six. Cars were also getting faster by the month as new developments manifested themselves and Sunbeam succeeded in keeping up with the leaders. He had been wondering about a commission and putting himself up for soldiering but had not had a chance to discuss this with Anne-Marie who would be aghast at the thought. Some secrets had to be retained.

Anne-Marie had also been considering the prospect of children. Love-making was a regular occurrence but she had to wonder whether there was anything wrong. Talking to other women, she realised that it often took months for a spark to ignite. There was plenty of gunpowder going off inside her and she revelled in the ecstasy that lovemaking engendered. Sometimes she was caught whilst in her corset and lovemaking just took over; sleep often followed, well encased. Oddly, enough, she liked the feel and tightness that the restrictive clothes added to the overall sensation. James loved the new feel and touch and wanted her dressed more than she permitted. Plenty of time to experiment, Anne-Marie thought.

Early in 1938, James decided to drive to Exeter and to call upon the Devonshires who had their main barracks, there. Whilst he did not know any single individual, he had been in the cadets whilst at school a few miles away and, of course, knew about army life from cadet training and drill. He left school as an Under Officer and had his cadet record with him. He was introduced to a Captain by the Guard Sergeant and invited to have lunch in the mess where he met a number of the officers who were not engaged in increased training. During lunch and discussions, James reached a decision: he would join up if they'd have him. He was duly welcomed and given a date for his junior officer training to start. He really dreaded returning to tell Anne-Marie the news he knew she did not wish to hear.

He felt that it would be wise to get in early and to know more than those who waited until the inevitable call to arms took place. He wanted to be ahead of the game. Mark, the captain at lunch, had agreed with his philosophy to be prepared and to be a leading scout. His abilities and his language knowledge would be invaluable if there was a conflict.

He never saw Mark again.

Anne-Marie was heartbroken at the news and railed at James for not having the sense to discuss it first. It took a week or two for her to realise that what he said did make sense. By this time he was away in Warminster learning a new discipline and military ways. He was interviewed by an officer who had travelled from London especially to see him. He said little but asked a great deal of questions about Paris, his father and he spoke fluent French with him.

'Does this interview take place with every new officer?'

James asked. He felt a little foolish when he received a knowing look in reply.

'I do apologise, Major.'

His superior looked at his watch and said the train would not wait for anyone.

Training over, he was despatched to the Regiment in Exeter and started life as a subaltern and had to learn the hard way just like his company who were also new boys. It was strange that they saw him as their leader when he was just as ill-informed as they were. He found, again, that he was a natural leader and was appreciated because he took time and trouble to help with his men's private problems—money, married differences, living difficulties, old jobs and unfinished business. This all took time and he neglected Anne-Marie and was unable to write as often as he had promised. His new batman was not the type who could help with his private life but did an excellent job with his Sam-Browne and pasting up his spats with the gunk they called Blanco. He preferred to shine his own boots which took hours of work. He felt he had to out-do his men. This was his way of leadership: work from the front.

He and Anne-Marie did manage two week-ends leave and she travelled to Exeter where he met her with his beloved Morgan and they went off into the wilds of Dartmoor—for times almost forgotten. They walked and saw so much; the views were incredible until one day, the mist fell like a cloud and they were disorientated. James carried his compass in his pocket but using it was difficult as training had been rather less than more intensive. He realised that he'd have to give rigorous tuition to his platoon and maybe others, too. He followed a river bank but failed to locate the Morgan that day. James was frantic to return from leave on time, otherwise he'd be carpeted for setting a poor example. So, early the following day, just as dawn broke, they set off at a brisk walk following the instructions provided by a local they'd met in an inn. Anne-Marie simply had to doff her tight foundations as she became quite breathless and sweaty. It was off with her stockings, as well, and she had to walk unprotected in her shoes. Her clothes went into James' shoulder-bag. As hoped, they found the car and it started like a dream and they were off towards Exeter via Okehampton. James dropped Anne-Marie off at St David's Station and realised, too late, what he was carrying in his bag.

4 The New Army 1938

There was a telegram awaiting his return at the barracks. He was instructed to leave Exeter and to report to an address in Sussex by 7am the next day and to tell nobody apart from his CO where he was going, not even his fellow officers and certainly not his troops. Sadly, he was not permitted even to say goodbye. The Adjutant suggested he should say he had to go into hospital for a minor op and would be back soon.

What on earth awaited him in Sussex, of all places? He had never heard of Shirle Place, or where it was located in a small village barely shown on his map. Even stranger, when he arrived, everyone was wearing civvies and he was despatched promptly to change. There was no bull and he lost his batman who was said to be unnecessary for what they were doing. 'How's your French?' a new colleague enquired, rather too casually.

After breakfast at about eight o'clock, James was taken to a large room where he joined about thirty other men and a few women, all clothed differently and instructions were given in a meaningful tone.

'There are officers and servicemen from several regiments and the navy in this room. Uniform is not to be worn. Saluting is not required and military routines you've learned so far, are to be quietly forgotten.

'Nobody is permitted to say where you are located and definitely not to spouses or partners if you have them. If really pressed, just say "Sussex".

'Spouses are to communicate in emergency only, via a WHI number to be sent to them by telegram from another staff office.

'Everyone, here, has been specially chosen for tasks ahead. I am able to tell you that you are exceptional otherwise you'd not be in this room. Each of you has a precise talent and, each individual may well know what that ability is.

'Homework will be intensive and examinations have to be taken so your progress will be carefully monitored. Work is the main ethic, here. You will all be learning a great deal and adding to what you already know.

'No-one is permitted to say what you are doing or to give any hint as to any activities you are asked to perform. Your work, here, is of a secret nature and that is how it must be regarded by everyone present. I do remind you all that sanctions will apply in default. There is an expression you must take to heart at all times "Careless Talk Costs Lives".

'Cars, if you have any, are not to be used under any circumstances without specific permission.

'You will be given plain special clothing if and when you have any need, or for exercises.

'If seen, you are to look like civilians at all times. You must never give anyone a military appearance or look.

'Surnames will be phased out, as far as possible, and you may communicate with your fellows and trainers using your first names or pet-names if you prefer. Just remember, civilians rarely use their surnames without a prefix such as Mr or Miss. If seen off-duty, make it obvious that you are not military personnel.'

Asked by a brave soul what they were going to do, here the lecturer said:

'You will all find out soon enough. For the moment, just assume you are engaged upon work vital for any future war work.

'You are all to report to a designated assembly room at six o'clock, sharp, every day until further notice is given to you.'

James thought that they were all classified as dead. He was exasperated and desperately worried. Sense told him that it would all become clear; this was still the army.

His only new information was that he was attached to The Artists Rifles, and that this differed from some of the fellow newbies, here. As an artist, this did seem to make sense. Maybe he was taken on to draw scenes from training or marching for use by the recruitment boys. But why the nonsense with the WHI number and nobody had given him a sketch pad, yet. It appeared that whilst he was in the army, he was not being treated as if he was in the army he knew. This was more akin to a prison camp: no uniform, no cars, no communication, no saluting, no batmen, plus homework—and he'd find that the list went on.

Taken by charabanc the next morning, he and a group were driven to a small hotel that had been taken over by people who were clearly not used to running a guest house of any description.

'You are here, this morning, to learn why you have been specially selected for duties that are important to the new efforts that are going to be necessary.

'You must brush up on your languages.

'Mr Compton, you are certainly the best French speaker here, as they tell me you have lived in Paris frequently. Oh, one thing more, James, you will be called upon to help others with their verbal French. I have to remind you, your German is not up to speed, so concentrate upon that and one other language of your choice—as long as it's one we teach here.

'Mr Fitzjohn, Bill and Mr Graves, Tony, your German will be similarly useful to James and others.

'Just a reminder, you are not all officers, here, but treat each other as equals, whatever your actual rank, regiment or service. Nobody needs to know your rank, service or regiment. That's your secret; keep it so.

'Remember too, that you are going to be treated as civilians here.

'Go, make yourselves at home and get to know each other as you'll need to support and to be supported by each other. And,

'finally, for now, I have some sad information. Your letters will be censored until further notice, so I suggest we all leave out the usual salacious bits or the sergeants—sorry, the censors, will be mesmerised. Just keep them totally bored out of their skulls.

Oh, don't be smart and write in any language except English. The black pen will obliterate any non-English words.

Suspected codes will also be eliminated, so don't use, say, the
sixth letter of each word spelling something imaginative.'

Still nobody knew what they'd be doing, apart from being at a
funny-school where they'd be expected to be fluent in another
tongue.

5 Another Leave

It made sense to meet Anne-Marie at Withdean and to stay with
Martha as James' location was not that far away. Anne-Marie was
bursting to know what he was really up to as his letters had been oddly
bland and uninteresting.

She really wondered if he had met someone else; letters were
infrequent as well as being distinctly dull. Even what had been written
had, in parts been blacked out.

She mused . . .

he simply cannot have met anyone else; they are so happy and
content together. The only smudge on the horizon was James' failure to
discuss joining up long before there was any real war.

At least she had a glorious job and worked so well with Coleen who
listened to her worries and placated her quite easily. She was worrying
about nothing at all.

Packing her things, Anne-Marie took the train to Brighton and a
taxi; Martha opened the front door of her modern mock-Tudor style
house which at least had enough bedrooms for the family. She was
frosty—not entirely unexpected as she was consumed with jealousy as she
felt James had been taken from her. Stolen, maybe.

'I have no idea when James will arrive; have you heard,
Mary? She never referred to Mary endearingly and never as
"Anne-Marie" the name which James always used.'

'No; he has to say as little as he can in his letters. They are
clearly censored and, as you know, we cannot speak on the

telephone. I had hoped that you'd know when to expect him here.'

'I am far from happy at this silence and his downright rudeness, Mary.'

When here, she tried to treat Mary as a servant and asked for what she wanted with barely a please or a thank-you. "It's time for tea" and she'd sit there doing nothing except fidgeting with a puzzle or a jig-saw. Mary was expected to go to the kitchen without being directly asked. In turn, Mary took ten minutes to show that she was not the new slave but slowly went in and decided to see what provisions were available.

There was a huge white rounded refrigerator which made quantities of rattling noises when it was doing what these machines do. It had a heavy door and several shelves but nothing much of interest was lurking within. Maybe she'd have to slip down to the local stores, so she busied herself making a list. On purpose, she did not make tea.

Let Martha come and ask—in an acceptable manner. The bottom shelf of the big white noisy machine had a number of Pyrex dishes—food had been made up but whatever dish Mary looked at was clearly made for just two people, not for three.

What a strange—no, unpleasant—woman. She abandoned the list and determined to take James into Brighton when he arrived; Martha could stuff her belly with a double helping of something.

Whilst unpacking, laying her things on the bed as there was no space for anything apart from James' things in his old chest and wardrobe, Mary asked herself what the future held in store. She hated this house and everything and everyone who was in it.

But just as she was getting thoroughly maudlin, the Morgan sound grumbled outside and she could not resist dashing down stairs; only to find Martha waiting for her son's arrival. She physically stood in the way of the front door so that Mary was almost excluded from any joyful meeting of mother, son and wife. Beastly cow, she thought.

James knew what his mother was like and he said nothing to Martha but moved her aside and hugged Anne-Marie as if he had been apart for a year or more.

> 'Darling, I have been longing to see you for—for—well so long I have given up praying for the day.'

> 'Mater, hello; it's good to see you, too.

> 'I'm starving, what's for supper, this evening?'

> 'I have forgotten to prepare meals for three. I'm forgetful these days and the dailies do not think.'

> 'We are going out for a meal; that's what you wanted, James, so it will not matter.'

James looked torn between his mother and his wife but Anne-Marie's glare told him to be on his guard.

> 'Let's go and get changed; you must be cold after the long drive and I want to hear your news, in full.'

After another huge hug and a lingering kiss, Martha called from just outside their bedroom door:

> 'Are you coming down? I much want to discuss a few things with James.'

Clearly, this imperative meant James alone.

> 'No Mater, I'm going to take Anne-Marie out, first, and when I'm back we can spend ten minutes with your problems. Will you heat up one of the dishes the dailies have prepared for you?'

So, the happy couple went out and walked down the hill towards the bus stop; busses were the most appropriate means of getting to Brighton and a Morgan was not tamper-proof. A Southdown decker came first, a shade more expensive than the red town bus but it was more like a coach and was clean and stopped less frequently.

> 'What shall we eat? Or would you prefer a drink, first? I think we should head for either the Queens or The Grand and we can eat and drink and have some peace.'

So, they walked along the promenade, towards Hove, holding hands and saying little even though there was so much to say. The Grand was closed: requisitioned by the military, as were most large hotels and substantial homes, too. They walked on, turned off the sea-front and found a small cafe, just three chairs and a small table were available.

> 'We'll keep this for our absent friend. Martini, wine, Tizer—whatever you'd like.
>
> 'I am going to have a long, cool beer, first.
>
> 'Now, tell me all your news.
>
> 'How's Coleen and Dress Battledress?'
>
> 'I've told you in letters all about . . . it's not Battledress—but I have not heard a single interesting thing about your life in the horrid army. Where are you stationed? Who have you . . . ?'

James interrupted and said:

> 'I am doing something for the war effort and I have to ask for your forgiveness as I am not permitted to say more than what I have written in my letters. The good news is that I'm stationed in Sussex and am learning a great deal but the work is hard and time-consuming.'
>
> 'But what you wrote to me was total tripe. Probably what your Mater is having for her supper tonight.

'No, your letters were really boring and you did not even tell me you half loved me.

'I wondered whether you had met a lovely army-girl, AST or something; these are new, I gather from The Times.'

Changing the subject,

'Have you remembered to bring my clothes with you? You obviously wanted to have my lovely smelly corset with you to keep you company when you dashed off at St David's; I was so cross with you and half decided to call at the Guard House and ask for my stockings and corset that Lieutenant Compton has taken from me . . .'

'I would have murdered you,'

James said with a wide grin and the whole atmosphere changed from being tense to relieved and relaxed. The drinks and some snacks arrived.

'Seriously, can't you tell me anything more about what you are up to, James?'

'In a word, no.

'I expect you will find out when the time is right but the papers have started to say one has to be aware of spies and Nazi Fifth Columns whatever those things are.

'So, please don't ask.

'I would recommend that you do take The Times every day but please do not start with Deaths and In Memoriam columns first.

'I am quite safe. I'm learning considerably. I do need some more clothes when we can get into Hanningtons, tomorrow. I look forward to leaves so much.'

Anne-Marie memorised what James had told her in what passed as her brain; she recalled everything as if it was a photograph.

He was not in danger; "safe" was what he said;

He needed more clothes; why? What was wrong with uniform?

"Learning considerably" sounded suspiciously like academic work rather than playing with guns and tanks;

She didn't like being told not to read the Deaths, first. That spelled danger, in her mind;

And, why the WHI number when he's thought to be quite local?

The word "no" means there is much, much more to find out.

She intended to listen to what was muttered in sleep. Maybe she'd make a good and valuable spy; but for whom? The Poles, the Russians, the French—not the Spanish as they are still killing each other . . . endless choice.

Secrecy led to leakages, she thought. It was virtually impossible to keep spouses out of range for long. There were bus tickets in pockets, for example. Receipts for essence for the Morgan. Oh, joy.

James found a copy of The Times which was not available at the guest house. He'd read it later, he thought.

Headlines said the government was at odds with everything and it was better to read the social columns and what little scandal The Times dredged up. He did like the advertisements and the fashion pages. There was no motoring news or articles but, anyway, he knew most of what was going on with makers and he had kept in touch with Don who was mad at him leaving so quickly when he was about to become one of the best drivers in the world—or so he said in his letters.

After dinner, a simple meal which was well cooked and comparatively superb food when compared with what the Shirle-staff were concocting.

They went out, returned to the promenade and started to walk in the Hove direction, again. Hove is so much nicer than Brighton, they both agreed. They turned around when they reached the new Hove Marina which was soon to be opened. James noticed there were a number of uniformed navy men there. It was not a boat-yard, there was no harbour nearby, so why the senior-service interest? He thought there must be something like Shirle going on.

He did mention this to Anne-Marie who added the snippet to her mental list.

The thought of being in bed with James with his mother just through the wall appalled her. No chance, whatsoever, of any larking about as she'd almost certainly beat on the dividing wall and that'd promptly quell any ardour. It was this-night-dead, already, of course.

Anne-Marie had some spectacular news, anyway. She wanted to tell James when the time was right but that never materialised, here, in his mother's home. She blurted out:

'James, I think I am pregnant; it's been . . .

6 Jane Changing 1938

'When could we come round to see you, Jane? We are in Brighton for a couple of days more as James is on leave.'

'Any evening; why not come and have a bite with us, here?'

'That would be excellent; would tomorrow be good?'

'What time do you suggest, Jane?'

'Mama normally has dinner ready for eight; why not come about half-seven?'

'We'll see you then, and look forward to it. It'll only take us about ten minutes, top, to drive round, James says.'

James and Anne-Marie decided to dress 'smart-casual' as dinner at home did not seem to be a dressy affair but they decided to take a couple of bottles of wine from the local Rolfes Stores in Tongdean Lane.

Anne-Marie decided not to discard her corset, yet, but felt that as she was about three months, she ought to loosen the laces by an inch— and then she'd be able to have a reasonable meal and feed for two, or will it be three?

She had been remarkably lucky and had not suffered any unpleasant sickness which was so common for early-days mums.

Jen had discussed the need for a proper maternity belt. This is similar to a normal corset but shaped differently and readily adjustable. She said that it's important to support the abdominal area otherwise the weight may stretch the skin and muscles and then your fabulous figure will be lost.

Coleen did not know yet and this was a concern; if she won a part during the later stages and after the birth, who would look after the shop? This needed to be resolved and, as it was Mary's making and problem, she felt she ought to start to look for a suitable competent assistant who'd have to learn the ways of Dress Address well before pregnancy became a real problem. Pity Jane was so involved with animals, but, anyway, she was too rural a girl to know much about London's ways and selling dresses.

Jen might be a possibility but could not fit the shop-work with her home visits. She'd be good and it could promote her foundation consultancy business as well. But she had to be discounted.

James also worried; who would look after Anne-Marie in the later stages, then for the birth and for some months afterwards. Mater? He could do nothing. But he knew that this idea would create a monstrous explosion—to Mater and Anne-Marie both.

She would have to be brought into play and this leave would be an ideal time to raise the subject and to see how his women-folk reacted. It will be Mater's first grand-child, so why shouldn't she try to be maternal for a change? It might just bring the four of them somewhat closer but he had only distant hopes. If Mater proved to be as selfish as usual, just what do mothers do when their husbands are away soldiering? Are there nursing homes or baby ranches?

Anyway, it was still early days.

'How lovely to see you both; do come in, please. James, you met my parents, briefly, didn't you?'

'No, not yet, but I've heard from Anne-Marie, of course. It will be interesting to put faces to tales; one always seems to have a completely clashing mental picture.'

'What did you see in your imagination, James—go on, tell me—you must, please.'

'Too late, thank heavens, and I was absolutely wrong, anyway.

'Good evening, you must be Mr and Mrs Palmer, how are you both?'

'A reasonable guess; you must be James Compton. We're Alfred and Mavis, James. We were sorry to have missed your wedding but, as you know, we had arranged a holiday some months' previously and we were longing to see the Grand Canyon and it could not be cancelled. So, we'll catch up on things, now. It's been ages since Jane saw Mary, as well. What news on your front?'

Moving into the sitting room, Mavis disappeared and Alfred prepared drinks for everyone and unusually, both Mary and Jane chose squash with squeezed oranges made up with lemonade—a strange mixture that Jane had taken to.

The house was larger than James had imagined and the sitting room had a French window looking out over the garden that sloped away from the house via some terracing. He wondered who the gardener was as it looked well-cared-for and attractive—yet it was only a mile or so from the centre of Brighton. The furnishings were modern but there were also some Chinese looking pieces that looked right in this setting. The ornaments were eclectic and dated from either work places or from longer holidays. What will be recovered from Arizona, James mischievously thought. The walls were papered and were supporting a number of paintings; some were probably relatives and looked, by the elegant dress, typically nineteenth century whereas others were clearly more modern but carefully collected and re-framed as several had the same design of strong gilt-edged frames which blended well with the room. James considered which of them designed the pictures and the furnishings; definitely Mavis.

'Mary, you look delightful; you appear to be taller and so slim. Married life must be suiting you a treat. What am I missing?

'Have you any good men in your parish, where is it, Ifield?'

'Jane, I think all the good men have gone off to join the boy scouts or something, as James has, of course. Please do not ask—he won't or cannot tell you where he is at present. I know so little, it's just not fair and it's putting quite a strain on our life, just when we need to be together.

'We have given up on the Ifield property and I now live in Maida Vale again which is close to my work.

'Why the strange drink; you used to be well into sherry or martinis, as I remember; you are well—you look absolutely blooming, your cheeks are bright and your hair is fresh and suits you well; a little colouring, maybe?'

'That's one of my secrets.'

'Jane, we know each other too well for secrets. Are you still in Poynings with all those lovely vets?'

'That's problem number one: You remember my friend, Archie, who worked in the oil fields for Shell-Mex?'

'What's happened to him, Jane?'

'I've had to write a terrible Dear John letter. It was awful and I did not know what to say as he's kind and gentle and there was no way I wanted to hurt him but, but—how can I put this?'

'What have you done Jane; tell me please.'

'Well, that's one little or not so little problem.

'You'll meet him a bit later as he'll be here, soon. Henry—prefers Harry—joined the partnership a few months ago after gaining some experience in the West Country and has taken over from one of the seniors who had to retire.'

'So, are you are going out together now?'

'Yes, we are actively looking for a home but are uncertain what the future will bring; veterinary surgery is not a protected occupation and he could be called up if they bring in conscription; he might even find himself commissioned as a military vet; they do keep some for the remaining horses and some mules.'

James said:

'Congratulations appear to be in order, so why the strange drink mixture, Jane, or are we awaiting Harry before bottles get uncorked?'

'Well, there's more. I'm afraid I could not wait and I'm having a baby, but not for about six months by which time, hopefully we'll be married.'

Anne-Marie was incredulous; she had known Jane for long enough to know that she was not exactly anti-men but not interested in anyone special apart from the occasional mention of Archie.

'That's fantastic news, well done on finding Harry and starting to produce.'

'We are in the same club: I am also expecting in much the same time and am also starting to worry about the future.'

Alfred stood to prepare some more glasses.

'Jane and Mary, shall we drink to your sensational news'

Mavis came in just after the announcement but may well have overheard the gist of Mary's similar news.

'I don't believe it: both of you. Must be something John Bull has put into the water. Mary, well done.'

'You'll like Harry, who'll be here soon unless a cow has let him down somewhere. We are so pleased for Jane and I'm longing to become a granny, at last.

'But, Mary, you are looking much slimmer than when we last met; have you lost weight—but you say you're well into your pregnancy, same as Jane.

'What are you doing, what pills are you taking?

'Jane has had a bad bout of early-day sickness and is completely off some food and does not drink any alcohol. She adores almonds, though. Strange.'

'Before Harry arrives, I'll tell you my secret for being slim. For some months now, I have been fitted for a firm corset and now I cannot live without it; I've loosened it a fraction and it conceals any sign of my bump but I must go and get fitted for a proper maternity version that gives support when and where it's necessary.'

Mavis said:

'Oh yes. I used to have two or three when I was expecting and they made life much less obvious and I retained my figure after confinement. They were horrid, unattractive things, oddly enough almost khaki coloured with straps and buckles; not remotely out of Hanningtons, for example.

'I think you must speak to Jane about corsetry, I think she needs something now. I make her wear a foundation in the evenings when she's home and particularly if we're going somewhere smart. But we do have arguments about this—but she looks so much better when dressed in good underwear. Where did you say you went?'

'I did not. But I work with Coleen, an actress friend and she recently finished a part where she was obliged to be trussed up as an Edwardian lady, all curves and bustles and she looked fantastic—less the bum-piece, maybe—but she did. When she finished understudying a principal, she wanted to keep the specially made corset but they would not let her have it. She decided to see a friend, Jennifer, and introduced me to her when she had placed an order.

'I was amazed at what a good fitting would do for me and here I am, wearing one of mine.

'James greatly likes them and went back from leave with one of mine in his kit-bag.'

James looked embarrassed.

'That's unfair. I did take one but it was a mistake.'

'I was mad at you and nearly called at the barracks asking for it.'

To gales of laughter from all,

'Do tell us more.'

Said Alfred.

'James, you didn't undress her and take it off, did you?'

'It was nearly dark and Anne-Marie went and hid behind a bush on Dartmoor as we were rushing back to my barracks and she could not walk as fast as I needed to run as being late would have caused a nightmare of problems.

We'd been fog-bound. Anyway, I stuffed her garments and stockings into my shoulder-bag and left Anne-Marie at the local station and forgot to give her . . . well that's my story.'

'It's time we went in to eat; I don't want it to spoil. Harry's not here, yet. No news I suppose?'

Queried Mavis.

'He never can tell; as a new partner, he gets all the nasty outings and must have his head inside a heifer or something pregnant.

'He'll have to learn how to deliver me soon, so practice makes perfect, I hope.

'There are not many telephone boxes in our working area and, anyway, he would not think of that because he'd prefer to get here rather than waste time finding a phone, money and using it.'

'He's impatient; most men are.'

It was about an hour before Harry arrived.

He had had to go via his flat as he was much in need of a thorough wash as he'd had to deliver twin calves, unusually, from a heifer with her first born and he had had to call out another partner as the animal had become distressed and they may have had to perform a Caesar on her. In the event, ropes and muscles had produced two calves, a bull calf still-born. Not a problem for a dairy herd as male calves went to the local hunt for hound food.

Harry was tall and muscular with a crop of light blond hair and a darker moustache which he said made him look older and wiser. He had a face that appeared older than his years—not lined but mature and he had bright blue eyes and fair eyebrows which was said to make him attractive to the opposite sex. He'd had a few girl-friends when in Devon and Cornwall but none that lasted more than a short time. Arriving in Poynings, he was instantly attracted to Jane and promptly warned off by a couple of the partners—who were both married and just plain jealous. Jane brushed Harry off, as was her manner. But one day they were out working together and driving along and they started to let their hair down a little and Harry asked her out for a drink. Unusually for Jane, she accepted, saying,

'I do have a close friend working abroad for Shell-Mex.'

She'd spurned every other vet in the practice, including some who were single. Whilst Jane was concerned for her oily-boy she found that she adored Harry and longed to be allocated to his round. But, she did not want to let herself fall into his arms; she had had a long running relationship . . .

It was late one evening when they were together and the weather was foul, so Harry suggested she camped at his flat. It did not take much persuasion for Jane to start to spend several nights a week at his Westmeston apartment, part of a large house that had been altered to make two additional separate homes providing an income for the owners. It was conveniently located for the Poynings practice and an ideal jumping-off point, now that a real home is needed. Being together so much, during the day and most evenings—and some nights too, brought Harry and Jane together quicker than had normal circumstances prevailed. Both families were so pleased, too, which was a real bonus and Mavis spent ages on the line to Harry's mother. So, it will be interesting when the two families meet—probably when they marry.

No plans have been made for a date and location, yet. Mavis is getting anxious as the banns have to be arranged at a suitable church nearby. As they are not regular worshipers, Jane is dreading having to show her face in church just to entertain the religious politics necessary for the three Sundays when the orders are read out. At some stage, during the banns business, Jane and Harry will have to discuss matters with the vicar who will also have to be told about their expected; that will raise a few eyebrows into the organ loft.

As a considerable number of guests have already been suggested, two likely churches have been promoted by Mavis, who is clearly taking charge of the matrimonials which is good as both Jane and Harry are dedicated to their work. She thinks that either St Peters or St Bartholomew's are likely and the less churchy St B's will be selected as it has lots of space and room for a small orchestra which is something that Mavis would love to have for her daughter's wedding. The interior of this church is like a vast hall, no pillars to interrupt the view for the congregation and the design has been said to resemble Noah's Ark but Alfred has told her that's a fiction dreamed up due to its vast size.

The problem with Bartholomew's is its location in an unfashionable area—but, St Peters is also similarly placed but on the opposite side of London Road and in a much more attractive island location. Final choice may rest upon how Mavis and Alfred interact with the ministers and their suggestions. The reception has also been worrying Mavis. She contemplates classy whereas Alfred is practical. It's a competition between The Royal Albert and The Pavilion and who knows which will win the day. Jane is delighted to be leaving this entire organisation to her mother who has a businesslike turn of mind entwined with expansive entertainment whereas Alfred is realistic and maybe a little hard-headed. Someone has to look after the pennies.

Dinner over, and after a lovely chat and catching up with everyone's news and getting to know Harry, it was time to return to Withdean and the little matter of their forthcoming offspring. James suggested taking Mater for a really good lunch at The Regency Restaurant on the seafront which was newly opened and which she'd enjoy and importantly, where she'd be less likely to cause a scene and where she'd be unlikely to know the other diners—a constant worry as her past was a closed book. Anne-Marie and James nattered about the morning's problems for an hour or more lying in bed, but more than a little restless.

Why was the natural event of having a baby such a problem?

7 Store and Staff

It was agreed that Mater would look after Anne-Marie in the later stages of her pregnancy but she would continue to live in Maida Vale and help the new assistant settle in at Dress Address. Feeling well was a surprise; one expected that having a baby caused the mother to be unwell, tired, sick and unable to work adequately. In fact, Anne-Marie had never felt better; pregnancy clearly suited her and she looked blooming and her figure with a new supportive corset was excellent, so much so that few knew she was even having a baby in three months time.

Anne-Marie thought she was plain fat and had been eating too much but, realistically, her fatness was much lower in her abdomen and whilst her breasts had become modestly rounded, her hips were no larger than usual.

Coleen had found a new girl to help her; Bronwyn was a few years older and experienced and called Bronnie for short. She was originally from Wales but did not have an accent nor did she speak any Welsh. She had worked for some years in a small department store in Sidcup but had moved to be with her husband who now worked in Bermondsey in South East London. She had two teenage daughters and was probably in her early-forties.

Bronnie was presentable, well dressed and had lustrous hair that she spent time and trouble keeping as immaculate as she could; she appeared to home-perm her locks at least twice a week. She was busty but had no obvious waist and rather larger hips. She always wore stockings and good sensible shoes together with a smart tunic or suit for work.

There was a natural ease between Coleen and Mary and they were just starting to get to know Bronnie. Coleen was out one day, and Mary and Bronnie were keeping shop and having a good natter—and the opportunity presented itself for some quiet woman-to-woman gossip when they were without any customers.

Bronnie was found to be a person who kept her environment immaculate; the simple Hoover cleaner was out every morning but she also regarded dusting as a priority that both Coleen and Mary had tended to neglect until needs must. The shop front and door also had its face washed every day and it was amazing how much street grime was collected on the damp cloth. Mary thought Bronnie was an excellent find and would fit in well as she improved aspects of running a shop that had been neglected. Interestingly, she never criticized what had been left undone. She just made things better without being asked.

'What does Coleen wear to give herself such a gorgeous figure, Mary?'

'I know it looks Victorian, but it is a modern design based upon the fashions that existed at the turn of the century—not long before you were born. Your mother would have worn clothes that attained a figure like Coleen, today.'

'You mean corsets and things, Mary?'

'Oh yes. Coleen is an actress—you knew that didn't you? She had a good but temporary part as an understudy for a well known actress for some six weeks or more in a central London theatre. She played an elegant Edwardian lady who was dressed immaculately and who also had the most gorgeous figure with a tiny waist, a huge bustle and an enormous well coiffed wig. Her part called for a lady aged about twenty-five who was shortly to be married to an Earl.

'Coleen hugely enjoyed being that part and had to be subjected to an incredibly powerful corset that made her figure take on the 'S' shape of that era; seriously curvy and really uncomfortable until one became used to the imposed restrictions.'

'But did she have to undergo all this discomfort?'

'Yes, that was the part; dress and strong corsetry went with the part—and remember she was to marry an earl, so total elegance was a major aspect of the role. She started to enjoy the feeling imposed upon her and although today the Edwardian shape is impractical, the similar Victorian image is readily adaptable to today's circumstances. So . . .

'Has she adapted, changed all her dresses and suits and given herself a tiny waist?'

'Oh yes, but we should not discuss her in her absence. She has been fitted by a friend with a really lovely corset and nowadays she is never seen without it. It fits her like a glove and it definitely brings business to the door because customers much appreciate her obvious smartness and, by today's standards, her unusual figure. She will tell you more; do just ask her. She won't mind telling you; I know her well, now. Please refrain from admitting we have had a gossip, though.'

'I'll say not a word; promise.'

'Hello, Mrs James; how are you? May I introduce you to Bronwyn who has joined us after working in the department store in Sidcup?'

'Did you work in Andersons, by chance?'

'Why yes, Madam. I was there for the best part of twenty years and they held my job open during the time I had my daughters. I started as a junior when I was just fourteen, I think. There was a really excellent departmental manager who taught me so much.'

'I must have known you there because I was often looking around for ideas when I lived in Chislehurst but I tended to buy dresses in Bromley or Croydon where there were larger stores.'

'That's a pity because I was almost always to be found in the ladies-wear department, so we just missed each other.'

'Did you say Bryony?'

'No, Bronwyn.'

'Sorry, I should have listened harder; a natural mistake.'

'Please tell me what you have in this excellent shop which I may use for a forthcoming christening: my grand-daughter.

My daughter-in-law will be wearing a well-fitted blue dress and matching shoes and accessories and she is always band-box smart whereas she has to nag my son, just a little. He is learning; any suggestions, here?'

The two were well matched and with Bronnie's past experience, she did find two suitable outfits that would not clash with her young family. She had to ask quite intimate questions about Mrs James' foundations as these were critical if she was to look equally "band-box" smart. She admitted to wearing Spirella foundations and had a figure better controlled than she wore today.

Bronwyn asked her if she could return wearing her Spirella corset to try on the two dresses, again to see if any alterations were necessary. A good fit was essential for a christening, she counselled Mrs James.

She agreed to return in two days' time and the dresses were set aside. The camaraderie was touching and the two gave the impression of getting on well and to be at ease with each other. As she left, Mrs James said,

'See you Thursday afternoon again, Bronwyn; hope you'll be here, then.'

'Of course I will.'

'That was an excellent demonstration of your craft, Bronnie. Coleen will be thrilled to hear how you managed Mrs James who often comes but rarely buys more than an accessory or a smart blouse or two. It would not surprise me if she did not buy both dresses—and they are quite expensive new stock which we obtained from a Jewish East End tailor who came over from Germany where he was a couturier of some standing—at least until Adolf messed things up.'

'Bronnie, I first met Aaron Katz whilst I was researching suppliers before this shop was opened. He has been a wicked friend and mentor for us. He often comes with things to show us and Coleen has found that what he brings, sells within days. Maybe we should order more, in advance; he is an excellent tailor and dressmaker.'

'Thanks for the background; I'll tell Mrs James the provenance of her dresses; it does help to cement a deal.'

'We were talking; I am also heavily corseted; had you noticed?'

'Yes I had but I know you are expecting and your figure is nothing like Coleen's. I assumed you had a maternity foundation, just like I used to wear when I had my daughters some years' ago. I only wear a light suspender belt now but my husband is always looking in certain intimate shop windows to my acute embarrassment. I must not ask him to come here and see Coleen; he'd want me trussed up as well; I know him too well, by now.

'Tell me, why does a young girl like you wear strong supports as you noticeably do?'

'I just wish I had been satisfactorily dressed with good foundations by my parents. My grand-mama would have had me appropriately corseted but I do not think she thought it seemly to mention such things to me and she left such discussions to the occasional brassiere, teddies, camisoles and similar undies.

'It was Coleen who suggested I should meet her good friend, Jen, who works for Mme Vermeuil, a well known expert corsetière and maker.'

The door opened and two customers came to have a look inside.

'Anyway, let's show these customers some dresses that they may like; we'll talk more later.'

'We cannot sell to everyone. Those two were clearly actresses and maybe friends of Coleen as they asked for her, in person. I think they will return because I told them she'd be in on Thursday and they said they'd be back then as they wanted some distinct advice.'

'Why then, did they not ask you what they wanted?'

'Here, customers—clients—do become attached to one of us and you'll acquire a new client in Mrs James.

'We find it is like being a hair stylist, but here we style our clients with suitable dresses and never, ever, over-sell or suggest something's ideal when, clearly, it's unsuitable. Clients have learned to trust us and our judgement. So they treat us well and frequently return.'

'Speaking of my pride and joy, I always go to see Angela, who is my favourite stylist; I spend my half-day with her every week as I adore having my hair prepared and regularly permed. It drives my husband, Henry, witless.'

'As I was saying, you like having an incredible hair style; I like having an incredible foundation which my husband, James, cannot seem to get enough visual contact. I suspect Henry may be the same?

'I find I am utterly lost when my foundations are not in place, well laced up and supporting my breasts from below rather than from the shoulders, where they used to sag, a little.'

'I noticed that yours were firm and supported well; is that one of your secrets?'

'In Victorian times, the corsets did four things—they reduced ladies' waists by several inches, supported their bosom, held their tummy and underpinned their hosiery. Well, today, the latest garments have the same requirements plus another vital aspect—they reach lower and contain their backsides.

'Foundations are made with much less rigidity today and what I wear is so comfy and, more often than not when James is at home or about on leave, I'll wear mine all day and keep it on at night too, as he loves the firm feel.'

'Are you quite serious, Mary?'

'Very. I feel inadequately dressed without my corset in place. James adores me in my bondage, as he rudely calls it.

'The tummy firmness is going to be reduced considerably from now on because whoever is living here needs more room to breathe. But I am now in a special garment with considerable adjustment—straps—built into the corset I'm wearing; I could not be without this, I can tell you. All my womanly curves are under control and there is no loose movement whatsoever. Do feel my tummy, for yourself, Bronnie.'

'It is so, so firm. I have all the stretch marks left from carrying two children, sadly'

'Firm but not tight; plenty of room for someone to move but you'll not see the kicks that I feel inside.

'May I make a suggestion, please? Bronnie, you would look spectacular with a little bit of figure assistance; you tell me you just wear a suspender but that does not assist your curves. You have a good upper figure but your waist should be proportional to your bust and hips. I assure you that after learning to live with a good corset, you'll never regret the change it impels upon you.'

'You are a dream to tell me this. I know you are right but I've put off the cause for years, now. I will have a short talk to Henry and see what he thinks. But he'll need to know what one will cost. Time to go home soon—Henry, you are in for a tight surprise.'

8 Soon to be Three 1938

Mary had so many feelings about being pregnant; happy to have part of James inside her; happy that her pregnancy was progressing well and that Dr Paul Bander was perfectly at ease with the progression towards the third trimester and that mid-November was the likely due time. As far as he could tell at this stage, he thought there was just one baby.

'Anne-Marie, my wonderful love: you are looking so well; pregnancy seems to suit you both and your figure has hardly changed at all; it's amazing.'

'James, it must be your influence upon you-know-who. He—or she—just knows how to behave and to treat mother with respect. I've had no awful sickness and the doctor says I look fine and ready for the November birth. I'm not looking forward to that, I can tell you. The things friends have told me and what to expect does not bear thinking about.

'Anyway, I'm still at work and getting on so well with Bronnie, the new girl who'll take over from me when I am off-duty. I expect to be in Withdean from October onwards. If nothing goes wrong, the baby will be born there, too. The doctor lives not far away in Varndean Gardens.'

'Mater seems reconciled to the forthcoming birth and she has had the dailies thoroughly clean the front bedroom and has arranged for adequate bedding, towels and things that you'll need.

'She has promised me that she will welcome you as a daughter and will not expect you to be her servant. She knows very well that I'll be so angry with her if I have to remind her of her promise. You are going to need her help as I cannot be released from my army commitments.'

'Oh, James; thank you so much for organising things for me; where would I be without you and your strong will? I need a safe, agreeable, happy home where I can be free of most worries. A new baby will need all my attention but all the dailies have had experience and will be offering their wisdom. They all love babies and they'll be so happy to help me.'

'Have you worked out what you are going to need? Baby clothes, perambulator, cot and lots of things like bottles, sterilising potions and napkins? Mater will enjoy taking you to Hanningtons and to other stores and pharmacies. She will lay on a taxi, I have no doubt.'

During an August leave, James was staying in Withdean, too. His base was not far away but most of his time was taken up with training and learning duties; at least this was established but he did not say much about his work as there was an embargo on open talk.

He had made contact with the Canadian troops who were stationed close to Martha's home. The Princess Patricia's Canadian Light Infantry were required to patrol the South Downs and to seek fallen airmen from any combatants. They were issued with motor-cycle-sidecars which were eminently suited to the terrain, access through gates and to be able to traverse ground that could not be driven over, even by jeeps. A gunner sat in the side-car operating a Sten gun. Flares were used to call up reinforcements if a casualty was located or if a German flyer was seen. Once James was known to be operating nearby, he was invited to take a few turns as the gunner which pleased him greatly. The PPCLI were under great pressure as they had a vast area to patrol and had limited spare crews.

'Darling, shall we all go into Brighton this evening? The theatre or cinemas are possibilities but I'd suggest The Theatre Royal would please Mater greatly. Let's look at their program and see if seats are available.'

'Martha, James suggests the theatre this evening; you know most of what's on, would you like to go there after dinner?'

'James, that'd be an excellent idea. A new production of GBS's Pygmalion has been scheduled for The Theatre Royal and given the cast list, it should be excellent. Would you book for us and try to get seats in the royal circle or mid-stalls. I'm sure Mary would prefer to travel by taxi, so please would you arrange that, too?'

'Mary, I remember all too well the time when I was expecting James. It must have been in 1912, I think. We were living in Folkestone and during the early stages I was pretty unwell but later, when things had settled, I was back to normal and we used to spend a great deal of time at theatres, good cabarets and dinner-dances, too. I enjoyed the time there but life was often quite strained as we had hoped that a new baby would improve our life together, but that was not to be.

'Socially, things were good but, privately, we were not blissfully happy and it was quite a job to keep matters away from the public gaze. Henri was much inclined to go and live in Paris but he would not leave me on the north side of the channel, so we ventured across on the train ferries a few times.

'When in Paris, Henri was always talking about where he'd want to live, which district and what he'd most want to see every morning when he awoke. Did he wish to be high towards the north like Montmartre or to the west like Bois de Boulogne. Equally, The Marais or the Sorbonne and Luxembourg districts all had creative wonders of their own. Personally, I'd venture no further than the Ile de France where so much went on day by day in the narrow streets and paths that were away from the national monuments like *Notre Dame* and *Sainte-Chapelle* which attracted tourists like moths towards a bright light. Whereas he could not take a fix and concentrate upon an area, I would have been satisfied with an apartment on the *Ile de la Cite* and to learn so much from the creative peoples. To prove my point, just consider how many street artists there were who congregated in this one small area of Paris.'

'Martha, this is the first time you have told me anything about your past; I am delighted to know something of your and James' background. We must speak again like this as it will bring us closer and we do have to live together and to share our fortunes and misfortunes as part of life. It will improve our happiness and ability to be close and active together. I would much like to be as close to you as James and I are; secure in the knowledge that we think alike and also know what the other is doing without being prompted. Maybe we are telepathic.'

'Tell me, have you two considered a name or names for the unborn, yet?'

'We have or rather we did when I first told James when I knew for certain that I had missed a monthly or two. James was directly into names and literally hundreds were thrown into the melting pot. He came up with so many classical suggestions and being thoroughly mundane, I rejected these as they'd have made life difficult for the child. Kids with strange names are more often teased. I recall Perdita and Antonina. They were called Ninea and Ditty whereas the Jane's and Anna's escaped that cruelty entirely.

'James was called Gumption as a take upon his surname, I suppose. I really do think that surname-takes are more acceptable than teasing names based upon first names. Nick-names such as Dusty, Tabby or Polly are a another matter; they are meant kindly whereas teasing names such as Ninea, pronounced Nine-A found a hurt girl who never recovered from this cruelty.

'Anne-Marie, I do not want to have a child who is laid open to stupid hurt. I have never given this much thought; I do think what you have said is true and we must all come up with a list for both sexes that will keep us happy.

'I came up with "James," as a name, whereas Henri tended towards French given names. In the end, we did compromise and James' names are James Maurice, as you know, of course.

'He is occasionally called Morris, of course, which he does not mind as he is into motor cars.'

'James, is all well for tonight? Where are we seating and what time is the performance?'

'Grand Circle, second row for 7.30 so we'll have to eat
no later than six as I've organised Streamline to collect us
at seven, prompt; so, Mater, is there something simple to
eat?

'What's in the white monster which we can heat up quickly?
I'll light the gas and find a suitable bottle to celebrate.'

9 Walking Jane

Anne-Marie telephoned Jane to see if they could share some time
together and to compare their feelings and findings.

'Jane, let's try to have some time together. I have so much to
tell you and to find out about your state. James wants to see
more of you, I know; is there any chance of Harry joining us
for a good walk by the sea, perhaps?'

'May I call you back having spoken to Harry, assuming I can
get hold of him? Are you in Withdean with James' mother?
Maybe she'd like to join us, too.'

With both Jane and Anne-Marie expecting at much the same
time and in the same Brighton area, talking and exchanging feelings,
ideas, findings would be normal and to be expected. So, a walk on
the downs or by the sea should be lovely and hopefully Harry'd be
available.

Meanwhile, James and Anne-Marie were at a loose end and rather
stuck until they heard from Jane. The weather was calm and sunny, so
an outing was sensible. Anne-Marie was longing to have a sympathetic
ear to discuss her feelings, her body, and her expectations and of course,
her worries: all potential mothers have worries. Martha was not the most
helpful or maternal of women. The telephone rang . . .

'Hi Jane; what news?'

'Harry can make it but not until about half past two, today. I suggest you both come here and we'll all have a natter until we are ready to go out somewhere.'

'Sounds sensible. When we go, we'll have to take two cars as our Morgan is limited.'

'Not a problem; Harry has a Rover and it will seat four with ease. So come now, Anne-Marie.'

Jane and Harry had been looking at properties for sale but nothing fitted the bill perfectly. This aspect or that space or the state of the property was not satisfactory, so looking was getting tedious as both work and duty came first, so fitting in visits was plain difficult and the agents were finding this couple impossible to satisfy and worse, any visits had to coincide with the sellers availability arrangements, too. It took a genius to fix up viewings. There was no urgency as Harry had a rented property in Westmeston to use until the jig-saw pieces slotted together.

James being away and Anne-Marie renting in Maida Vale to be close to Dress Address, there was no need to purchase at this stage of uncertainty. There was also doubt regarding Harry: if the politicians fail to reach any agreement concerning Nazi Germany, he may be conscripted. On James' advice, Anne-Marie read The Times avidly and was keeping abreast of news—or what news was being published, anyway. So much was secret, as James was finding, that he could not communicate effortlessly with his wife; more than enough to put fatal strains upon any reasonable marriage. Luckily, both Anne-Marie and James were strong, single-minded and firm in the belief they had in each other. Simply, they were devoted to each other with a strength that was astounding.

Anne-Marie wanted to find out more about Jane and Harry.

The walk took the group onto The Downs, starting at Devils Dyke, where the hotel was closed and taking a circular route via Fulking and either, longer via Brook House and some agricultural land or, more directly towards Poynings and then up to the Dyke again. It depends upon how the two heifers feel, Harry suggested rudely.

'Jane, how are you feeling?'

'Well, I suppose. The doctor has given me the all-clear, so far.'

'No, I meant how do you find your body with all that's going on inside?'

'Strange. My breasts are much larger and are feeling quite firm. Mother had to take me to Hanningtons to get me fitted for new bras and she talked me into getting a stronger girdle thing to support the lump. I have two, so that one can be in the wash. My lump feels strange and I find I cannot do the work I used to do with ease.

'Also, I'll soon have to give up being too close to cows. Whilst I am supposed to understand them, they do not seem to have feelings for me, in my state. One barged into me the other day and gave me quite a fright. I'm reliably told that our bodies are well constructed and able to take quite large bumps without any cause for alarm. I am eating well but some things, like almonds, I crave. What about you, Mary?'

'Well, starting at the top, my hair feels much more wiry compared to the fine feel it had. This will pass, I'm told. I seem to worry and my brain misses James enormously and it keeps me awake. My upper shape is much the same as before but I have always had it firmly supported from below, as you are aware'

'I admire you for wearing such incredible corsets; my mother does, too and she urges me to do the same but I have resisted—apart from the supporting girdles.'

'I cannot tell you how much I enjoy wearing my foundations, as Jen calls them. They give me a really fantastic feeling of closeness, they buoy me up and prop me up and give me a much better profile and a straighter back as my shoulders are held back. I'd urge you to try.'

'I cannot wear anything like you do on a farm; I have to bend, take my clothes off to inspect cows rather intimately and how would that seem to a man-vet—unless it was Harry?'

'I'm finding my bump is getting larger almost by the day. Jen had me fitted with a special supporting corset which has four adjustment straps which I can manoeuvre in the morning when I get up and later, in the day, when needs must. It looks horrific and James really does like to help make changes that he thinks will help. In practice, it is a matter of trial and error. I do find that if I confine my charge too much, I get a good kicking. Work is not a problem for me and I still look much the same. I'm remarkably well contained and my clothes seem to fit as before but soon I will have to get into something called maternity wear that looks shapeless and ugly.'

'James, are we keeping up the pace to your satisfaction?'

'Yes, fine. Harry knows this area like the back of his hand and he is pointing out the farms he knows and we have already deviated from the sign-posted paths twice. Are you two in need of refreshment, yet?'

'We can go the quick way to Poynings and The Royal Oak or stop now at The Shepherd and Dog, here at Fulking. You three choose the route and the stop. I do know the area quite well, now.'

The walk and stops progressed and there was much conversation between the men and the women. It gave an ideal time to be alone with each other and to exchange intimate feelings and findings which would be difficult over a dinner table or even in a sitting room.

Walking time passed without a hitch and nobody became in the least tired but the upgrade towards the dry chalk combe of the Dyke was to come and there were no good pubs after The Royal Oak as the Dyke Hotel, where the Rover was parked, was closed.

'The view is spectacular.'

'Yes, it'll get better as we climb towards the Dyke.'

'Who has a good appetite—don't all put your hands up at once.'

Chapter Four

1 Seven years later, 1945

*M*ary stopped short when Martha called out for her. Her pain had returned and she needed some help with her medication which was supposed to help but really did only a little. Martha was angry, upset and wishing that Mary was not about although she needed her more than ever. Mary, herself was far from happy; husband gone forever—without even a good-bye. Peter was a form of anchor but was quite unable to give the affection his mother needed. His needs were demands. Martha had also lost her only son but was far too concerned for her own health and self-satisfied interests to care much, let alone to comfort Mary in her great distress. She did tolerate Peter but normally passed him onto her dailies who acted as loving childminders. Mary had reverted to her anglicised name and rarely used Anne-Marie, especially since August 1944 when the light went out of her life.

Mary had had another indication from mystical Eleanor. Mary did not call her own mother "Mater" but Martha was known as Mater by James and James alone. Nobody else dared to call her by that familiar. So, how did Eleanor know the familiar? How? Martha did not even know the woman. She did not even know her immediate neighbours because they were in trade. Martha knew few people locally as she had moved to Withdean to escape from her past. She bought a large semi-detached mock-Tudor styled house in the early thirties. Almost as soon as Martha had moved into her new bolt-hole—for that was what it was—Arthur Whitstable, who lived a mere hundred yards distant, called to see the person he knew as Martha Redgrave.

'Martha, how lovely to see you . . .

'I'm Martha but I do not know you; have you made a mistake, perhaps?'

'You are Martha Redgrave; Martha who lived in Rangoon with Francis Redgrave . . .

'I've never met you and you are mistaken. I'm Martha Compton. Sorry, I cannot help you. Good day.'

Arthur had not made a mistake. Puzzled, he could not understand why Martha had denied all knowledge of their past association. The Whitstables and the Redgraves were running rubber plantations in Burma: of course there was no mistake. What was Martha up to? Arthur was quite certain that he had not made an error and returned to his bungalow in Valley Close—a very confused man.

Martha used the local Rolph's Stores in nearby Tongdean Lane on few occasions as her dailies did most of the shopping and cooking. Her interests were theatrical and occasionally cinematic but she ventured into Brighton and regularly visited Hanningtons, the comprehensive general store where she researched fashions for herself. She had dressmakers and corsetières who came by appointment to attend to her personal needs. Shops and stores were a means for research, to see latest trends, to feel fabrics, to view colour schemes. On rare occasions she did make a purchase on her account and always had the goods delivered. Apart from the large store, Martha used to venture towards the Palmeira area of Hove or George Street looking out for interesting shops and quieter small outlets which displayed the unusual from which she dressed her home with furniture and soft furnishings.

She had a strange passion for small jade or carved ivory elephants. This dated from her time in Burma living as Martha Redgrave. She displayed her collection on the many shelves available, often above fire surrounds and window cills. Imported items such as these were valuable and likely to appreciate considerably; this Martha knew. She had a good eye for potential value and could determine the capable from the worthless. Occasionally, a daily dropped one whilst dusting shelves: it was always "a special one" and she was far from pleased. She and her daily staff were distant and distrustful of each other and the only link was via Peter who never quite understood why many came and left so soon.

Otherwise, Martha read library books and completed The Times crossword every day. Years before, she and James used to vie with each other to complete the cryptic clues within seconds of reading the text aloud. Between them, they'd feel they had failed if the entire puzzle had not been completed within twenty minutes. Targets were frequently set when they worked as a pair and the most recent was just 15 minutes, achieved once but not regularly—yet. Alone, Martha would expect about 30 minutes for completion. Illness affected her otherwise alert brain and she slowed and often could not see or work out the compiler's thought process. So, many puzzles remained part completed. Just one missed clue was the cause for great angst.

There was another fad—jigsaws without pictures which were maddeningly difficult to assemble. The pieces were made of four-ply wood and were quite chunky but beautifully carved and finished and every piece unique. Martha did it by touch, alone, and it would consume some hours of her life. James had disliked these blind jiggers. James was now just a memory.

Martha felt that she had lost her son to a wife who had stolen his affections for her. This was unforgiveable. Mother and son had been close but during his teenage years he had been at boarding school and rarely did he come home because his mother was usually away trying to keep her marriage alive. Holidays were usually spent farmed out with caring teachers who were glad of the company of an undoubtedly bright pupil. Longer breaks were spent in Paris with Father. Home with mother was a time devoted to what his mother wanted to do and never what her son wished to see or to do. Time was wasted doing endless puzzles and maybe going over a few papers that had missed clues. Was it wasted time? James' brain was incredibly alert for one relatively young.

Mary was the thief of her life and of her son.

Martha could not begin to forgive her. Not even when she produced a grandson in 1938. The war with Germany had also intervened and the few times that James returned on leave, his time was spent firstly with Mary and their son and what was left with his ailing mother.

Mary now lived with Martha, somewhat unwillingly but for essentially practical reasons. Work was not feasible as Peter had to be appreciated and Martha demanded attention and help with her illness and Mary was the solution. For Mary and Peter it was accommodation and food but not a real, loving, home.

The long and interesting garden enabled an escape from household chores and the incessant demands from her mother-in-law. Mary began to like plants and propagation of seeds and cuttings.

Peter had been sent to boarding school in Brighton where he was unhappy and always distressed when he had to leave home at the end of the usual school holidays.

Mary often pondered Eleanor's latest statement and whilst it was obvious that Martha would die relatively soon, she could not understand "and there's a new existence." This was puzzling, indeed. Whilst these mystical pronouncements were said upon chance—there was disturbing truth in what Eleanor had to say. She was right about James, right about Francis who lived a few doors away and right about Martha's pet name, Mater. There were more accurate hits. So, Mary did wonder more and more what was meant by the new existence which seemed a more definite change than a local event such as getting a new job in Brighton, or even London.

Mary's interests were fashion, dressing well—unless hiding and working in the garden when she did manage to dress the part and often worked with the gardener who came three days a week. Osborn was a Sussex man, aged about 50 but who had suffered gas attack whilst a sergeant in the First World War so was unfit for any active service in the second war. He had an instinctive love of plants, read journals and passed a great deal of wisdom onto Mary who thrived in his company but only from a gardening viewpoint. One thing that attracted Mary to Osborn was his distance; he never made any approach and he retained a master-servant relationship which was strange as they often worked closely together and discussed how and where to establish shrubs, which annuals were to go where and how they would be shown off to advantage. Together they maintained a flower cutting border towards the top end of the garden; dahlias were a speciality. Mary was an attractive woman but she never gave any hint whatsoever about her past and for Osborn her life was a closed book apart from the times when Peter came to see what was going on or needed his mother. Mary felt safe with Osborn; she did regenerate in his company; she learned a great deal from him and knew, just given time, that there was a great deal more which she could eke out of his knowledge and memories.

It was customary in Martha's house to dress and to appear smart in the morning seated for breakfast and certainly in the evening. When gardening, Mary simply had to change her outerwear but retained the customary firm corsetry. She felt un-dressed without the foundations which she wore—and had so done since the mid-thirties. There had been changes during pregnancy using special garments that provided adequate lower abdominal support. Newer designs and garments were now available and Jen and Mme Vermeuil had yet again worked wonders. Mary never went to anyone else and still had a close relationship with Jen who visited frequently and also attended upon Martha who was a long-term wearer of strong foundations.

Rather than having one long garment, she now wore three—an under-belt over which fitted a firmly laced corset that controlled her body from her lower ribs to below her hips and her suspenders. Her bust and the area below her breasts were held in place with a long-line brassiere that met and clipped onto her corset so as to give one long covering from shoulders downwards. Some boning was inevitable and adjustments were made by tightening and loosening the criss-cross lacings depending upon how firm Mary wished to feel encased. She felt closer to James when firmly dressed: he adored her foundations and by tightening her laces, she felt a strange closeness—one that could never be shared with anyone, not even Jen who did wonder why Mary demanded garments that were so firm and over-constrictive for her fairly slim figure.

Whilst she had a really good natural figure, she had lost some tone because of childbirth but the made-to-measure control garments were fitted so that her waistline was reduced by several inches from her naked form. Dressed casually, Mary frequently wore a polo-necked jumper, a belt to cinch her waist and a skirt or slacks worn with a pair of flat soled or garden shoes.

She and Martha would often dress each other for dinner. They never exchanged garments because Martha had a matronly figure whereas Mary was svelte and did not need to be contained at all: but she preferred it. She liked the feel that foundations gave her; the hug and the feeling of control and the sense of poise provided together with far better uplift for her breasts that could not be achieved with a simple brassiere. Stooping was managed: one had to bend from the knees rather than the waist. Sitting was better given a firm chair rather than a sofa but Mary had long been used to the necessary slight differences. There was never any discomfort unless there was a slight mis-alignment in one of her foundations.

Just like Coleen, Mary also had a gorgeous Victorian re-design made from violet satin which she frequently wore for dinner and almost always if she and Martha were to go out for a formal meal somewhere or out for dinner together. She could lace this by herself but if Martha was feeling amenable she'd ask for help and maybe help her mother-in-law correctly into her unfamiliar supports, too. Martha did like being held firmly, too. It took her to an age when rigid garments were *de-rigueur* and always worn every evening without question, however hot the weather. The women had sumptuous dresses that required the necessary foundations that provided a shaped form, small waist and rounded hips and well-contained breasts to be shown off to perfection but with due modesty.

Martha's illness was starting to have an effect upon her figure and she had to relax the firmness of her foundations—much to her disgust but her doctor insisted on a less harsh regime and the visiting corsetières, customarily Jen, adapted some and had new garments made, better to suit her needs.

2 The Ballet Years, 1946/48

Maybe Mary's "new existence" had arrived; she was back at work in London. Peter had been sent to a preparatory school and to Martha in the school holidays. Martha was often quite ill and the daily helpers would become child carers by default. Mary had left Coleen some time previously but was frequently retained for her advice. Bronnie had taken over the running of Dress Address admirably as Coleen had won several good parts and a few film auditions and was currently in California with a Los Angeles based studio where the producers were enamoured with her and her dress perfection. She also had a good relationship with a film director and it was likely that she'd stay in the US for some time. Her letters spoke of her happiness and her wish to marry soon and to have children. Much information came to Mary via Bronwyn who was always quite open with her gossip.

Bronwyn had a natural flair for running Dress Address but she did have ambitions and wanted Coleen and Mary to consider larger premises, more stock and staff to assist. Coleen asked her to wait until some real cash was likely when she'd need better to invest it. She had instructed Bronnie to start looking out for a larger shop and had asked Mary to liaise with her if she found anything likely.

Mary had launched herself into the theatrical world, specifically ballet and opera, where her expertise in locating materials for the stage became a by-word as Get Porter. She never used her married name. She had made good connections with the Jewish community whilst researching for Dress Address years previously and fabrics were her real *forté*. Tendrils grew and expanded; everyone within the trade knew of her and her business notes and cards proclaimed Get Porter. Her valuable clients were the theatrical couturiers. Living in London, again, she had found a flat-cum-small-office near Victoria so that travel to Brighton, to see Peter and Martha, was simpler.

She also retained an assistant, Vera, to look after her business and to take messages. Vera had been in the rag trade before the war and was a widow, too. She had some invaluable connections but was nearly sixty, so did not want to start a new business by herself. She and Mary had met via Coleen, strangely and had hit it off wonderfully. Vera lived in Battersea and often the pair would discuss the day's business over a snack meal in a small cafe that they habitually monopolised—and thus drew new custom, too.

Fabrics were quite hard to find in the post-war years. Imports were restricted but there were warehouses that had retained stocks that could not be marketed during the hostilities when staff were engaged in essential war work. Many firms failed for lack of money. Stocks were either stored by senior staff or directors or were impounded by debt and default agencies. Mary's task was to locate such stocks and she became remarkably successful at researching the formerly successful businesses that existed pre-1940. Much was lost in the blitz of course but like refugees valuable stocks were transported from the perilous city storage vaults to cellars and even private homes and garages. The day would come when such stocks could be converted into cash. Mary was a conduit. She gained a great deal for the Royal Ballet and Ballet Rambert who were the couturier's clients. Astonishingly valuable gifts were bestowed upon her for negotiating deals. Gifts were, of course, not financial but clothes, cases, handbags, lingerie and, on a few occasions, small jewellery gifts in pretty presentation cases which she and Vera treasured.

Living alone was not a happy experience. Married life had become a memory for Mary. She was bombarded with propositions but nobody came near to matching James, the true love of her life. She became rigid when approached and could sense an impending male assault without seeing the formation. She was an attractive woman; she dressed immaculately—she needed to be presentable and thus able to see those that mattered in the fashion business. As she was a valued conduit, the fact that she was unapproachable did not matter. Her reputation for being sexually unattainable preceded her and some may have ranked her to be lesbian. What mattered to Mary was that she was left alone and business was what really mattered to her, her clients and to the sellers. Time was also moving on; British stocks were starting to dwindle, other buyers had joined the search and it became necessary to travel much further to find satisfactory locations having the quality and quantity demanded for the London stage.

Vera was utterly invaluable. The pair thought alike, trusted each other and both had incredible resources based upon past work and the human connections which did seem to inter-mingle and thus lead to more threads which Vera exploited with charm and vigour. Her hours increased and she was at the flat-cum-office almost before seven each morning. Sometimes, Mary was so tired she was not yet up and dressed but this never proved to be a problem and then they'd enjoy breakfast together—just toast and marmalade with coffee or, if they felt dramatic, a croissant or two.

Mary had to see and to feel fabrics; it was never enough to hear the quality over the telephone or from suppliers' lists. This was an area that Vera did not feel as adept as Mary. Colour was also important and some demands were made for textiles to be seen under stage lighting which did alter the hue considerably depending upon the spotlight filters used. So, large samples were collected and taken to major theatres for critical consideration. This made for a great deal of taxi-travel as time was often short and material racks and rolls could not be held on appro for long—at least, a morning was feasible but longer was out of the question. This demand was telling upon Mary and demands were inevitably made by Peter and Martha, with her worsening illness, too.

3 Martha's Demands 1948

Martha became really ill. Mary recalled Eleanor's mad prediction many years previously. "You'll be glad when it's over; it's your Mater, this time . . ." Martha had demanded that Mary attend to her and to ease her pain, something that the daily staff and the new night nurses could not do. Martha was incredibly rude with her staff and a succession of nurses who looked after her in exchange for money and offered no human care beyond the minimum necessary. Mary knew Martha well enough to let insults slide over her. She did care; she was her husband's mother. She was devoted to James and missed him inconsolably. The connection between Martha and herself was almost a lifeline—though a one-way lifeline.

Exhaustion soon took over. Mary was eating badly; the doctor was extremely concerned for Martha's carer's health rather than that of his patient who was clearly dying and lingering, thus making others suffer in her last but one wake. Martha had been selfish for many years, of course. She was a miserable and unhappy woman. "You'll be glad when it's over . . ." Mary could not see the Eleanor connection. She had a job with endless work that also tired her considerably—to the point of exhaustion.

Martha had made certain that her wealth passed to her grandson apart from the Withdean house—and had made no bones about telling Mary what she had willed and entailed into a trust fund.

Martha died of an overdose prescribed by her doctor and Mary recalled, years later, that she was asked,

'Shall we make it six months or six weeks?'

Responding, Mary had said, simply,

'I am past caring.'

The doctor took the humane route and Martha died some six days later. Mary became strangely ill and suffered an almost complete collapse which her doctor—the same Dr Barnes who had looked after Martha for many years—just could not diagnose. In all probability, he thought it was a form of mental weakness. How wrong he was.

Again, with time and the benefit of hind-sight, Mary realised that Martha had had an influence over her young life even after her own miserable and painful death.

No doctor would have realised this was the cause of Mary's obvious illness that presented as total exhaustion. It really affected Mary when living or just staying at the Withdean property. Had life not again intervened, Mary would probably have died from an unknown complication or malaise; she was acutely ill with no organic reason.

Paul and his Swiss wife, Giselle lived next door to Martha's old home. Paul was in trade and socially unacceptable to Martha, so they had not communicated. Mary became coolly friendly with this couple who also had a son much the same age as Peter. Both children were confined to different boarding schools for much of the year.

Giselle was concerned for Mary who was clearly ill and listless and did not appear to care at all for Peter who was almost a prisoner, either at school or in his room when at home. Giselle's son never played with his age-related neighbour and remained separated by the timber dividing fence. Giselle and Mary used to talk over the fence but never went into each other's home. Martha had set the scene for this restrictive attitude to those in trade and it did affect Mary's relationship which was businesslike rather than neighbourly.

Paul was a bit of a mystic and one day asked Mary if she'd like to hear what the future said in the tea-leaves. This was a quaint way of suggesting she see a clairvoyant but the connection was not obvious. Even the Eleanor experiences did not manifest in "tea leaves". Giselle actively persuaded Mary to meet a member of Paul's shop staff for the essential tea party.

4 Three for Tea 1948

Tea time Sunday was almost forgotten. Vera was also under considerable work-strain and Mary's brain had become a distant relative of its former clarity and it was Peter, home from school, who reminded her that someone was coming for tea—just as the door knocker rapped softly. Standing there was a young woman who looked just like the dailies who had worked for Martha for many years. Olive Weeks was a local Sussex woman, plain but with a sparkle in her eyes but looking somewhat drab, dressed as she was in her funereal best for this important tea-party.

> 'Do make the tea with your usual Mazawattee leaves.' Olive suggested. 'Please use an extra spoonful, though, madam.'

Mary had failed to buy a cake but had managed to prepare some sandwiches but few were eaten as Olive was edgy or even a bit nervous. She was unaccustomed to meeting anyone of a professional class and she had few graces until she started on her mission. Then she became strangely really animated.

> 'What is your name?'

Olive asked of the young boy who had joined them for tea.

> 'I'm Peter and Mrs Compton is my mother but please do call her Mary.'

Olive nervously stated:

> 'Tea leaf reading, technically Tasseography, is considered to be a creative and intuitive form of divination dating from ancient China but the quality does depend upon me, the

seer or reader. I have to concentrate and maybe move away from myself so that I can interpret the symbols that present themselves. Clairvoyance is essential as is a quiet and peaceful atmosphere.'

Everyone had a cup of tea, taken as they would normally. Olive insisted that Mary shook the teapot before pouring and positively refused to let the strainer be used. As the first cups were drained, Olive gave the pot a thorough shake, not a stir, and some tea spilled out of the tea-pot lid.

'Please leave the spill; it's vital',

Said Olive, who had clearly taken charge of the proceedings. She was almost a transformed person and was no longer the nervous soul who had arrived. She must have studied her craft over some years.

'Please finish the last of the sandwiches.'

Olive requested of Peter.

'I need the plate to help me with the session. Would you please both drink all the tea just leaving the tea leaves in the base of your cups. Don't choke on the leaves and try not to eat them as they are essential.

'When you've finished just give your cup a gentle swirl and then hold it but you must not let anyone else touch it. Hold it tight, please.

'Shall we start with Mary's cup?

'That's interesting. I am not certain that I can see what I am staring at. It does not make much sense to me as you are living, here, in Brighton. I see water, and no, it is not the sea because I see you travelling under a vast section of water.'

Peter could not resist offering

'The Thames, maybe?'

'Much larger; I see a really large expanse of water. It's above you. I do not understand what I am seeing. You are both travelling and I see vehicles and a big bus or a train maybe, but there is steam forming so possibly a train but I cannot understand why the water appears to be in the sky: it is definitely above you and that is so clear but I cannot connect the scene to what I am being shown.'

Mary had been quite silent so far but was a little irritated by the strange journey being formed in Olive's mind. Mary recalled Eleanor's last statement when she had said "there's a new existence" which she had never managed to understand. Martha's death was all she had been able to muster in her mind.

'Please continue, Olive, this is fascinating.'

'You are going away and you are never going to return—either of you.

'Yes, Peter, you will be going, too.

'Peter, we will look at you shortly but clearly, you are both going away—separately—and it is clear neither of you are returning here.'

As Peter was at school, there was no possibility of an early release from the awfulness of his prep school which he hated so much. The bullying; the brutality of the masters; the spiteful teasing . . . So, he placed his hands on his hips and listened absently and thought how he could escape this mad tea party.

'Mary, I have some words of strong warning and you really must listen carefully. What I am seeing is so clear that I could almost touch the people that I see. Mary, you are with an older woman who is kindly and down-to-earth and another woman who is tall and elegant but who conceals a nastiness I cannot describe.

'All I am told to say is that you must be on your guard, Mary, and you must use all your powers to protect the woman standing in the middle who is being mistreated in some way that I cannot understand. It's not danger or violence but it appears to have a connection with money.

'I do not understand because I am not seeing a shop; it could be a farm as I see a field but there are few animals apart from horses. It must be country, somewhere.'

'This is quite incredible, Olive. I have no connections with the country and nothing to do with horses or the countryside. I was born in East Anglia and have lived in London for many years apart from those spent, here, in Brighton. Are you sure you have not muddled the tea-leaves?'

'May I have a look at Peter's tea cup?'

'Peter, I see you so much happier. You are enveloped in a mountainous area with trees and a huge watery area nearby and I also see rushing water as if it's a waterfall; definitely a waterfall with substantial noise, a rushing noise. Ah! I see young boys and I think it is a classroom with a lovely view over distant water. It is now less clear.

'My experiences do not work as well if we take another cup from the pot. That is about all I can tell you. I tend to forget what I have been shown so I'm unable to give you further help this time. Sorry.

'Please let me have the plate; it has been connected with our session.

'I see, strongly, a silver-haired woman, no, two women and one's frail and I am given that they are sisters; strange. I cannot offer you anything more. This is clear but I'm forgetting it already.'

'Please tell me a little about yourself, Olive. How did you learn to read the tea-leaves? Have you a few stories to tell? When did you know you were clairvoyant?'

Mary felt she had to know more and now that the tap was turned off she was more inclined to know what Olive had in her upbringing and work, maybe.

'I am a local girl and I work for your neighbours as a packaging assistant—blue sugar packets, mainly but I am learning to slice bacon with a big machine with a huge red and silver wheel and I'm terrified I will lose my fingers . . .

'So, you work in a grocery shop, do you?'

Peter asked having suddenly awoken at the thought of fingers being entangled by a vast machine.

Mary asked if Olive had been on holiday, recently and Olive said that she had never been any further away than Worthing, just a few miles from Brighton.

She had never been on a train and rarely travelled on a bus. It was clear that Olive had limited experience of life but she had managed to say so much in a short time and what she had said did not fit clearly with anything to do with her own experiences.

No; she could not have made up this as a fable. But, Mary thought, it simply cannot be true. She pondered:

'Peter in the mountains near water;

'All of us travelling with water above us, as if in a submarine, maybe;

'Strange ladies, one of whom must be watched with all my hawk eyes;

'And a horse.

'And two sisters, as well;

'And we are never coming back . . .

What utter nonsense. I will have a word with Giselle.

'Good-bye Olive, Peter will see you out. Thank you, and here is a little something for your trouble.'

Later, when the atmosphere had calmed, Mary was ready for bed as she was feeling utterly drained. She had felt really ill for some time, now, and she was not given to being ill. There was nothing physically wrong with her, as far as she could tell apart from the loss of her periods but Giselle had noticed that she looked tired, drained, overworked, maybe. Vera was noticing that Mary was not the Mary she had joined to help run Get Porter. Mary needed a holiday. That's it: a holiday.

In bed, Mary could hear a sharp rattling noise from the landing and then a crash which was clearly from downstairs. What's Peter up to, she thought. Getting up to investigate, she found Peter fast asleep in his bed. Downstairs, a picture of James, Mary and Peter had fallen from its hook and smashed. Strange.

5 Businesses 1945 - 1950

Mary had been too busy to meet Jane frequently in the past year; they had spoken and Mary had sent presents for Heather as she was her god-mother. They still lived at the flat in Westmeston as they had not been able to find what they were really seeking. Harry had not been called up, or conscripted but he had received forms that were not proceeded-with when returned; his work was seen as essential. Both were still working for the practice and soon Harry was to become a leading partner.

Jane's mother, Mavis, looked after Heather during the day and took her to kindergarten which she greatly enjoyed but was shortly to leave to go to preparatory school, The Drive School which was not far from the Palmer's home in Dyke Road Avenue.

Jane had been moved within the practice and she was now the office manager which suited her well; she understood the outdoor life, farming practices, the ailments, drugs and illnesses that were common and thus she had an excellent rapport with the clients who treated her as if she was a vet—asking questions which should have been referred. One of the few tasks she could not do was to sign prescription forms which used to irritate farmers who urgently needed some tabs for a sick animal and who had to await the return of a veterinarian. Fuses used to blow on occasion until Jane persuaded the Senior Partner to leave some pre-signed scrip's for emergency use by Jane. The farming community took to Jane and trusted her which was good for all concerned.

The operation of the practice had changed and was more up-to-date with methods and treatments. The War Ag—a government organisation—laboured farmers, vets, services and corn merchants unmercifully. Rules and strictures were considerable. Its proper name was County War Agricultural Executive Committee or CWAEC but War Ag in common parlance. County authorities were empowered to requisition land, premises, factories, farms and almost anything that was regarded as necessary for the post-war effort including demanding farmers to produce a specific minimum quota with a sanction in default. Properties and land for airfields, railways and roads were just requisitioned. Throughout Britain the War Ag was an all-powerful and demanding organisation and was much feared.

The Poynings Practice suffered as some farms were taken over and others gave up dairying and implemented beef rearing which cut income considerably. Jane had had to learn a great deal about land orders and practices and she had taken the time to become an authority on the majestic and lengthy rules that applied almost without question.

The local farmers used to telephone Jane to discuss any problem that had developed which they did not understand—a frequent problem. Then there was the Tithe Act which affected many farms with nearby church and parish connections—and more learning was necessary. Jane was becoming an authority and with a little more self-inflicted training would have made a good solicitor; something she and Harry seriously examined as she was vital in the farmers' eyes and several new clients had joined the Poynings Practice simply because of Jane's expertise, help, guidance and authority.

Harry's position had also grown and clearly he would become the Senior Partner within a few years' time. He and his wife were regarded in the same breath and both were regularly invited to dinner with clients which gave both an even better understanding of their professional work.

Harry worked part-time at the local abattoir where meat had to be examined and signed as fit for purpose and this took hours of his time. He was also the Auction Market Veterinarian and every week had to attend for most of a day to ensure that animals were well treated and that there was no obvious disease left to spread. Their combined income grew, of course and finding a property for them and Heather became a necessity. Something would turn up soon, given all the connections they had attained.

Mary did not feel relaxed with Jane and Harry because she was a widow and maybe something of a marital threat. Many, many widows felt the same stigma and Mary simply did not want to be a pawn in that game. However, Heather and Peter spent time together, more often than not staying with the Palmers in Dyke Road Avenue during holiday periods. Mavis enjoyed having two children—something she had been unable to do, herself. This was a blessing for Mary as it gave her a break and being cared-for by dailies was not ideal for Peter as they could never really leave the house apart from a short walk to the local Rolph's store in Tongdean Lane.

Mary was working with Vera and she and Vera had taken on a young assistant, ostensibly, to help Mary with her work but this also extended to helping Vera considerably. She was good on the telephone and, amazingly, could operate a typewriter fast and accurately which pleased Vera, so releasing her to do more of what she liked doing.

Bronwyn had found a new shop premises which she and Mary thought ideal. It was much larger and needed considerable fitting-out which Coleen's father dealt with admirably as he was a carpenter and a building works foreman. They divided the shop into three sections—the dress department which operated much as before, a large fabric department which had, literally hundreds of rolls of materials and textiles which Mary could have run admirably but was otherwise occupied with Get Porter. Lastly, Jen had joined Dress Address and she managed the new foundation-garment department with much admired displays of corseted mannequins which attracted custom. The new shop was almost like a department store and if it prospered, that would be the next move. It was still in the same area, but a street or two away. It had been able to keep its COV telephone number which was a blessing, but had to extend its phone network with more, unconnected, numbers which was a bind and they had to employ a telephonist who also operated one of the cash machines.

Coleen was committed to the stage and was living in Hollywood, and engaged to be married. She maintained a strong hand on the shop finances through a firm of chartered accountants which oversaw most fiscal duties. Their fees were extortionate.

Bronwyn now dressed like Coleen and Mary; Jen ensured that Bronnie was a real example for Dress Address. She stood out like a beacon wearing strong foundations which she had found to be a real asset as they gave her an authority over the shop assistants as she preferred to work by example. The practice of staff wearing some of the sales stock continued as it had been successful in the previous premises. The assistants liked this as, instead of a uniform, they modelled outfits and that improved their confidence and which helped sales. One by one, the general assistants also chose to be fitted by Jen, typically to improve their waistlines and firmly to support their breasts. Bronnie's husband was also delighted with the new shapeliness achieved by his wife.

Any new forms of corsetry that Jen found were tried by both Bronnie and Jen. The new Camp corsets were arriving and they made the wearer look trussed up with something called fan-lacing. These corsets were immensely strong and constricting and often could not be worn continuously for more than a working day. Both suffered for their cause and as they earned so much from custom resulting from their demonstration, they felt it to be worthwhile.

Many women had matronly figures and they were delighted with the results of being dressed so competently with their figures restructured so effectively. Jen gathered that some marriages were saved as a direct result; their wives looked so much better, dramatically improved after a lifetime of child-bearing and too much starchy food. Being so tightly and firmly enclosed also acted as a form of diet for many women, helping them to reduce a dress size or more—and dress sales rose as a consequence.

Coleen was still well remembered by the theatrical corps and many actresses chose to make appointments with Jen who had photographs of Coleen dressed in her wickedly powerful Victorian-style corsets. It was well-known that she had attained film parts as a direct result of being well dressed so it was natural that other actresses wanted to follow suit.

6 Wild Call 1950

Mary received a call from her friend, Nesta, who lived in Hassocks, urgently asking her to call to see her about a matter of life and death, or so she said. Nesta was severely asthmatic, so Mary naturally thought that she was literally on her last legs and agreed to visit her the same week even though she was pre-occupied with requirements for vital materials required for a forthcoming opera production.

'Nesta, you look remarkably well. Tell me more'

'I'm quite well, considering. The wheeze comes and goes but it's not me this time. I need to see you about my sister who is in a hell of a state. She fell off her horse and landed on her head amongst other places and, unless she is tended carefully, she may not survive. So, I thought that if you did not have much to do, you may like to spend a week or two with her.'

'I am literally overloaded with work and would normally love to help. I simply cannot, on this occasion. Do you have anyone else up your sleeve, perhaps?'

'Unfortunately, not. I have already tried everyone else I know, but as you are about the furthest away from where she lives in the furthest outpost of West Wales, I left you until last. So I am asking you because now I am desperate and on my bended knee if I could stoop so low.'

'I tell you what I'll do. May I use your telephone and I'll telephone my colleague Vera and see if she can cope.'

'Vera, I have a problem. How would you feel if I asked you to manage for a week or ten days without me? I know that we have to find the material for the ROH. Any suggestions?'

'Mary, you are in luck, a rep for Anstruthers came in today, and bought a sample that may well be right up their street. The cloth has a sheen, it is the right colouring, they have an adequate supply and I have asked them to reserve it for three days—Oh and its measurements are exactly within the parameters they require to dress the chorus of forty people.'

'Vera, you are a wonder. Could you have it taken round by taxi and if it's satisfactory—give them just 24 hours to make up their mind—then order it and ship their requirements to them. I assume they have enough rolls available. Bye.'

'Nesta, you may just be in luck. I need to farm Peter out somewhere—probably with my friends the Palmers who have a daughter of a similar age and it's half term. So, I'll arrange for Peter to be shanghaied. Tea did you say?'

'Mary, that is good news. Let me tell you what's happened. My sister, Olwyn keeps a riding school and a small farm plus a market garden. She was out exercising a horse and it was startled by a passing van and reared and threw Olwyn who landed in the road—hard.

'She staggered to a nearby house and asked for help and an ambulance came and she was in hospital for a few days and released after severe concussion. The horse found its own way to its stable. She has been really rather ill for some time since and is not looking after herself but, she also has a problem with a tenant who is being awkward and wanting to manipulate the lease. She'll tell you more.

'Here's tea and some sandwiches. Now, this is her address and number and she'll meet you at Carmarthen railway station and to get there you'll go via Paddington and it is quite a long journey.'

'How will she know what I look like?'

'I've described you in minute detail, my dear. Just let Olwyn know the train time at Carmarthen and she'll come for you in one of her cranky vans; one is a black ex-RAF ambulance and the other's green and a little rusty. Cars and such are still difficult to obtain.'

'So, what's Pembrokeshire like? I have never been. All I know is that Wales is full of coal mines and slag heaps . . . it sounds dreadful.'

'You'll find out, soon enough. There are neither mines nor slag piles so you'll be happy. It is lovely down there, the sea is close and there are several ancient castles and an island where they keep some monks and there's a mad poet who lives along the coast, in Laugharne according to The Times. Go, and have a good rest; you look as if you need it badly. I have never seen you looking so drained and out of sorts, Mary.'

'You are right. Since I have been looking after Martha, who mercifully died recently, I thought I'd be better with less of a workload—nursing, washing and keeping the other staff happy and protected from the bad manners Martha used as a weapon.

'It is strange; since she died and I have had far less to do and I won back my freedom, but my health has collapsed. I feel utterly exhausted, sleep poorly, there are strange noises in the house and the doctor says he is concerned about me and that unless something changes he said I will not survive much longer. He says medication will not help; just "do less" or I'll be in a mental hospital.

'And here you are—asking me to take on more.'

Peter was happy to stay with Mavis Palmer and Heather. Mary's business was running well with Vera and she did not have to worry, at all, about Coleen who had a superb manager in Bronwyn and, of course, with Jen, there too.

So, in August, Mary set out for Paddington and the express train terminating at Fishguard Harbour—wherever that was.

On the journey, the train went into a tunnel that went on and on for far longer than, say the Balcombe Tunnel on the London to Brighton line. Mary turned to a passenger and asked where they were.

'This is the Severn Tunnel and it runs for nearly five miles, most of which is under the River Severn., It is dripping wet inside the tunnel and water pours in constantly and you'll see the windows will look as if it's been raining when we enter Wales.'

'Thank you; that description has been surprisingly interesting. Have a good journey'

Exiting, the carriage window was smeared with rain and smuts. Mary suddenly recalled the tea party when Olive had said, so strongly, that she saw Mary travelling under water—much more than just going under The Thames. Mary shivered; what else had Olive said that would come true?

She became chilly and was really shaken by this unexpected event. How could Olive foresee this? And Olive had no experience of life beyond Worthing and what made it stranger was the fact that Olive had difficulty trying to describe what she had seen, clearly in her own mind. "The water appears to be in the sky: it is definitely above you and that is so clear but I cannot connect the scene to what I am being shown". How weird. Then there was the sisters connection . . .

Olwyn met her, as arranged at Carmarthen Station, and she had her shabby green van and no sooner had they sat in the elderly vehicle, which was quite noisy, chatter started as if they had known each other for many years. Of course, Nesta had spoken of her sister whenever Mary had been to see her in Hassocks. As sisters, Nesta and Olwyn were quite close but chalk and cheese characters.

'We have about thirty miles to drive from here to somewhere called Redberth which is near Pembroke; do you know of it?'

'Sorry about the racket but it is still impossible to buy good new cars. I am still a little deaf after my fall, so you may have to yell to be heard.'

'I feel quite relaxed, already, Olwyn. I have been feeling increasingly exhausted since Martha died.

'Strangely, it is as if she had a hold over me or a malign influence of some sort. I am a strong woman, not given to any form of lassitude but I have to struggle to get up in the mornings when I stay at the Withdean home where Martha died; if I stay in London, I feel refreshed when I wake. I feel better for the long train journey, too.

'Mary, I understand what you are saying—I understand without you having to explain the phenomenon. I am completely at home with what you have experienced and later, I'll tell you more.'

'Olwyn, what do you do at White Lodge? I know you have a riding school but little else; Nesta keeps her counsel regarding you and never gossips.'

'Thank heavens.'

'All I know is what I have gleaned from her, about your accident and you having some tenancy problems which worry you greatly.'

'Well, I have been unwell due to concussion and back-ache and have been unable to work for some time: the house is in a mess but the garden is OK because I have a helper. She lives with me so has been doing what passes as cooking, so we don't quite starve.

'The horses do need proper exercise but they are otherwise well. A local girl runs the stable and the school and we take in livery animals, mainly for those who hunt. I have about one hundred acres and take in another farmer's cows, keep some sheep and rear some calves; nothing exciting. A contractor makes some hay and does any work that is needed on the land—something called rotation. I'll show you round in the morning and you'll meet Slug.'

'Slug—is that a pet?'

'Pet, no. Slug is my nick-name for my garden helper who moves slowly and one day I said, rudely, a slug would move faster and it stuck. She is quite elderly and slow but thorough and knows market gardening backwards but she ain't no cook, as you'll find out. She can just about break an egg to fashion a lettuce omelette.'

'That sounds horrible. I can cook; thank heavens, so we'll see what I can fabricate.'

The road from Carmarthen was supposedly a trunk road but went through a mass of little villages such as Bancyfelin, St Clears where hold-ups were inevitable and on to Llanddowror where road-works are practiced day and night. Red Roses, the next named village is at a junction between Narberth and Pendine, so the lights take a month to change to green.

After a rough ride in an elderly van with a seat vastly unsuited to her firm foundations, Mary was stiff when she arrived at Redberth and White Lodge. It was dark but the van's lights showed a substantial property—far larger than had been anticipated from what either Nesta or Olwyn had intimated.

'Are you hungry after the journey?'

Olwyn asked.

'Let's see what Slug has left—if anything. This is the cook-house and, yes, do look; she has worked wonders for us and it looks like a beef and vegetable stew which just needs to be heated. I'll put the kettle on and see if the Rayburn has any heat left to revive the stock-pot. Then I'll take you to your quarters and we can relax.'

Olwyn did not appear to be unwell but concussion does not show; neither do back problems but Olwyn did not exert herself and thus risk a painful spasm. She did need looking after and it was clear that neither Slug nor Olwyn were home-makers let alone used to chasing a vacuum cleaner. Mary asked herself where the tenant came in; was that Slug, perhaps?

Doubtful. The tea-leaf reader, Olive, had suggested someone who was younger, tall and attractive and that differed from the Slug-description Olwyn had promoted. Anyway, Slug lived with Olwyn and tenants do not normally share a home with the landlord; a problem for later or tomorrow.

Mary was glad to divest herself of her tight corset which had formed several marks on her back and sides due to the long train and van journeys. On the whole, she really did like wearing really firm foundations which kept her body feeling secure and her breasts taut and well supported from below—essential when in the ancient van which had been a bread-delivery vehicle and was well rusted as a result. But, this evening, it was doubtful if Olwyn would notice Mary's shape and unsupported breasts whilst they had supper. Olwyn, herself, was dressed as if for the farm and even had wellington boots on over a pair of cord trousers. Her own figure was well, sagging somewhat. Clearly, she was not a follower of fashion. Was everyone in Wales similarly dressed?

The 'quarters'—a quaint name for a guest room—comprised a single bed, a chest of drawers, a sofa that had seen better days; a carpet that was positively ragged, but clean; a fireplace that made howling noises, a creaking wardrobe which had a cracked mirror and a curtain-less window which had some nets for security, maybe. Mary determined to make this room somewhat more homely if she could.

It rather depended upon how long she was needed at White Lodge. A day or two was sufficient given what she'd seen and heard so far. Maybe she'd telephone Nesta later to say she'd arrived and quietly speak of her first impressions if the receiver was not to be overheard. Nesta had said that the telephone was a Party Line, whatever that was and that it could be overheard by others.

Mary dressed for the part: she knew it was a farm, so came prepared with suitable rural wear and put on a chemise and basic underwear over which she wore a cotton dress and a cardigan; no stockings, so hopefully it would not be cold even though it was August.

'What do you want me to do for you whilst I am here? Nesta said you needed to be looked after and she inferred that you needed a nurse, maybe?'

'I don't need nursing; had enough of that fussing when I was detained in the local field hospital after the fall. I do need help with catering; the house that's begun to feel run-down and I want to discuss a personal problem when you've a moment to listen.'

'Is that a personal, personal problem or something to do with Slug or a tenant, maybe?'

'Oh, you have much to learn about what goes on here. I am fine in wind and limb, apart from my back, maybe, so do not need help with my water-works or anything—what did Nesta suggest I needed?'

'Slug is totally self-sufficient and she is not a tenant; she lodges in her quarters, and has been here for some twenty years, now.

'The Silvermans are a worry; they occupy a large but separate part of White Lodge and are choosing to be tardy with the rent and want me to renovate large portions before they will pay. Work does not need doing urgently according to my builder, Halbert, so they are being awkward and I am seriously worried. Is that what Nesta mentioned?'

'Nesta says little'

'the less the better, I feel.'

'She said my visit was really urgent and that if I failed to drop everything and come promptly that you'd shortly be dead.'

'She is naughty. I am reasonably fit, now, as you can see but the house and the Silverman tribe are getting to me and I sounded at my wits end when I recently spoke at length to Nesta.

How long have you got available to stay here?'

Mary started to tell Olwyn what she did in London and where she lived in Brighton and how she had looked after Martha during her final illness and what the Withdean house felt like, especially after the end when mirrors and pictures started to fall off their hooks for no imaginable reason. She had not really listened to Peter who said the furniture rattled, particularly at night, and that he did not like living there at all.

Work was what mattered to Mary, now that she was a widow. She and Peter were not very close as she had had to send him to boarding school and even in the school holidays she had difficulty finding time for him as business always loomed and took the forefront. When Martha was alive, she and the dailies used to be the childminders-in-chief. She thought about how Peter would manage down here, if she had to stay on for longer than a week or so at most—beyond that Peter would be an imposition upon the Palmers.

Back in her quarters, Mary slept admirably. Unusual for her, being in a new bed, new surroundings, new tiny noises, water in pipes, wind in the windows, bird noises up the chimney. But she did rest well, something that had not happened in recent years. Frankly, Mary was exhausted and it showed to those who knew her well, like Nesta. Olwyn had suggested breakfast at eight, so Mary set her inborn clock for six-thirty and it invariably worked well; she often marvelled how this bodily function worked. Animals, birds and even insects all had similar abilities.

Mary washed and found the water a little wanting, slow to flow and long before it ran warm: something else to sort in due course. Maybe this was what the tenants wanted fixed as well.

She decided to dress and stepped into her stockings and pulled them up to her thighs so that they felt smooth and firm on her legs: a feeling she loved with the latest labels that were now available. She had come with just one extra corset as travelling light was sensible. She pulled it up to her midriff and then wriggled so that the upper section enclosed her breasts comfortably. This was not a firm garment but a corselette or all-in-one made principally of elastic with a few stiffening bones and under-wires. Then she attached the six suspenders to the stocking-tops.

At last she felt elegant again and ready to face the world. To Mary, it felt as if she was intact and under control. She did wish she had brought one of the new firmly structured corsets that she normally wore when in London as these gave her a shape well beyond the capabilities of a mere corselette. If she had to deal with anything of a menial nature, the lighter garment would be ideal.

She dressed in a skirt and twin-set and went downstairs to the kitchen area, wondering what Olwyn would call this as in military speak; probably cookhouse. Olwyn was down and had just finished porridge and suggested Mary foraged for what she could find. Slug had just gone out—and as yet she had not met her. Cold stewed porridge seemed to be the best bet for the new girl on the block.

7 Sabotage 1950

Olwyn started to tell Mary about the house and how it was divided. As Olwyn lived alone, she felt that having a tenant would ease financial pressures and would make good use of the too-large house. Apparently, it had twelve bedrooms and several living areas, at least three kitchens and an uncountable number of loos and bathrooms. From what Mary had seen already, there was no wonder why it all looked a little depressed and in much need of care and attention. Something Mary felt she could assist with ease if Olwyn so wanted. But time was against Mary; she had a business in London that needed her expertise.

The Silvermans had started to tell Olwyn that the house was in need of expensive structural alterations. They felt that parts of their apartment were literally dangerous which both Olwyn and Mary felt was somewhat far-fetched and beyond the truth. White Lodge was a substantial and well-built property and these small mansions were not given to falling down overnight.

Mary wanted to speak to Nesta and she decided to await Olwyn going out to look at her horses before using the telephone. The instrument was in the room used as a study and she sat and picked up the receiver and heard talking and almost put the receiver back onto the rest.

But she did not; she listened, somewhat surprised. She did not know any of the parties to the call but she did understand what was being said. She was horrified and wished Olwyn was there with her.

"Look Mr Halbert, all I want you to do is to do as I have told
you, precisely and nothing more. To repeat myself, you go to
Miss de Vere and tell her simply that the whole section of her
house will fall down if she does not take immediate action

to shore it up and then to rebuild the wing of White Lodge. Understand?"

"Yes Mrs Silverman"

"Then you can start on the drains; they all run across the garden here to the pit. I want you to block them with cement so that they overflow . . ."

"But the mess and the smell . . ."

"Exactly, Mr Halbert. That is what we want you to do. Smell and mess and worry. You are getting paid well to do this, just do it exactly as I have told you."

"Yes Mrs Silverman."

And the telephone clicked and there was no further sound. Mary put the receiver down.

Now she understood why Nesta had asked her to go down to Pembrokeshire to sort out her sister's problems. Now she knew what she was up against. She could not speak to anyone on this telephone for fear of being overheard by the Silvermans as the line was something called a Party Line, used when the GPO had limited resources in some parts of the country, usually in the more rural areas where there were less available resources.

Mary found Olwyn in the kitchen garden working with an elderly lady, she assumed Slug.

'Hi Mary, come and meet Slug–Jean. We are preparing the ground for spinach and chard seeds. Want to help?'

'Olwyn, I need to speak to you before I forget what I have just heard'

'Oh? What's the problem, Mary?'

'It's back at the house; I need to see you there, please'

Mary recounted, as best as she could, what she had inadvertently heard. Olwyn was horrified that she had listened and chastised Mary roundly for daring to be so rude. The Silvermans were her friends and her tenants and were not to be discussed as gossip overheard either by accident or on purpose.

Anyway, what was said over the telephone was private. Olwyn stalked off and Mary was utterly chastened and mortified. Nonetheless, she had heard what she heard and determined to do what was right in her mind even if Olwyn had other ideas.

In the war, it was quite normal for information to be obtained by all evident means and the telephone system was known to leak like a sieve and conversations to be overheard by spies, authorities, government or whoever. Mary felt a little better with this realisation—even the government had listening posts.

She returned to the study and found pencil and paper and wrote an account of what she'd heard. She was certain that it would be of use, later, if not sooner. When the drains overflowed would be sooner, she felt. And who would have to put matters right, and who would have to pay? Olwyn, of course. Mary decided to walk into Redberth and use a telephone box there. There was sure to be one, somewhere.

She'd confide in Nesta and see what she had to say—and hopefully advise.

Nesta was horrified. She knew of Halbert who was the local builder and he had done work for Olwyn whenever she had needed his services. As for the Silverman family, Nesta had little or no time for them. She was certain they were trying to take over the whole of White Lodge by hook or by crook. More by crook, she reinforced. Nesta suggested that, by using the trusted Halbert to impart devastating knowledge of building failure to Olwyn, he'd be believed. Further, if the drains failed, as they would, she said her sister would have monumental costs that she could not really afford.

Nesta decided to call in some artillery. Olwyn was being perverse and talking to her would only result in a rebuff for her too. A few days later, Olwyn's cousin, who lived in Carmarthenshire, telephoned and said he'd be in the area and wanted to discuss a family matter and he'd be there at noon on Thursday. He said, mysteriously, that he also wanted to meet Mary.

> 'My cousin, Jack, is coming and wants to meet you; do you know him, Mary?'

> 'No. Who is he and what does he do?'

> 'I thought something was fishy when he wanted to see you.'

Must be something Nesta has said–Jack must be her cousin, too, Mary presumed.

> 'Quite possibly; Nesta has been putting her oar into things again. I must talk to her.'

Jack de Vere had been a colonel in the Grenadiers but had now returned to run his estate and acted for the military only in an advisory capacity for the Territorial Army. Arriving just as he said, at precisely noon on Thursday, Olwyn was at her most prickly and thoroughly alarmed that Jack took Mary aside as soon as he arrived and had a meeting alone with her lasting about an hour. He asked Mary to stay whilst he spoke to Olwyn but not to say anything unless he asked her; he knew his cousin was high-minded and it might be difficult to make her see sense.

> 'Olwyn, you are in severe trouble. Your tenants are making difficulties and their actions will cost you thousands . . .

> 'Jack, you have been listening to Mary and to what she has inadvertently overheard. I want nothing to do with dishonesty

and kindly, you may take Mary to Carmarthen Station and put her on the next train for Paddington.

'Mary, please go and pack and await Colonel de Vere.'

'There is nothing dishonest in overhearing a party line. Intelligence services used the telephone as a major source of important information during the war . . .

'We are not now at war, Jack.'

'You are at war with Mrs Silverman, Olwyn.

'The sooner you listen to what I have to say, the less their activities will cost you; how well do you know Halbert, the builder?'

'I'd trust him with anything and there is no way he'd go behind my back. He has served me well for years.'

'He has two masters, now, Olwyn; one who can afford to pay and one who cannot afford the consequences. This is what we are going to do. I have already spoken to Halbert and asked him to be here at two o'clock, precisely.

'He'll be here, mark my words. I told him you have a problem with the stables after a horse knocked over a support beam in its pen and that the hay loft looked like it was falling in. I will deal with him when he arrives and want no argument from you, Olwyn. Now, let's find something to drink and see if there is anything in the larder.'

Mary went into the house, feeling mortified.

'That is grossly unfair. I've heard that Mary has come at Nesta's express wish and to look after your interests because she knows that something is up and something's not right.

'You have some serious apologising to do but from what little I know of Mary, I think you have a really excellent witness to what took place. She could never have casually made up what she told me when we briefly met, and further, what she told me tallied almost to the letter with what Nesta had told me over the telephone. I am used to dealing with military intelligence and when I hear the same story told by different individuals, I listen for errors and variations in the underlying events. In this case, I have nothing to suspect, except for Halbert and the Silverman woman.'

'But it was Mary who must have told Nesta and Nesta told you.'

'You seem to forget that I had a short and valuable meeting with Mary as soon as I arrived and I was alone, purposely, so that you could not intervene and try to upset what she had to tell me. If Mary had been making the matter up, then she should have had a job with military intelligence. 'Mary was unbelievably accurate and when you realise she has never met the principals in this story, she has no reason whatsoever to make up a fictitious turn of events. What has she to gain? Nothing. Now, let's go in and await Halbert over a cup of tea. You can then bring me up to date with your life, Slug and the animals.

The door bell rang at a few moments before two pm. Jack asked him to come in and he, Olwyn and Halbert went into the kitchen and Jack asked him to sit at the table as he had a problem to discuss.

'Do you normally work for Miss de Vere, Halbert?'

'Yes Sir, I do and have done so for some years.'

'Why, Halbert, are you having discussions with Mrs Silverman and her husband?'

'I am not, Colonel, Sir.'

'Halbert, May I read you a transcript of what was heard over the telephone by way of intelligence?

'Shall I start or would you like to re-consider the serious position you will find yourself in default?

'Halbert, you have denied discussions with Silverman family. I now require you to tell the truth or this matter will end with a call for the Police to attend. What, now, have you to say in answer to my repeated question? Halbert, are you having discussions with Mrs Silverman and her husband?'

'I am in the wrong. I have had some calls and talks with the Silvermans and I fear I have not been truthful or fair with Miss de Vere and I am deeply sorry.'

'Halbert, why have you gone behind my back? I have used your services and trusted you for years, now. What have you to gain by this tom-foolery and, apparent nonsense by the silvermen?'

'Well, it's like this, Madam. I've known that you have a lot to do here; this is a big property and I know that whenever I give you a bill, you choose to pay with post-dated cheques. Silverman offered me five thousand to attend to you and to tell you that there was a defective beam in the West Wing and that, if it failed, you'd be forced to rebuild much of the house and the conservatory. The drains were an afterthought. The cess pit is just beyond the house and a serious blockage would be quite costly to put right and that would earn me a few bob more with the Silverman's help and guidance.'

'You have seen me taking a written account of your statement, Halbert. Is there more that you wish to say before we consider asking the local force to call on you with a view to their taking proceedings for fraud?'

'Yes, they told me that they want to take over the whole of White Lodge and that if they could force Miss's hand they'd see me right in the future'

'Now, Halbert, please leave and I must caution you not to speak to anyone, particularly the Silverman family or their lawyers or, in the alternative, I shall see that you serve a long time as a guest of His Majesty. Do I make myself clear? Do I have your total understanding of the seriousness of your behaviour, Halbert?'

'Yes, Colonel. I shall say nothing. May I apologise Miss de Vere?'

'Just leave, as Colonel de Vere has asked, Halbert.'

'Now, Olwyn, go and find Mary.

'I wish to see her, again. I think it is high time for you to apologise, this time. According to cousin Nesta you really do need her here and I think Nesta has her head firmly screwed on to her shoulders; it is a pity, only, that she is not well enough to travel down and to sort you out better than I am able.'

Olwyn was so upset by the turn of events; she was in tears—quite unlike her normal self as she had been commissioned in the women's army during the war and knew what went on behind the scenes. But, she was high minded and preferred to trust her instincts rather than evidence at times. She had trusted the Silvermans both as friends and excellent tenants. It hurt her dreadfully that she had been so abysmally let down.

Jack required Olwyn to write a letter to Silverman giving him just fourteen days fully to move out, but requiring him and his family to move away and into hotel accommodation within the next twenty-four hours and never, ever to set foot at White Lodge again for any reason.

Further, contractors appointed by Olwyn would be tasked to remove all furniture. In default the matter would be taken much further . . .

Jack suggested that the wholly independent Mary should be asked to ensure that all their property was removed, loaded and transported carefully.

> 'Mary, I have been sorry that you've been put through this scene. I am well aware you are still upset but Cousin Olwyn now understands that she needs a rock, like you, to support her through a number of difficulties and hopefully to try to help her get this lovely property into good running order.
>
> 'Do you think you can do this for me? Here is my card: you are to telephone or write if you are ever in any difficulty with any of the de Vere family. I thank you for taking the sound and wise action you did. I think that you know that once the de Vere family have dealt with the Silverman family, no further action is likely, unless . . .
>
> Jack took it upon himself to hand the letter of notice to quit to Mr Silverman and to ensure that they knew the situation they now found themselves and that a charge of fraud would be upon them with vengeance if they did not quit and leave for an hotel with immediate effect—and never to come to White Lodge ever again nor to make any contact with any of the de Vere family, their staff or the contractor, Halbert.

An hour later, Jack saw the Silverman's car leave.

8 Into the Melting Pot

Mary and Olwyn were wary of each other, with good reason.

Even so, much needed to be done; the financial situation required serious consideration as income had been lost upon the tenants' departure. Neither the riding stables nor the market garden produced much income but letting some acres from the farm did bring steady income but hardly enough to sustain the large property and inevitable repairs and expenses.

Luckily, Olwyn was reasonably forthcoming about finances and the pair put their heads together to try to devise a workable plan for the future. Olwyn admitted that she lost her cool because she was concerned at the potential loss of income rather than the potential cost of repairs.

She had no idea that the whole scheme was devised to force her out of her home and to reduce the price if she were forced to sell.

White Lodge was a lovely property but it did need a great deal spending on it to make it attractive and presentable. It would sell either as a whole or in parts—the land and the house separately. The house could be used as a guest-house or maybe as a small hotel but the cost of conversion and the location ruled that out of the question. Maybe, part of the large building could be divided into three or four apartments for rent. This would cost money to arrange. Running a business in Pembrokeshire was not realistic for geographical reasons but it was in an area noted for its beauty, the coastline, its ancient monuments and castles and all this affirmed, in Mary's and Olwyn's minds, that the best option would be to realise the cash tied up so that Olwyn could attain an income.

There was a new oil refinery being built in Milford Haven and there could be senior engineers needing suitable homes. Olwyn talked to both Jack and to Nesta and the decision to call in Frank B Mason as selling agents was obvious. There had been a narrow escape from the Silverman deceit as they would have purchased but at a much reduced price.

Olwyn asked Mary for her opinion about making a living. A new home—somewhere—few contacts, no real occupation except running a loss-making riding stable and a market garden which were both judged out of the question. Mary had a business that was thriving but was undercapitalised and she hated the property in Withdean.

Olwyn was about as far from up-market fashion or textiles as imaginable: she dressed for the farm and the country and almost entirely lacked dress sense. What was clear was the dependency that Olwyn had seen in Mary. Nesta had seen her sister's need for someone competent: Mary. Had Mary not arrived in the nick of time, Olwyn would have muddled on, slowly but surely losing her capital tied up in the property even if the potential fraud had failed or been detected.

Mary looked into Olwyn's personal interests, hobbies, ideas, even her dreams and past occupations, which were effectively negligible as she had been supported by her father who owned White Lodge before his death. His capital was divided between his children but Olwyn took on the property as part of her share. Only time will tell if this was a sensible decision: at the time it did seem the wisest course as Olwyn was making use of some of the land and the stables.

Thoughts were now vital. The future for Olwyn was thoroughly abstract and Mary decided to set out a list of possibilities.

At 46 with no previous experience apart from being a third officer in the forces, employment looked unlikely but re-training was entirely within range. She had had an excellent education in Cheltenham but did not attend university as this was not realistic for women in the 1920s. Interests included medical and health practices but, of course, the professions were out of the question. This left what were termed fringe interests such as nutrition, homoeopathy and improbably, chiropractic or osteopathy. Olwyn had always been interested in faith healing but that could be practiced at any time but lacked the necessity of income as those in need never felt the obligation to pay for the help and service they somehow assumed was heaven-sent. Practicing as a nutritionalist maybe the best option and courses were available. This left future location as an essential consideration.

Mary had, by now, been in Pembrokeshire for three weeks and it was time to return to London, Vera and her work. She dreaded returning to live in Withdean and Peter was a worry, too. School started soon, so that was one less worry to be of concern.

Olwyn had, even in this short time, become dependent upon her new friend and Nesta encouraged her to do her best to maintain a close connection although neither could see the future and the lie of the land.

It would take some months to sell White Lodge; Slug was there to give support and company as well as a modicum of security as living alone was never wise in a large property. To be fair, Mary was lonely and her inner being was starting to mutter and to call for a man in her life, again. She had been so fortunate to have a brilliant husband and really asked herself whether this was repeatable.

Olwyn told her that there were many fish in the sea but she had never married and her experience was limited. For her part, Olwyn was not interested in sharing a small home with any one person. It felt alien for her; so far, her own company had stood her in good stead.

Her best advice was to do what she had found when confronted with impossible problems; simply to pray and to ask for guidance from those above. She had done this when she spoke to Nesta, saying she felt desperate and Nesta took action and suggested Mary. Jack had turned up when her life seemed again to be in crisis and, of course, she had asked what she called the-powers-that-be for help but Mary was not involved in that request. Mary was not into any form of prayer and did not really understand the "powers that be". She'd watch and see if that line of help worked.

Mary had inherited Martha's home in Withdean but she loathed living there as it was full of unhappy memories and, according to Olwyn, was spooked with a poltergeist and her best option was to find somewhere to rent having sold the semi-detached mock-Tudor home awash with its troubles; another decision taken.

Jane and Harry were still unmarried but had found a superb property in the village of Steyning and promptly offered a temporary home to Mary to be custodian as they could not move for a few months. It would help because considerable work needed to be carried out and redecoration was essential and Mary would be well able to keep a watch.

Brighton agents were instructed to sell the Withdean property. Properties were sought to rent in London. A deluge of property for sale and to rent fell through the Steyning letterbox for Mary.

Both Jane and Mary had children of a similar age and both were at boarding school. Jane was again pregnant and would soon have to stop her work for the veterinary practice where Harry was now a senior partner. So, a nursery room was needed, as was a refitted kitchen, revised heating and new electrical wiring throughout the Steyning property.

A multi-disciplined building contractor had been engaged and their site agent took over the day-to-day running of the refurbishment contract, so releasing Mary to conduct her own business and yet to offer security at night and weekends for Jane and Harry who came over frequently to provide company and to discuss progress.

Life did seem to be on the change for Mary. She decided to do as Olwyn advised and she asked for help in her own way. Coleen was rarely in the country as she was securing many parts in films in Hollywood and she was likely to marry, soon. Bronwyn and Jen were still running Dress Address in London and this was proving to be an incredible investment and Mary sometimes thought whether she should copy the scheme: she had the experience.

She added to the deluge of post by asking for details of commercial properties to let in the Home Counties. Thoughts. Sometimes, thoughts and ideas just wasted time. Mary had an excellent business but she depended upon the aging Vera and locating fabrics was starting to be less demanding as more new cloth was being imported. Just how long could her unusual business be required? Maybe a new shop was not such a bad "thought".

Pity one could not ask for Men for Life, she reflected. Maybe she should ask "them above" for help. She had to cease being the Professional Widow.

9 Seeking and Finding 1951

Mary decided to ask Bronnie and Jen out for a girlie evening and both jumped at the chance. Where shall we go? Mary needed to be close to Victoria so that she'd be able to travel to Steyning, so all agreed to meet at the Grosvenor Arms and the Underground was also convenient for Jen and Bronwyn.

Mary was longing to know more of Dress Address' fortunes and they both told Mary how a simple shop had become much more like a store and they had even been able to secure a lease on the shop next door which Mary knew about, but had not had any active involvement. Jen had fitting rooms upstairs in what was a flat above the shop and this suited her specialised business where privacy was of paramount importance for a corsetière.

There were seven sales employees, now, some part-time but most with a precise knowledge of the fashion business, and a telephonist-cashier. Bronwyn was the overall manager with Jen taking over during holidays or occasional illness. Coleen was rarely to be seen but was always welcome when she returned to England for short visits and for a longer period when she was filming in West London for some weeks. She found the income from the store to be excellent and it smoothed out the ups and downs of otherwise lucrative filming work in Los Angeles as well as at Pinewood.

Jen had made arrangements with more corset makers as Mme Vermeuil had also taken on other fitters, so could not cope with all the work brought in by Jen who also had good business connections with Camp, Spencer and Spirella who were bespoke makers of superb corsets. Women—and occasional men—came like moths attracted by a bright light to Dress Address which had developed a reputation for providing excellent advice for a demanding clientele.

Jen, of course, did not have to waste time travelling to and from locations all over London as was her custom when she started helping Coleen and Mary and many others. Her diary was filled with appointments for fittings with ninety minute intervals throughout the day and the last would often be after office work finished in the City and six pm and seven-thirty were the most popular. These City clients were also comparatively well-heeled and had no worry about spending considerable sums on the best new foundations which were necessary to co-exist with the latest fashions coming onto the market from France and America.

This era was to be the renaissance for corsetry which had almost died with the start of the First World War and had literally flapped around in the thirties and the forties had impossible supply restrictions overcome only by makers such as Mme Vermeuil who had managed to acquire and to store good stocks of suitable fabrics and necessary hardware components in the thirties.

Jen so enjoyed seeing a figure walk in and the later leave dressed superbly in firm foundations and a client literally beaming with delight at the transformation which was eminently achievable and functional. When an appointment was made, she did insist that a selection of outer-wear was carried in a suitcase, together with suitable shoes to match. Jen explained to Mary:

> 'Fitting is becoming much more than just showing what was feasible. Integrating the finished ensemble of shoes and clothing with suitable corsetry to enhance their bearing and the hang of their dress is essential.
>
> 'Clients see themselves before and after fitting as they would be seen in public. Where else can they get this service?
>
> 'I frequently see the same customers at least twice quarterly and they never go elsewhere.

'Some first visits, all of ninety minutes duration, are spent discussing what is needed, where they see their own problem areas and no fitting is carried out. Of course, I show them examples of suitable foundations and discuss what it may feel like and how best to wear it and when to remain suitably dressed. A corset is not for occasional use or for part of any day and they need to understand the necessary regime. This gives customers great confidence and secures them as clients of Dress Address, indefinitely.'

Mary listened carefully and said:

'Jen, you have brought your work into focus; of course clients appreciate the difference they can achieve by seeing you as opposed to grabbing something off a Marks & Sparks rail. The difference between an off-the-rail garment from any shop and a personal fitting is profound and having seen themselves when they walk in and later . . . walking out makes clients' smile. I know; I recall your first fitting with me when you took such care and time did not seem to matter. My comfort and confidence was all that mattered to you.'

Mary changed the subject and asked for their advice on her future as well as ideas they might have for man-location as she was now approaching forty but still had eminently good looks and an astounding—well corseted—figure.

'I am starting to feel lonely. When there is a form to complete, it seems to ask "profession" and being born naughty, I respond "widow". I am paid—a pittance—for being a widow, so the answer is not as asinine as it seems. The truth is, I am feeling my age, feeling lonesome, feeling discarded and I now regard myself as a Professional Widow.'

'You have a fantastic business, Mary. You helped me so much when I first joined Dress Address and I'd never describe you as "lonesome or discarded". You have so, so much to offer the right man and I'd urge you to start to keep your eyes and ears open. You admit you have been repelling all comers in the past. That was quite right; you were then a new widow but, again, upon your own admission, you are now a professional widow and it's time you were not.'

'Thank you, Bronnie, for that vote of confidence.'

Jen had few ideas as she was mainly involved with married women but Bronnie also had suggestions that were to prove interesting.

'Mary, you do need to expose yourself to meeting new people and not just those you see at work. New contacts are never, ever, going to knock on your door. You must knock on theirs but at a public location where classes or lectures are held.

'Bridge is a possibility but it's played by pairs, so not suitable for your purpose—to meet a suitable man. You need to select evening classes where there could be a good chance of there being single men so dressmaking and cookery are not on the menu. Try art appreciation or book discussions, just as examples.'

Then Jen had a spark of enthusiasm:

I have a regular customer who never, ever dresses without his corsets. He's a widower, I think quite handsome, well dressed, has a career and is always keen to get information on the latest foundations—few are made exclusively for men, but he has his expertly adapted for his use.

'Jen, who does this man work for; do you know by any chance?'

'An engineering company, I believe, but I cannot say much more than that. I also know that he is based in the City and lives in . . . I'd have to look in his file for that and my records are confidential.'

'Interesting; we'd seem to have a common interest. Just why does he wear corsets—unusual for a man, today? I know many military personnel wore them in the late nineteenth century but not nowadays, except in special circumstances. Did he have a back injury, perhaps?'

'Mary, you are probing a little too deeply. If you worked for Dress Address, that might be all right.'

'You have a telephone contact number, Jen?'

'Obviously; but I cannot let you have that.'

'No, I would not ask but you could make contact and ask him if he'd care to meet a fellow enthusiast. You could ask him to come to your studio to see some new developments and then have a quiet talk and watch his facial expressions.'

'Well, I could but I'd like to sleep on it and then decide. See what my mood says to me.'

'Jen, its time I had a consultation, anyway. I'm not entirely happy with these new elastic girdles—all-in-ones, I believe you call them. They are firm but the feel on my body is so divergent from the feel of a rigid corset.

'The elastic garment constantly squeezes me whereas, once in position, a rigid, laced corset relaxes its pressure and I find that much more agreeable although I am fully encased. I suppose I like being squeezed less than before.'

'Mary, I totally sympathise with you'

Said Bronnie, with some feeling, adding:

'I am never without my rigid corsets, nowadays in the shop. I am expected to be formally dressed and Coleen is always delighted to find me thus when she calls.

'Mary, strange you should prefer the rigidity of the older styles.'

'Having tried the elastic girdles I do agree; they are not for everyone or for every occasion. They are better worn where a woman has to undertake some active work as part of her job. A rigid corset is not suited to manual work: bending, stretching or lifting even though the spine may be supported to some degree.'

Jen said:

'It is why I take so long interviewing my clients and when they understand, they really do appreciate the service I offer.

'Mary, I'll telephone you to make an appointment and we will discuss what is best suited for your frame, in a couple of days, probably. But it will cost you.'

The evening had been a great success and there had been a lot of catching-up and it was time to take transports back to home and families.

§§§

Mary thought about the handsome, widowed engineer but had to leave this line of enquiry entirely in Jen's hands. Whatever Jen suggested, Mary did not want to be introduced directly to him; just not the way she worked or felt. She recalled, sadly, the way James had been able to introduce himself on the train all those years ago. That meeting was so natural and was not contrived. It formed one of her most precious enduring memories. James never knew but had he asked to see me more in the short taxi ride, the answer would have been an immediate yes. Adoration on sight. Could it ever happen again?

Bronwyn's suggestion for widening the field did appeal to Mary. She did meet a number of textile representatives and some businessmen as well as many connected to the theatre and opera.

One could not walk around with a notice stating "Hunting" and it was much more the man's duty to ask rather than for a woman to mention need.

Evening classes were an ideal route to be able to meet without having to sell one's self. From past experience of meetings, Mary recalled that when a group introduced themselves the patter typically ran "I am Johnnie and I'm a surveyor and live in Pinner with my wife . . ." or "I'm Jessica and also live close to Pinner and I'm interested in making the most of our garden . . ." Such personal introductions would enable Mary to find out, who was single or a widower—at least, it would furnish a few clues.

Bridge was popular but Mary had never taken any part. Life had been too busy, then there was Peter to consider and anyway, she realised that most bridge players had partners and the game did not really suit singletons . . . and she was a paid-up member of that club. But, there must be bridge schools where those interested in starting met and learned the cards; A possibility, perhaps.

Mary decided to look for classes and bridge schools being held in the Steyning area, close to where she was currently living, and sought to find those that had artistic merit such as Watercolours for Beginners or Advanced Dressmaking—but that would not bring in many men, so dressmaking was abandoned. Musical Appreciation was a good possibility but, again, this genre would not appeal to men in their thirties. French for Beginners or Business and Management or Sales Marketing courses would appeal to younger men and women. So, it was a question of finding out what classes were available and then filtering out the non-starters such as dressmaking, history or cooking classes that would appeal either to women or to older men. She thought that, even with so many war casualties, it was not simple to locate available men.

Quite by chance, she recalled seeing a board in Kensington—in Adam and Eve Mews, rather fortuitously, which stated it was a "Fellowship Agency", a quaint name; was it for meeting people? She decided to call there, when next in Kensington.

Back in work routine, Mary was travelling all over London seeking materials for enquiries that Vera had amassed. She had time to think and to wonder what to do as the Withdean property had been sold—quite quickly for about £25,000. She no longer felt tired and washed-out living in Steyning. The problem with Jane's new home was the incredible dust that accumulated and Mary was for ever having clean and re-clean surfaces. Even her bed felt coarse from dust and it was nowhere near where work was being carried out.

A volume of post came every day and Mary tried to sort the wheat from the obvious chaff, often during the train journey up to town. A change at Horsham was always necessary as there was no direct line and papers frequently became muddled during the platform manoeuvres. In all probability, Mary thought that renting again would be preferable as she had no idea where to put down her permanent roots.

Peter would be finishing at prep school and would need a senior school, somewhere. His fees were met from the Trust Fund set up by Martha upon her death. Maybe where his father went and became Head Boy in the early 30s, provided they did not entertain barbaric caning practices, as in the past.

Peter was not at all happy at the Brighton prep school and his reports started to be poor for his age. He was working but was so unhappy and he found he was watching his back too much to concentrate.

A story horrified Mary.

Peter was in a classroom that had tiered levels and the master had a long oak table in front of the large blackboard which stretched the width of the classroom. The lesson was Geography and Masson had drawn a crude map of England and Wales onto the blackboard. He started to ask boys what fish were to be found off the South West, in the Bristol Channel, near the Dogger Bank and he came to Dover.

> 'You, boy, pointing at one of his charges, what's to be found in the Channel narrows, Boy?'

> 'Ker-kippers, Sir?'

> 'Down here, you insolent brat'

Masson placed the boy's head under the end of the oak table and walked back a few paces and took a short run and kicked the poor miscreant until he came rolling out at the other end of the long table.

This story, told by Peter but reinforced by a fellow classmate, was quite enough for Mary to decide upon change. She reported what she'd heard to the Headmaster who flatly refused to listen. She approached other parents that she knew and word spread. Several mothers took their children away; the Head resigned—or was forced to do so by the governors.

Mary went to Gabbitas Thring, an educational consultancy which had many, many years' experience.

They interviewed Peter and established that his competence was well below what one should expect at ten; there was no chance of his attaining a satisfactory mark at Common Entrance, the public exam necessary for entry into any good public school.

They recommended a cramming school that had had good results. It was called Lapley Grange and was located in mid-Wales close to the Dovey Estuary. Ivor Cross was the headmaster and he enforced a rigid but kind discipline and also training in most regularly played forms of sport—hockey, cricket, rugby but not soccer. Athletics were important, specially running and swimming. Every day, the boys had to run up part of the local mountain, Foel Goch and dipped in the stream, Mynydd

Coronwen except if it was too icy. It was located near somewhere called Glandyfi which was some eight miles east of Machynlleth. Fees were expensive, but the classes were small and there was almost an excess of staff to pupil ratio but past results in public examinations were good, if not outstanding.

Peter passed the interview and he was to start there in the Spring Term, 1950. Quite extraordinary, but tea-leaves-Olive, some years before, had seen Peter at a school near a mass of water, where, she said, he'd be happy. There was no conceivable way that Olive had fabricated this story. A new school near Worthing might be dreamed up but on the far coast of mid-Wales: improbable; but true.

Jen telephoned and left Vera a message to say she could not give Mary an appointment for about five weeks. This was strange as, previously, Jen had been able to accommodate Mary at almost a moment's notice. Never mind, she thought. I'll wait. June came and Mary thought she ought to telephone Jen and confirm the time. Knowing she held strictly ninety minute meetings, starting on either the hour or the half hour, she was surprised to be asked to arrive no later than 10.20 as she was meeting a representative first. The meeting dragged on longer than it should and by 10.30, Mary was anxious about the over-run since Jen was a stickler for timing. Never mind; there were magazine copies that were always interesting. Jen and her rep came out ten minutes later. He must have done good business, she thought.

'Mary. How good to see you. You look incredible, as usual. What have you got on today, may I ask?'

'I'm in rigid corsets again and this is one I bought from you, probably a year ago when I may have been a little lighter. It is tight, today. But you know I like them firm.'

'Come in. I had a long meeting with Charles: you saw him just now when he left.'

'He looked pleased with himself; you must have given him a boat load of business.'

'No, we were talking about you. I asked you to come early as I wanted you to see him, casually.

'He would like to meet you and was fascinated by your story and why you originally started to corset at quite a young age. I gave him no details about you and treated the discussion with loose threads rather than handing him all your patter on a plate.'

'I was watching him carefully the whole time. I showed him the latest styles available from the American firm, Camp and I think I'll get a sale for one of their incredible fan-lacers, which are extremely powerful. He must like a bit of discomfort as this design can be quite demanding from my experience—which lasted just one day and that was more than enough. They are quite incredibly supportive, though, and better suited to ladies carrying a large posterior and a weakened tummy.'

'Jen, please tell me more about him; I was not really looking when he left—you did not warn me to have my spy-glass at the ready. He stood upright, dressed well, suited, looked businesslike had neatly cropped hair and a small moustache which made him look quite handsome, I felt.'

'Mary, you missed little from a casual glance. He had no idea that you were awaiting his exit, so would not have examined you. He is far too well mannered, anyway.'

'Mary, I can tell you he was Marlborough educated, trained as an engineer working his way up as an apprentice and then decided to specialise in oil-field work where he was initially a roustabout on drilling platforms in harsh conditions. Later, he needed more geological information and decided to leave and to take a university course which lasted three years. He is now about 45 and has worn corsets since he suffered an injury during the last days on an oil rig. He has no back problem now, but really likes the feel and containment offered by really extreme corsets. He lives in the Home Counties but I cannot tell you where; he will have to tell you. Oh, he now works in a City office, driving a desk as they say. When would you like to meet? The three of us, maybe, so that nothing alarming will happen.'

'Well, Jen, I do not want to seem over-keen and also, James is still very much alive, within me;

'I am sure you can understand what I am saying. I did have a discussion with Olwyn when I was in Pembrokeshire recently, and I asked her what she thought I should do because I did not want to be a professional widow for the remainder of my getting-older life.'

'Mary, I can well understand. I'll not hurry things along.'

'Olwyn, herself, is simply not the marrying type. She prefers her own self, had an affair many moons ago but has never recovered from the experience and is not in the hunting field, save for foxes—or other women for that matter.

'But, she did say that she'd have a little think. Quite what that infers, I do not know. I'll discuss it with her sister Nesta, whom I know quite well and she lives locally, in Hassocks.'

'Jen, I have never had an opportunity to ask much about you, personally. You are married and, maybe, have children?'

'Yes and No; when working, I do tend to concentrate on what's in hand and as you know, I work to earn a living and thus concentration is essential so I don't bring Herbert into any discussions. You have never asked, before, so I have never raised my home life with you.'

'I have to support our household as best I can as my husband was badly wounded in the First War; he is older than I am and we met and married in 1932 but he's getting increasingly infirm and we almost never go out. I love him dearly; he is kind, considerate and still has a great sense of humour. When I'm out, he reads and listens to the gramophone, so buying him a present is quite easy.'

'Like you and James, I shall be lost without him or a partner one day. He has not much longer, regrettably, as his organs are slowly failing according to the physician. So I now live to give him the best that I am able and to look after him just as if he were my baby. He is no baby, though. He does for himself when I'm working but it will take him a good half-hour to boil an egg, for example.'

'That's amazing; three minutes, tops, so sadly he must be infirm now.'

'I need the companionship that I receive from Herbert. I am surprised at how long you have been alone: sorry, leaving Peter out of the equation. I will not become a professional widow as you rather disparagingly call yourself.'

'I really do wish I'd known more, much earlier, Jen. But you do not wear a ring.'

'Just a foible of mine; of course I do have a ring and we were married quietly, in church but I think that having a ring in place leads to questions and, apart from close friends and some colleagues, my life is compartmentalised; silly foible.'

10 Nesta's Call 1951

Nesta wanted to hear all the news first hand and asked Mary to come to Hassocks as soon as she could travel. The sisters had had long talks, and the business with the Silverman dynasty and Jack had been explored with some vigour. But Nesta wanted to talk to Mary to hear her side of what had been happening and all the quite momentous news.

Olwyn had also mentioned that Mary was quietly looking for a new companion in her life and were there any ideas.

'Mary, Dearie, it's lovely to see you so soon and I owe you so much for helping Olwyn though a pestilent time. I could not go into much financial detail before you went down there but I gather you do know the situation quite well now. Olwyn lives on her rental income and has limited capital apart from the value of land and property.

'Mary, you realised she could not live at White Lodge without more income and that could not be conjured out of thin air and selling up was just obvious; has been to me for some years, now, but Olwyn is a stubborn so-and-so and would not attempt to listen to her busy-body sister.'

'You are being unfair on yourself. Olwyn would give anything for you to have lived there . . .

'We'd have fought like wild-cats, Mary. Impossible; I am quite infirm and Olwyn is sprightly and active. I would not have wanted her to wait upon me and she would have done so because that is Olwyn and she'd have made it her duty. So, no; that route was out of the question.'

'Did she tell you that I have decided to give up being a professional widow? Nobody in mind but some friends have made some suggestions, mostly where to look rather than who to look at.'

'There is someone we both have in mind. You met Jack de Vere and he took quite a shine to you as you proved yourself to be businesslike and competent in a difficult situation.'

'But Jack's married; he told me what he and his wife were doing, holidaying somewhere warm.'

'Oh yes, not Jack, lovely as he is.

'Jack and Caroline have a son, Robert who is just a tad older than you are and he is still unmarried; by the way, his name is Bob for short.

'He was engaged to Louise and they had a son but sadly she was killed serving on a bomber station when the control room took a direct hit. Their son Andrew, has been brought up by Louise's parents and Bob has been reticent about looking around; anyway, he has a career in the FO and that has to take precedence if he is to advance. I consider he is now free, able and eligible and Olwyn tells me he is due for some leave from the Russia House in Moscow and Caroline has great plans for him when he lands back in the UK for a few months.'

'Jack de Vere's son was mentioned but I see a big problem. Although he has a daughter, Caroline is certain to want a further grandchild and I am getting a little long in the reproductive tooth, so I have ruled him out—much as I'd love to meet him as he sounds fantastic.'

'Mary, I think you are quite right; let him make all the running and I'll find out Caroline's views. If you rush headlong into a relationship, it may take up some years for both of you to decide and if it hits the buffers you will have lost vital time as

I'm sure it does get harder to find a mate when you'll then be forty plus.'

'Nesta, what wise words you speak. I'm intrigued, though. Nesta, you have not said much about him. On purpose or just being perverse, perhaps?'

'Just cautious, my dear; he may have some Muscovy duck in his sights for all we know. The lassies over there are incredibly attractive but are watched day and night and cannot mingle so it's unlikely he could put one in the diplomatic bag; would you like me to have a few words with Caroline?'

'Why the devil not? But don't drop me in it too far. I can foresee a huge problem: my age.

'Robert—Bob may have thoughts on having another baby. Caroline would like that, I'm sure. So, although he is about forty, a much younger wife might be better suited to his needs and those of the de Vere family.

'I am getting ancient for new babies.'

Nesta said there had been quite a few couples coming to view White Elephant—Nesta's private name for the Redberth estate. None had expressed a definite interest apart from an American engineer working for Esso. However, there had been no requests for a second look.

Olwyn was not concerned and was assured by Frank Mason, the agents, that the property was eminently suited to someone and time was necessary in all such cases where there's a large central home and land. The acreage is too small to farm but would suit a family who have a number of horses or plan to expand their current stable. The agents did warn Olwyn that it would be unwise to split the estate into two or more lots. Leave such arrangements to the eventual purchaser, if they so wish.

'What does concern Olwyn is what she should do following a sale and just as importantly, where she should live. She is resigned to taking a rented property whilst she searches for an occupation and a real home.'

'I'll make some time to go and see her. Peter is at school near Machynlleth and I'm sure he'd like me to call on him one day as I rarely went to see him during term time in Brighton. I'd like better to see the school and surroundings and to take in the atmosphere. I was there for his brief interview but he has told me a little in his letters; some things amaze me and he is growing up so fast, now.'

'I'd love to see some photographs of his new school, Mary and you'll be able to tell me so much more when you have been there.'

'How will you travel to the wilds of Wales and then get to Pembrokeshire?'

'Yes, I have looked into this and London trains go to Machynlleth, serving mid-Wales and on to Dovey Junction before winding north towards Barmouth.

'From Dovey Junction a rather slow train runs south via Aberystwyth to Carmarthen and then on to Kilgetty, in Pembrokeshire, where Olwyn will collect me if I manage all the connections without getting hopelessly lost.'

'As Olwyn wants to meet him, and for his holidays, Peter is going to have to manage the trains by himself but he'll enjoy that responsibility as he is fascinated by locomotives and timetables. No decision has been made about senior school after his Common Entrance; it's too early to make a final choice but I have put him down for the Devon school where his father went in 1926. I expect they'll take him because of the parental connection. He will have to manage a new set of trains if he goes there.'

'Has Olwyn discussed what she wants to do—career wise—since my last visit?'

'No, nothing has come to light; she did not mention the subject when we last spoke. That means she is undecided or has put the thought to bed. It must be a worry for her. I do think you ought to try to start the thought process running when you next see her, Mary.'

'When James and I first met, it was like an explosion inside me; I'd have said yes, then and there, on Brighton Station, if he had dared to ask me to be his mate for life. I suppose I am again seeking the same chemical reaction, and if it does not happen I may well walk away. Oh, life is difficult at the moment. I also have a young son to care about and how will he get on with a new father-figure?'

'Mary, being young does lead to lots of complications. I never had these problems because I decided in my teenage years that romance was on a distant planet and, as I could never have children, I went out of my way to avoid serious male contact and here am I today, a professional spinster. It's time for you to get to Steyning or it will be dark.'

Mary left Hassocks by train and had time to marshal her thoughts as Nesta always managed to illuminate her life so eloquently. That was why she liked to spend time in her company.

11 Man Hunt

Mary did not sleep well. There were too many thoughts, all having a whale of a time in her mind. Upon waking, she decided to visit the place in Adam and Eve Mews. Forgotten what it was called for the moment but a decision was taken.

Jen's man was also a possibility as a shared and common interest was always a good sign but she felt strangely nervous about meeting him. She had seen him fleetingly and he did look smart and quite attractive. But; but what? Another decision taken, she'd have a word with Jen and ask her to arrange a threesome. Correction, why not a foursome with Herbert who did not get out too often?

It was just seven minutes past six when Mary had a memory surge.

What had tea-cup Olive said about Peter; she wished she had written down what was said soon afterwards.

"Happier"; "mountainous area with lots of trees and running, no, rushing water and noise with a lovely view and many young boys." Yes, that's what Olive had said. But just how could she know?

She'd never been further than Worthing; no rushing water there apart from the sea. The sea goes in and out but does not rush. She had also mentioned "a waterfall".

Mary was chilly with this astonishing memory recall. Analysing what she recalled, "happier" came strongly to mind. Peter had really hated being at the frightful Brighton prep school where bullying and sadistic masters were rampant. As long as he was really happier—that mattered greatly to her. Mary recalled, with some horror, that she had used schools as childminders so that she could enjoy her work.

She felt really cold, not just chilly. Now, more than anything she wanted to talk to her closest friend, Jane who would be able to help her in her acute distress. Mavis also; she needed to talk to Mavis who had often looked after Peter with Heather, her grand-daughter. Incredibly, the relationship between Peter, Heather and Mavis was harmonious and like a second home for him.

Olive had read tea-leaves from a cup. Just how had she been able to dream up quite so many accurate scenes? Her descriptions were clearly naive but, she thought, if you gathered ten people to watch a soccer match where a goal had been scored and then afterwards asked the group a number of questions . . . you'd get ten varied views or flashbacks. What numbers were on the shirts? Where was the ref? Who tried to tackle the scorer?

Olive was so correct; indecently correct. Amazing. And Mary recalled that she had been quite rude when Olive left the Withdean house. She did not believe a word that had been said and Peter was only interested in "long journeys", "under water" and losing her fingers in the bacon machine.

Mary determined that she'd try to meet Olive again and maybe she could shed some light on her future. She knew where she worked in St James's Street and put this high on her mental list.

A bath was needed; she was chilled and anyway, it was now well past her routine time for starting her day. She had to see Mavis, Olive, Jane, Jen and her male customer and possibly Herbert, too. Her brain was muddled, again. But Mary was far from muddled.

Bathed, and dressing, she had to have more information about the new school—what was it, Lipley Garage? She had to set out a few questions for Peter asking about what the rushing water was; was there a view? Was it mountainous? Some of Peter's letters had attempted to describe the surroundings but his letters dwelled more upon what he and his new chums did during the day. The telephone was not useable, unless there was a genuine emergency.

Mary decided upon an older corset today—one that was not rigid but which held her closely. She picked out the one that she had worn when on holiday in St Albans with James. It was just a little tatty but intact. Obviously well made but it had had a good deal of wear and she was larger than she was nearly seventeen years previously—and pre-Peter, too.

Another thought occurred to her, she remembered what Olwyn had said. She regularly asked for help from "them above" or something like that. Of course, James. He was "above". She dressed as if she was going to meet James; in the right foundations and did she still have the skirt and top she wore at the Inn they stayed in. Probably not, now, but she asked James what she should wear now. Was she daft, she mused?

She picked out clothes from the cupboard and thought,

'not what I'd normally wear.'

but she had asked and this is what was suggested for her. The corset fitted surprisingly well; it could not be laced up as tightly but it was going to do a really excellent job. It was firm but fitted her body well. It enclosed her and gave her real shape, almost better than the rigid garments she had become accustomed to wearing day after day.

Her normal bodice was missing but her breasts were supported differently and they felt strangely odd. Less squashed into the rigid shape but more defined into two definite rounded shapes. This had taken more time than she could readily spare but Brighton was her calling ground; Olive and Mavis. Jane was unlikely to be there. An important letter for Peter which she wrote whilst having a coffee and a boiled egg for breakfast.

'Mavis, have I been cruel with Peter?

'You were looking after him, the awful school being a childminder? Mavis, have I been a dreadful mother?'

'Mary, just what has entered your psyche, today?

'I have never seen you quite so distressed and looking physically altered, too. I remember when you did look like this ages and ages ago. Are you ill or am I seeing something unusual about you, today?'

Mary burst out laughing and then had a fit of streaming tears. Mavis was not sure whether to crack open the sherry or the tea-pot and decided upon a good proper coffee made from beans—still a rarity as hardly an essential during the rationing period.

'I have to admit, I spoke to James this morning and I put on an old corset I had worn when we stayed near St Albans and I asked him what clothes I should wear today.'

'Well, Mary, you look unfamiliar but now I come to think about it, attractive, too. What threw me was the difference. You are always immaculately and severely dressed with a tiny waist and a bust to die for. Now, you look like me. Firmly corseted I expect, but with a modified outline; just unexpected. Sorry to be surprised.

'Now, Peter. He has always been happy, here. He fits in so well with us, as a family. He knows the routine we have; he helps as if it is quite normal. The times he was really upset was when he had to catch a bus back to school when he had stayed over from boarding. That often resulted in floods of tears and I could never understand why. I did ask but he would not let his guard down.'

'Mavis, I have not seen you recently but I've changed his school. He is now at a crammer in mid-Wales as there was a dreadful case of sadistic behaviour by a staff member who kicked another boy through or under a form table during a lesson. That school was a hell-hole of bullying . . .

'Now I understand so much better. He did try to say what he wanted and Heather had thoughts on what he had said to her but I did not really understand. Why do boys clam up on such important things in their life?'

'Mavis, you have just told me why. You said "their life". Their world is a closed environment; one does not talk. Even his father would not talk about what he was doing in his army school—where he was a trainer—and Peter may have picked up his feelings, although he was young then—little more than an infant but impressionable, nevertheless.'

'If you were to have a close talk with Heather, one day, when she is deeply upset about something silly, you may find a whole truth and a contrasting truth lies inside her normal daily self that she keeps far from anyone. A psychiatrist could help explain what is happening with clammed-up children.'

'I am going to try to see Olive, again; she who gave me so much accurate details about Peter and my future. I did tell you but you put it down to a bit of nonsense when I was distressed.

'I have written a letter to post to Peter as I want to check what Lapley Grange School is really like—the view, the waterfall, the estuary, the mountain, the trees. Olive mentioned all these facets that she "saw." I do hope Peter can write me a good, detailed letter. The boys there are forced to write home every Sunday after church service but the results are pretty dismal. On Monday we did . . . One Tuesday we did . . . and so on. Boring stuff but that comes from writing an enforced letter rather than one written with the spirit of dialogue moving your right hand. The boys just want to get on with their sport.'

Walking up St James's Street, Mary found the grocery store on the left and went in and scanned the shop for the big red-wheeled bacon slicer but, no Olive. An assistant was standing near the back of the shop and, nervously, Mary went up to him to ask if Olive was still working here.

'Don't I recognise you Paul; Giselle is your wife, isn't she?'

'Right on two counts. You are Mary Compton who lived next door to us and who sold the other half of our property after old Mrs Compton died and you disappeared and did not return, according to Giselle. Even when the removal van came from Dor-to-Dor, you did not attend, she told me.

'You did not even come and say good-bye.'

'I am so sorry; I was not being intentionally rude but I became ill and never wanted to set foot in that house ever again. I recovered my health just as soon as I was staying elsewhere. It was uncanny; Martha had a hold over me and she upset Peter, as well—I mean after she died.'

'Mary, I have some uncanny news, as well.

'Next door sold quickly, as you know. What is strange is that the new owners moved in and within a week had ordered the removal vans and they moved out and it was for sale, again. They could not stand it. By all accounts, so Giselle tells me, there were strange noises and their furniture moved and they thought there had been an earthquake or something.

'Pictures they had arranged carefully also fell to the floor and glass broke.

'I never got to know them, but the wife was terrified; hence . . .

'Peter had furniture shaking and knew nothing about it when I went into his room to ask him to stop making such a racket: he was asleep. So, I heard it but assumed it was Peter so did not go straight away to look.

'Do you recall the day he had a small party, your son came round? Well, it was that night; come to think about it, a picture fell as well but I put that down to high spirited children who must have disturbed it, somehow.

'What's odd is that the picture was nowhere near where the kids were playing.'

'Mary, I am not in the least up with things like this but have you heard of poltergeists?

'Giselle has more knowledge than I do and she says it is a classic case and with what you have now told me, reinforces it. The only way forward, for the house, is to have a service of exorcism carried out.

'There are priests who have definite knowledge and are directed if someone asks the local clergyman. There is nothing in the Book of Common Prayer; the service is akin to the Catholic faith, I think. Giselle is catholic and she knows a great deal more.'

'It is not my problem, now. I do not wish, ever, to see the property again and the ghost may start to influence me again if I get near. You knew that Olive came and read the tea-leaves, didn't you?'

'Yes; she has an uncanny knack and is said to be extraordinarily able; certainly she's psychic.'

'She came to me for tea and announced a number of changes that appeared utter rubbish at the time. For instance, she said "you will be going away, never to return, going on a strange trip with water above you and you'd meet . . ." and "there'd be problems and to watch out". Well, everything she said has come true, uncannily true and I am here to ask her to see me again.

'She told Peter, clearly that he'd be going to a school close to water, with a view and where there was rushing water. He is now at school in mid-Wales and I was there only briefly so did not take in everything but, again, what Olive said . . . Quite beyond belief.'

'Now, where is she? May I see her for a few minutes, please?'

'I wish. Out of character, she came in one day and said she was off and never came back again.

'Another girl said she had moved to Rottingdean and had an attachment.

'Attachment?'

'I think she has found someone but nobody really knows. If you do want to see her, I think I'd try the grocery stores, there, in Rottingdean; that is the business she knows but of course, she could work in any shop that would take her. Start there and just ask after her. It is most unlikely that she's taken work far from Rottingdean.'

'Do you have her old address?'

'Of course, but I doubt she'd be there. It was just a small flat, quite near here. As you know her, I'll just give you this address, but, I'm pretty certain she will not be there. Do have a look around, ask another neighbour if there's a forwarding address. You'll know what to do.'

'Thank you for your help, Paul. Please give Giselle my good wishes. Here is my temporary address in Steyning.'

Mary was stunned. What a development: two developments, the haunted house and Olive's man.

Bit between the teeth, she caught a bus to Rottingdean with no knowledge of where Olive may be. She recalled her name—Olive Weeks, that she was quite young and maybe a little plain and that she had worked in a grocery store in Brighton.

Rottingdean was quite close to Black Rock and was an older village, regarded as a part of Brighton and also close to other settlements such as Saltdean, Woodingdean and Ovingdean. So, without some good luck, there may be some shop research to carry out. She decided to make the query simple. She would go in and just ask for Olive Weeks and with no encouraging answers, walk out with thanks and onto the next retailer. Maybe she should first eliminate the grocers and similar vendors.

She was on the point of giving up and moving to Woodingdean, which had a number of shops, when she walked into D R Evans Grocers and there she was, large as life and Olive instantly recognised Mary.

'Olive, I'm delighted to see you again. How are you?

'Why did you leave Paul's shop?'

'I met the man in my life. He works on a farm near Rottingdean and I decided to join him and his parents and we are living together but awaiting our marriage before things go too far. Luckily I have a room to myself, well, a cupboard more like, but we all get on well and I love him, dearly.'

'Olive, would you kindly read my tea-leaves for me, please? You were unbelievably accurate when you came to Withdean.'

'I remember nothing of what I said; I never recall what I have been shown. My job is to describe what I see as best as I can but then the whole experience goes blank—so your secrets are quite safe with me.'

'I have no secrets, but you were so accurate that the only person I'd trust to give me another reading would be you and you alone, Olive.

'When could you make a tea time, but in Steyning where I now live, temporarily?'

'It would have to be on a Sunday, when Mark has some time off and he'd love to drive me over there and he'll go off to have a look at the Parish Church and the old tombstones.

'You laugh. Seriously, his hobby is old churches and reading the notices inscribed on the stones and memorials. He has books and books on old churches and I do find them boring but he sees so much that I would miss. I expect he will convert me into loving his passion, too.

'I must serve a customer.'

Mary arranged for Olive and Mark to come to Jane and Harry's home in a fortnight. They may or may not want to meet Olive. Harry is a hard-headed man and not into the ethereal in any way.

The small sitting room felt ideal for just the two of them and she made some sandwiches and had baked a chocolate cake. At least she knew the form and decided to take some notes this time, provided Olive agreed. Mary thought it a pity Peter could not be in Steyning, too.

'You may take notes if you wish; I see with my eyes switched off but I do find it difficult to describe all I see in understandable words. I was not a school person and essays killed me. I'd clam up after writing a dozen words and used to get an Omega Minus for not thinking. My abilities do not need me to think up a story or an essay. I just have to describe what I see and that's a doddle for me.'

'Yes, I can understand that. You told me I was to go on a long journey and you saw me travelling with water above me. I did travel and went under the Severn River in a train tunnel. I recall that foxed you but you were so correct. I'd have had a job describing that event, Olive.'

Tea progressed and Olive settled down with her thoughts; peace was necessary for her and she said she liked this house. She felt it was old and yet calm, without any malign influences.

'There is considerable change for you. More moving but normal moving and you are with a new man, no, I see men; this one is new because I see he is careful to do everything for you and to be polite. He is lovely but he must have been injured in the war, maybe, as he is standing so erect as well as being well dressed. He is like a living statue.

'I see you with another group of men. You are in a sumptuous hotel or something and strangely, it is rolling around. There are many, many people; everyone is carefully dressed, as if for a formal dinner-party. There are two notable men, there. Both have strange names; I do not understand that. They appear to be attracted by you. I am getting the impression that you like one of them and are content in his company.

'I am seeing a huge factory; no, not a factory where they make goods for sale but water tanks and chimneys and many yellow bull-dozers pushing mud around. It's fading, I'm afraid.

'I see you changing your work; like me you are going to work in a shop, I think. Not a normal shop that sells things but a shop that makes things; I see clothes and some things like my grand-mother used to wear under her dresses. I remember being fascinated by her strange garments but that is what I see, quite clearly, Mary.

'You are moving, as I told you, you are going to help to run a lovely small home in the country and I am seeing a walled garden and a small orchard with, I cannot tell . . .

'You are going to have to watch your health, carefully, as I see a hospital but one where they have many women in beds. But they are not ill. I cannot understand why they are there if they are not ill.

'You are going to take up a new and uncommon hobby; I hear music and people are moving. I thought people sat for a concert, but not here. Everyone is in pairs and happy.

'I am in Jane's new home; please ask her to have a cup of tea with me.'

'Jane, I see you with two children, one older and a babe in arms.

'You are happy and so close to your husband.

'What I do see, clearly, is many, many books and you are writing something and working hard; I think you are learning something as I see a school or maybe a college building with older people all over the place.

'I think I see a set of scales, old fashioned ones like they used to have on shop counters but you are definitely not in a shop.

'My scene is getting less clear and I am tired. Another day for you, Jane.'

Olive and Mark took themselves back to their home and Mary and Jane were left to ponder what had been described. For both, it was clear.

Jane wanted to study and maybe become a solicitor. Scales of justice, maybe? There would be many books if she were to study.

As for children, she was pregnant and maybe Olive could have seen her shape but, to be fair, she did have her eyes closed until she got up to leave.

For Mary, the reading was clear in places. The "statue" was clearly Jen's customer wearing his corset. She was concerned about health and as she was nearly forty this was not uncommon but why so many women—women who did not appear to be ill. Jane said,

'You are a mutt! They are all there either to have, or have had babies. No babies about because they keep babes in a separate nursery except for feeding-time . . . Be careful, Mary, you may find yourself in calf again.'

Mary asked Jane if she remembered the shop in Alfriston—the one that sold clothes and corsetry. I think that Olive said that she saw a shop that made things rather than selling things. But she could not foresee herself making corsets; far, far too difficult. Whilst she could sew, it was elementary work, running up a dress from a pattern, maybe. Olive was quite clear about seeing corsetry and called them strange garments according to the notes taken. But shops were there to sell. No, they are there to advise, as well. That is what Jen does upstairs at Dress Address. It was time to talk to Jen and to fix up a meeting for four.

Chapter Five

1 Fellowship Agency 1951

*M*ary was at work with Vera and catching up on requirements and any outstanding missing requests. She found herself on the road, again—at least mainly the iron road of the Underground, as she was searching for a discrete fabric and a colour that simply could not be substituted, if not found. It was for a forthcoming production of Swan Lake and costume production had to start no later than three weeks' time or the director would have to make some drastic changes to the concept for this production. It occurred to her that locating material was like being a detective and sifting through clues or going over previous evidence from earlier searches.

She decided to go back to her earlier enquiries, set them out as a list and mark the findings with a score. Some could be readily eliminated. But someone might have misheard the original enquiry and may have given an erroneous answer. Alternatively, they may have been occupied on another enquiry and failed to give the time to Vera for a good and proper answer. Or?

Mary listed the top possibilities geographically and took herself off to Harrow where there were valuable contacts in North West London. Time being quite short, she hired a car and driver for the day and rephrased her questions so that a wider set of answers were likely—that may lead her to try a swatch of what was—now—available. The first three wholesalers still had nothing suitable but it was useful to renew acquaintances and she was taken out by Richard Jaimes for an early lunch or elevenses by the third call she made.

'Mary, I've known you for many years but you do not often appear, here. Have we done anything wrong or is there anything more we can do for you?'

'Absolutely nothing wrong, Richard. I am here because I need a fabric that seems unobtainable and I put the potential suppliers into an order and your firm came third: not a bad mark. So, as the Americans would say "we luv you babe".

'As for what more can you do—yes, you could start to trade between yourselves, other wholesalers and maybe some firms that are not known to be large outlets but just could have hidden reserves.'

'Do you know, Mary, this has been a topic of discussion in our offices as business is tight; rationing is still having an effect. This idea of yours could open a few magic boxes. When war started, many rolls of fabric were spirited away from the bombs and for safety as they were valuable. We have been receiving a number of unasked-for enquiries which we normally turn down simply because the small firms do not have accounts with us.

'I know what you want; I have a picture of it in my mind and I'm going to call a meeting to discuss how we start to approach the lesser mortals.

'Does Vera know where to contact you if we do come up with a lead, or two?'

'Yes, of course. I must go.'

'It has been a good and valuable meeting with you as new ideas are often so valuable and we have failed to see what's under our noses.

'Just an impertinent thought; you still a widow?'

'A professional widow, sadly. I could not begin to see or even want another man until recently. James was my life, love, soul-mate and I still talk to him but I believe he wants me to have a new relationship.

'Are you starting a club for sad war widows, then?'

'Might be another good idea of yours. Are you going to be prospect number one, for me?'

'I really must go. Bye, Richard and thank you so much again. "Prospect number one"—me?'

Catching the Underground, taking the Bakerloo Line, there was a problem and Mary had to change at Paddington and, just because she had a few minutes to wait, she travelled to High Street Ken and walked the short distance to Adam and Eve Mews to have a look at . . . Yes! the Fellowship Agency and to see what her senses told her.

A number of small offices or businesses were found in this area, an old stabling area from the days when horse-coaches were the main means of transport. So buildings were altered, changed or re-built but what she was looking for, The Fellowship Agency, was clearly to be found in what was once a hay loft with rickety stairs leading up and then along a passage and linking with a much bigger building which was sub-divided into quite tiny rooms with frosted glass walls but which looked impersonal and uninviting.

Mary had a strange shudder and was not at all happy to be in this building. But, a young and attractive woman materialised and said, charmingly,

'May I offer you any assistance; this passage is long and uninviting.

'Who did you have in mind when you came up, please?'

'Well, I'm a war-widow and I was looking for "Fellowship".'

'You have come to the right place; I'm Virginia, Ginny for short, but you really ought to meet my principal and I'll have a look and see if she might be able to see you. Please will you wait here?'

The reception area, for that was what it looked like, was impersonal but it had been decorated with fresh flowers—just a small vase, it was a gesture, there were magazines including Picture Post and The Illustrated London News.

There was not much evidence of other fellowship guests and the telephone remained silent. The walls had some reproduction paintings but, sadly, no photographs of successfully matched couples. Mary thought how she would start to change this place when Ginny strode in with a wide grin.

'Mrs Sutcliffe, call her Helen, please, would like to meet you. I'm sure you'd appreciate a pot of tea. Am I right?'

'That would be excellent, Ginny; thank you.'

'Mary Compton, do join me in my lair. I'm Helen, as Ginny will have told you. How did you find us?'

'I work in London seeking specialised fabrics for the theatrical market and I am always searching for names, businesses, premises, changes and your name gave me a thought whilst exploring Adam and Eve—nothing to do with work. The thought was for me, personally.

'I have now been a widow for many years and wish to give up being a professional—widow not a . . .

'We are well off the main road pavement but a surprisingly large number of people wander into the Mews just to have a look and a wonder why it has such an unusual name and then they see us, just as you did.'

'Sorry to disappoint, Helen but at least I was keeping my eyes well open. It was some weeks ago when I first noticed you but only a broken down train made me change course and land here today, as they say, on spec.'

'Mary, we look after a number of people who are currently feeling lost, for lack of a better word. Many war widows either come or are sent here but sadly, men appear to be fewer and a little far between and hence the name: Fellowship.

'I do wish we had long lists of available people but we take our guests to private informal functions where there is a talk, some eats and drinks and we do our utmost to steer people towards someone we have an idea that togetherness may work.

'I work intuitively whereas Ginny is hands-on and she has a gift for sorting people who do turn up here.

'I rarely see people, like you, as Ginny has a number of forms, as you'll find out.'

'I assume she goes by dress and bearing.'

'It tells us exactly what we want to know. You, for example, have superb posture and are clearly dressed for a business meeting and appearance is so, so important for a potential meeting of minds.'

'Of course, I know nothing about you but I assume you are a widow; you would not be here if you were married and you are still wearing a ring.'

'How did you meet your late husband, Mary?'

'Good perception. He was dashing and sat opposite me on a train from Victoria to Brighton and I was smitten, just like that. I remember watching him, intently, in the mirror image formed by the carriage window. He offered to help me take my valise down from the overhead rack when the train reached Brighton terminus. There's more; he offered to find a taxi and we travelled together—and at last could exchange names.'

'I always try to ask; manners and behaviour are vital for this business and the more I store in my mind the easier it gets to be able to make sound and happy introductions just as you two managed for yourselves.

'I am a war widow, too, and know just how difficult it is to meet good, kind, happy and capable men. A major rule here, I keep my seeking well away from this office.

'I also believe in "what will be" and that a considerable element of a helping hand is necessary.

'All Ginny and I do is to help the helping hand a little. Do you understand my concept?'

'Yes, perfectly; live and breathe the "helpers above".'

'Mary, I hate paperwork and wish I could rely upon my brain, so I'm going to ask Ginny to take over from me and ask her to come in here and have a paper-natter. See you soon, Mary.'

Ginny was a sweet girl and she was thoroughly organised. Rather than shuffle forms and then start at the top of page boring one, she did seem to know the papers inside-out and just asked questions and wrote answers onto a paper pad which was much less formal. It was noticeable that when she asked a question or if I gave an answer that was not strictly what Ginny was wanting, she'd use the second paper pad for the waffle. It occurred that the waffle pad would turn out to be the more beneficial. She did track onto modern music and finding a brick wall tried classical and then onto operatic sequences and then she was writing like a demon using the waffle pad.

Similarly with art and appreciation but when she asked what James liked, it was pad one, again.

So, pad one was for factual answers and pad two for casual and maybe off-the-record points.

Ginny was an absolute delight to talk to. She found out so much about me, what I wore, why I liked to be dressed rigidly, adding that she had been encouraged by her mother but preferred to be unstructured; except when it was to meet someone special with her parents. She was surprised to find James was a racing driver and engineer and had clearly expected an accepted profession.

That was for Pad one. Joining up pre-war was a huge bonus, shown by her facial expressions and the fact that he was a trainer, was a linguist and engaged in secret war work caused some rushing between pads of paper with annotated notes. Solvency was something of import and she did seem to delve a little too much; Mary was unused to having her finances explored in detail and had no bank statements or papers with her.

Having spent a good ninety minutes at Adam and Eve, it was time to go and tell Vera today's news, both personal and business.

2 Office Calls

'Your friend, Jen, telephoned but she wanted to see you informally rather than for a new fitting. And, if I may be so bold, you do not need more new corsets: you look amazing just as you are. Most women today are so unstructured and just look dishevelled and utterly plain and not at all interested in life. You look immaculate and ready to take the world head-on. Mary I do not have a go at you often, do I?'

'Vera, you are my closest confidante and if you say something, it is always with my interests at heart. You are like a mother hen to me, if I dare say so. This business would fail if it were not for you and your typist. I have never really got to know her. What's her name, Vera?'

'Jeanette. She's a school leaver and is just seventeen and learning fast. I can rely upon her to make more than tea, nowadays. Errors in her typing are few now, which is admirable as our customers do not appreciate scruffiness; talking of being scruffy, would it be wise to consider giving this so-called office a bit of a revamp? If customers came here they'd not be impressed.'

'Vera, this is quite the wrong area to have a theatrical office, for that is what we are really. I would assume that a bolt hole in Soho would be expensive and off Bond Street prohibitive and all three of us would have to scramble through the Underground masses on our way to Victoria or Battersea. I think we should ask some of our customers and suppliers what they suggest. If the general answers are to economise, then we know what to do.

'But we could find a smarter flat or apartment, maybe somewhere like Grosvenor Gardens where we could have an office and set up a flat rather than vice-versa. The area is smart enough and miraculously survived the bombs, bar a few broken windows. We'd have to keep the caretaker sweet if I lived here occasionally, but we'll have to see what lands on our doorstep. Did you know I had been receiving masses of props-to-let leaflets?'

'Mary, how did you get on in Harrow, today? I gather you went for a snack with Richard Jaimes; he told me, and sounded happy with the time you spent and he said you'd had a great idea. Please enlighten.'

'Well, I am pretty certain that the big boys like Richard do not do business except with fellow wholesalers rather than stooping down a few inches and finding smaller fry who are trying desperately to get ahead. These smaller firms just may have secret stocks retained since the blitz.

'Richard asked me if I was still a widow. I thought that a little strange but times are changing and becoming more enlightened, I suppose. Told him I was a professional widow—which is how I do feel.

'I would really like to have a new soul-mate, just as James was, and I am certain that that is what James would expect of me. We did discuss this, only once, because we were both certain that our lives would carry on indefinitely. He told me that if I were to die, he would not expect to remain unattached and therefore, the same applied in the event of . . .

'I did ask Richard if he was starting a club for sad war widows which just popped out when he asked if I was still available.'

'I wonder whether he has anyone in mind, Mary. This country alone lost a million soldiers and many more civilians but no one really knows an accurate figure. So, there are quite a few lonely people many of whom would love to be re-attached.'

'Vera, did you know that I stand to lose my miserable war-widow's pension if I re-marry? Every year I receive a form that I have to return to the War House declaring my marital status with the caution that if I am fraudulent, I could end up in Holloway Jail, receive a huge fine or both upon conviction; the cheek of it. It makes me cry whenever I receive the letter; I can now recognise it without opening the envelope.'

'I had a meeting today with The Fellowship Agency in Adam and Eve Mews near Ken High Street tube station. The two girls I met were lovely—Helen and Ginny. The owner, Helen, is also a widow and quietly looking and hoping. She has a receptive mind and does not seem to miss a trick. Ginny runs the office and does the paperwork and is a forms-fanatic. She has a card-index system to help weed the wheat from the chaff. I got the feeling, clearly, that they were interested to meet me and that their systems would be eminently good for my search.'

'How do they make introductions, Mary? It sounds a little churchy, fellowship, a guild, maybe.'

'Not remotely linked to any church; they never mentioned religion except for a question Ginny had to complete on one of her forms; my protestant answer was not discussed. More like a club, I felt. They arrange meetings for fellow sufferers and until I go to a sorority meeting I'll not know.'

'Not many men will be at a sorority meeting, Mary; I think it's for women.'

'Well I forget what they did call meetings but I am certain that they will invite suitable candidates of both normal orientations.'

'Strangely enough, I have only recently given my professional status much thought. So much needed to be arranged, Martha's passing; Peter's schooling; selling the Withdean house; meeting Olwyn and trying to sort out her problems; helping Jane and Harry quite apart from helping you to get this business back on its feet again.'

'I'm nearing a crisis age and I really do wish to share my existence with a live partner again. James is always in my thoughts but I wonder how I will manage with two men at once. This is a paradox I had not remotely mulled over; any ideas or suggestions, dear long-suffering Vera?'

'Take life as it comes, is my immediate thought but that's an inadequate answer. You must never attempt to weigh one man against the other. I feel that would be a disaster-recipe and jealousy is corrosive and leads to resentment and distrust. Talking between yourselves, don't keep repeating "James would have done this . . ." or "what wondrous times James and I had . . ." Time has moved on, and James, sadly, is no longer a part of this life and you really must do your utmost to separate your past from any potential partner you are lucky enough to meet.

'He will have another man in your life, anyway: Peter. Being a step-father is going to be difficult as well as a constant reminder that someone's been here before.'

'Vera, you speak such wise and sound words. Words I had never even appraised. Clearly, with a few scenes looming on my singles situation, I do need to clear my brain and talk privately to James and to ask for his help and guidance. At least I am not wearing widow's weeds like Queen Victoria in her gloomy fusc.'

'No, Mary; you look so elegant and I do know that you are much admired by those who meet you. Richard said so, only hours ago. Your posture speaks for you so loudly and Jen's creations do more for you than you conceivably imagine. I do not know how you do manage to wear such firm foundations all day, every day but the results are remarkable. You tell me about Coleen and her success and now forthcoming marriage. Corsetry has definitely changed her out of all recognition and literally moved her from Bethnal Green to Hollywood via Dress Address—and that's a winner, too.

'I must write names on small pieces of paper and throw them into the air and do as you suggest: "take life as it comes." Maybe I must start to be a professional huntress rather than a professional widow.

'Much more fun, I think. I hope I may use you as a sounding board when I do have something or someone to discuss. The only sighting I have is Jen's customer, Charles who I have seen but not met: we passed on the stairs. He wears corsetry so we do have something in common but I need to know a great deal about his activities, his work and indeed why he dresses extraordinarily for a man.

'But then I dress bizarrely too and if my stance and shape has brought out some good in me, maybe it has with Charles too. Add Coleen, Bronwyn, Jen and a couple of the shop workers too and we need to tell the world:

"buy foundations and wear your figure with pride."

'Anyway, isn't it time you visited Jen?'

3 The Huntress' Tale

With one name in the paper chase Mary felt she needed more to give herself a reasonable chance at finding a suitable man without having to look back later with regret if the wrong choice was made. The hunting period had to have a good and fair chance of success. She set out her own parameters and wrote them down.

She felt her senses to be critically important. Peter had to be weighed up as a fundamental parameter.

A wider list would have to include dress, hairstyles, bodily hair, shoes, socks, sports, mental abilities, sight and glasses, hearing, sense of smell, driving ability, writing competence, capability with hands, cooking and menu choice, dancing and musical choice.

But this was being too pedantic, too organised, and too utilitarian. Love matters most and with James—must stop harking back—it was literally upon sight and none of the senses or concepts were evaluated. They were taken as read, as far as could be remembered.

Love and attraction were most important and how would one score love and attraction out of ten?

No, a list was impractical because scoring was subject to one's moods and hormones which would cloud the issues and make a score differ from day-to-day. That would be unfair for everyone concerned. Discussion would have to take priority but she'd need some form of record. A diary came to mind but that would be a record of what had happened upon a definite day or entry.

It was not a thought-record it was a fact-record.

A chronicle entered her thoughts; she was not sure why or from where the idea formed in her head. It just did. Why not keep a chronicle? Why not indeed?

Not so much a daily record but more of a statement of thoughts; impressions set down for later discussion and consideration. What was the most important consideration? One's emotions simply had to be number one.

Lists were irrelevant, marking was impossible for a variety of reasons. Quantifying emotions, impressions, thoughts or any abstract nouns were out of the question. What would occur would arise from discussion. To discuss something would need information, recollections and reminiscences: in a word, "chronicles".

But, just how would she apply pen to paper to record a chronicle? A fact such as "went to the pub" would have no viable use in any ongoing discussion, whereas "Joe's frame of mind was upbeat . . ." could lead to useful interchange. So, any chronicles must be related to impressions, thoughts, and feelings, preferably some that came from the love interest.

How he felt, behaved and appeared; What appealed to him? What reaction he had when something was said or an action taken . . .

These thoughts made Mary nervous; she was not a psychologist and had never tried to keep any form of diary, let alone a "chronicle". Practice would be necessary but a decision was made: the chronicle would start now and it would fire up any discussion with Vera and Jane and hopefully the quality of such wisdom would start to improve with the necessary practice.

> My mind is a blank. I have no clue what to set down.
> I have been alone since the last war started, not when James was killed.
> Why do I feel I need a new husband? What are the benefits?
> Are there any detriments?
> Do I have a physical need, if so, how does this manifest itself?
> I do need tenderness, a closeness, hugs, physical contact.
> My brain needs stimulation from fellow contact.

Mary felt she could start to write what was revealed in her mind and she aimed to write six things at definite points in the day—morning, noon and night to begin with but additionally, during and after any meeting such as with Richard, a matter of hours ago.

Richard was interested in me, as a person not as a customer.
He was clearly undressing me in his mind. That put me off.
He wanted to touch my waist, to know why it was so small.
Are you still a widow, he asked. A little personal?
Richard was on the point of asking me out, again.
Not sure if he is married; no ring visible.
Interested? Interesting? Not sure, probably not.

Jane and Harry were still out, but that was quite normal; maybe out to dinner, somewhere. Mary's mind was churning and one thing was certain: she wanted to meet Charles so she decided to telephone Jen.

'Jen, how are you? I have reached a decision and have decided to cease being the UK's number one Professional Widow. I liked what little I saw when I was last in your lair.'

'What have I done—something you want to wear, or someone you want to meet?'

'Both, but primarily to meet Charles. Could you arrange a suitable get-together with the four of us?'

'Just leave the arrangements to me, Mary. I have no idea when Charles will be available but he'd like to meet you so he'll not take long giving me a date.

What did you want to see me about, professionally, Mary?'

'When we last met, I told you I did not much like the new elastic girdles and all-in-ones and prefer the rigid corsets. I want to see what is available from the American firm, Camp as well as anything else you know about. I have to be firmly and tightly encased, as well you know.'

'Mary, you will be amazed when you see and feel a Camp creation but Bronnie did not like the feel, though. I'm not certain that you'll like the fan-lacing, either.'

'Why?'

'Well, fan-lacing suits women who have a large figure problem—which you do not. They are extremely powerful due to the fan-effect and they control the waist, lower abdomen and posterior admirably and give curvature where shape had disappeared. Allegedly, men love it; their wives look so much better. But you, Mary have little or no excess weight to control. I'll show you, but I do not think they are for you.

'There are some other lace-up designs that are a cross between elastic and rigid which I think you'll really like; extremely firm and they give a magic new shape to the designer figure. You!'

'If I wore something new, do you think Charles would notice?'

'Well, he has not seen what you wear, anyway, so the matter is irrelevant. But, do choose carefully when we arrange a meet. Consider first what look you wish to achieve, so select the outerwear, then which foundations will best show off your figure under the chosen dress. You need to be relaxed, used to wearing the selected corset and most importantly, it should not be obvious that you are encased: don't be rigid but do appear curvy and well shaped. With your experience, I do not need to teach you these things. I'll be in touch, shortly.'

Although advice was unnecessary for Mary, it calmed her down and lessened her natural excitement. She realised she was feeling that life was moving forward again and that maybe the missing part of being married may just come to an end, soon.

She longed for companionship, someone to talk to, a man who would be able to discuss daily life, what had happened, where things were going, who was being seen and then to be able to cling to each other and to be close just as life with James had taken its natural course. But the James-marriage had been so terribly interrupted by his being away for almost all the life and time supposedly spent together.

The realisation that professional widowhood had started in 1938 came almost as a shock. She'd have to learn to live with a man full-time. She had become used to her own company, managing everything that the day threw up and having nobody to discuss the daily grind, the queues, the lack of food and clothing, rationing and making the best of what was available.

Peter suffered as a result of rationing, hardly seeing his mother, being far away at a remote school and having to write forced letters that must be a bore for him to concoct and an utter chore for me to read. Must arrange my time to give more to Peter.

Food did not present an obstacle as eating was a necessity rather than a pleasure; one's figure was vital, so less food was preferable.

Even so, clothing was a major stumbling block and whilst she could now make many dresses, slips, nightwear, the sources of supply and materials was still difficult and if she was not in the business she could never appear so well dressed.

She realised she had thought what she now needed to write down: her chronicle.

These thoughts would give Vera and Jane more than enough material to be able to have a sensible discussion. She felt more relaxed and for the first time since dreadful 1944, she was able to look ahead with pleasure and some real hope.

Lists and diaries were clearly out and chronicles were in. With thoughts on paper, she, Vera and Jane could consider matters rationally.

She thought of Richard; as an experiment, maybe. She did not appreciate being undressed mentally by an almost total stranger and this had put her off. But why? Surely this was a perfectly normal feature of being a woman who dressed well—who dressed unusually well. She created the interest he noticed so, was she being unfair in criticizing him for looking just a little too intently? At least he did not reach out and touch her; he did not put his arm around her waist even when they parted. Maybe he was married and being good but why did she get the feeling he wanted to take her out? Maybe she'd have a talk, soon, to see if he had found any material she still needed. Richard would be an interesting companion and one who would understand her work and they'd be able to supplement each other. This had occurred already; it was suggested his firm should seek new connections well outside the normal relationships; more thoughts to chronicle.

Immediacy was going to be a problem and this was to require a new discipline. A photograph could be taken but recording words needed large, expensive instruments. Notebooks would be small and able to be carried in a handbag wherever she went and pens were messy so soft cored pencils would be best. Writing would have to be done in a train or on a bus as and when vital thoughts came into mind. A chronicle had to have that "immediacy" otherwise it would appear to be a mere diary. The next test would have to be Vera; she would read what had been put to paper and her criticisms would be invaluable.

The clinical approach had been fine in theory; in practice, it was not the way people met and fell in love. When Mr Second-Right was first seen, she'd know instinctively. Wouldn't she? Vera, Jane and maybe Jen would all wish to help with her choice—but without having a chance to meet him; this would prove to be impractical if not impossible.

Peter was too young, yet, to be involved, and he was the most important consideration. Oh, why did she have to start this impossible quest? She was so happy with James. Tears started to flow; she had not really cried like this for years. Was she unhappy at the thought of seeking a new partner? Was she missing James and unable to ask for his help? Were the tears a display of uncertainty or tears of turmoil?

Mary knew she'd need all the help she could muster from her close friends and would have to talk with everyone who now mattered in her life. But she was not used to talking about her personal feelings and maybe airing her innermost recollections. But what are real friends for, she deliberated. They must be asked; it is unlikely that they'd offer guidance without being asked. Just not the way things were done.

Living in Jane's house, it should not be difficult to find a suitable moment when daily stresses could be set aside for an hour. Jane was high on the list. Vera would be a valued source of experience. Ginny may well be able to offer reasonable help. Nesta was an incredibly wise soul. Amazingly, Mary realised that she knew many people but had few close friends. Jen was a possibility but she had always kept her personal counsel—until recently. Coleen was abroad and, anyway, her relationship was more of a business nature and personal matters were only related to underwear and what was worn—a passion they shared. Coleen had not turned to her to discuss her latest conquest and probable marriage.

4 Bronwyn's Life

Bronnie and Henry were delighted with the way life had turned now that management of Dress Address had changed their lives—better income, happiness at work, improved clothes and, as Henry found, superb foundations which he adored.

This considerably improved their private lives; he found her corsetry to be a wild turn-on and Bronnie asked herself why she had resisted the cause for so long. Making good, proper love had made her feel like a new person, happier in her work, brighter with her children and her revised mood improved home-life immeasurably.

Jen had arranged for rigid corsetry to be adapted for both daily wear and to enhance Bronnie's shapely figure which would be unsuited to a normal Victorian hourglass-figure corset. She had a large bust and a wide waist that was not readily trimmed to be in proportion to her bust and hips. Firm foundations gave Bronnie a figure that imposed authority by improving her stature and making use of the main asset—a really strong bosom which she, literally, carried to great effect. She used to say in an unguarded moment that she felt like a galleon in full sail. She never had staff problems as the dominance observed carried great weight. It also made her popular and several of the older staff made appointments with Jen and could then be seen in the store more suitably attired. Bronnie always gave those who tried a new dress allowance—a pay rise in all but name.

Henry insisted that they took good holidays and they often went to Wales where Bronnie had her roots. Although originally from the valleys, they always went to coastal areas such as Cardigan, Aberystwyth and towards Caernarvonshire.

This year they were booked to stay in Saundersfoot and Pembrokeshire had a great deal to offer: incredible sea coast, islands, castles and several harbours but Pembroke Dock was a large RAF defensive area and Sunderland flying boats were much in evidence and the general public was still prohibited from access to some installations. The South coast had so much to offer, including Stackpole Quay and Bosherston with St Govan's tiny chapel, and was largely unaffected by the hostilities except that training took place near Castlemartin and that was akin to Salisbury Plain except that it specialised in armoured vehicles and battle tanks surprisingly, for a stunningly beautiful location.

Their daughters had left school and both were successfully employed in London as they had learned shorthand-typing but had also chosen to take additional courses so that they'd be eminently suited to work as PAs which then led to improved salaries and future prospects. Bronnie had wanted them to take up some form of medicine but neither felt that the medical professions were for them. They had steady boyfriends and marriage was a certainty in the sometime future.

Bronnie had taken over the management of the new Dress Address store which had moved to new premises and had taken over the next-door vacant shop and the flat above. Coleen still owned the business but was the sleeping partner but she still relied upon Mary for advice and a stable voice in London in exchange for a modest salary whilst she had made Los Angeles her home.

To smooth the way, Coleen had been advised to incorporate Dress Address so as to limit her personal liabilities. The business was profitable and Coleen's remuneration was healthy.

She felt that the principal managers, Bronwyn and Mary, should have a share in the newly limited company. But this left Jennifer, who ran a separate foundation garment division without a share and Jen also took over the day-to-day running of the business when Bronnie was either on holiday or unwell. This inequality was felt to be impossible, so the newly issued shares were split between Coleen, the major shareholder with sixty percent and thirty percent split between Mary, Jen and Bronnie with the last ten percent held for the store staff and issued as a productivity bonus—which also included the three managers, so their overall shareholding would rise with time.

Coleen and her accountants felt that employee stability was important and it was decided to operate like a partnership but under the limited umbrella. The business would trade as Dress Address but would be controlled by Dress Address Limited. The landlords were not entirely pleased as their properties could be at some risk if there was a failure in the future. The solution was to agree to an extension of the leases as well as an agreement not to increase rents for a two year moratorium and then to keep increases linked to no more than a government linked index.

Business stability was just as important for the landlords as it was for the employees. Bronwyn was to hold the position of Managing Director with Mary as Chairman. Coleen would take an office more usual in the USA as President and Jen would be Personnel Director. Mary and Coleen would be responsible for agreeing all staff and directors' remuneration.

The employees, now twelve including the eight shop-floor workers were asked to come to a meeting starting at normal opening time on the least busy morning, which happened to be a Thursday for some unknown reason. The store opened late at 10.30 am. Bronwyn always ran her staff as a happy group and whilst all knew something was developing, they were greatly looking forward to being included in Dress Address' future. None of the new directors had any previous experience of company management and the accountancy firm agreed to attend the initial meeting and early board meetings to help, guide and ensure smooth operation; they would also report to Coleen who could not attend in person.

Bronwyn took the floor and formally introduced the new directors, who were well known by everyone and the one new face, Arnold, from the accountants who would report to the missing director, Coleen. There was no reason for the meeting to run into any difficulty and, quite the opposite, the eight floor staff gave their overwhelming support and were aware that details such as productivity, bonuses and future share issues could not be concluded today. Bronwyn had been concerned that there would be lengthy discussion but in the event it ran smoothly because none of the floor staff had much business experience, so could not argue from a strong standpoint.

Importantly, Bronwyn and Jen would continue to take daily charge of the business and its divisions as if there was no immediate change. All that the staff would notice was pay came from a new company and that at least one new department would be created following the success of the foundations division.

This was to be renamed the Lingerie and Corsage Department to give a modern, fashionable designation. Corsage was a play upon words as the term "corset" was seen as restrictive, although necessary. Lingerie had a French feel and all women appreciated the French influence upon their underwear which also needed to be seen as fun garments both in and out of the boudoir.

Until now, "fun" was never associated with corsetry. The range of lingerie was poor and bras were abysmal and the American influence was vital for the future. Both Jen and Mary felt that a great deal of work was necessary to change foundations into lingerie and that the best ally they had was Coleen.

These changes could not be accomplished via either letters or the telephone system and it was agreed that Mary should travel to New York to meet Coleen and to explore the possibilities across the pond. Trade fairs were not frequent even in America. In the UK fairs had not yet started.

Bronwyn would take a holiday and combine this with an investigation of what Paris had to offer: something that would appeal greatly to Henry as a bonus. Jen could not be considered because Herbert was frail and could not be left for a fortnight and he was unable to walk the distances that might be encountered on a working holiday. As Bronnie had to go to explore fashions on the continent, Jen would take over shop management—a task she was well used to in Bronnie's absence. Fortunately, there was a new member of staff who worked with Jen in her department.

Alice had joined Jen as the foundations department could not operate single-handed. Alice was older and experienced in all forms of corsetry having worked most of her life in other stores where such departments were usual. Jen learned a great deal from the new and experienced member of staff but Alice was not used to dealing with representatives and she had never been employed as a buyer.

She had a gift for being gentle, caring and helpful with clients. She knew exactly what would suit their current needs and readily agreed to wear good modern corsetry as demonstration was often key to a new sale.

Alice looked spectacular in one of the latest Camp fan-lacing garments as she had a mature figure which had been childbearing in younger years. With the Camp garment, she also wore the latest long-line bras that were starting to appear; these supported her medium-build bosom and lifted her breast-height. The overall effect—a smaller waist, raised bosom, controlled hips and posterior was spectacular. She became used to the firm feel of fan-lacing and wore her corsetry without question every day—and she admitted to Jen, well into the evening, too.

Bronnie and Henry took a fourteen-day holiday at once and arranged to travel by boat-train to Paris. Neither knew the city but, sensibly, chose to stay centrally. The travel agent booked a small hotel near Chatelet which had more Metro connections and it was close to The Seine and to central Paris.

The agent suggested that if they wanted to explore the shopping districts, particularly for fashion, they should first look at Rue du Faubourg-St Honore which was where luxury dealers held prominence, specially couturiers and dressmakers. Secondly, seek the Boulevard Haussmann which had many stores with general departments. He said that Paris had a maze of streets and small shops which were often a good source for all descriptions of garments, prices and quality.

Neither Bronnie nor Henry spoke much French—school at best and they were advised that most natural French workers did not speak any English so it was with considerable trepidation that they were setting off into the unknown armed with a simple phrase book which made them feel and to seem rather foolish. In the past, Henry had managed to communicate with Arabs, and he found that drawings were always useful so Jen made sketches of intimate ladies-wear for Bronnie and she also took pictures cut from catalogues. Sketches and the phrase book should help considerably. Prices, of course, were all in Francs and they devised a workable means for translating Francs into Pounds. All this was theory but practice was to come.

Jen felt a little left out of the researching but it was obvious that she had the task of running the store and its departments when Bronnie was away; Herbert could never be left alone for too long, anyway.

5 Mary and Coleen New York 1951

Mary took the sea route from Liverpool to New York. The liner was modern but utilitarian in its fittings and state-room furnishings were not opulent but perfectly adequate for purpose. Most ships had seen some war service transporting families and service personnel across the North Atlantic before being refitted and returned to civilian use. There was just one class and the service was operated by the White Star-Cunard group. Business passengers expected to travel west on one ship and to return on another going east. In the post-war years there was considerable change in shipping fleets and airline travel was a threat to liners. Sea crossing was seen as the preferred option for most travellers as it was safer and gave users a break, relaxation and good well prepared food with a wide choice of wines, too. Coleen arranged to meet Mary at the Port Authority's terminal and both were booked into the central Algonquin Hotel and had secured adjoining rooms which was convenient.

Mary looked tired upon disembarking. Many queues, waiting for luggage to be off-loaded and then checked, waiting for the immigration process but at last she could just see Coleen waiting in the arrivals hall.

'How fantastic to see you again, Coleen; it has been ages since we last met in London. Please tell me your news—are you married, yet? Possibly children?'

'Well, yes—and no to children, but we are happy together. Eugene and I married last year and you may have heard of him as John Hackmann. I am now Mrs Eugene Meyer and we live in Burns Park which is in Los Angeles, towards the north of central LA but south of the Hollywood area.'

'That's wicked: congratulations, Coleen.'

'Thank you.

'It's not too expensive, it's a good area and we love it for the time being. Who knows what will happen in the future. I am getting a number of quite good film parts but am awaiting a big break. Eugene is also waiting for his call from a studio wanting the special abilities he offers; his leaning is towards historical movies but nowhere near any crime or sci-fi. I also like historical themes and that is how I managed to leap from

London to LA after my part as an Edwardian lady about to become a Countess.'

'Coleen—I hope I don't have to call you Mrs Eugene'

'Heavens no, he calls me Collie, so I'll answer to that with pleasure.'

'I see you are still dressed firmly and have a terrific figure.'

'Yes, of course; Eugene loves me all trussed-up and for him, the tighter the better and my waist is now down to 18-19 inches when I want it that small. I eat much less than I did simply because I have a much smaller stomach, now. But you are also looking so elegant but I think you have strong modern elastic, am I right?'

'Yes; I did not know what the steam-ship would be like and if I was heaving with sea-sickness I did not want to be trussed up as you are, now. I adore being well-fitted and will not go anywhere without something really firm. I caught this malady from you, of course, Collie.

'You would be astonished how the desire to be well corseted has spread throughout Dress Address. A good half of the staff are always rigidly dressed these days and the customers notice it and many take a trip upstairs to see Jen.'

'The strange thing is that a good, well fitted corset is so, so opulent and once the body is used to the fit it feels awkward when unadorned. Anyway, Eugene will not let me be seen bare.

'I am certain that I get parts because of my appearance and am so often asked,

'Why? and,

'What does it feel like? and even,

'Does it harm you?

'I tell anyone who asks, often leering men,

> "you just have to try it for yourself to find out how much better you will feel and that standing straight will enhance your health."

'Unlike elastic garments, there is no feeling of being compressed all the time. It is difficult to tell someone who has never tried a corset or even a girdle what it really feels like. Some ask if it's like a bathing suit and I mischievously suggest wearing, say, ten at once, then you might just come near.'

'You know why I am over here, apart from just seeing you; Jen's department is being renamed Lingerie and Corsage Department and we need new stock to live up to the name, specially lingerie which infers lighter garments and a modern edge as well. There are no UK trade fairs yet, and the average bra that's available is just plain horrid. Bronnie has gone to look at Paris to get a feel of availability and I've come to NYC to do the same with you.'

'How well do you know New York, Collie?'

'I live some four thousand miles away so, not well but we will have to explore, ask questions, seek lingerie and corsetry stores and see just what is on the market.

'The Americans are well ahead of the Europeans simply because there are more of them and demand is greater. Take the major corset makers, Camp, Spenser, Spirella and Royal

Worcester—they all started Stateside and have factories here. American women present a really huge demand. This is influenced by their eating habits. There has been no rationing and their size and weight is greater and their need for corsets is determined by body mass.'

'Collie, I cannot help because I live a similar distance to the east. Left to my own devices, I'd start by looking at directories, similar to Kelly's in the UK and a library will be a good bet.

'I'd find out where the fashion districts are and the hotel concierge should know that. Smaller foundation-wear shops are often a great help as they do not know what we are seeking and they'd think that we are personal shoppers and are inclined to say more than they ought and thus give away trade secrets. They would know when and where trade fairs are being held. Just ask nicely, is my secret. Remember, that is what I do in London all the time. However, I am not seeking lingerie in London but fabrics, as you know.'

Collie and Mary spent a week researching New York and came away with a fantastic grasp of what was available. As expected, some smaller shops were remarkably helpful and their comments led to more points of call and these spread when names were mentioned. It was quite extraordinary how helpful people were inclined to be when shown kindness and a little generosity.

Both Mary and Coleen purchased garments that suited them and fitted well. Some of the fitters in shops were astonished by Coleen's figure and said they wished they could do the same for some of their customers. Giving details and trying to help them led to a much improved exchange of information and in some cases, names of wholesalers which will prove invaluable.

Mary was very well suited by one shop where she purchased the latest design of an all-in-one corset that had not yet crossed the Atlantic.

She liked the slimming effect, the tightness imposed by structured lacing which was also found to be superb. Her breasts were also supported better than she had been used to with UK-made garments. The overall line of these was far better and there was an absence of any bulges and it was impossible to see the lines of corsetry through the outer dress fabrics—a real no-no for any well dressed woman.

Collie was less inclined to change her foundation-wear from rigid to elastic-based apparel. Eugene was not a fan of what he called "smellastic" and he wished he had been born so that he was in his twenties in the late 1800s.

A number of well structured bras caught Mary's eye but she only bought half a dozen and then thought when she'd be able to wear them unless combined with a corset. Her corsets were all made with breast support built-in but a bra could be worn first to form better overall structure and to improve comfort; in fact she felt better with a bra under a corset because the bra materials were much less stiff and the rounded construction enhanced the visible effect. Shoulder straps needed to be worn neatly concealed or carefully cut off.

Supporting the breasts was unnecessary as the corset provided all the uplift needed—one of the reasons why she loved being in rigid garments and another reason why she could not explain to men the feeling she attained from wearing corsets.

It was soon time for Mary to board the liner taking her to Southampton but she had achieved her mission—to gain knowledge for Jen to be able to make business enquiries and to source new stocks for the Lingerie and Corsage Department. Mary felt that she'd soon need larger premises and that custom was certain to increase as a result of the research. She wished she could ask how Bronnie had managed in Paris.

6 Bronnie in Paris 1951

Bronnie found that she could speak quite a few words and phrases she had learned from the little book but both she and Henry were stumped when they received a gabble of spoken French in return.

What they did find was the friendliness of the native French people who had suffered greatly during the occupation. The English and Americans were seen as saviours and they were treated kindly and when diagrams were used. Everybody comprehended what was needed or which direction to take. Money was a major source of hands-on difficulty—the way prices were displayed with lots of noughts and commas. They were fortunate to find a fellow hotel guest who kindly explained the French currency method and after that short talk Henry had an answer to most money matters, except when it came to travel on the Metro.

Paris was a city where they could easily walk. Metro travel was fine but one saw nothing of interest and what they most needed was shops selling lingerie for Jen's department and what the French called *gaines* and *soutien-gorge*, commonly SG in their parlance.

For example, England simply did not have similar SGs. She did not much care for English bras which were unattractive, weak and did not support her ample figure at all well.

The French, particularly the shops in *Rue du Faubourg* had an upmarket approach and Henry was bored stiff whilst Jen tried numerous garments in the fitting rooms—where he was strictly prohibited from entering. She purchased some as examples but they were highly priced and she questioned whether customers even like Mrs James would afford French Francs converted into Sterling.

Importantly, what Bronnie did find was that comfort was much improved and the support offered by both girdles and bras was significant. Names on labels meant nothing and it would be necessary to try to source makers via the telephone book. Garment sizing was also out of the British ordinary and a table in the phrase book proved helpful as asking for a typical 40E met with incredulity by the French where it appears she scored 105F but this was an average and to be well fitted trial and error was necessary and the selected label may typically range between 85 and 95 and the cup sizes between their D and H.

Days evaporated and they had not been to see any museums or galleries. The *Tour Eiffel* was not open at all as were many listed major sights. The streets were full of construction operations, too. Many shops were closed but this did not seem a great problem as there were more than enough to satisfy their needs.

Bronnie made lengthy notes relating to what she had seen and noted maker's names. She spent most of a day studying the directories and despatched Henry to look at galleries and museums. There were no fashion trade fairs being arranged in France; only leading couturiers were showing their latest, expensive, wares which were unsuited to Dress Address' needs and in any case would soon be copied by lesser fashion houses who sold to the mass markets. Bronnie would have liked to be invited to a show but that could not be arranged as seats were secured by invitation only.

Henry found several museums and places of interest were closed and that Paris had a great deal of work to accomplish before recovering from hostilities and the German occupation. Works of art had been removed to places of safety many years previously and no doubt museum staff and experience had been lost until management had explored all possibilities for regaining normality.

Churches were open and were well peopled and Henry enjoyed seeing *Notre Dame* for the first time. He also wanted to know what Bronnie was up to but, of course, could not communicate but he had found an excellent *bistro* located on the *Ile St Louis* where he had had lunch and booked them in for the evening and he was assured of a warm welcome and some excellent French fare—for the victors. This was a short walk to the hotel in *Avenue Victoria* but it would be dark and few street lights worked but it was hardly worth taking just one or two stops on the Metro.

All too soon, it was time to return to *Gare du Nord* and the boat train to London.

Bronnie was pleased; she had collected a mass of invaluable information for Jen and, of course, had some actual samples she could demonstrate. England needed to improve its lingerie manufacturing and vitally, its design techniques. This would be useful for Mary to know as she had substantial contacts within the competent Jewish fraternity who were inclined to be into design and manufacture.

7 Hunting Continues

After New York, Mary was anxious to start to look for a new companion. She had seen nobody who leapt out of the shadows and gave her cause for a fluttering heart but, to be fair, she was not looking in downtown NY and she had Collie at her heels most of the time.

Her life with Collie had been businesslike from the start of their relationship; it was never based upon close friendship but, having said that, she did get on well with Coleen. Their backgrounds were mis-matched and their training and education were poles apart.

Mary reviewed her possibilities, again. Jen's customer, Charles, was high on the list but Ginny had to be asked, too. There had been no time to join clubs and institutions but on the liner she had met two men who were possibilities. Whilst they did not know one another, they were both American oily-boys working for their conglomerates and active on refinery infrastructure in separate locations.

Brent was going to be based in Pembroke and Chester in Southampton. Oddly enough, both given names seemed like place names in England and she thought this would lead to confusion.

Mary maintained her Chronicle and wrote down her thoughts and feelings which were later to be important.

She liked Brent Collins. He was tall and slim, unmarried but committed to his career and he had clearly stated he was not able to spend time "womanising" as he ungraciously put it. But there was a softer side to his apparent hardness and Mary liked this aspect. Long-term, he did not wish to settle outside of his home country. At least he could discuss this, so he would not be averse to having a family to support. His home town was in Wyoming, wherever that was. Not much excuse for Mary to be able to work in the fashion business.

Mary wrote:

> Brent's tall and slim, unmarried but committed to his career;
> he has not spent time womanising; Arrgh!
> There is a softer side to him. Liked this;
> He did not wish to settle, long-term, away from his country;
> He lived in Wyoming, where was that?
> Probably not much fashion business there.

Brent Collins was to be based in Pembroke. He looked tall, slim and dressed well and had very short, cropped hair which gave him a real American look. His breath was interesting; he must use some form of spray with a cinnamon component. He did not get close and did not speak to my boobs.

Chester, on the other hand, was previously married and he said he was divorced because he was unable to give his wife the home-life she so needed and she had gone off and found some local guy which had given Chester considerable angst and grief because of her intense sexual needs.

Many men found that their lives were connected either to firms working abroad, in the services or the mercantile marine where they were apart for long months at a time and if their womenfolk could not take the lonesome life, then disaster was inevitable.

Chester needed a new close companion and he was absolutely taken by Mary and demonstrated this at every given opportunity. They did get on jolly well. She was immediately attracted to him, liked his manners, kind attitude towards her and a definite need for close companionship. He had two children, so Peter was unlikely to prove a problem.

He liked the way that Mary dressed but this was not a good example as she had not brought excessive outfits since this was essentially a business trip. He did not appear to notice her corseted state or, if he did, he did not make any comment: he must have felt her structure on a few occasions but, maybe, he was just not accustomed to talking to women about their underwear. He held her closely when they danced—too tightly she felt, but maybe this was because he liked the feel of her foundations and the apparent tautness of her breasts or alternatively, was this the American way?

Chester Becker was in his mid-forties, a senior design engineer specialising in refinery projects and aiming for higher echelons of management. His marital status was holding him back in the succession ladder. Directors saw stability as a key component for advancement. His home-base was in Virginia and any future home had to be state-side if he were to advance unless he changed his employer.

All too soon Liverpool loomed out of the gloomy mist with the sound of ships' sirens and tugs' hooters, an increase in crew movements and the sound of chains, heavy ropes being deployed and winches under power. The big liner moved slowly and steadily into place at the appointed dock and the operation took about an hour before there was a final whooping whistle as the tugs cast off. The last breakfast was being served and there was no urgency to leave as customs had not released the passengers.

Mary had breakfast with Chester and other passengers so there was no chance of any intimate or private chatter. She noticed Brent and he tried to get a place at the same table but all were taken. She gave him a warm smile but she thought he realised she was close or attached to Chester which was inevitable on board a ship as, short of meeting in a cabin, all places are public, particularly dance floors and restaurants.

Chester expressed a firm wish to meet Mary again, and passed her a note of his business address. He did not have a private address as he needed to find something to suit his needs and the work location. He did not know Southampton or Fawley and he said he wanted to explore possibilities before being cast into whatever his office thought best.

He did ask Mary if she had any spare time to help him with his search but that was not feasible as so much needed to be discussed with Dress Address directors whilst her findings were clearly in memory. She thought Chester realised that this was not a casual excuse—after all she had been in NYC on business.

Once in Liverpool, Mary escorted Chester to Lime Street railway station where steam trains ran to London's Euston Station. He purchased first class tickets so that they could be relaxed and, importantly, be able to chatter freely. The train had both bar and restaurant facilities.

She promised to meet him the following Sunday and Monday and asked him to find a room for her. Coyly, she conjectured what he would do with this request.

Would he be tempted? Would he find a separate hotel? Would he arrange an adjoining room?

Mary would have liked to spend some time with him in his room but she was not ready for any intimacy beyond a close cuddle. The room arrangements he made would tell her much about him and his morals which were important to her. Being with Chester and looking at what houses or lodgings he chose would also fill in gaps about his life and working arrangements. The new refinery was not in the city and nearer to The New Forest as it was to the west of The Solent.

Chester is going to work in Fawley;
He was married but unable to have a home-life;
She went off with someone else;
I like Chester, a lot;
He is well mannered and obviously cared for me;
He is kind and gentle and needs close companionship;
He dresses smartly, even on ship;
He does not smoke, nor drinks a lot;
I like the twinkle in his eye and the ready smile;
He does not keep looking at other women, good!;
I do not think he is possessive, another Good;
I must find out about his children; ages etc;
Has two children, so Peter unlikely to be a problem;
Liked my dress but did not notice corsets;

Maybe he was not used to women-wear;
Held me very closely when we danced;
Noticed my firm breasts;
Shared a liking for similar music;
He's mid forties and a design engineer;
Seeking senior management posts;
His home was in Virginia;
Would I need to live and settle in USA?

8 Chronicles and Meetings

Mary was at Dress Address early the day after she landed at Liverpool. She had checked to see if this was convenient for both Bronnie and Jen. Alice would stand in for Jen if she had any appointments. These were going to be difficult meetings as she and Bronnie would have to condense their findings into a competent verbal report before the written account was prepared.

Mary said that she'd met Coleen—who now liked to be called Collie—and neither of them had any idea about NYC and where to go. Collie was married and was now formally known as Mrs Eugene Meyer.

Having researched the libraries and directories, they had a plan of campaign and sought shops specialising in foundations and corsetry where they found the owners or staff to be remarkably helpful and forthcoming. Hailing from across the Atlantic they were not seen as a business threat and were told which lines sold best, which fitted and supported better and what garments and makes were best avoided. Mary had full notes which were scribbled as soon as they left every shop.

Mary described the textures, fabrics and constructions they had seen. Bras were so much better in New York and women were well catered-for compared to those visited upon the unfortunate British population. Mary recommended Jen to look into trying to arrange supplies from wholesalers or makers where she had been given names and addresses. Mary had purchased a number of bras she liked and which would probably fit her and some that Bronnie, Jen and maybe some staff would be able to try. She had them in her case and passed them round for all to examine. Mary had told white lies in the shops about the varied sizes she requested as being for her mother or whatever, as it was essential to conceal the real reason for their visits.

Foundation garments were much the same as Jen was used to providing in the UK—imports from USA but there were some differences. She opened her case to demonstrate a new design that had not reached these shores yet. It was a complex design, rather like the fan-laced Camp, but made by Sears, another maker and somewhat improved as far as comfort was concerned. It had lacing which enabled the corset to be adjusted by the wearer and it gave excellent support. Mary said she'd put it on and give the others a demonstration of its effects and power. She felt just a little alarm at doing this in public but everyone knew so much about each other—so why worry?

The UK was not well provided-for with new garments called girdles. Almost every American woman had some and wore them and insisted that their daughters were properly fitted with their size and different designs, too. These were all-elastic, some with a few bones to stop riding-up and others with zips where tightness demanded a means of entry and escape. Girdles came in several lengths and one was observed which stretched from waist to just above the knees. Everyone giggled at the thought.

By all accounts, girdles were worn by young girls so that boys were prevented from having their way effortlessly, as before. Mary had brought some girdles to try in a few sizes to suit the others. Corsets which used to be worn were just a tad too restrictive now that youngsters were emancipated after the war years.

Another find was long-line brassieres but not many were available yet. They looked forbidding and everyone who saw and felt them did not think they'd sell to the British as they were formidable, to say the least. Mary said they were definitely supportive but she had not tried one for a full day's work.

'So, what do you all think of my finds?'

'Mary, you have done wonders for my department. What do you think Bronnie?'

'In time, the whole of your department will have to change to accommodate samples of the new designs. A problem I see is that for every type of bra, we'll have to stock fifty odd sizes to be able to fit anyone from a 32 to 38 in the usual cup sizes, A to E. If you show, say, six varieties or colours, the cost of ordering will be high and space will be difficult to find.'

Jen said

'If we are going to be a competent lingerie retailer, we have to provide the stock and the varieties'

'Quite so',

Said Bronnie

'But I feel we must test the marketplace first before committing ourselves to ordering, say three hundred or so.

'Jen, do you know which sizes would sell better than others; that might enable us to have either a wider range of bras or fewer ordered.'

'I'll look into that suggestion, Bronnie, and come up with a potential order.'

Bronnie had a similar but shorter report to illustrate her Paris visit; her main finds were SGs and some *gaines* as bras and girdles were called across the Channel.

'I foresee my finds adding to Jen's difficulties and maybe Jen really does need to make a careful list of recommended sizes used by most of our customers.'

Bronnie had been impressed by the range of attractive lingerie, teddies, slips, knickers and other items of what she called comfort-wear. She had brought a selection of SGs and comfort-wear for all to see and to try.

Mary asked what had been spent on garments during the NYC and Paris adventures. It was quite considerable—literally thousands when converted to sterling but Jen was certain she'd be able to sell most to her more demanding and wealthy customers; this somewhat relieved Bronnie.

Mary had to leave to don the new corset she had bought and went off to see Alice and to ask how she was getting on. She may well need some help to fit into this new design. She removed her usual stiff corset by unhooking the studs and eyes that ran down the front of the garment; Alice picked it up and loosened the laces a little as she thought it would be needed when Mary left.

Alice did look solid and well formed in her new foundation. She said it felt really good, was incredibly supportive and that she wished she had taken the plunge earlier as it was not in the least uncomfortable; quite the reverse, actually. She enjoyed having to dress each morning, slowly closing the fixings and laces before putting on her business-wear. She felt she looked spectacular: competently supported and with much improved curvature. She loved working at Dress Address and felt she was well looked after by both Jen and Bronnie.

Dressed just in her knickers, Mary let Alice try to fit her into the new and complex design. It was like an All-in-One or a corselette but had unusual lacings so that various parts of her anatomy were able to be restructured. She chose to have considerable force applied to her lower abdomen and backside which was not covered by her regular corset. This felt strange. Her waist was also reduced, rather like the rigid corset action and this garment did have substantial boning to assist. Finally, the upper or bodice section had to be closed; this supported the breasts from below, as did her corset but, again, there were differences and her breasts surfaced rounder and separated whereas, in a corset, they were mono-shaped or were seen as one rather than being two distinct entities with a cleavage as found in the Sears creation.

'What do you think, Alice?'

'Well, it seems to be very tight, indeed; can you take that compress? It certainly gives you a superb figure but how will it feel after a few hours of wear?'

'Alice, we shall see; please would you kindly wrap up my rigid corset and I'll carry that home with me.'

She liked the overall feel. She went into the meeting-room for a demonstration.

'Please take off your suit, Mary',

Bronnie asked. Hands weaved from all quarters as they examined and felt the new design.

'Mary, how does it feel?'

Asked Jen with some surprise.

'Spectacular; I am going to keep it on for the rest of the day and give it a working test.

'Do you think we can obtain more from the supplier, Jen?'

Meeting over, Mary wanted to see Jen for a few minutes before she set off to see Vera and find out how her Get Porter empire was managing in her absence.

'I've arranged a meeting date with Charles and cleared this with Vera.'

'Will you bring Herbert, too, please? Will you also make the booking with a suitable place near where you live?'

'I'll confirm the date and time and location, soon.

'I must say, you look incredible in this Sears garment; and it was not made-to-measure. How does it feel after about an hour?'

'Frankly it feels both very tight and very comfortable, too. Only a good test will tell me how it fares and I'd like to examine my body when I take it off later tonight; pity you will not be there to see and to advise. I'll telephone you in the morning to give you the latest news—and whether I am wearing it then.'

Mary trembled a little as things were starting to move forward; she had Chester lined up as well and Ginny had been in touch with Vera, so assignments there may be on the cards, as well.

Oh, why not just stay a simple widow, Mary pondered. She again recalled how she and James had met; so simply, just across a train carriage. After all, she had met Chester and Brent in a similar manner.

She'd see what came forward; she had been longing for companionship for some time, now. She sat down to write her Chronicle; not absolutely necessary, but to keep in practice. She needed to recall the expressions and hand movements made by Jen and Bronnie as each verbal report was given. It had been a most enjoyable and amusing meeting.

Just sad that Jen could not have gone either to Paris or to New York.

Notebook ready, she took the Underground to Victoria and was looking forward to a good rest. But, first, the Chronicle: It was interesting to watch Bronnie and Jen whilst they examined the goodies.

Bronnie's hands were a joy to watch; they
were like a conductors movements, holding,
feeling, touching, stretching garments and
seemingly taking in all she could feel.

Jen, however, appeared to be more clinical and laid bras out flat, stretched them, felt them all over and mentally made notes, I assume. She felt the wiring and stiffening and places one or two onto her body to assess, too. She put them into three piles; again, I assume the good, the bad and not so sure

We'll see from her written report.

We are at Victoria, now.

Chapter Six

1 Chester in Southampton 1952

*A*rriving in Southampton, Chester had felt distinctly lonely and he so wished he could have remained with Mary whilst he found his way around and secured somewhere to live or to rent.

He found Mary to be a marvellous and strikingly attractive person and he decided he would do all in his remit to attain her as a partner and probably a wife. He knew he had never been with anyone who switched him on as well as Mary and also, he knew that she'd be a major asset towards his aim for promotion to the highest levels within the firm.

What did Mary think of him, he asked himself, rather too often, maybe?

He was worried. Dames like Mary did not grow on trees. She was so unusual and talented, had a good job running her own business and was patently busy. He wished he could have some leave before starting the essential work he was sent to the UK to organise.

A huge new refinery was being developed at Fawley, across The Solent from Southampton and it was located nearer to the New Forest so housing would be attractive. He so wanted Mary to be with him, to help, advise and to see things through feminine eyes—which he naturally lacked. However, she had agreed to meet him on Sunday and Monday and, like a little boy, he was excited.

Mary had asked him to locate accommodation for her and he decided to find a suitable country house hotel in Hampshire. He knew it would be vital never to seem pushy or to upset Mary with foolish arrangements that might cause her to feel uneasy. He settled upon the Logan Hall Hotel which was just outside Lyndhurst and was a late Regency property, now interestingly converted to a boutique hotel and restaurant. He selected and ordered two double suites, one better furnished for a woman with more facilities and not too close to his selected suite.

Chester started to see land agents in Lyndhurst: he had to begin somewhere and this was relatively close to Fawley. He knew what he wanted. He had a picture in his mind and although he did not need five bedrooms, he preferred space and comfort. He would have to employ a housekeeper and a property with separate staff accommodation would be sensible. He needed a short-list by the weekend when Mary was joining him in the search. He had just four days to find something as his work started just as soon as he could be on site. The Monday was a public holiday and many workers would be off-site so that was not a difficulty except that if something was found, the agents may be closed. He deemed that, given his senior post and the cost of a property, he'd be able to expect agency staff to be available for him, whatever the imposed breaks.

Saturday came and he went to Logan Hall to check that what he had ordered was in order. He wanted to view both rooms, again, and ordered some wine and champagne to be in Mary's suite as well as three bouquets of flowers and some special soaps and bath water toiletries. The hotel was used to being asked for luxuries which pleased him. He was used to the best that could be arranged in America. He also decided to meet Chef and to discuss what the menu may offer on Sunday. It may be necessary to order some meats or fish so that they were in stock. Chef was delighted to have someone demanding who cared what was on offer as this gave him a chance to excel with a special menu from which choices could be made.

Chester had noticed what Mary ate on the liner, so knew what to avoid. He thoroughly enjoyed the hotel visit and was, in effect, doing his normal job but for himself and Mary rather than for a huge oil company.

Check, check and re-check was a mantra literally distilled into his being.

A final thought: he organised a limousine to go to Steyning to pick Mary up from her home and to arrive promptly on Sunday morning at Logan Hall for eleven o'clock. He had also retained the car and driver for his use over the weekend. He did have his own company car but he was not familiar with the twists and turns of UK roads in the New Forest where there were more turns than twists, it seemed. The car was a limousine with a dividing screen so that he and Mary could talk freely and be in some considerable comfort. A little funereal, perhaps, but businesslike.

'Mary how dandy to see you, again. I have been so looking forward to be with you.'

'Me, too. But I was expecting you to pick me up, although the car and driver were brilliant; I am not used to such luxury.'

'Let's just arrange for your cases, have a coffee and then start to look at what I have found, so far. You'll love the area; it's green and lovely with sudden good views.'

'I need to have a quick wash and brush, please, so will you take me to my room, please; I'll need just fifteen minutes as I know you are anxious to make a start and time is short.'

'May I have a porter, please?'

'I will not come to your room as I do have to check my papers and arrange the best route to take with Joe, the driver.'

A list of potential properties was handed to Joe who came in and had a coffee whilst the itinerary was developed between them. Chester liked Joe who was a former soldier attached to the Parachute Brigade and well suited to Chester's needs. He lived in Totton so knew his way in the New Forest area. A good choice for a car hire firm.

Mary descended just two minutes later than expected and said:

> 'What a spectacular surprise: the room is fabulous and so well fitted out with wines and luxuries which will give me a really good stay here. Pity it could not be longer. Let's get going as I'm so keen to see what you have organised. Oh, thank you for the flowers: they cannot all have been put there by the management. They are beautiful and so many thanks for the kind thought.'

Joe was entranced by Mary and her gift with words. And her looks and dress were something else. He had never seen anyone so well turned out even when he worked on functions in the Officer's Mess where women were expected to be immaculate partners of their men-folk when in Dress Uniform.

Chester assumed he had done everything correctly; had he missed out on any item? He was unused to organising hotel accommodation but more competent at getting contractors on site, on time with all their requirements. By Mary's looks and gestures, he felt he need not worry.

They set off to look at suitable potential properties that were available for rent and also saw some that could be purchased but that was not the real intention as much more time would be required for major capital expenditure. Rentals for a year or so would give time and an opportunity to see much more of the area and to see how the job and work progressed.

Mary was mentally writing her Chronicle and wondering just what she should commit to paper. She did not find the prospect effortless but knew it would be invaluable later. She was utterly captivated by Chester and his obvious abilities. She refrained from comparing him with James: they were so divergent but there were similarities. No, she must not compare—but Chester shared a liking for things being just so and in motor engineering at the level James aspired to, it could mean a top position in the field or ending a race as an afterthought. She was desperate to know what Chester was like as a lover. Oh, she did miss this close companionship so, so much. Mary wanted to get out her notebook, now, but that would seem rude, so put the idea aside. Just what would Chester think if she had started to write her nonsense?

Much later, when they had parted and gone to their rooms, Mary sat down at the desk and wrote:

> *Chester, Chester: what am I going to make of you?*
> *I am entranced by you. Competent, organised,*
> *masculine and attractive,*
> *well turned out and a strong character.*
> *I have never been so pampered by someone I hardly know.*
> *He must like me; it is not as if we have just met.*
> *The liner gave us time to look at each other, too.*
> *His clothes are immaculate, well pressed and the*
> *shirt and tie match well. I like his choice of shoes and*
> *socks—a particular need for me. I used to have his*
> *shoes or boots immaculate, too.*
> *He is not overpowering in choice of cologne: good!*
> *His hair is carefully groomed and he does not wear a*
> *wig . . .*
> *I like his blue eyes; they seem to notice everything, too.*
> *His table manners are excellent; noticed on the ship*
> *and during the incredibly good meal in the restaurant*
> *this evening.*
> *What do I dislike: what would I change?*
> *He has the start of a tummy. A corset for him, maybe?*
> *He does seem inclined to give orders rather than ask*
> *gently.*

Would this become a problem if we married?
I would hate to be ordered. He has not done so with
me, so far.
He is quite clueless about women's fashion—why not?
He said he wanted help with his suiting and shirts.
I did notice he had a little ear wax; then J did, too!
I would trim his eyebrows, slightly and maybe suggest
he grew a moustache.
He did have two children, aged six and ten and they
were in the USA with their mother.
He said he much wanted to meet Peter
and would like to see his quaint school with rushing
water.
He still did not notice my firm corsetry. A surprise.
I know that he appreciated my firm breasts, though.
He watched them just a tad too often. He did not
look at other women and there were some very
attractive diners. He was clearly interested in me, me,
me and me, alone. Marks out of ten?
Eleven, probably but wax, eyebrows, no corset, no
moustache clueless about fashion—say nine and a half.
Some training needed.

She felt so much better now that she had committed thoughts and findings to paper. She looked at what she had written about Chester a few days earlier and it added up and was not disorganised in the findings and messages. Could she live with him? Consider the prospect; think seriously; there was a real spark but what was it?

2 Jen and Charles

It had never occurred to Mary that finding a man and ending her lonesome widowhood would be quite so traumatic and arduous. Chester was excellent, but, was he too good to be true? How would she manage to add up the mental scores achieved by Charles and who-knows-who from Ginny? Then there was an outsider, Bob de Vere and a remote chance in Richard from Harrow. It was getting a little too involved but she treasured her Chronicles which were like photographs in print. Vera and Jane needed to be shown her writings and she wanted their ideas and comments that they'd bring to the fore.

She started to simplify her relatively short list of prospects. Bob de Vere sounded really lovely but he was in Caroline's pocket and urgently in need of new offspring which she might not be able to pull off in her late thirties. Then Richard; she knew so little about him as they had had a business meeting and personal discussions did not take place. Was he married, for instance? She knew nothing whatsoever about Ginny's findings.

Jen had arranged a foursome in a local inn near where she lived. This was to be an ordinary meeting, so that Charles could just meet Mary without being overwhelmed by ostentatious surroundings. Mary and Jen had agreed to go 'Dutch' and share the cost. Herbert would no doubt enjoy an evening out as Jen rarely took him because he was quite frail. It was not going to be a dressy affair and smart-casual was suggested for everyone.

Mary had no idea why, but she was not looking forward to this meeting but determined not to show her inner feelings; Jen might notice because they knew each other so well although they were not close friends. It gets like that when you've seen each other almost naked from time to time. The meeting was arranged for seven-thirty but Jen, Herbert and Mary agreed to be there by quarter-past at the latest so that they could welcome Charles without everyone being huddled in a doorway. Jen, the one who knew Charles, was going to be the look-out. The appointed time came and went: this was quite strange as it was not polite to be much more than ten minutes late at most. By quarter to eight, Jen decided that they would have to order some food as Herbert had had nothing since a light lunch and he tended to get a little feeble when hungry. By eight, Mary and Jen were a little anxious and could not think what had delayed Charles. He definitely knew and Jen had confirmed the time and the place on the telephone a day or so ago. He knew the name of the inn, so could have telephoned if there was a problem—telephone enquiries would have assisted. Mary wondered if, maybe, Charles had just had an attack of seriously cold feet.

At just after half-past eight, Charles turned up, looking frantic. His train had been involved with a delay on the line, the cause unknown, and everyone aboard had to sit and chew lemons awaiting some information from the train guard. Some passengers were mighty angry and this did not help the atmosphere. The guard said that the only messages had to come via the line-side telephone box operated by the signalman in cases such as these. Charles had fortunately bought a copy of the evening newspaper, so he had something to read and he re-told a story he had found:

> "Quick: it's my husband back early; hide in the wardrobe. A quiet voice suddenly broke the silence in the wardrobe, saying, it's damn dark in here. Who's that, said the man who was still naked. Hand over £20 and I'll not call Dad and tell him who you are. Thinking this was a reasonable means of escape; he handed over the cash and made a dash for the nearby window. The youngster returned home a few days later with a new trannie. Where did you get that? I never gave you money to waste, said his mother. Saying nothing, he was ordered to go to confession where he was bundled into the box and she slammed the door shut. It's damn dark in here, the boy said. Oh! Don't start that again, said the priest"

Which lightened the atmosphere a little.

'Has anything like that happened to you Charles?'

Asked Jen.

'Well, now you ask . . .

'You must be starving, Charles. What would you fancy; the menu is here.'

Mary tried to lighten the general mood and asked Charles what he had been doing today before the train problem.

'I am in charge of emergency aid for the rigs we operate; when things break down, it is impossible to have everything on site to effect repairs. It is my job to assess a situation, what's needed, and how best to get the rig working in the quickest manner without having men and equipment standing idle.

'Today, I had to arrange for an injector pump to be sent to the Gulf by chartered aircraft; not just one plane, but three as no one aircraft could manage the distance alone. The engineer on site could not be certain what make and model the pump was, so I had to source three different possibilities. Quite involved. We cannot use the airlines because customs delays make the loss prohibitive.'

At least Mary now knew something about what he did at his City desk; and she thought it had been financial, bean counting, maybe.

'What do you do, Mary? I know nothing about you as Jen is secretive and she has told you nothing about me as her clients' affairs are confidential, so she tells me. But I know she's mentioned that I wear corsets regularly and that's why we meet at her office. I assume you wear corsets and that's why you know Jen. I have not been able to assess your figure this evening because I was late and you remained seated when I came in. Correctly remained seated, I must add. So, what do you do, secretly?'

'I hunt fabrics and textiles'

'There must be more to what you do. Jen did mention you were extremely busy in your work and finding a pair of socks cannot be that difficult.'

'I search for the almost unattainable, a little like you do when seeking an injector pump. My "pumps" are needed by leading ballet companies and with rationing and the ravages of the war, bolts of material are hard to find; colour, texture, weight and quality all have to be taken into account—as well as more of a technical nature dependent upon what the theatre director has in mind. Stage lighting always passes through coloured filters; coloured fabric can change under certain lighting. Tests are vital. I have often to travel all over London and the Home Counties when I am on a mission.'

'But you used to work at Dress Address, didn't you?'

'Yes, I was there at the start, with Coleen—have you ever met her? It was a small shop and located in the Covent Garden part of London.

'Coleen is an actress and that is how I managed to get compressed into tight corsets. She was dressed for a part as an Edwardian lady and found that she adored the feel and constriction offered by what she had to wear. When the show closed, she decided to talk to Jen who readily had a superb Victorian garment made for her—and she has worn a corset every day, ever since.'

'But what gave you the need for corsets?'

'Coleen, of course. I liked the look that she attained and decided that if she can do it, so can I. So, a few weeks after she had her new corset, I was seeing Jen and decided to venture into the exo-skeletal fashion.'

'You never told me that.'

Said Jen.

'I assumed you realised, Jen.'

'We do have to be careful as Coleen cannot be discussed, here. Confibs and all that please, all of you.'

'Few women wear corsets today. I just wish they did, like the norm in earlier centuries. I think they look superb on a woman and on many men, too. I'd ban pot-bellies if I were a member of parliament.'

'Why are you corseted, Charles? Do you have a pot-belly as you call male tummies?'

'Simply because I injured my back on an oil rig—my last day on one—and liked the support a corset offered. A dreadful thing; it was prescribed by my doctor. I still have it but would not be seen dead in it.

'When my back recovered via physio and some acupuncture, I decided to find a supplier who'd not laugh at me and eventually I met Jen via a woman friend who took pity on me. She was a regular wearer and had heard of Jen and is now a good customer.'

'Stop', said Jen.

'Cannot include her, here, please. I do know that you two do know each other and that she'd probably not mind but I have strict rules and a little breach leads to a cascade if I'm not careful. I do not even tell Herbert anything about my customers; he did not know who was coming here, tonight.'

'Mary, I like the feel of a rigid corset that I wear every day. As Jen might tell you, I have a collection of garments and she keeps me posted on what's available. I have a good income, doing what I'm good at, and corsetry is my hobby. So, I wear what I like and I suppose some discomfort is my penance and maybe I enjoy a little physical torture.'

'But I do not feel this is torture, as you suggest.'

Mary said.

'I so enjoy wearing a corset as it gives me an enhanced figure; a closeness that I love to feel; an improved structure to my body; and a framework that my soul loves—to make me work—better and harder.

'It's a strange desire. My late husband also loved to see me dressed appropriately "in bondage" he used to say, sometimes I even wear a corset at night. He used to love me wearing one in bed.'

'This is getting quite intimate, you two. You'll have me telling you about my dress, soon and that'd never do. I do not even tell Herbert what I wear.'

'So, Charles, tell me a little about yourself apart from what dresses you have.'

'Now you are making fun of me. I am not remotely into "dresses" and anything to do with cross dressing. I'd get thrown off the planet if my employers thought I'd turn up as a fancy woman. They do accept I have a bad back and in the office, that's where it stops.

'I have been married but she died and I'm a widower, now. I have two grown up children who have been living with my mother until recently. Difficult to hold down a job with teenagers when I was abroad and working the hours I do in the City would have been impossible; so I do not see much of them, now. I live near St Albans in a village called Marshalswick.'

'Charles, that is amazing. A coincidence if ever there was one. I spent my first night with a man in the Blackbury Duck many years ago. We had separate rooms and he became my husband, James. He was killed in the war a few years ago.'

'I know the Blackbury well. It needs a new coat of paint, and more, but the landlord and his wife do a good trade there. I doubt if you'd remember them.'

'We could have met there as I know it and it's not far for Jen to come, either. I assume your train broke down or was delayed coming from London.'

'Yes. It would be nice to have a dinner there, sometime, Mary. I do not drink much but go there for the atmosphere and cradle a soft drink after a beer, at most. I drive, so that's my excuse for being un-inebriated.'

'Do you travel on holiday, much?'

'Not really; I do not like being alone on holiday, so I don't book. Also, the costs of single supplements put me off. Maybe I'm mean but why charge more for being alone?

'I do play board games some evenings at the Blackbury and I used to be a dab hand at darts but gave it up as I'm terrified of hurting my back; a lot of twisting is needed to succeed at the level I used to achieve.'

'We differ quite considerably, Charles; as you are a man I'd have expected that. I have unusual likes and going to a pub is not in my habit except in case of need.

'Charles, may I have a look at you, standing, please? You'll be able to see my figure, too.'

Mary and Charles stood to have a look at each other. Charles was naturally slim and his corset made him stand erect with his shoulders held right back. It must have made him stand taller, too. He looked at Mary and said he much admired a well dressed woman who stood well, had a good shape, a well supported bust and trim waist and hips.

'It's all down to Jen, Charles. She has been my guiding light for many years and I owe her so much for her advice, kindness, and support and help when needed. I am her Chairman, now, appointed by Coleen but I do not work in the shop any more.

'How do you find Alice, if I may ask?'

'Alice is really lovely; I was a little concerned when I first knew I was to meet her but she put me entirely at ease; she measured me without any embarrassment and discussed how best to fit me into a new design that I wanted. As I do not have a big bum, it has not come to pass.'

'I think I know what you were looking at. Camp fan-lacer?'

'How did you know?'

'It was not from me, Charles,'

Jen exploded.

'I also wanted to try one, so I guessed. They are best suited to well rounded women with posteriors that are in need of entrapment and encasement—and neither of us fit that bill.

Alice clearly knew her job and I'm glad she was good and kind with you.

'I speak as The Chairman, now.'

Soon, it was time to part company as the staff wanted to close for the evening. Charles and Mary exchanged contact details and farewells were said.

On the train home, Mary started to write her Chronicle:

There was no apparent spark of enthusiasm;
No wonderment and that wonderful inner
feeling.
Maybe it was all spoiled because of Charles
late arrival.
His joke was a bit feeble and I think I've heard
similar before but it did lighten the atmosphere.
Any story would have done.
I think Jen was a little heavy-handed with us;
she was on ceremony the whole time and this
did not help the atmosphere. A mistake to have
Herbert, there;
He did not utter many words at all but he is a
sick man.
Charles did not look at my figure, nor did I see
his until we were almost ready to part for the
evening.
We did discuss why we both love wearing
corsetry.
Charles said it was his hobby and he had a
good collection.
He plays pub games and used to be an ace
darts player.

He does not go on holiday much, as he hates
being ripped off as a single traveller. Does that
make him mean?
Am I being a little cruel?
Charles failed to ignite my dreams and I
wonder whether we should meet again.
Strange that he lives precisely where James
and I had our first nights together in separate
rooms. I ought to arrange a dinner at The
Blackbury and give this one last chance. I think
I am disappointed.
I had been looking forward to meeting Charles.
But I did have reservations just before the
evening. Strange; "them above"?

3 Ginny and Mary

Something was brewing as Ginny had been trying to make contact as a matter of some concern.

'What is it, Ginny? I have been in America and dealing with matters arising from the trip and then I have had a couple of nights away in The New Forest with someone I met on the liner coming from New York. Now I am all yours.'

'Mary, I had a superb example of virile manhood on my doorstep and I wanted you to be entranced but I've had to pass him onto another candidate. I do not think they will click as I had expected you two to fall for each other. My charts and calculations said YES, YES, YES to me but maths is not necessarily the answer to all my selections. Helen also thought that you and this guy were ideally suited'

'Ginny, there will be another man, another chance and another time. Please do not be alarmed. I know that my role as a Professional Widow is coming to an end as I feel this in my bones. Since we first met and I was so impressed by your competent note-taking, I have met three men—one casually, one with high hopes on my part and a third, yesterday, who shares some of my weird interests but unfortunately he just does not crack my whip.

'I have started to write a Chronicle and this is beginning to give me a record and an insight into whom I am meeting and I'd much like you to read some of my entries, if you have time. I only have my notebook and I cannot leave that with you, so it may be best if I read you a bit of it.'

'Sounds good; please do read it to me as I'm not too hot with script.'

Mary began with Richard, followed by Brent. These, she said were targets to try to get the feel of chronicle-writing as it's not plain sailing. Then came Chester, for the first rendition. Having had a splendid day or two with him, more was written and Mary stopped for breath.

'What do you think, Ginny?'

'Well; it's not what I am used to doing but if I can get candidates—that's what we call you, by the way—to keep excellent records, it should help them to find their hearts desire coupled with my mathematics. My method is plainly clinical, yours is esoteric.'

'Please tell me a little about the star you wanted me to meet, if you can without giving anything away.'

'He was an athlete nearing the end of his career, due to age. He is much the same age as you are and was educated at Oxford and was a Blue. He runs his own consultancy business, specialising in business crises which need to be sorted out quickly. He has an excellent brain and is a fast thinker. He does not have a great deal of ready cash; he rents his home in London; cannot say too much more.'

'Well, that's helpful and interesting.' James was athletic and played for his school but never went to university but he was a motor racing driver which is an athletic sport where one needs to think fast and react like lightning. My work is also a form of crisis management; I am called in when leading stage directors cannot find fabrics they are seeking and I have to work fast to satisfy their huge demands.'

'I think I gathered that when we met. This would be why the maths added up between you two. I really do not think there is much in common with the lady I sent him; she is not an academic but is classy, her father has a title.'

Interesting, Mary thought. There are men out there so it is a matter of finding the one. Need I worry? Chester is clearly interested in me. Why me? He is near the top of his career. What have I got to interest him? Maybe we shall see.

4 Chester and New Forest

Last Sunday and Monday simply fled by and both Mary and Chester had to be at their respective offices the next day. They agreed to meet again for a weekend but starting on Friday evening, arriving at Brockenhurst Station so that they'd have all Saturday and Sunday together and that Mary would travel to London on Monday morning. The journey to and from Steyning would be quite mad—changes at several stations, so going via Waterloo was the best option. Chester had not yet arranged a property to lease so the hotel rooms were re-booked as they were known to be satisfactory and the staff had begun to recognise their guests and their individual needs.

Chester was uncertain what time he'd be able to leave his office and it was decided that Mary should take a taxi from Brockenhurst—maybe have a walk around first—and then go to the hotel to rest, read, have tea and await his arrival. They decided that they'd probably go and find an inn or a restaurant somewhere not too far away unless he was delayed past eight o clock when Mary would use the hotel restaurant. She had made this proviso after the last time she awaited James at Marshalswick when he turned up hours and hours late through no fault of his making.

She had time for a walk in Brockenhurst which was a simple small town and its redeeming feature was St Nicholas' Church and some splendid oak trees which, during the run-up to the Normandy landings, sheltered armoured vehicles from sight-seeing enemy aircraft. The taxi took just twenty minutes to get to the hotel which was well known. Had time for a quick bath and change when there was a knock at the door and a message.

Chester was downstairs.

Mary was ecstatic to see him again and it must have showed in her facial complexion as he took hold of her by the shoulders, pushed her away a little and beamed at her, taking in the beauty he so enjoyed seeing. Moving away from the reception hall, he held her hand and took her out into the grounds, just away from the hotel windows, and gave her a really strong hug and she ventured to kiss him first as she was certain he'd be reticent—being on his best behaviour.

Oh! That was lovely, she thought. No man, apart from Harry, had kissed her since sometime in early 1944 and Harry's peck was on the cheek, anyway. No; she recalled that Richard had given her a discrete peck, too. She really hungered for intimacy and closeness with someone she admired. She was not certain that she loved Chester, yet, but it was starting to get close. The weekend together may prove to be a turning point.

Mary was a woman who had to, and was able make up her mind quickly. She was determined to keep this fact to herself and to her

Chronicle. She had her Chronicle in her mind at all times; there were a few lines to write—right now—but someone was in attendance.

'Where would you like to go?'

Asked Chester; he went on:

'We did see an interesting hotel and restaurant in Brockenhurst, I think it was the Montagu Arms but I may be mistaken; let's go and see if I'm correct and we can always mooch around if it's closed or full.'

'That would be fine; I like mooching around and being foot-loose, so let's keep our eyes peeled but don't slam on the brakes when I drop my arm to indicate I've spotted a gold mine.'

'May I be fancy-free too?'

Asked Chester.

'I want, so much, to be close to you. I loved the way you treated me with all those gifts and with the respect that I had longed for. I need to get closer to you but we must both take our time and yet . . .

'How has your time been down here?'

'Fawley is a really huge site and I have not yet mastered it all by any means. There are hundreds of contractors, all doing their speciality work as it is being transformed from a storage depot into a full-scale oil refinery which will not be in production for about ten years.

Esso has taken on a further 3,000 acres and there are yellow excavators and Cat D8s appear to be transforming what was good farmland into a sea of congealed mud whilst they clear the way. That's not my problem, thank heavens. I'm in charge of refinery engineering and my day is taken up with meetings from dawn to dusk but I do have a staff of about fifty to help me. My two PAs keep superb notes so that I am kept on target all the time; without them, and a further one joining soon, I'd be utterly lost as each contractor expects me to be every inch in-pitch the moment they walk into my meeting rooms—I have three of those, so you can just about imagine what life is like.

Infrequently, I have to balance two meetings at once, maybe where a couple of contractors have similar or connected projects. They are being held up now because the infrastructure—underground installations, such as water, sewerage, electricity and even roadways—are all fighting each other for space. I have to argue with my oppo, sorry, opposite number, so that we do not receive extra charges for delayed working. It's a huge balancing act but I have reservations about Esso in USA which dived in too fast: do not ever admit this if you happen to meet one of the bosses.'

'Chester, you must be exhausted; how are you this evening?'

'I'm OK, thank you; I've been so looking forward to seeing you again and am already invigorated but tonight I do need a good night's sleep, so no time for any harum-scarum. Shall we say, bed by ten at the latest, please?'

'I, too, have had a long day, going to wholesalers all over North London instructing them to take a new approach to our needs. This exercise came about because of a meeting I had with a leading firm run by Richard Jaimes who I've mentioned. He likes bits of me, so I gather from his eyes which never left my breasts alone.'

What is it about breasts, Mary reflected, not for the first time. The last time, now?

'My mind has been in turmoil: looking forward more than you can imagine to being here with you, again.'

'See that place? Does it look interesting? Shall we get out and explore the menu and see if they've got space for us?'

'Game pie seems unusual and inviting; it probably grew up in this forest.'

'No room, I'm afraid . . .

'For how long will we have to wait, please; this may assist you.'

Chester handed over a large note which was the American custom.

'May I suggest that you pop across the road and you'll find the inn will have some excellent wine and I'll see you here—say forty minutes; you mentioned game pie; I'll have chef reserve some for you'

'That was well handled, Chester.'

'Money does seem to talk when it is necessary. The hotel understood my requirements when we first stayed there.'

'I do not like flashing cash around; it is not a British habit but, maybe, one that I'll consider living with.'

'That sounds as if I can relax just a little. If we really do start to love each other, who is going to be the first to say so, I wonder? I'd hate, more than anything in this world, to make a complete fool of myself, Mary.'

'Tell you what; I will take complete charge of love-moves as you have a huge exercise on your plate and mine withers into sweet Fanny Adams compared to your responsibilities. Just do not expect me to move like lightning. I'll try ball lightning, first, maybe. Just you wait.'

'Do you know, you have a wicked sense of humour and a competence that I could do with in my office. My PAs are good, but they know nothing of what I have to do; they take copious notes and cross-check with each other but know nothing apart from what they have learned on the hoof, so to speak. I think you'd have vastly better abilities and intellect.'

'Chester, I would not work with you as it would confuse the angels who look after me so well. Soon, I will tell you about "them above" who seem to guide me wherever I am going. I use them constantly.'

Game pie was really excellent and chef had done his utmost to please, with the aid of a shared tip. The wine was good but Chester could not take too much as he was driving and States law prevailed with him and his demanding conscience.

This impressed Mary as irresponsibility would diminish him. They were both in bed by ten-thirty and would meet at nine o'clock for a buffet breakfast which was excellent on previous occasions.

Mary was impressed that Chester had not attempted to ask if he could share a night-cap. Another thing, he still had not mentioned her tight underwear; maybe he disapproves? Surely he's noticed, by now?

The Chronicle had to be written:

> Chester is quite amazing. I have never known
> any man like him—and I
> include J, too. However, they are poles
> apart and nothing will ever
> diminish my feelings for the past.

Chester: you behave with utmost good manners.
I admire what you are
doing at work and do wish
I could work there, with you
but I suspect it would destroy us before
long, so I'll not suggest it.
If the moment seems right, I will express my love
for him and see what his face says or does, then.

I am getting quite good at reading his
inscrutable boat-race-book.
Although he was at work, he has managed
to dress immaculately and was shaved and
cologned with a different flavour: spicy today,
which is a sign of caring for me.

Chester is thoughtful and sensible; I liked his
decision to go easy with the wine. He is a man
who does lead from the front.
I am tired and this is enough, dear Chronicle.
Good Night.

No, some more:
He has not noticed my corsetry, yet. And he did
not attempt to ask for a sun-downer or whatever
they call a quick drink—and a cuddle before bed.
Yes and No! Bye-Bye, again.
Some more thoughts:
I do like his soft American accent; it's growing
on me because it is not too hard
and brash.

"Nos da", as they say in Pembrokeshire with a
curious lilt.

5 Morning Time

Mary was awake quite early and thought how Chester felt after his hard day's work. She considered wandering to his room and surprise him but felt she just did not know him quite well enough, or, perhaps, she was not adventurous enough. She decided to have a deep bath and then think . . .

Quarter to eight; bathed and refreshed and the usual light make-up applied with some Chanel No 5.

She did feel like exploring the hotel jungle; she knew roughly where Chester's room was, just up one floor and along to the right. Taking her room keys, she ventured out. She was dressed only in her nightgown and the hotel bath-robe. She tapped softly—he may be still asleep, but he came to the door at once, expecting housekeeping or maybe a message from reception.

A look of total surprise and pleasure showed. He grasped Mary by the shoulders again and walking backwards, escorted her into his suite and parked her on the settee, releasing his grip. He then dropped his jaw and blurted out:

'You are prettier than housekeeping!'

'I never dreamt that you'd have the courage to come and find me; I am so, so surprised because I have been awake since six wondering whether I should venture to your apartment—and here you are with the same thoughts.'

'Chester, I am terrified of upsetting you, my dear.'

'I am far from upset. Let's set up the ground rules so that you—and I—can relax in each other's company without fear of going too far.

"Bed is out of bounds;

"Undressing apart from our robes is not permitted;

"Kissing—but for no more than two minutes—is allowed."

'Will you add to my laws, Mary?'

'Well, I had hoped to hop into your warm bed, take off all my clothes and kiss with total abandon but then . . .

'Rules are there to break. That's why we have policemen. Hunky great men with muscles. And truncheons.'

'We call them night sticks, Mary.'

'Chester, we are both being naughty. Where's your night stick, then?'

'I ain't a copper, as you call them over here.'

Chester sat next to Mary and took off her bathrobe and put his right arm around her shoulder and drew her to him and moved his face close enough for her to make a move towards his cheek and eager mouth.

Mary's face took on a stiff appearance just to test him and to see what he'd do next.

In return, he pulled her closer to him and planted a really gentle loving kiss directly onto her lips.

Eagerly, Mary responded as if bitten and took hold of him with wild abandon and then broke Rule One and pulled him up and marched him towards the large bed and just lay still, alongside his amazing mind and body.

She thought this was quite awesome. Chester showed no taste for taking any advantage but just lay there looking at his prize with an appearance of adoration and happiness. Then he smiled and went towards her face, again and connected his lips to hers. Mary had not had such affection for years and needed this closeness so desperately. She took his lower lip and carefully bit it and held on tasting and smelling him.

Parting, they coupled their mouths and she started to breathe in and out together which caused Chester to become so excited and she noticed his hardness. Breaking, Chester said,

> 'This is quite sublime; you are a competent lover and I do not know what to do—or what not to do. I had never intended to make love to you until we had advanced our affair and maybe agreed to marry. To make love now may cheapen our relationship and I do not wish to do that; I think you do know that.'

> 'Chester, I am all yours, now; I need your close love— lovemaking—but, as you say, we ought to await our feelings which are overwhelming us, now. How is your tummy, is it aching?'

> 'Of course it is;

> 'I have never, ever, had a woman quite like you who knows all these things. Maybe I am a little naive and the only person I have slept with, who mattered, was my ex-wife who ran off. She was just a body, a lovely body but without much of a mind.'

Mary took his large member and stroked it and removed his nightclothes and placed hers with his on the floor.

> 'Take me, please, Chester; I cannot wait and I know that you will be ill with pain if we delay.'

> 'This is absolute heaven, Mary. You are firm, well juiced and I have seen your curvaceous breasts for the first time. They are spectacular and look solid when you are dressed; how do you manage that?'

Chester moved in and out of Mary with long, slow strokes and he was desperate not to ejaculate too soon and to spoil the event but, as happens, his climax was just too soon for his happiness; he had wanted to reach his crowning point at the same time as Mary but this was not to be. He felt it was vital that she reached a climax, too and had to use his fingers to continue to arouse her senses but there was one more way that he thought might work for her. Chester was determined, at all costs, to make her achieve her result which he knew she needed so, so much.

He slid down the bed, kicked off the top sheet and blankets and placed his mouth near her vagina and nuzzled her and found an area that caused her to gyrate with enjoyment, just above her vagina; there was a small area and this may be the 'G' spot that was spoken about in some articles he had read.

Mary squirmed and wriggled and suddenly she drew him tightly towards her and gripped his body with her legs so as to stop him moving further: he had had enough; she had reached her climax and once was more than enough. More, now, would spoil the fantastic effect.

> 'That was magic: blissful, wicked. Thank you Chester; thank you, thank you.'

They both relaxed and lay back and cuddled together, her breasts lying close to his mildly hairy chest and their mouths breathed together in that marvellous exchange of happiness that can occur after real lovemaking. After lovemaking as it should and must occur. This was memorable lovemaking.

Mary was so, so happy and she knew that Chester was utterly overwhelmed by what he had achieved.

She loved him. She clearly loved him. He was so gentle, kind and thought for her during the whole time they had spent on the bed. He had not taken any advantage or forced himself onto her: quite the reverse. She had taken the lead as he had earlier promoted.

An hour passed and it was nine-thirty and time to get on with the day: breakfast was needed first.

'Chester, please throw some clothes on and come down to my suite, please. I want to ask your advice about something.'

With that, Mary slipped on her nightdress and robe and took off into the corridor to be met by a chambermaid who just said a good morning without a hint of showing she knew. This was a good hotel.

Mary had a chance again for a quick bath and grabbed her damp towel but found that there was another clean and dry, so brushed herself dry in a matter of a minute or so. Her face was still glowing and she cleaned her teeth with care and removed the last sense of Chester-taste from her teeth and mouth.

There was a tap at her door and she expected Chester but it was another chambermaid who made her excuses and said she'd call back. Chester appeared as she left and Mary let him in.

'Chester, have you noticed my clothes and the firmness I effect to wear?'

'I had, yes but in polite society a man does not discuss what underwear his girl is wearing—until she raises the subject.'

'You are right, but I need your help and understanding.' I wear tight and supporting corsetry not because I need to do so but because I want to do so.

'Now that we know each other intimately, and upstairs was quite superb, Chester, I need your full understanding and maybe your liking for what I wear every day. I have brought three corsets with me and need to explain what they do to me and for me and how you might twig.'

'Twig? Are they made of wood and whalebones, too? Mary, doesn't it rather depend upon what you are wearing on the outside for the day?'

'It can do, but I do not know what the weather is like, yet, so I make a choice and stick to it. I am now so used to being tightly encased that I can change outerwear in a few moments whereas my corset can take ten minutes to fit onto me.

'I now need your help. At least you are unlikely to become aroused again, so soon.'

Taking the newest garment that Jen had had made for her but which she had not worn after the first fitting, she passed it to Chester to feel. He expressed astonishment at its weight; it was far from being a flimsy, feminine or remotely sexy item. He held it and then placed it near his nose and liked what he sensed then took it and thought just how this mad melee of laces, hard bones, elastic and sensuous satin or silk could readily encase any woman. He was to find out and help Mary with the lacing and tightness.

Mary was, of course, more than capable of managing for herself after years of practice. She reached for her stockings; a new pair straight out of the light card packet which she unravelled from the inner tissue-paper and rolled the first so that her fingers reached the toe seam correctly and slipped it onto her leg and up her thigh. Chester became aroused, again and bent to stroke her other thigh which she loved almost more than anything that had already happened. She leaned back and gave out a low moan and a sigh but realised they had work to do, so grasped the other loose stocking and started it around her other toes and stood to make it and its mate gain height and tautness on her legs. Cool stockings were always a pleasure.

Chester clearly was aroused again; a good sign.

'Chester, we have work to do; that is why I am down here. We'll make some more love this evening and that's an order, not a threat. I so, so need you.'

'Mary, I cannot express myself except when I am inside you. I am supposed to be the boss-man, in charge; taking control . . .

'No, this is keeping house: my department.'

Now it was corset-time, again. She stepped into the lower section and wriggled so that it rose over her bottom and up her tummy until it covered her as far as her rib cage. Now she attached her suspenders onto her stockings with the six clips. Chester looked utterly entranced. He had never, ever seen such a performance. Mary was still naked and her pubic hair was in full view. Knickers are the last item to wear as one needs, at times to take them lower during the day. Her modesty control took over and she turned through a half circle towards a wall.

'Now you can help me, Chester. I need to tighten the corset around me by closing the three sets of laces. One set is at the back and there are two at the front. I normally leave the rear one more or less closed, as it is, but today, I'd like it considerably tighter, so please undo the simple knot, like the one you have on your shoes, then pull the lace pairs until the garment closes a couple of inches. Can you see what I mean?'

The corset became tighter and felt more secure and he asked,

'Is that enough?'

'Yes, I think that will do. I have two more laces to adjust here.'

Turning towards Chester with her pubic hair seeming to rustle in front of her, she said:

'Please adjust these evenly; it's quite difficult but with my help we should be able to achieve the necessary balance—neither side tighter than the other.

'Try the left set first and I'll say "when".

'When!—I'll hold the laces whilst you do the same to the right set. The whole corset should start to feel firm soon. Just a little more; it is really tight and this garment has not been run in yet. This is its second outing. Corsets are a little like motor cars: have to be "run-in".

'Ooh! This is enough. Please tie a shoe-lace knot, carefully and don't let any laces to slip loose. I'll then do the same to the left.'

Mary now needed to fit and to close the bodice section and it also had lacing to close at the back but, having had many years of practice, Mary could do this in the dark and blindfolded. Chester said:

'You look like Houdini in a straightjacket. Surely this cannot be easy, Mary? Are you doing this just for my benefit?'

'It is wonderfully restful after about half an hour when it has become used to me and I have settled into its power and control; I do not notice it unless I have applied it incorrectly then and only then it may dig into me.

'As for your benefit—no. I am wearing my corset solely for my benefit because I wish to look glamorous especially for you, and to be seen as women should be seen and admired.

'I now have breasts that are well supported, firm and controlled and higher than normal, but not sagging at all and never bouncing, whatever I do.

'Now, please help me to choose from the day dresses I have with me; suit or long dress, Chester?'

'Knowing what we are going to do, I think a suit would be preferable for agents but I'd prefer a dress.'

'A tweed suit is what you'll see, today, Chester'

Taking a light tweed suit that she'd bought from Dress Address some months ago, she slipped on her knickers, blouse then the skirt, zipped it up and was helped into the jacket by the attentive Chester who also helped to close the front buttons of her blouse whilst she felt him finely touch her taut breasts. That touch was quite exquisite. She had never, ever allowed anyone else, apart from James, to be quite so intimate with her body for all these intervening years.

She considered she was now disqualified from being a Professional Widow. Did she have to write to the War House and tell them the truth? Of course not; she surely had to be married but recalled what the regular missive had said. "If you marry or choose to live with anyone, then you are disqualified from receiving your state annuity" This recall annoyed her and somewhat deflated her arousal. The impertinence.

> 'Mary, I am utterly astonished. I do not believe you are relaxed, but you say you are, so that must be. Do I like what I see? Of course; you look so elegant and I feel unworthy to be in your presence. I now appreciate what I have been seeing since we first met. All women should wear fine undergarments—'

> 'Foundations'

> '—like you do; women need to be supported, so as to bring out the best from their natural curvature. Most American women do wear girdles and things nowadays. It seems to be a rite of passage for the younger element—for my American PA, whereas my Brit . . . well!

> 'Breakfast time, if they are still serving. We can also let the poor chambermaid have another bed to make.'

> 'Do you drive, Mary?'

'Yes, but I do not have a car, nowadays. I have a little red book which gives me a licence to use the roads but I'm out of practice. I never had to take any silly test, thank heavens. I'd have failed it. Do not expect me to be much good; I need to go into a field to drive around in circles to get the feel, again.'

'What's planned for today, Chester?'

'I need your help with some more properties that are available to rent; I wish we had Driver Joe, but we'll have to manage. Can you map-read?'

'Positively not and no, I cannot understand maps. James used to twist and turn his map almost inside out.'

'Then you will have to take the wheel and I'll navigate.'

'No, no, and positively no, Chester. I will be a liability to all wildlife, foxes, pheasants and darling deer. Oh, and a danger to you.'

'Then, let's just find an open space; plenty round here as much of this is what's called Common Land, so they say. Then I'll start to teach you American style.'

'That's in return for your instructive lesson in bed with me this morning, Chester. You are an amazing lover and attentive to my needs which were just as great as yours. How is your tummy; does it ache?'

'No, not at all; but if I had not received the release, then I'd be in dire pain. Must be a bit like what you have every month with your curse. By the way, we did not take any precautions. I did not come prepared. Do you think we are safe?'

'I should be safe as my last period was just a few days ago. However, I'd really love to have your baby. My fecund time will soon be over for ever.'

'Mary, I had not intended to ask you if we could marry because I take important decisions with considerable thought. That is my training and my practice. I'd just love to ask you, right now, but I feel we must at least get this weekend over; we hardly know each other and for all I know, I might have a competitor.'

'No competition, Chester. Even if there was, you'd take the winner's podium. No, you'd share the winner's podium, sorry about that, but someone else came first.'

'Of course. I also had a first wife, so we are equal on the togetherness stakes. Come, let's get driving round and round in circles.'

The car was a Sunbeam, oddly enough, but not a racing model; a plain ordinary car, suited for an executive with leather upholstery and wood panelling wherever the makers could find a tree to cut down and affix the bark. It had a bonnet that was long, like a Hurricane's front fuselage where the pilot sat. This car had a high roof-space and a boot which would probably take a ton of cement if called upon so to do. The headlamps were striking, fixed to the front wings and they shimmered in the daylight.

It even had a starting handle, according to Chester. Something that the Americans had long since left by the roadside as their motors were too vast to twist into life by hand.

Mary got into the driving seat but was far too far from any of the pedals; she was also too low and had to peer around the huge headlamps; one of them, at least as she could not see the other.

'Hop out and I'll see if the seat can be adjusted. Yes, here we are. I think we have to sit in the seat and slide it forwards and backwards until it reaches its best position. I will do this for you. Does this look better, Mary, my love?'

'I can now see the winged whatever on the radiator cap and also both lamps. Hop in, please.'

'Now, you are not practiced and this automobile will seem vast versus the pedal-car you last drove. So, expect to stall the motor. I did when it was given to me.'

# Chapter Seven

1 Richard Jaimes

*B*ack at the office in London, Mary was surprised by a call from Richard who was insistent that they met, soon.

'What do you have for me, Richard?'

'No materials, but a business proposition and a personal matter you may like to hear.'

'Sounds interesting on both counts; when shall we meet—and where?'

'I'll come down to Victoria, this time, as it's my turn to travel and I rarely come far south. Ideas where to meet in some privacy?'

'The Grosvenor Arms is good and it's central to where I work. We do not meet people in my office as it is my flat and we've hived off a section for Vera and her assistant to work.'

'May I suggest Wednesday lunch time say 12.30, Mary?'

'Good; see you there then; meet in the bar area?'

What had Richard in mind? She looked at her Chronicle entry, made several weeks ago, and it reminded her of her feelings and thoughts. Richard did want to alter the tone of that meeting to a personal level and he was clearly interested in her figure and she had the impression he was mentally undressing her which she did not like—it put her off him.

Also, he could only just stop his hands touching her waist to explore just why it was visually small. So, whatever personal matter was in store, his agenda was going to be deflated. The business proposition interested her but whatever could he have to offer or to suggest? Richard and Mary's businesses were quite different. She felt that her work was at odds from his textile stock-holding. There was little common ground except when she needed a few bolts of material—like any other of Richard's customers. So, having settled her mind, she had a short discussion with Vera about Richard and awaited Wednesday with both interest and alarm.

Mary had not mentioned what took place in the New Forest but Vera had to be told. Where to start? Her reputation for keeping an extreme distance was soon to be in tatters.

'Vera, I have an admission to make.'

'Good heavens, your face is flushed quite pink; whatever have you done—or been doing whilst you've been away in the deep, dark forest?'

'I've been a really bad, bad girl.'

'I have been longing for you to let your hair down for so long but could never mention anything personal for fear of having my head chopped off; just what have you done, then?'

'You know I met Chester on the ship and since then we've been together three times. Vera, I took myself to his room at the hotel and I'm no longer a professional widow.'

'Well, that's the best way I have ever heard someone tell me they had slept with their beau. Did you really, Mary? Are you pregnant or anything, perhaps?'

'No fear of that—but I'd like to be, though.'

'So you did, did you'

Vera said, smiling broadly and obviously wanting to hear the grisly details in full.

'Go on, please.'

'Well, Chester looked after me admirably. He behaved with utmost dignity and calm and was quite definitely attracted by my mind and probably my body, too.

'Never once did he ever attempt to get close or personal and you know that I like that approach.

'Consider Richard, who just wanted to undress me. None of that from dear Chester.

'Anyway, I woke early on Saturday, had a bath and decided to find his room and knocked softly; he was already up but still in his hotel robe. His face was a picture and he was both surprised and overjoyed to see me. He took me by the shoulders and placed me on his settee.

'Again, no attempt to force himself upon me. He set down some rules such as the bed being out of bounds.

'I had already breached the rules by coming to his apartment . . .

'So I decided to take every initiative and stood and took him to his bed.'

'Mary, you are incredible; naughty, skittish—and I like it. I did not believe you had it in you. You have kept every man you know at such a distance that you are really regarded as not just frigid but men would take odds on your being a lesbian; you knew that, didn't you?'

'Vera, I know my reputation; it is the armour I wear to keep them at bay. But I needed his visible and tangible love and to be handled by a real man who knows exactly how to behave. I have been alone for far too long, now.

'His handling of me in bed just proved that he is what I'd expect from James, had we had more time together. Chester was kind, caring, and gentle and saw to it that I reached a climax that I so desperately needed.

'Needless to say, he reached his far too early the first time, which is understandable.

'Most men are unable to carry on; forgive me, but something goes a little limp. He used other means, means that had never been tried on me ever before. Vera, I am embarrassed.'

'I can see you are a bright colour of pinky-red and it's time to bring out the tea and to celebrate your achievement. Bottle of champagne about?'

'Chester had never seen my undressed state, without my foundations, and after this junket, I asked him to join me in my room, sorry, suite. The hotel is lovely, by the way.

'After another bath, which I needed, I can tell you, I determined to ask him to help to dress me so that there were no alarming secrets between us. I was quite worried about what he'd think. I cannot change my habits and the liking of what I wear but it could have put him off so, he needed to be exposed to the facts.'

'Once again, he was incredible; he dressed me, or helped, even putting on a stocking, lacing my corsets as tight as they'd been made to slice into me and was quite overcome by my breasts which, when encased as they are—all he wanted to do was place his face between them and to breathe the aroma that must have been pouring out of their satin enclosures.'

'He was a real joy' He mentioned his sudden liking for corsetry several times over the remaining weekend, we had all Saturday, Sunday and Sunday night together so there are no hidden dress problems to overcome, now.

'I really do feel that Chester is going to be my second husband. But, I want your advice and help as well as Jane's feelings. It is unfair of me to use your advice and then to turn you off just before taking a momentous decision.'

'Mary, I know how strong a person you are. You do not need my help, or Jane's wisdom, either. The decision must come from inside you—based entirely upon what your gizzards tell you.

'Seriously, Mary, if you cannot tell the truth from what you have experienced, then you are not the boss I have so enjoyed working with for all this time. Mary, go with your instincts. Look at your Chronicle and read, re-read and bring up any aspects you have concerns about. Discuss them with Chester. Listen to what he has to say about you, too. But you do not need to ask anyone else. As they say, "your call" You do have my entire blessing and I wish you every happiness.'

'Shall I tell Richard that you have just become engaged?'

'I think that would be wise. I do not feel happy with a guy who
has tried to undress me; would that stop if we were together
and he saw someone better looking? No.'

Richard called off the entire meeting and Mary never found out
what he wanted—apart from asking her out. Quite what the business
venture was, well, it died, so must have been connected with his need
for my body, she thought.

2 Steyning Night

As usual, Mary went home and hoped to see Jane, there. Sometimes
she and Harry came home too late to have a natter but she determined
to let her hair down for the second time in the day.

The telephone rang and it was Chester; it was nearly ten-thirty
and he hoped Mary was not already in bed; he had had a lively day
at the oil-works and was dog-tired but had been hoping Mary would
ring—unlikely as she did not know his number, yet.

> 'Mary I feel so incredible. I have never felt quite so physically
> complete except when I am with you, with you, whatever we
> do together.

> 'Even when you nearly managed to mow down that huge tree
> but that was my fault because I wanted you to stop looking at
> the shift lever.'

> 'Chester, I feel the same. I have been waiting for Mr Right
> to appear since the start of the war. I lost James then, not in
> 1944. It has been about fourteen years . . .

> 'I vividly recall Peter, when he was quite young, asking me
> "Mumby, who's that strange man in your bed, Mumby?" How
> do you imagine I felt, then?

'There was nothing I could do; his leave was spasmodic and he had to take it as it was available and there was never any notice, so I did not know from one day to the next whether or when he'd appear.

'I've had one of the most miserable times that anyone could endure. I was even told, by a clairvoyant, that my husband would not come back from the war. I dismissed her talk as just stupidity on her part but she was so right, not just once, but twice. I believe in clairvoyance, Chester. I have been close to things I cannot understand not just from Eleanor but from Olive Weeks, too. She read my tea-leaves so, so accurately.'

'I do not believe in ghosts, spooks and things that happen supernaturally, Mary. I am a practical man and I know what I can see and touch and smell, maybe. I need to be convinced about things that go bump in the night. You will have to tell me much more and I'll need strong persuasion.'

'Chester, we have so much more to discuss and one day we will get round to it. For the time being, I have told you and let's let it rest. I have no need of more visits to have my tea dregs analysed.

'Now, I just want to help you to establish yourself at Fawley. With my help you'll live in a place you grow to love. Maybe, you will grow to love me, too. I'd like that, so much, Chester.'

'Remember, Mary, the initiative must come from you; we agreed that course of action, remember?'

'How can I ever forget that?

'I have just turned down another man—at least Vera telephoned him—whom I'm convinced made an appointment to tell me what he thought of me and to ask . . .

'I have nobody else lined up in my gun-sights—or should that be radar, these days?

'I could go on hunting, searching, looking and feeling my way and each day I will age another day and days become weeks and weeks months . . .

'I think you are in the same vacuum; alone, unloved and missing what life should be all about.'

'Chester, when do we meet again? Did you say Friday, again?'

'Yes; Brockenhurst and back to the same hotel which is my base for you until we sign up for what we want. Do note the "we", Mary'

'I did.'

'Are you still trussed up in your extreme bondage, may I ask?'

'Yes, of course. I am out of my suit and ready for bed and will just loosen it a bit and go to sleep.'

'Surely not in your foundations?'

'Oh yes; I will be reminded of you if I wear them. I love you, unreservedly, Chester. I want to feel you around me all the time, night and day; do you have any idea how I feel?'

'I am just starting to understand. You are one amazing piece; I want you to be close, closer, and closest to me at every imaginable moment. Did I hear voices?'

'Yes, Harry and Jane have just come in and I must go, now. This call will have cost you a fortune.

'No; I am still at the office. Good night, my darling one.'

'Have a good rest, Chester, my dearest; Good Night.'

§§§

'Jane, How good to see you. Hi Harry.'

'Mary, I have missed you for days and days; what have you been up to, if I may ask?'

'Today, routine work in London, but I have been staying in the New Forest with Chester, a new man in my life.'

'You are not permitted to have anyone in your life without my agreement, Mary; please tell me about him. Is he English? What's his name? I heard you say "Chester" as you signed off and that's not an English first name apart from being a town in the wet and windy north, near Crewe.'

'Jane and Harry, I have so much to tell you and I need your advice, as usual please. When I returned to England on the liner from New York, I met Chester Becker and another guy, called Brent.

'Both were coming here to work for oil companies but I preferred Chester and spent time with him, especially in the liner's restaurants. He is divorced, in his mid-forties and a senior design engineer for the new refinery being built near Southampton. He is one of the top people at the huge site. As a guide, he has three PAs and seems to spend his life chairing meetings with contractors, so it's intense.'

'What's he like as a person—nothing to do with work, Mary?'

'I have written my Chronicle and to take in the answer to your searching question, please will you both have a read. That is why

I have been labouring over my whimsical writings several times a day, if I am able.'

§§§

'Well, he appears to be comfortably off;

'you stay in a suite at his hotel;

'he hires a limo to collect you;

'He does not impose upon you and is careful not to have a quick grope, sorry, grasp—which is a good sign. I think respect is all important and he looks towards you with care and gentleness and does not seem to take any advantage. You both appear to be getting on well, together. Any arguments? Rows, even?'

'Only when I tried to bulldoze an oak tree with his car and he nearly had apoplexy, Jane;

'otherwise, none whatsoever, but it's early days and I am going down to Brockenhurst this Friday. We, I should say, "he" is looking for a good pad until he can buy what he wants. Together, we are searching the New Forest via land agents but have not as yet decided which to take, if any, of the current offers.'

'We had a lovely time in bed last Saturday morning . . .

'You didn't, Mary. You devil. I'd never have thought you as being capable as, whenever I see you with any man, your guard is so far up that I cannot see your face!

'I am more than well aware that James was your life, soul and mate and you do not wish to dilute his remembrance in any way.'

'You are correct, Jane. I did ask James—you know I talk to him—for his help as I am tired of being a lonesome widow. So, my guard is down but Chester never took any advantage whatsoever. He was unaware that I dress in heavy corsets. He had never touched me intimately—well apart from a few dances on the ship.'

'Please go on, Mary; tell us more. I am wildly interested and I think Harry is too.'

'Yes, don't let me interrupt you.'

Harry muttered, just awaiting the next salacious bit . . .

'When I awoke in my room, no, my suite on Saturday morning I thought I'd have a bath and had decided not to go near his room. Bath over, and dry, I had a fit of the devil and went off to find his suite in the jungle.

'I tapped on the door and his face was a scream. Surprise, happiness and real joy all rolled into one expression. I was in my bedclothes and room robe, still. He took me by the shoulders and marched me to the settee and sat me down. No attempt to kiss or to cuddle and he maintained his distance.

'Then, after a while, he asked, quietly, if he could steal a kiss. Moving closer so that was do-able, he enjoyed the experience; as I did, too. Then, Oh I forgot; He made some rules like "no bed; "out of bounds" and a couple of others, too.

'Anyway, I just became too excited; I have not been in a man's close company for some years now, and I needed to be close. I need creature comfort, Jane. Do you understand?'

'All too well. When I found Harry, we were all over each other. I had been desperate and Archie was so far away. All that's history, now; I am so happy with Harry and wished the same for you. Go on; I interrupted . . .

'The devil was in me, I now know for certain; it took over and I leapt up and ran to the bed: he followed and, well, we had a sensational time together.

'I am still tingling at the thought.

'Jane and Harry: advice, please.'

'Mary, neither of us can give advice as to what you should do. Your decision; you'll know. Do as your inner self suggests and I repeat what you say, so often: "ask for help".'

'Typical: ask friends for advice and they turn you down!'

3 Vera in Office

Mary felt really alive; still tingling as she had described her senses to Jane. Why had she been such a fool for all these years? Why had she not realised that we are here, on earth, for a limited time and every moment should be enjoyed or at least used with a purpose in mind, Mary's inner self muttered.

"You have wasted so many years; you have shown your back to so many admirers; you must now pick up the pieces and make someone else happy; then recover your own senses and repair the damage you have inflicted on your body, your brain, your memories—and remember—thank James."

With that monologue spent, Mary burst into floods of tears.

'What on earth has happened, Mary? This is just not you. Has Chester said something?'

'No. My inner self gave me a good talking-to. Much deserved, I know.

'Tea or coffee, now, Vera?'

This gave Mary a moment to dry her eyes and have a look in the mirror to repair the damage and to try to wash away her red eyes—as Vera had said, "this is just not you". Usual tea made, Mary took the cups to her desk and passed one to Vera.

'So what brought on this introspection, Mary?'

'In the past, I have been foolish. I am so happy with Chester and that has demonstrated how foolish I have been. As you know, many men have looked at and admired me and what have I done in return? I have snubbed them by putting on an air of being untouchable. That's why I have won the accolade "lesbian".'

'You are about as far from being interested in other women as any I have known. That is not you, either. You have been loved by James and his memory for longer than I have known you and this relationship seems to have guided you in almost everything you have achieved—for good and less good.

'By "less good" it is you, and you alone who has suffered. Now I am able to see a real future for you. Chester is an able man. He earns enough to be able to support you in a style you have never previously been able to achieve.'

'Vera, I know; I have become used to having to live carefully. I have not been successful like Coleen with her fabulous business, Dress Address, and her own personal success with Eugene Mayer.'

'You have one of the most successful stage-connected firms in London. Why do the leading directors and couturiers beat a path to this humble office almost every day? They need your incredible expertise, Mary. Nobody else has your ability to know, instinctively, what they need. They contact us by letter or telephone and try to explain in words what they are visualising and what happens? You hear and somehow translate their needs from whimsy into fact and go find exactly what they have in mind.'

'I know; I do seem to have a gift for reading their minds; not directly as would a psychic maybe, but by instinct and an understanding of the London stage scene. They describe what they want and for which production and my sixth sense and experience takes over and I translate that into bolts of fabric . . .

'Then you take over and deal with the practicalities of delivery, payment and book-keeping for me. We work as a team, the three of us.'

'Tea break is over. What's on the books today?'

'You have a board meeting at Dress Address Limited where you have to keep proceedings under control. That's the Chairman's function. You must listen, digest what the others have said or need and refrain from giving advice or taking sides with any faction. You guide what's happening, rather as a ship's captain. You are neither on deck nor in the engine-room. You keep order, you maintain the proceedings via the agenda and you only have a say if and when there is a vote that is deadlocked. I expect you will also need to take notes as there is no company secretary, as yet.'

'Yes, that is on the agenda. Also pay structure, expansion of Jen's department, expenditure on new lingerie and new marketing requirements as, with expansion, we have to tell more people we are here, waiting to see them and to show how new lingerie will comfort them.'

Mary and Vera attended to Get Porter's current requirements for the stage and Vera made a list of contacts she needed Mary to telephone and to turn requirements into orders. Some, Mary would have to see before ordering and these would have to await the morning. Today was timed-out and the board meeting would run well into the evening. It was the first and, frankly, Mary was a little concerned at how it would operate.

What wise words Vera has given today. How must I behave at the meeting? Nobody will have a clue how to proceed and they'll be nervous to start with. The accountant will be there to assist, which will be good. As ship's captain, I have to be the guide, the authority and to encourage the others.

As she was about to set off for Dress Address Ltd.—

'Call for you, Mary.'

'Hi, Chester; why the bell this morning?'

'Only that I have a few minutes between meetings and I want to say how much I need you down here. I cannot attend to my personal affairs and run this refinery expansion. Do you recall my telling you that the only thing stopping my career in its tracks was my lack of a family life? This is weighing heavily on my mind and we need to discuss this at the weekend. Are you ready for Friday evening?'

'Longing for the time to pass and to feel the movement of the train racing its way south. Meanwhile, I need you here to help me run a difficult and complex board meeting. Vera has just briefed me as to my duties but I lack vital experience.'

'Mary, you told me that the accountants would be there to help and to guide proceedings from a formal pattern. That is their job; they appreciate that you are all amateurs—but wage-earners become salaried staff by experience and that is what you and the others have to achieve. Put simply, it will be a learning process and the teachers are there, so stop worrying. I know you are on edge; I know you better now than you know yourself. Just to say, what a peachy person you have become with me. I turn to you for almost every decision we make together: where to go, what to view, what to say to agents. You are incredible. I'll leave you, now, as I am being pressed into service by a PA.

'Love you.'

'I love you more . . .

4 Board Meeting and Away

Mary took the chair and opened the meeting introducing everyone, mainly for the benefit of Ivan and Spencer who were from the accountancy practice. Everyone was asked to give a short account of their experience, when they joined Dress Address and how they feel that their contribution to the Board will progress the business.

Ivan was asked to explain the duties of directors and he concentrated upon the roles that each member was expected to take charge. The legal points and responsibilities and confidentiality related to being a director were also explained. Ivan preferred board meetings to be run on a formal basis and that even though the business was small, the responsibilities and confidentiality aspects were to be regarded as if the business was much larger.

Mary asked Ivan to run this first meeting as everyone present had to learn by example. Notes would be taken by Spencer but each member should also write down points made that reflected upon their department or office.

> 'Good Evening; I am Ivan Hughes and my colleague is Spencer Acres who is a trainee within our practice, typically called an Articled Clerk. I am a fellow of the Institute of Chartered Accountants and have the letters FCA after my name. I will endeavour to run the first few meetings on behalf of your President, Coleen Meyer, who cannot be here today. She will receive a full copy of the notes Spencer is taking and he will have them typed up. You will all receive a copy, too, and these must be regarded as strictly confidential and never to be released from your close possession unless in this building or in your own homes, but kept locked, safely. Let's start.'

Each Director gave their own reports and was glad when matters concluded as being in a formal board meeting for the first time is quite an experience. Ivan was sensible and helped at the moments when there was a sticking-point. There was not a great deal of finance to discuss as there were no monthly accounts, yet but these will be available for the next run. Initial talk of what orders would be needed for Jen's department were formulated. Marketing the revised business was also a major discussion point and Ivan suggested that there was now a need for close budgeting. Overall, the meeting was not as daunting as had been expected. Bronnie and Jen had work to do before the next meeting—which will be when first decisions are taken by the Board as a whole. Mary, as chairman and director in charge of salaries must report on her proposals. The post of Company Secretary also needs to be filled and suggestions will be required. She knows who will help her with her deliberations.

Mary closed the meeting and thanked everyone for their valuable time and input. Time, now, to return to her apartment, collect her case and make her way to Waterloo and the train leaving at about ten in the evening. She felt acutely nervous even though she was like an adolescent schoolgirl before going on stage. Mixed up emotions mingled with a longing to be with Chester, again. He had said in a quick telephone call that he was being put off his work ethic and that he must get a grip on himself.

Enough time to change, have a quick wash and attend to the ravages of the day and the practice Board meeting. Hair was just so, as Mary had been to her usual dresser on Thursday who had been requested to put on a really good show. Not that she could see her hair apart from peering in the mirror, it felt unusual; somewhat prepped and in a new style and even a mild colour change from dark to just going a little blonde. She must try to grow her locks to get full advantage and at the next appointment a tad more colouration and styling will take effect.

Mary pondered whether Chester would even notice the transformation from mild mouse to alley-cat.

Jen had given Mary her new corset which she said she'd much enjoy wearing in the country. It was made in America and consisted of a made to measure all-in-one garment, which covered all her figure from below her spine upwards to include her breasts and it was closed via a long row of hooks and eyes to the left, under her arm. That was not all.

To give strong control over her tummy, it was constructed with a firm under-belt which was stiffened and was about nine inches wide and also closed with a row of hooks and eyes but was unseen under the outer layer but she knew it was there. The whole garment was good; less restrictive than any of her laced-up corsets but positively firm enough to give her good figure a substantial help to effect the overall hourglass shape she had come to expect.

As she walked out, carrying her case, she felt the pressure of the garment and liked the new sensation and overall control it gave her; it was jolly expensive but beautifully made and supported her breasts as if she was born inside it. She especially liked any corset she wore to lift her bust an inch or two higher than most women chose to, or had to wear theirs. Would Chester notice this change, she mused, as she jumped aboard the bus platform, helped by a kindly conductor, taking her case, who said

'Waterloo is it, Madam?'

'Yes, I'm aiming for the 10.05 for Weymouth.'

'Plenty of time; please take a seat and I'll grab a few coppers, soon.'

Train journeys were a real pleasure; not many passengers at this time of the evening but a somewhat wild-haired man entered the compartment and Mary decided to get out and find another place where there were some women passengers. The train had no corridor and she wished she had asked for a first-class ticket. At least the strange man did help her with her heavy case and this gesture recalled her memory when James first spoke to her at Brighton Station all those years' ago. Just memories but no room for getting maudlin. Use the memory to build upon her longing to reach Brockenhurst again and to receive a hoped-for kiss and a generous hug.

No Chester waiting at the station; this was not surprising as he was often late as he was never able to control his time to the minute. Every time he left the refinery site, he was delayed by one or more colleagues who had an invariable "urgent" matter which could await a week or more. He thought he needed to start to train people in the American way of performing their duties where people on the move and clearly off duty were never delayed; just good old fashioned crackajack manners.

Mary made for the Waiting Room but refreshments were closed but at least the stove was still quite warm and a few people were still milling around, so she felt safe. Chester dashed in about thirty minutes later than he had expected and instantly noticed her new fresh appearance, took her face into both his warm hands and moved her carefully, as if she were a china doll, so that he could give her the longed-for kiss. The hug was lost because of her coat but that could wait.

They had decided to take one suite at the Logan Hall as they both knew each other somewhat better, now. It would be great fun to be able to wallow in each other's more intimate company and to be able to discuss what to wear and even to help each other with their choice.

The visit had a lengthy agenda; a property had to be finalised until there was time to find a permanent berth that could be purchased. Chester did not wish to be hurried with this major choice and, in himself, he also wanted to be settled with Mary, first. He was quite ready for the next big step between them but was Mary as far advanced with her thinking as he was? His job was making decisions. Did her work involve thinking on her feet 25/24? Time to raise the important matter when they had had a cuddle in a few minutes time.

'Have you eaten, Mary, my love?'

'Nothing; I forgot about grub altogether.'

'Let's see what Room Service can rustle up; I could wolf a fillet steak; what about you?'

'Try them for a mushroom omelette, please, and a bottle of Sauvignon Blanc. I think apple pie and custard to finish unless you'd prefer a cheese board. Leave it to you.'

'Mary, my love, we have not had a cuddle, yet. How was the train journey? Any problems?'

'I settled into a compartment in an old non-corridor train and a scruffy man came in and I decided to scarper and find some women passengers. But, he was helpful and sad he was being deserted; you can never tell and I do not take any risks after a chap did attack me and wanted to rape me in Tongdean Lane Brighton some years' ago. He did not like my stiletto heel into his cheek which must have bled like the pig he was; I was covered in blood when I reached home after a fast run.'

'Please promise me that you'll always travel First Class in future. Third is risky when there are no corridors on ancient rolling stock. Try to get a porter to escort you, as well. For a tip they'll find you a safe seat and with a corridor if you ask.'

'Having organised Room Service, we've got half an hour for rattle-snake time; do let's see what you feel like, tonight, my adorable, beautiful soul. I have been waiting for this moment ever since last Monday. Time to be with you cannot come too soon for me'

'Me too, Chester. I have something new in place tonight. Can you detect what I am wearing?'

'You look much the same, good waist, high bust, trim backside, adorable stockings, smashing hair, bright eyes, meltingly good mouth and lips. What more could a randy American ask for? Come and lie with me, just as we are, until the chap arrives with eats or *chuck* as we say stateside.'

Chester and Mary loped over to the wide bed and fell into each other's arms and she kicked off her shoes—harder for laced up business-wear Chester had matched with his suit, so he dropped to his knees and undid his shoe-laces. Mary noticed and asked him what was wrong. On the bed, together, both put their arms around each other and Mary was startled.

'Chester, what have you got on? You are all stiff and solid like I am. Take off your shirt, now.'

'I went to Portsmouth to a firm called Vollers and had myself fitted with a foundation for me to take control of my ghastly tummy—the result of too many good dinners, eating out and trashy *chuck*. Told you I would and I'm not for being upstaged constantly by your magnificent shape.'

'Please stand up and let me pronounce my verdict on your bodywork.'

Chester was a little embarrassed, stripping to just his new corset and knicks. Mary turned him around and admired every angle. She poked and prodded a little but the fitter had clearly done a good job. Chester knew that he must have one made-to-measure and Mary found she could not squeeze her fingers inside the laced-up corset which reached from just above his lower rib cage to his hips and it had front lacing which made it simpler to don and to doff. It was black and not really noticeable under his normal grey vest and pants. But, his figure was much, much improved and there was no evidence of any roly-poly tummy.

'How do you feel, encased into this thing?'

'After the first half-hour, I simply do not notice it at all. It does not squeeze me; it is just there and does not move, so my body accepts it as if it had always been there.'

'Has anyone noticed your slimmer contours, yet?'

'Yes, one of the PAs asked what diet . . . and I received enquiring glances from the others—so they had patently gossiped.'

'What are you going to say, when they ask?'

'Doctor's orders; I have suffered since the days I rode in a rodeo—and this thing helps.'

'Now you will begin to understand why I prefer the rigid corsets I wear *de rigueur*. Today, you'll find I have a new one for your benefit, too. It is not a rigid Victorian device but a brand-new example of American construction.'

'Please let me see, Mary.

'So, how do you like the new streamlined me, then?

There was a knock at the suite door and the night porter entered with a large tray which he placed on the side-table and went out, again, to fetch a small round table. He uncorked the wine and placed it into the ice-bucket having poured two measures. He wished both a good evening and a meal.

'So, how do you like the new misshapen Chester?'

'Very much, indeed. You look far better, you're standing better, and your slight slouch has vanished and there's definitely no sign of your vast pot-belly which used to overtake your trouser belt.

'No complaints at all;

'You were desirable before you were entertained by the voluptuous corsetière—but now, you are indescribably sexy. You look so, so much better and I'm really proud of you for taking the initiative to go and be mauled by the fitter—an expert fitter'

'Well, she was expert, considerate and understood the many men who also needed fitting. Oh, she was not exactly "voluptuous". Just competent. It was not in the least embarrassing and was just like a visit to the physician.

'She asked why I needed a corset as most men do not wear them now and I told her there were two reasons, you wore rigid Victorian corsets and I needed to tame my beer-belly.

'"quite right, too" she said and added she'd have mine made to measure in just thirty minutes as I was a fairly normal un-corseted shape, so that the team would have little difficulty changing a standard male design to fit perfectly.

'She asked how I knew to ask for M2M as she called it. Again, I said you'd always been fitted with utmost care and precision to which she added her refrain "quite right, too".

'So, Chester, what do you want to do with it now? Eat or take it off?'

'No, I'll wear it and maybe eat a little less. It does have a control over what I stuff down my gullet. Put food in front of me and I will be ready with knife and fork feeling waste-not-want-not.

Are you remaining shut-in, Mary, dear?'

'Oh, yes, of course. But I am well used to being "shut-in" as you call it.'

'That's another of those American expressions which just confuse you. I am remarkably relaxed, but I'll just put my robe on as it's a spot chilly half naked. We missed out on the cuddle. Have to have grub first, though.'

Wine and supper finished—at least, there was a good half of the vegetables left on Chester's plate and they discussed what was on the agenda for the morning.

Chester explained that, after the last weekend when they'd seen several properties, he asked one of the PAs to make appointments with the agents concerned and a time was agreed for each call, starting at ten-thirty, so they'd need to be on the button come morning as there was a twenty-minute drive.

'Chester, are you going to sleep in that thing?'

'If you wear yours, I'll try mine, too.'

'I dare you to keep it on, after you've bathed, and I guarantee you will have me in mine and maybe we can try to make love and see what it feels like.

'It's years since I have received anyone in one. I will warn you, I am tighter when a corset is in place as, I suppose, everything inside me is squeezed a little.

'It will not affect you, though, apart from having to push a little more. I have brought some lube with me, just in case. And a horrid rubber thing for you to use—unless you want me pregnant.'

'We'll have to talk about that, soon.'

'Mary, last night was spectacular—again. You are magnificent in bed and I have missed so much being celibate all these years. You have, too, I imagine.'

'I cannot tell you how much I have missed the feeling of being moved to a climax; you perform this act of kindness with an expertise that really surprises me. Sorry to say this, but James was always exhausted when he came home on leave and was so ready to reach a climax that matters were at an end before he had begun, poor thing.'

'Oh, Mary, what can I say? He was a wonderful man, by all accounts, and you were let down; not his fault at all. I should know because I was impotent, at times when with my ex. Work took precedence, tiredness had a miserable effect and when I had had a good meal she had prepared, well, it took the stuffing out of my desire. I ate less last night, so we were

OK. I enjoyed it with you dressed in your fundamental, sorry, what is it?'

'Foundation.'

'Definitely you were tighter and I nearly, so nearly, came before my time but we did it together, which is quite incredible. Thank you, so much. You are amazing.'

5 Home Finding

Breakfast over, Mary and Chester were ready to leave by nine-forty-five. Mary drove whilst Chester read the maps and amazingly, there were no silly spats or near misses with giant oak or elm trees.

The first property to see was the furthest away at Bistern Close, roughly south west of Lyndhurst. One of the best on the list but it was a good hour's drive to Fawley which was going to be a huge disadvantage. Mary had seen it before but had not been inside. The agent was on time, thankfully and took over the visit, using the keys she had. Inside, it was quite light, had six bedrooms and adequate living rooms and a place for a study which would be essential. Chester would have to have a live-in housekeeper who would also have the kitchen as her domain, leaving food prepared but ready to warm up each evening. She would need at least two bedrooms, one to sleep and one as a living room. Depending upon movements, a PA may also have to stay over if work had to be prepared before morning; so this property had the necessary space.

The principal bedroom was well appointed and had what was known as an *en-suite* bathroom which were built only in good hotels. It was the distance that killed this lovely house, though. Speeding was impossible at night in case a large animal loomed and stood transfixed by the headlights. So, they gave this one just seven out of ten.

The next, in Setley, was with the same agent, so she led the way in her car, driving a bogglingly complex route where the direction of travel kept changing; first east, then north and after a point, back south again or so it seemed.

Big property, again, and it had five bedrooms and a servant's quarter. Not as attractive as a property but that would not matter greatly. Inside, it was practically furnished, had a reasonable kitchen, just a little dated from the 1920s and in need of a refit soon. The main bedroom overlooked a gorgeous section of old forest with mature English oaks and other deciduous specimens. Bathrooms were all separate and floors were wooden without any carpeting. The journey would take about thirty minutes. Marks out of ten, seven again. Parting company with the agent, they went on their way to the next way-point and viewing.

The next was on the coast, near Lymington, and Chester had high hopes for this one and was looking forward to showing Mary as he felt it had something indefinable about it. Took just fifteen minutes to reach it from Setley but the last quarter mile or so was up an unmade track which could be treacherous if not a competent driver. Never mind, we shall explore. This property had four principal bedrooms and an annexe for staff. It had five bedrooms but one had been cut and made into two bathrooms for two of the main bed-chambers. Views from several rooms were out across the Solent estuary and towards Yarmouth on the Isle of Wight. The bedrooms were all carpeted and homely. The kitchen was utilitarian and had good work-surfaces and lots of copper polished pans and a huge range and water heater which was coal fired like a railway locomotive. Clearly, a housekeeper would be necessary but she'd need to negotiate the difficult drive to reach any shops in Lymington unless there was a small store in Keyhaven, nearby. After much thought and mild argument, Chester and Mary agreed that eight was the score. Would have been a clear ten without the bumpy drive.

There were three more to view and none achieved more than a score of five, at best, so were discarded. One was right next door to the refinery but was small and ill-equipped and more suited to a relatively junior member of the staff.

It was decided that the coastal property near Lymington would be taken and the agent was advised by telephone just before their closing time.

The evening and all of Sunday was free for enjoyment and maybe a walk, literally in the forest. Both were quite tired from the viewings, taking mental notes and driving all over Hampshire, so it felt. The hotel restaurant was chosen and they decided to retire, first to the suite for a couple of hours.

Chester was aiming directly for his side of the bed when they came into the room; the view was enchanting and Mary decided to spend ten minutes taking that into her memory. Her flat in Victoria had no scenery to explore except for other dingy properties; Jane's home had no views from the room Mary used but Steyning, itself, was quaint and viewable. Dress Address, of course, was a commercial building and across the road was an insurance company office block and more than a little dull. When she lived in Withdean, there was a long garden and mature trees to the rear but just similar properties looking to the east.

'Mary, please come and join me; I need you and I'm kinda hungry for a big hug and a bit of closeness.'

'Are you still in your new waistcoat?'

'Yes, of course. I'll wear mine until you let yourself loose from your imprisonment.

'I like it; it gives me some warmth and it really does feel good and firm; I cannot, yet, describe how it feels except that it is, as you have said, like wearing a constant hug and then I think of you.'

They lay on the bed, together and enjoyed the closeness of their bodies and the feel of their corsets which made both conscious of the other and their positive need to want to fumble the other's body. Both decided to take off their corsets and Mary said she'd change into rigid stays before dinner.

Chester had no choice if he were to clamber into his garment for dinner: he would do so as he copied what Mary did in this respect. He took her lead.

He utterly adored Mary and so wanted to broach the subject which was on both their minds. But he chose to await Mary's move.

Undressed, they slipped between the sheets and were soon so close to each other that coupling became inevitable and hugely enjoyable for both. Kissing, suckling and moving softly between each other was normal and lovely for both.

The feelings were indescribable and both wanted the orgasms to extend for much longer than was permitted. Permitted by whom, Mary wondered, whispering into Chester's ear. An hour and a half passed as if it was minutes and they both had pangs of hunger. Mary probed Chester in the ribs, making him squeal as she had hit a definite avoid-spot in his back. Had he suffered an injury at some point, she presumed?

Chester helped Mary dress and put on stockings and her corset which required him to lace her into it with care and precision. She loved being dressed by another so much and always liked it when Jen or Vera helped her but Chester was something else; his fingers were much stronger and his expertise was novel, to say the least.

Dressed, or should that be trussed, Mary turned to the naked Chester and placed his corset round him and closed the busk front with the five studs. The lacing was to one side of the front and it was faintly difficult to make the fabric move all the way round anti-clockwise whereas in the other direction the corset closed with ease. This was because it was designed for a man who was not expected to have a dresser. Door-knobs had not been reckoned as a means for self-help closure. His next garment . . . Well, Jen would have an input.

6 Sunday's Decisions

Both awoke at about six o'clock and were into each other's arms right away. Both had slept in their garments and were rested but Chester had had to get up and walk about to ease the pressure and slight irritation he was experiencing as he was new to corsetry and night-use.

Better after a bathroom visit. The morning looked set to be fair but it was still quite dark and they had agreed that a walk would be useful—to re-energise their systems and to have vital exercise and contemplate the earlier events. Chester was immensely anxious for Mary to ask him something but was damned if he was going to take the initiative; they had agreed.

Mary was in charge of matrimonial matters.

His corset started to feel hard again; obviously he was not used to it—or it was not used to his body. He had been told by Vollers' fitter that both it and his body had to get used to one another. So, it came off readily and he wriggled into bed with Mary and put his arm around her breasts which felt so firm and contained.

He wanted, now, to make love again and he was starting to attain an erection for, was it the third time in twenty-four hours, or was it more? He moved further up the bed and nuzzled Mary's ear and then breathed into her ear so that she slowly awoke to feel him close to her side. She knew, instantly she was awake, what he wanted and rolled onto her back so that he could enter her and give her the most exquisite pleasure—again.

Mary knew that she would be utterly lost without Chester at her side but obviously considered which way to turn. Which way would her business take her? Would she be able to work from nearer Waterloo? How long would the train journey take at commuter-time? Would she need a business if she shared her life with one earning more than enough for two and able to pay staff as well?

Oh! Why was life so damned difficult and yet the answer was painless: just ask him.

Both were extremely happy and felt exhausted from their exertions and yet fulfilled. Mary was still corseted and it felt a little damp and needed to be changed—and washed. Chester made a coffee for both of them and they discussed where they should take themselves for a hand-in-hand walk. The sea shore at Lymington towards Keyhaven was obvious and it would give them both a better insight towards where one or both was to live for the next few months, if not a year or more.

Oh! Please ask me, Mary. I am mentally begging you. Can you not see how I feel about you?

Up and dressed, Mary wearing her new garment and Chester trussed into his, they went down to help themselves to the usual spread of the buffet breakfast and more coffee. They sat looking into each other's eyes and Chester was hearing Mary almost purr with contentedness.

Ask, damn it, he thought.

'You know I have to be at the office quite early on Monday, my lovely one. I'll have to run you to Brockenhurst by about seven o'clock, so we'll have to be up, packed and away by half six. We have to be ready.

'Let's go find the sea and frighten the sea-weed, Mary.'

'Come, then; I have been so happy this weekend and hate the advance of Monday. How the troops stationed around here must have been so worried about the prospect of being carried across the water to fight on landing back in 1944.

'James may well have been here, or close by as he was in charge of a section of special anti-tank tanks which had been fitted with superior armament capable of destroying anything that the Hun had to throw at them. I learned all this from his fellow officers after the war ended in Europe.

'I have never spoken to anyone else about this. One day, I'd like you to take me to Caen and to find where he was killed by a mortar shell. I am not into morbidity and I cannot take him back but I can and will honour him with a visit, one day.

In one of the cemeteries, there is a white tombstone with his name engraved on it but there are no remains below; he was blown to pieces, I was told.'

Mary was in tears; tears had not been shed since 1944 when the telegram arrived. She did not open it for some years but knew what it said.

Even the poor postman who delivered it said "I am so, so sorry, dear". It had been his misfortune to deliver maybe a hundred similar missives to widows. Then there was Eleanor who had predicted this accurately. How?

'I am really honoured to have been told this. What can I say to you? Please give me your hand; I want to be a part of this memory with you.'

So they sat on a bench in the hotel garden for about an hour and Mary woke up from her memories and said:

'Let's be off. You have been kindness itself, Chester. Please will you marry me?'

7 Momentous Moments 1952

'How soon, Mary?

'I have been mentally begging you to ask almost since we first met on the ocean-liner. I'm an impetuous man, as you realise and I am capable of making good, quick decisions.

'That is why Mr Esso keeps me.

'I need to buy you a ring but I cannot do that with you beside me but I would like some guidance, please.'

'Do I really need a ring? Surely the wedding band will be sufficient to tell the world?'

'No, this is my call and people will think I am a miserable devil if I cannot give you at least a cheap fair-ground prize-gilt-imitation-diamond. Plus a goldfish.'

'Why not do just that, Chester? Is there a fair on this evening, anywhere; it'd be fun to see what we can get by hook or by crook. Let's ask a policeman—he'd be sure to know where all the rogues are a-lurking.'

'I am so, so happy that you have asked, at long last, Mary. There is so much we have to attend-to.

'The first priority is to get our home as we wish to have it. We need a houseful of furniture . . .

'And, do not forget the furnishings, sheets, pillow-cases, rugs, table-cloths, dish-cloths and all the things that men never consider.'

'Sorry, that is what I keep you for.'

'Now, now, don't be naughty, Chester.'

'The home is your province, Mary. We need to discuss finances and I'll arrange for my bank to transfer a monthly lump so that you'll be able to afford cheap dish-cloths. I do not have a proper English bank, yet. Mine is still stateside and in dollars but it will save me having to carry a wad of English with me.'

'I had asked myself why you Americans do seem to have a penchant for oodles of cash. I need comparatively little in readies but use my cheque book constantly.

'I'd like to get a feel for your taste in furniture—and furnishings. Like the ring-thingy, I need some guidance from you, this time.

I propose to come down from London and to meet you in Southampton so that we can visit a few furniture stores just to get your impressions of likes and definitely have-nots.'

'Better, idea: I will arrange to come to London; there are certain to be more stores and I believe you have something called "Heels" in "Tattenham Corner", so the PAs have told me.'

'So, you have discussed our marriage with them already?'

'Oops, sorry. I have put my three feet in the glue, already.'

'No, I understand; marriage has been on your mind night and day. They'd be foolish not to notice your thoughts are elsewhere.

'It is Heal's and they are in Tottenham Court Road—some way up from the Underground Station which is at the cross roads with Oxford Street.

'You will need at least three wads of cash with you but the quality and designs are excellent.

'I will meet you off the train at Waterloo Station but you must ask a PA to telephone Vera to say, definitely, what time you'll arrive. I do not want to have a wasted morning awaiting your release from Hesto, or whatever you call your employer.'

Mary had already had ideas of her own. When they visited the Lymington property, Mary was planning where to put furniture, what to buy and what colour schemes would best suit the walls and timber work. She knew she'd marry Chester well before asking him. Naughty to have kept him on tenterhooks for longer than necessary, but she—and he—had to be certain. More than certain.

Vera and all the others had to be told of her engagement; the first thing they'd ask to see would be the ring and maybe later today she'd be able to sport a sparkler of some sort.

There was a fun-fair in Christcurch—quite a big affair so rumour had it—so they agreed to see what it had to offer as prizes.

'Chester, you have to put that wooden ring over the prize you select without it snagging the stand. It will take you too long and cost too many dollars unless you brighten up your act, here.'

'May I have a go and see if I can avoid hitting the oak stands?'

Mary, you seem to be quite good at this; just need to perfect which prize you really want; do we need a teddy-bear, yet?'

'Are there any other prize stalls? I'd like a dipper ride, first. It may knock some sense into my feeble brain.'

'James used to like the Wall of Death where he rode a motor-bike at speed in a sort of steel-mesh container. He used to come out all spinning and he simply could not stand upright for a while as he was so dizzy.'

'Mary, let's just take a wander around and see what takes our fancy. I am so, so happy this evening. There is so much we have to discuss but it will all wait. We now must find a ring, here.'

'Proud owner of a miserable one-eyed bear.'

'Chester, how good a shot are you?'

'Pretty good, at one time, but they bend the barrels at fairs so that winners do not scoop everything.'

'Spend some time testing the weapon of choice first and then have a go to win. James used to tell me how the odds were stacked against the punters at fairs in England.'

'Mary, the odds are well agin us as I have to kill the bull three times to win a lovely ring. I get a fish first, then a sloppy teddy and then the ring . . .

The test over, and a worried stall-holder standing anxiously and menacingly too close to Chester, he fired.

Splat!

He had a gold-fish.

'Re-load, please'

Splat!

He'd won the teddy bear

'Re-load, please'

Splat!

'Now will you do the honour of marrying me, with this ring as proof of my troth, Mary?'

'I shall treasure this ring more than you can ever imagine, Chester.

'Vera will be able to have a really good laugh. I am so, so happy, Chester. Home to bed now, please.'

Lightning Source UK Ltd.
Milton Keynes UK
UKOW04f0941011013

218258UK00002B/145/P